HER CLAIM

LEGALLY BOUND BOOK 2

REBECCA GRACE ALLEN

Rebecca Grace Allen Enterprises

Her Claim

Copyright © 2018 by Rebecca Grace Allen

Digital ISBN: 978-0-9978792-7-8

Print ISBN: 978-0-9992066-5-2

Editing by Jennifer Miller

Cover Design by Romantic Book Affairs

HER CLAIM

*S*he's no princess. He's no prince. Then again, they never wanted a fairy tale.

Legally Bound, Book 2

Cassie Allbright takes no prisoners. A half Cuban ball-busting attorney, she's too tough to admit what she wants in bed. But tough is the only way to cut it in her high-powered firm, and Cassie doesn't need a knight in shining armor. And she definitely doesn't need Patrick Dunham—an arrogant, chauvinistic man-whore with a knack for pissing her off.

Bound to the helm of his family's publishing house, Patrick is shackled to a life of power and wealth he never wanted. Seduction is his only distraction—his nights of pleasure always temporary, because happily-ever-afters are *not* for him. But while luring a woman into his bed has always come easy, the high-and-mighty Cassie has never succumbed to his charms.

Their verbal sparring turns to foreplay, but instead of scratching an itch, it only whets their appetites. Patrick gives Cassie a taste of what she's secretly craved, and Cassie's dark desires stir up things Patrick never knew he wanted. Enchanted, he offers to fulfill her most dangerous fantasies. She agrees, with an iron-clad escape clause: her heart is off-limits, and so is his.

Funny thing about hearts, though. They have a way of ignoring the fine print.

Warning: This book isn't for the faint of heart. Disclosure includes angry, vying-for-control hate sex and one steamy weekend in Miami. Ready? Break the caution tape and proceed.

AUTHOR'S NOTE

As I said in the warning, this book isn't for the faint of heart. It contains breath-play scenarios, consensual role play depicting non-consent and references to alcoholism. There are scenes of violence that may bother readers with past trauma. I don't want anyone to be shocked or triggered by that, so please don't read this book if you think it will upset you. I myself had difficulty writing it, and parts of the story are very personal for me.

I recognize that anything involving power imbalances, especially those sexual in nature, is a highly visible issue these days, and I want to be sensitive to my readers. I promise that everything the characters engage in is desired, thoroughly discussed and mutually agreed upon. And at its heart, this is a story of two people working through shame and heartbreak, and finding acceptance in themselves through one another. It's a story about love, sex and healing.

Now that I've fully prepared you, play some Marvin Gaye and read on...

XOXO

Rebecca

Spanish Glossary

Besos: kisses

Buenos dias: good morning

Calle Ocho: Eighth Street, the main strip of Little Havana, Miami, Florida.

Carajo: fuck

Churros: A fried dough pastry. Long and thick, they are often dipped in chocolate and sprinkled with sugar.

Cojones: a man's testicles; balls

Conquistador: One who conquers; specifically a leader in the Spanish conquest of America and especially of Mexico and Peru in the 16th century.

Dios mío: oh my God

Empanadas: A stuffed bread or pastry, which is baked or fried. The stuffing can consist of a variety of meats, vegetables, or even fruits.

Flan: An open, rimmed pastry or sponge base, containing a sweet or savory filling.

Gente: people

Hola: hello

La calle: the street

La cama: the bed

Livin' la vida: Living life, or living the life.

Lo siento: I'm sorry

Machismo: A strong, aggressive or exaggerated sense of masculine pride.

Medianoche: Similar to a Cuban sandwich, it consists of roast pork, ham, mustard, Swiss cheese and pickles, but is made on a soft, sweet egg dough bread. It is so named because of the sandwich's popularity as a staple served in Havana's night clubs right around or after midnight.

Mi amor: my love

Mi vida: my life

Mojito: A cocktail made of white rum, sugar cane juice, lime juice, soda water and mint.

Niña: little girl

Pastelitos: Cuban puff pastries, traditionally filled with cream cheese and guava.

Pero: but

Querida: dear

Quinceañera: The celebration of a girl's fifteenth birthday.

Sí: yes

Tapas: Small, savory dishes, served both hot and cold.

Tía: aunt

Tres Leches: A sponge or butter cake soaked in three kinds of milk.

1

---

*C*assie Allbright had never been so pissed off in her life.

Storming through the bar, she searched until she found Lilly at a table in the back, then slammed her bag down and yanked out a chair. "You would not. Believe. My day."

"I was wondering why he'd called you in so late in the day." Lilly passed over the blood-orange cosmopolitan she'd already ordered for her. "Talk."

Cassie sat, lifted the glass and took a sip. Best friends were a godsend. "Schaeffer told me I was off partner track."

Lilly's jaw dropped open. "You've got to be kidding me."

"Wish I was."

When she'd been summoned to their boss's office at a quarter to six, Cassie had thought it was a sign she was finally going to receive that coveted offer of partner. That she should stay the course and keep billing. But instead, she'd been sucker-punched and told the opposite.

"What did he say?" Lilly asked.

"He told me I haven't made myself 'invaluable to the firm,' since I haven't brought in enough business."

"That's ridiculous."

"Technically, he's right."

She'd worked hundreds of cases, reorganized and liquidated dozens of companies, but as a seventh-year associate, she still hadn't landed a big matter yet—the multimillion-dollar kind with a company so completely fucked it needed an entire restructuring to stay afloat. Those always went to the male partners, a fact of life she'd grown to loathe. Cassie knew her shit as a bankruptcy specialist, but The Law Offices of Forrester, Schaeffer and Pierce were run by three old white men, and she'd been battling the gender gap and racial bias for as long as she could remember.

Lilly's eyes were wide with concern. "Was he...?"

"Firing me? No." Those conversations took place in HR's fluorescent-lit cubicles, not in one of the partners' cushy offices that overlooked Boston's Charles River. "But he did say I should weigh my options."

"So you can decide if you're going to hop firms in the hopes of finding better luck elsewhere."

"Bingo. Which is impossible without a book of business." Cassie raised her glass. "Happy fucking Friday to me."

Lilly wrinkled her nose. "I'm sorry."

Cassie shook her head. Someone else might've felt like all hope was lost. Not her.

She wasn't depressed. She was determined. And pissed.

"Don't be sorry. All we need is another housing bubble, a second government bailout, or for some broke dumbass who's totally screwed his company up to ask for me personally, and I'll be golden." Cassie sipped her drink, waiting for the cool liquid to dial down her fury. "Will Jack be joining us tonight?"

"He's on his way."

Lilly lifted a hand to absentmindedly trace over the silver chain around her neck. It wasn't a necklace, it was a collar—one that locked in the back, only able to be opened with a key her boyfriend owned. Did Lilly even call Jack her boyfriend? Her

Dominant? Dom-friend? The world of trust and rules Lilly happily embraced made Cassie's head spin.

But it was a world she wished she understood, too, and a world she remained too afraid to dip a toe in. Because the idea of acknowledging the desires she kept firmly at bay made her more nauseous than a bad day in court.

"What about Brady and Samantha?" Someone else needed to be coming because Cassie didn't want to be the third wheel tonight.

"No Sam. Just Brady."

"Bummer." Jack's younger brother Brady was comic relief in human form—or at least he had been until recently, but Cassie liked hanging out with Sam. She was the only person Cassie knew with as much of a high-heel-buying habit as her. "Are the two of them—?"

Her question was interrupted by the sound of her phone ringing. She fished it from her bag and growled at the missed call on screen. *"Carajo."*

"Your mom?"

"How'd you know?"

"Because you always curse in Spanish when she calls." Another sign of true friendship. They'd only been close for a year and a half, but that was enough for Lilly to have become well-versed in Flóres-Allbright family dramas. "I still remember how surprised I was when you said you were half Cuban."

"You mean it wasn't clear from my stubborn persistence and tendency to fly off the handle?"

"I thought those were part of your sparkling personality."

Cassie huffed out a laugh. With her Cuban side's unusually dominant blue eyes and her Caucasian father's light skin, most people were shocked to discover Cassie was Latina. But since she'd moved to the Northeast, it had less to do with the way she looked and more with the way she acted.

Lilly fiddled with the straw in her drink. "You going to skip calling her back?"

"No. She'll just try me again if I do. But I need to find someplace quieter. Be right back."

She stood as Brady showed, waving at him before making her way to the rear of the bar where it was slightly less crowded. There was a game at Fenway tonight which meant people who hadn't gotten tickets to the stadium next door would be here, watching on the flat-screens. For the moment, however, she was only surrounded by a few locals and a bunch of guys in Harvard crimson polos. Preparing herself for what was bound to be her second inquisition of the day, Cassie returned her mother's call.

Three rings in, she picked up. *"Hola, mi amor."*

The noise in the background had Cassie placing her mother's surroundings immediately. The hiss and sputter of something frying in a pan. Buena Vista Social Club playing in the background. The house in Miami Cassie had grown up in hadn't been home for twenty years, but it brought back memories nonetheless. It was as comforting as it was aggravating.

"Hi, Mom."

"Lo siento, can you hear me?" her mother asked, bouncing back and forth between English and Spanish like she always did. "The kids are here."

"I can hear you fine, Mom."

"Good. I'm putting you on speaker." There was a pause, followed by a loud, *"Niños,* say hello to *Tía* Cassandra."

Two tiny voices responded in a sing-song, *"Hola,* Aunt Cassie."

"Hola, Antonio, *hola,* Annalisa."

One of the Harvard guys gave her a hard once-over, in a way she'd seen before: part shock, part accusation, part uncomfortable appreciation.

Got a problem with my Spanish, pretty boy?

Cassie shot a look at him until he glanced away. Tension coiled in the back of her neck as her mother switched the call off speaker, then began a report on everything her niece and nephew were doing. Cassie sighed and kneaded her neck with her free hand. It wasn't that she didn't love her brother's kids, but Jesus Christ, couldn't she get the CliffsNotes version or something?

"Listen, Mom, I'm in the middle of stuff. Was there something you needed?"

"Yes, yes. You're very busy. I know."

And those words implied what they always did. That despite being the first person in her family to go to an Ivy League college or graduate from law school, it didn't measure up with her siblings' choices. Cassie's younger brother had married a nice Cuban-American girl, and her little sister was engaged to a great guy from the Dominican.

Which, Cassie was sure, was about to be the topic of conversation for this call.

"Well, I don't want to keep you," her mother continued, "but we need to talk."

"About what?"

"Elísa is concerned you don't have a date for the wedding yet."

There it was. "I think you're more concerned than she is, Mom."

"Your sister has enough to do without worrying about this. You want to be the only one at the wedding without a date?"

Cassie's fingers tensed on her neck. Marriage and babies were another place she'd gone off-track. She was the eldest child in the family, and the only one not paired off, which was a cardinal sin as far as her mother was concerned.

She wasn't the only person Cassie heard it from, though. The question was a constant at Bar Association meetings, new employee orientations and committees she'd been assigned to.

You have kids?

Nope.

Husband?

Nope.

Cat? Dog? Small aquarium?

Nope. Nope. Double nope. For the moment, it was her and her work. But now that Cassie was approaching the ripe old age of thirty-nine, all her mother could talk about was her single status, or the lack of productivity of her uterus.

"I don't need a date. I'm the maid of honor. There's a guy ready-made to walk me down the aisle."

"That won't always be the case, *mi vida*. The clock is ticking, you know."

She knew. They'd had this discussion so often, Cassie couldn't look at a clock without wincing. It wasn't that she didn't want a family—at least, she wasn't sure she didn't—but she'd put the decision on hold while she'd pursued her career.

For half her life, she'd put her job first. How nice, to see how well her hard work had paid off.

"It's only September, Mom. The wedding isn't until Thanksgiving. I have two months to find someone."

For a date, not a husband. She could at least find time to do that much.

As her mother launched into an update on All Things Miami Wedding, Cassie's phone beeped with a text. She pulled it away from her ear and thumbed over the screen.

"Just warning you," Lilly's message read. *"Patrick is here."*

Cassie's lip curled in an involuntary sneer.

Looking up, she searched through the pub until she saw him. Patrick Dunham, otherwise known as Jack's best friend, wingman and a man-whoring chauvinistic pig. She'd been forced to share oxygen with him since Lilly met Jack and Patrick had become part of their circle. And there he was, sauntering into the bar like he owned it.

Scanning the room for his next victim, no doubt.

A publishing magnate, Patrick was your classic playboy—rich, privileged and born with a sense of entitlement. He expected women to drop at his feet because of his money and apparent talent in bed. Not Cassie. For months she'd watched other unsuspecting fools fawn all over him, watched him leave with a different one every night, never committing to a single one. He didn't try to hide it either. The very first day she'd met him, he'd proudly admitted to never dating the same woman twice with an egotistical, blasé and satisfied smile.

She wasn't sure any man had infuriated her so much.

Across the room, Patrick saw her and met her gaze with the conceited smirk she'd seen too many times before, his thick shoulders stretching the confines of his button-down shirt as he crossed his arms. Cassie's body heated as she glared back. He was attractive, but there was no soul behind that mask of green eyes, the thick black hair and goatee which showed no hint of grey despite him being midway through his forties. If every other woman in this room was his prey, Cassie was the one exception. She'd become his natural enemy, impervious to his good looks, smooth talk and cunning wiles.

It hadn't always been the case.

Once she'd enjoyed the quipped lines they exchanged like a good debate or a cross-examination. It was passionate. Exciting. And there was that one night at a party months ago, when she'd imagined that aggression turning into something hot and sweaty and desperate. But he'd quickly proved he was nothing but a tease. A fake. No ambition whatsoever except the chase. Men like that didn't get under Cassie's skin, or her sheets.

He smiled at her before breaking eye contact and disappearing into the crowd. Good. Let him disappear. She wasn't interested anyway.

And her mother had been prattling on about dates and weddings all this time.

Cassie switched into Spanish, firing out words to quickly wrap up the conversation.

"*Mamá, me tengo que ir. Hablo contigo mas tarde.*" She had to go. She'd talk to her later.

Much later.

"Okay. *Besos.*"

Blowing a kiss, Cassie ended the call and marched back to the table with her chin held high. Tonight, she was going to enjoy her drink and her friends and ignore the shit out of Patrick Dunham. She didn't need his attention, or her mother's approval. She didn't need a husband or a baby either. What she *did* need was to make partner, and she was going to get there, somehow.

She'd busted her ass to get this far, and she'd be damned if she let anything get in her way.

2

---

*B*arrel 'n' Flask was packed.

It wasn't a shock, not on a warm, early September night with a game starting at Fenway. This time of year had more people cramming into the popular pub than usual. The line by the bar was three people deep, the air thick with music and conversation. Which was exactly the way Patrick liked it.

A virtual smorgasbord of possibilities waited for him here— blondes, brunettes and redheads of every shape, size and color. He'd caught a few of the lust-drunk glances he'd become accustomed to over the years, then paused as three women dressed in tiny shirts emblazoned with the Red Sox logo offered him sultry grins.

He'd grinned back. They could offer him a night of fun for sure, but an orgy wasn't what he was into tonight, although he'd done that before. He wasn't hunting for a sleek professional either, the kind of woman who'd seem out of place in a sports bar, eager to escape as soon as he whispered the words *You wanna get out of here?*

He'd had enough of those types this week—willing women who'd sidled up to him at the Society of Book Writers fundraising dinner and the New England industry trade show's glitzy charity ball event. The suited, tight-lipped publicist he'd made scream the night before had been too easy to entice.

No, there was only one woman he was looking for. And once he'd seen her, all shining brown hair and bright blue eyes, Patrick did the one thing he always loved to do around Cassie Allbright: he made eye contact, held it, then went straight to those Red Sox groupies and got not one, but all of their phone numbers.

"Overachieving a bit tonight?"

Hearing his best friend's voice, Patrick glanced up and grinned. "It's been a slow week."

"And a slow week for you is only taking a woman home three nights out of seven?"

Buddies since they were teenagers, Jack had long ago stopped blinking an eye at Patrick's desire to spread the wealth of his looks and sexual talents around. He hadn't been like this in high school, or college either, but Jack had never asked why. Like a good friend should, he'd taken Patrick's one-eighty in stride without question. He'd also provided the only sense of normalcy Patrick had ever known.

"Exactly," Patrick said. "I'm making up for lost time."

Jack chuckled, then looked to the petite blonde standing by Cassie's side. "So am I."

Across the room, Jack's girlfriend, Lilly, blushed. Patrick watched them hold one another's gazes and pocketed the napkins with feminine handwriting scrawled on them. "If I were a different kind of man, I'd be jealous."

Jack glanced his way. "But you—"

"Are not a different kind of man."

Patrick was happy for Jack and Lilly, but commitment wasn't for him. Sure, he'd believed in happily-ever-afters once, when he was foolish enough to imagine finding a soul mate to go off into the sunset with. But those were childish fantasies. Besides, why would he want one woman when he could have all of Boston?

"I know better than to get into this with you." Jack nodded to the Sox girls. "Which one of them is getting ensnared tonight?"

Patrick was about to answer when Cassie threw her head back, all big smile and white teeth and sexy, badass confidence. *Not the one I want.* "We'll see. It might not be any of them. The night's still young."

They purchased their beers and made their way to the table their group was gathered around. Cassie ignored him as usual, busying herself with her drink and her phone. Jack's younger brother Brady, however, greeted Patrick like an eager Labrador puppy.

"Three women in under ten minutes." He saluted Patrick with a bow. "You're my idol."

"You'd better be glad Samantha didn't hear you say that."

Brady's smile faltered for a second. "Yeah, well, she's not with me tonight, is she?"

Bravado if Patrick had ever heard it, and a sign of trouble in the suburban paradise Brady shared with his wife, but that was none of Patrick's business.

"I guess not. Which means you're my wingman on my next round. See if you can't help me double my scores in half the time."

Cassie made a disgusted sound. Patrick glanced her way to find her staring at him in what could only be described as revulsion.

"You're a pig," she said.

It wasn't the first time she'd called him that. He didn't mind. It meant he'd gotten her attention. "Jealous, are we?"

"Jealous of women who don't know you're leaving them high and dry in the morning? No, I'm smarter than that."

Patrick's grin grew wider, his body winding up with the same charge it always did when he and Cassie clashed. A gorgeous, curvy lawyer with brains and a biting sense of humor, she was as standoffish as she was sexy, and the one woman who'd been able to resist his charms. It was amusing as hell, having her insult him, and their verbal sparring had become his favorite way to kick off the weekend. It was also a nice change of pace. Seduction was an art Patrick had become a fucking Picasso at by age forty-six, and he loved a challenge.

"I prefer to be upfront with my conquests," he said, enjoying the way Cassie's eyes narrowed at his choice of words. "I offer women what they want: a night of dirty, no-strings-attached sex, and I haven't heard anyone complain yet."

"Maybe you're not listening closely enough."

Listening closely was Patrick's area of expertise. He had an uncanny ability with observation, a sixth sense on picking up body language and clues. That was how he'd gotten to be so good at seduction, women practically begging to dish out their most illicit fantasies. He'd bet he could do the same with Cassie if she weren't such a sniping, closed-off bitch.

He moved into her space, close enough to get a whiff of her perfume—a sweet, floral fragrance that would smell damn nice on his pillows in the morning—but leaving enough distance to show her he wasn't interested.

"I listen. To every whimper, moan and sigh that proves they are one hundred percent satisfied."

Cassie rolled her eyes and went back to her phone, but it was clear he'd gotten to her. The apples of her cheeks had gone pink —a color that stole down her throat and to the hint of cleavage at the opening in her blouse. Provoking her was childish, but it was the only time he ever saw a break in her composure, and he enjoyed pissing her off.

Other than that heated flush, however, she remained as polished as ever in her skirt and high heels. She was hard up, probably from being so cold, aloof and superior.

Time to push a little bit harder.

"Maybe that's your problem, Cassie. A lack of...*satisfaction* in your life."

Her gaze snapped up, and those piercing blue eyes grew even angrier. Victory blazed in the pit of his stomach. No one else triggered his mean streak like Cassie did. It was such a rush, getting her like this, and knowing he'd hit a nerve revved him up even more.

"My only problem right now is the empty glass in my hand." She shoved off her stool. "Excuse me."

She brushed past him and stalked toward the bar. Lilly turned on Patrick.

"Do you have to give her such a hard time? She's had a bad day, and you're not helping."

He held his hands up in surrender. "I didn't do anything but speak the truth."

She jabbed a finger at his chest. "That's not what you do, and you know it. You say things to make her angry."

"Well, yeah. But it's so much fun."

Lilly narrowed her eyes until Jack reached up and lightly tapped her hand. She glanced at him, and something silent passed between them. Patrick didn't have to have been Jack's best friend, or active in the BDSM lifestyle, to know her behavior was that of a well-trained submissive. It was clear in the dynamic between her and Jack, as much in their unspoken glances as the padlocked heart around Lilly's neck.

Patrick had never been into that kind of play full time, although it was an interesting way to spend an evening. He'd been both dominant and submissive, been tied up and done the tying, begged for release and brought women to the point of tearful pleading for the same. Whatever their fantasy was, he made it happen, escaping from reality for a night of pure physical pleasure.

But that was where it ended. No relationships. Just sex. He didn't get involved in their lives, and he had good reasons for keeping it that way.

Lilly wrinkled her nose and lowered her finger. "I'm not wrong," she said to Jack.

"You're not. But be nice."

"Yes, Sir." She made a face at Patrick before going to join Cassie. Jack sipped his beer as she walked off.

"Lilly's right. You do like to rile Cassie up," he said.

"It's only because she's such an easy mark."

Brady snorted. "She's a *mark* you've been trying to hit for months."

Patrick shot the kid a glare. Yeah, Jack's little brother was still a kid to him, even though the guy was well into his thirties—but Brady wasn't deterred.

"You can deny it all you want," he added. "You want her, and she can't stand you."

Patrick turned to watch as Cassie leaned over the bar to give the bartender her order. The move put her full, heart-shaped ass into view, the silky ends of her hair grazing her neck, and he wondered for the thousandth time what fantasies lingered behind her steel exterior. All too often, he'd imagined what she was hiding behind her sarcastic mouth, and how enjoyable it would be to tease that information out of her.

He'd almost gotten there, one night months ago when he'd been able to cut through her snark and *talk* to her. But the next time they met, she'd resumed her customary bitchy ways, so he'd gone back to his regularly scheduled programming as well.

"She can go ahead and *not stand* me all she wants," he muttered. "The feeling is mutual."

"I think it's time for a subject change," Brady said. "Patrick, I'm hoping I can pilfer our connection and ask you a question about publishing."

Patrick turned away from his view of the bar. "What am I the V.P. of a huge corporation for if not to offer free services to my friends?"

"Family," Jack corrected. Patrick laughed it off.

Growing up, Jack had made sure to make Patrick feel included, inviting him over for meals when being in the Dunham home was impossible. He was doing the same now. Patrick appreciated the sentiment, but it wasn't necessary. He'd spent years cultivating a life where he was dependent on no one, where he could come and go as he pleased. He had friends, money and sex. Family was overrated.

He sat on the stool next to Brady. "What's up?"

"You know how Samantha is always taking pictures of healthy meals and putting them on Instagram?" Brady asked. Patrick nodded. "She's been doing more of that. She's got a ton of followers, and I thought maybe it would be cool for her to get them published."

"Is that something she's interested in?"

"I dunno." Brady shrugged and looked at his glass. "She hasn't been happy lately. Bored, maybe. I think she might need something more than taking care of the kids."

Patrick and Jack shared glances. More signs of trouble for Brady and Sam.

"It's a possibility," Patrick said. "The editorial team is always looking for new get-healthy books they can market after the new year. If she's got a following already, it might be something we can do."

And something no one would challenge Patrick on if he brought the concept to the team. Dunham and Strauss Books was his company, but he was mostly a figurehead without any real clout. What interested him didn't matter. He was needed to optimize strategies and generate revenue. That was what filled Patrick's days—running the global sales department of his father's legacy of a publishing house. He didn't spend time worrying about quality literary content, art or good books. Just dollar signs. Not that he filled his time with reading. Still, even though his job allowed him his expensive apartment and the lifestyle he'd become accustomed to, every day he stepped into the building with his namesake stamped on the doors sucked a little more life out of him.

Regardless, glossy hardcovers like the one Brady was after sold well. Years of strategic planning had taught him that much.

"Give me a call on Monday," he told Brady. "I'll find someone to hook you up with."

"Of course you will." Cassie snuck up on him as she returned from the bar. Patrick turned around with a start. "Hooking up is your forte, isn't it?"

God, she was obnoxious. She'd caught him off-guard and she knew it.

"We were talking about work, but you're right. It *is* my forte. Thank you for reminding me."

"No problem." She motioned toward his seat. "Now if you'll give me my chair back, I have a drink to enjoy."

Another woman would've used him taking her chair as a chance to flirt. But with Cassie, he was being summarily dismissed. Patrick glowered at her. Exchanging banter with her was fun, but only up to a certain point. After that, he either needed to work out his frustrations on the tennis court, or between the sweaty thighs of a writhing woman.

His next match with Jack was days away. And he had three phone numbers burning holes in his pocket. Something he intended to flaunt to Cassie right the hell now. Patrick stood and leveled her with a defiant stare.

"The chair is all yours. It's time to find the woman whose night I'm about to make."

Cassie lifted her chin and glared right back, hot and caustic like the air before a thunderstorm. It was such a turn-on, and so completely fucking aggravating.

Leaning in quietly, he said, "I'm sure your night with your drink will be as *satisfying* as mine."

She winced, like she'd taken a slap to the cheek. He turned from her quickly, nodding at Jack and Brady before heading into the crowd. The charge he'd felt before had vanished, and all that remained was a sickening disgust for being so mean. But fuck it. There was too much to be enjoyed tonight to spend it growling at someone who hated him. And even if it was the same damn thing he'd been doing every weekend for years, he'd take that over lusting after a woman he couldn't have.

He'd learned his lesson about that long ago.

Patrick went to the bar, found the Red Sox groupie he'd decided on for the evening, and offered to buy her a drink.

3

*P*atrick woke up well into the afternoon on Saturday. Eight hours of sleep, and he still felt like shit. Not surprising though, since he'd stayed out past dawn and hadn't bothered to undress before collapsing into bed.

Now the light was streaming in, too bright and glaring and bouncing off his whitewashed walls. He didn't have any curtains in his bedroom. Who needed privacy when you were this high up? And anyone lucky enough to see into this room should sit back and enjoy the view.

But right now it was annoying as fuck.

He grabbed his phone from his nightstand and unlocked the screen. Sixty new email notifications, plus the unread ones he'd ignored the day before. Couldn't he get one goddamn day off? It was the weekend, for fuck's sake.

Dropping his phone on the bed, Patrick rolled over and stared at the ceiling.

Last night hadn't been as enjoyable as he'd hoped. Sure, he'd had sex, but his head hadn't been in it. He hadn't been present, barely enjoying the sounds of pleasure he'd wrung from her, and leaving before finding any himself.

Red Sox Girl had pouted as he'd gotten dressed, saying it was late, he should stay, they could have brunch at some little place she knew of in the morning. That was always the hard part—when they wanted more. Because Patrick had nothing more to give.

So he'd gently reminded her what he'd said on the way to her place—he didn't do relationships and was only there for the night. He was honored to have fulfilled her fantasy, and stroked her cheek once to get a smile out of her before he left.

Needing to get the day going, Patrick threw off his comforter, took off everything but his boxers and threw his clothes on the floor. Not the best way to treat his luxury dress shirt and merino wool slacks, but it wasn't like he didn't have a closet full of designer clothes if a few needed dry cleaning.

As long as he was trapped in this lifestyle, he might as well enjoy it.

Hitting the floor, Patrick began his daily push-up routine. Once he got through a few hundred and his shoulders began to burn, he stripped the rest of the way down and made his way into the en-suite. Switching on the shower, he stepped into the glass enclosure and moved under the hot spray. He closed his eyes, crossed his arms over his chest and let the water douse him.

The tension was still present, his limbs tight and his body worked up with the familiar edginess that was always banished by a good hard orgasm. But to be honest, he'd been bored the night before. Super-slow sex had been Red Sox Girl's fantasy of choice. He'd been happy to oblige, but like the other women he'd bedded lately, her request hadn't excited him.

"Blindfold me."

"Take me from behind on our sides, like they do in porn."

"Let's do it up against a window for all of Boston to see."

The last time that had actually been interesting was when he'd done it on a fifth-floor fire escape because it gave him the challenge of making sure they didn't plummet to their deaths.

But their fantasies were all mechanics. Stage directions. It left him restless, which sucked because sex was the only thing that shut his brain off.

It was his blessing and his curse, this mind of his. His aptitude for remembering and noticing everything was the superpower behind his ability to seduce, but it made him crazy too. He was either constantly overanalyzing the present or fixating on the past. Sex was his drug of choice, the best elixir because it didn't cost him anything and it stopped him from *thinking* so goddamn much. Detaching from his mind and being fully immersed in his body was his only distraction from the endless time loop that was his life. For a few blissful hours, he put on an act, becoming their fantasy and turning into someone else—a man who wasn't shackled to a future he never wanted because of a past he couldn't change.

The need to pace had him getting antsy despite the steady stream of water. There was too damn much in his life he couldn't do anything about. Too much he couldn't control. Too much that pissed him the fuck off.

And, once again, Patrick's thoughts drifted to Cassie.

She made him angry. He didn't know what it was, but something about her brought it out of him. She was a homing beacon to his most base self, drawing out the worst parts of his personality, and truth be told, he hated her a little for it. He felt like shit when things got nasty, but it kept happening over the nine months he'd known her, and he couldn't make it stop.

Nine months. Nine goddamn months of banter as they watched their best friends fall in love. Months of seeing how smart she was, how passionate she was about defending her clients. Of having her poke fun at his cavalier lifestyle with her holier-than-thou loathing, yapping at him that women deserved more than to go home with him only to discover they were getting a one-night stand.

She didn't know how he ran his life. And he didn't feel like correcting her, so he'd kept to his usual game. Upped it even, whenever he was around her, because after a while, he realized he'd started doggedly going after women to get to her.

Getting a rise out of her was as close to sex as they were going to get. But it wasn't the only reason. He'd been waiting for something—a spark of jealousy in her eyes. Some kind of admission that she wanted him too. For a while, Patrick had told himself she was cold. Frigid. A woman that beautiful should've been married by her age, or at least dating someone. It had to have been a personality flaw, but he could never find the proof. She was fiercely protective of Lilly, loyal to a fault. She cared about a select number of people in her life, giving those close few everything.

And Patrick wasn't one of them.

The dissatisfaction ate at him, like an itch he couldn't scratch. It shouldn't have mattered—he didn't get involved, and certainly shouldn't with her. A one-night stand with Cassie would've made the dynamics in their group incredibly awkward, so he'd settled for despising her instead.

But he wanted her. With a kind of aggravated lust he'd never felt before.

He didn't just want to seduce her, didn't want to only prove he was the best she'd never had. He wanted to mess her up. To get in her face when she was mouthing off, and pay her back for all the times she'd been snarky by finding all her little triggers and reducing her to a helpless, whimpering mess. To force her to admit that yes, there was something fucking *there* between them, even if she hated him for it.

And now, standing in his shower, he was suddenly harder than he'd been with a naked woman beneath him the night before. From thoughts about a woman who couldn't stand the sight of him.

Fate had a goddamn twisted sense of humor.

When he was dressed and feeling human again, he started a

fresh pot of coffee and read through his emails. A note from the board of directors was at the top of the list. Delete. He didn't want to deal with their shit today. They'd send another email with the same crap on Monday. He scanned through the next few with even less interest: His head of marketing, having another panic attack over their global market share. Strauss wanting to go over the next year's budget forecast Patrick had already looked at a thousand times.

Scroll, scroll, scroll. Delete, delete, delete.

Finally, a familiar name stopped him—one he hadn't heard in years. A guy who could've only sounded more like the prep school bastard he was if he'd had a III tacked on to the end of his name. Hudson Grant had been a prick when he and Patrick were fraternity brothers at Princeton, and Patrick would bet he still was now.

He supposed he was about to find out. Because Hudson Grant, trust-fund baby and investment addict, wanted to meet for a drink.

* * *

The bar in the financial district was one Patrick hadn't been to, half because it was steps from his office, and half because of the decor. Chandeliers hung from the ceiling. The rich, dark furniture matched the even richer clientele, who must not have found the giant images of blown-up dollar bills on the walls as tacky as he did. Sure, Patrick had money, but he didn't like to flaunt it, and certainly not at places like this. But this was where Hudson had wanted to meet and Patrick hadn't bothered to suggest an alternative.

He found Hudson seated at a table, blond hair in the same stupid ponytail he'd sported years ago, a glass in one hand as he chatted up a waitress who looked beyond uncomfortable. Back at school, he'd exclusively dated sorority sisters and thought the only reason women went to college was to find husbands. Nice to see the guy hadn't changed. At least the wedding band he'd worn to their last reunion was absent.

Patrick approached the table and shook Hudson's hand.

"I seem to recall a beautiful heiress on your arm the last time I saw you." He nodded to the waitress. "Not that you're not beautiful, of course."

She blushed, looking at ease for a moment. Hudson took a sip of his drink. "Nah, unlatched myself from that bitch years ago. Have a seat."

Patrick ordered a scotch, neat before the waitress seized upon on her opportunity to get away. He pulled out a chair and sat. "So, Hudson. What got you looking me up?"

Hudson tilted his glass around until the ice pinged at the sides. "I'm looking for advice. I'm having some financial struggles."

"Again? I thought you'd been doing well."

Hudson snorted. "Digital-only publishing isn't what it used to be."

"You're telling me." The last time they'd talked, Hudson had wanted Patrick's thoughts on what he'd called *that whole e-book thing*. Patrick had offered a few ideas and gone on his way.

"You're feeling the heat too? You're the one who gave me the idea in the first place."

"I told you to invest, not open up your own house."

Hudson had forged his own press, Grant Books—an elite house that only published biographies and autobiographies about wealthy and successful men like him. Not the path Patrick had suggested, but he shouldn't have expected anything less.

"Well, I did. And now I'm having trouble paying my bills."

There was the rub. "And you thought I'd be able to help you out."

Hudson lifted his glass in a toast. "Zetes forever, right?"

Ballsy, to call on their Zeta Psi brotherhood after years of radio silence. The waitress returned with Patrick's scotch, and he took a long, slow sip before answering. "I'm not going to just cut you a check, Hudson."

"Come on. You run an international corporation. You're telling me you couldn't move around some money to help out an old friend?"

Patrick stiffened. Hudson wasn't someone he'd consider an *old friend*, but he made himself relax, forcing a smile the same way he did at sales meetings. "It doesn't work that way."

"Don't act like you don't have that kind of power. Your name is on the fucking building."

"Doesn't mean I can do whatever I want with the company's assets."

And that was the truth. His hands were tied in a way few people knew about, other than Strauss, the legal department, Jack and his dead bastard of a father.

"I'm sure you could make something happen on the side. An account here, a stock liquidated there..."

That was why they were here. Mishandled funds. Patrick put his drink down and leaned forward in his chair. "Tell me what's really going on."

Hudson sighed. "My company is falling apart."

Yeah. He'd figured that part out already. "You want to expand on that?"

"I made some bad choices, deals that went south. And now I'm about to lose everything I have. Every book with my name on it. Every partnership I've made in the last five years."

"And screw every author and editor working under you while you're at it too."

Hudson scowled, more likely because he was annoyed at having to remember that other people would be affected by his decisions than he was ashamed. "There's no way you can help?"

"Sorry. Wish I could—" no, he didn't, "—but it's not gonna happen."

Hudson knocked back the rest of his drink. "I should've kept that bitch ex-wife of mine around. At least then I could've fucked some money out of her."

Patrick's stomach roiled. He might have kept his distance when it came to attachments, but he couldn't imagine talking about a woman that way.

Hudson didn't need money. He needed someone to teach him a lesson. About his business, and about women.

And Patrick knew exactly who should do it.

Smiling at what remained in his glass, he took one more sip before standing, threw some cash on the table and took out his phone.

"There's one way I can help." He drew up his contact list, then began typing out a text. "I'm sending you a woman's name and number."

"A woman, huh? That'll take my mind off things for a night."

"It's for your business, jackass. Not your dick."

Patrick hit send. Hudson glanced at his phone. "And what am I supposed to do when I call her?"

Patrick smirked. "Whatever she tells you to do."

4

"*M*aybe *that's your problem, Cassie. A lack of... satisfaction in your life.*"

Cassie huffed out an angry breath and punched the stop button on the stair climber. When it stopped moving, she snatched her water bottle and took a sip. The liquid was tepid after an hour sitting in the cup holder.

"*I'm sure your night with your drink will be as satisfying as mine.*"

She growled through her swallow. Picturing Patrick's smug grin, the way he mocked her, insinuating how boring her evening was going to be while he was off getting laid, had anger flooding her system instead of the endorphins she'd been hoping for.

No, asshole, her night hadn't been satisfying. And neither was this water.

She sucked it down anyway. Making her way to the treadmills, she stepped onto the empty machine next to Lilly's.

"Training for a marathon?"

"Actually," Lilly said, only somewhat out of breath despite her speed, "I might sign up for the next one."

"Don't you want to ease into it or something?"

"I eased into it when I started. Now I want to see what I can do."

Lilly sped up to reach the end of her mile, then slowed the machine down. A former track star, Lilly had stopped running completely after college, picking it up again this past spring. She'd joined the gym Sam belonged to along with Cassie at the beginning of the summer, which was good, because as content as Cassie was with her hourglass figure, she needed to rein it in before that hourglass became a bell jar.

"I'm sure you'll rock it." Cassie paused. "Thanks for meeting me, by the way. I know it interrupted your weekend with Jack."

Lilly and Jack spent their weekends "in role," as Lilly had explained it—in the mindset of Dominant and submissive for hours of both sexual and nonsexual play. Cassie had felt lousy, texting Lilly and asking if she'd join her at the gym, but she'd needed to call in the best friend card. After spending Saturday knocking around her apartment, company was essential before she punched something.

Lilly had borrowed Jack's car, picked up Samantha and driven from Cambridge to Brookline without a second thought.

"You didn't interrupt. I think we all needed some girl time." Lilly hit the stop button and toweled off. "Besides, Jack's classes started this week and he needed time to prepare his lectures. I would've been watching TV or cooking if you hadn't called."

"Don't talk about food. I'm starving."

"So am I. Let's get Sam and go eat."

They caught sight of Samantha's fiery red ponytail at the weight rack, then went to the locker room, showered and got their things. Heading out into the midday air, Lilly stretched her arms and turned her face to the sun.

"I love how warm it still is," she said.

Cassie frowned and rummaged through her bag for her sweatshirt. "Your version of warm is debatable."

Sam shrugged. "Seventy degrees feels pretty warm to me. It's still technically summer, you know."

"For like twelve more days."

Cassie could already feel a mild chill in the air, especially with her hair still wet from her shower. Lilly had twisted her blond locks into a braid while it dried, and Sam's hair had gone from a ponytail to a messy bun, but Cassie's was too short for her to do either one. Once she'd kept her hair longer, but that was back when she still lived in Miami and the hot sunshine dried it within minutes.

She'd chopped it off when she'd moved to the Northeast for college, and while she loved New England for its seasons and its charm, sometimes she missed the warmth of southern Florida, missed how summer started at Easter and lasted well past Halloween. There were days when she longed for the sight of palm trees, for the feel of tough grass under her feet and humidity so thick she could chew it.

She missed other things too. Like the spicy sweet smell of her grandfather's cigars—hickory and toasted almonds and tobacco.

She sniffed the air hoping for a whiff of it, and tears sprang into her eyes unbidden at the loss. Every once in a while, she tasted the scent of cigar smoke on the air, and the ghostly aroma made her feel his presence even though he'd been gone for years. It reminded her of his warm, leathery arms and the scratchiness of his stubble when he kissed her good night. But taking trips home didn't bring her grandfather back, so she hadn't visited much. Not when all being there did was get her stressed. The last time she'd given in, impulsively buying a ticket home, all she'd gotten was a week of lectures from her mother.

"How long are you going to keep putting your career over getting a husband?" she'd bemoaned. "*¿El que dirán?*"

What will people say? As if Cassie gave a rat's ass about that. No, being here was better for her, away from the pressures of her family. Her layered, long bob cut was better for her too. She couldn't be bothered with fussing with her hair when she had companies to reorganize.

She tugged her sweatshirt over her head. "Okay, where do you two want to—"

"Aw, take that hoodie off, baby. No need to cover that pretty body up."

Cassie paused midstep and whipped her head in the direction of the male voice. A tank-top-wearing, muscled dumbass she'd seen once or twice at the gym was smiling at her.

She didn't smile back. "Excuse me?"

"I said, don't cover up." He said *covah* instead of *cover*, dropping the final *r* in a way typical of native Bostonians. "You've got a beautiful body. Don't hide it behind a sweatshirt."

Adrenaline rushed through her, her fingers tingling with her fuck-the-flight-and-fight reflex. "I'm not hiding behind anything."

"Yeah, you are." He pointed at her shirt, his grin lazy and stupidly large. "I'm reading it right now. It says Boston University on it."

Despite his local accent, he reminded her of things she didn't miss from home. The *machismo*, men coming on to her at every street corner and calling her *"gordita."* Affectionate expression or not, she'd hated being called "little fat girl," and she didn't like this guy man-splaining her own goddamn sweatshirt to her now.

"It says Boston University School of Law. I'm a lawyer, not some piece of ass for you to drool at. So unless you want a restraining order issued on you, I'd suggest you get the fuck out of my face."

He stepped backward, his hands in the air. "Whoa. I was saying you were pretty. That's all."

"Yeah? Really? Is that all?"

Cassie turned on him like a small whirlwind, but didn't feel as intimidating without her heels on. Whatever, she'd take him on anyway. She was about to step into his space when Sam's hand closed around her arm.

"Okay, we're going. Bye now." She yanked Cassie in the other direction from Mr. Muscles. Lilly followed, and Cassie allowed herself to be tugged away. She cooled down as they walked in silence, which was probably a good thing. It wasn't that guy she was angry at. She was upset at herself. And her boss. And Patrick. Not necessarily in that order.

After a few minutes, she finally muttered, "The guy was a jerk."

"He was," Sam agreed. "And you certainly put him in his place. But you might want to take it down a notch before you end up needing Lilly to represent you for ripping someone's head off."

They went into Cassie's favorite café, a cozy neighborhood spot with decent lunch fare, baked goods and coffees, and got in line. Wishing for one of the pastries she could only find back home, she ordered a fruit croissant. After growing up on *churros* and guava-filled *pastelitos*, Cassie had an unhealthy relationship with carbs and powdered sugar. Screw the workout. Whatever assets she didn't feel like shaking she could hold down with some industrial-strength Spanx. But she discovered after sitting down and biting into her treat that it was neither flaky nor fruit-filled enough to be satisfying.

"That's your problem. A lack of...satisfaction in your life."

She grimaced and dropped the pastry on its plate.

Lilly raised her eyebrows over her soup. "You know, not eating completely defeats the purpose of destroying your workout."

Cassie had to laugh. "You have a point."

Sam swallowed a bite of her sandwich—a healthy mix of whole-wheat bread and greens that put Cassie's croissant to shame. "You want to talk about it?"

"Talk about what?"

"Whatever got you ready to put your fist through that guy's head."

Sam's comment was punctuated by a knowing look in her dark brown eyes and a tilt of an eyebrow. Lilly, the more hesitant of the two and less likely to push, simply smiled and waited. Cassie envied them—Sam's calm demeanor and Lilly's hazel-eyed, freckle-faced innocence. They never seemed to lose their tempers the way Cassie did. But this was why she'd asked for their company today, so it didn't seem right to clam up now.

She tore off another piece of the pastry and chewed. "I'm pissed."

"About work?" Lilly asked.

Among other things. "I've busted my ass and now it feels like it's been a waste of time."

"It hasn't been a waste. It's what you want to do, isn't it?"

A paralegal up until a few months ago, Lilly was at the beginning of her legal career. Now she was eagerly anticipating the results of her bar exam and a chance to practice law.

"Of course," Cassie replied. It had been what she'd wanted to do since she'd beaten her grandfather in a game of dominoes, and he'd told her she was going to change the world.

Casimíro Flóres loved arguing almost as much as he loved his wife, cigars and Cuba. His name was Spanish for peaceful, although he was anything but. He was bullheaded and opinionated, and discussed everything heatedly, from dominoes to baseball to the Castro regime. He'd fled his homeland and come to America with nothing, worked hard for what he had and paid back every dime he'd had to borrow. Despite only being half Cuban, Cassie was born like him—pushy, determined and strongly averse to taking advantage of anything resembling charity.

"You're going to change the world, Cassandra. I'm counting on it."

He'd passed before she'd had the chance to prove it to him. She clawed her way through the lowest-ranking Miami-Dade public schools anyway, getting top grades and a scholarship to Brown. She worked part time at Boston Legal Aid while getting her JD, then started hacking her way through her student loans clerking for a Massachusetts Supreme Judicial Court Justice.

When she'd gotten her offer letter from Forrester, Schaeffer and Pierce, she'd thought the finish line was finally in sight.

"I've worked doubly as hard as my male counterparts, done all the right things demanded of me by the system, but despite the talk of diversity and inclusion I still can't get anywhere."

"You think you're not getting anywhere because you're biracial?" Sam asked.

"Yes. No. I don't know."

It was hard to talk about the blurred line of her ethnic heritage. Growing up, Cassie knew her family was different, but it became more apparent when she moved north. Acting Cuban with her Latina friends never felt comfortable, and acting American with Caucasians wasn't a perfect fit either. There was no way to be both. Society forced her to choose, to split the way she behaved, and somewhere along the line, she'd become two separate people.

She didn't know if that was the problem at work. It wasn't as if she was "Cuban Cassie" that much at the office—no one asked what her ethnicity was unless they heard a Spanish curse slip out. They assumed she was white, so she let that assumption stand, coasting by on her appearance. It was hard enough to get somewhere in the legal marketplace as a woman. Let her Latina side show, and that glass ceiling might get even farther away.

But parts of her had been erased in the process, and she'd been the one wielding the pencil.

"It feels like no matter what I've done, it's not good enough. I work hard at the office, it gets me nowhere. I try to make something of myself, my mother puts it down because I'm not making babies. I try to relax on a Friday, and I get Patrick telling me my life is unsatisfying."

Sam raised an eyebrow. "He said what, now?"

Cassie sighed and shook her head. "Oh, nothing. He was being his usual dick self. But the worst part is he wasn't wrong."

Lilly frowned. "You think your life is unsatisfying?"

Yes. "No."

"Then fuck him," Sam said.

No, Cassie didn't want to do that.

Well, maybe a little. But only as a means of shutting him up.

"Patrick, I can ignore." He was a bug. A mosquito flying around her head that needed to be squashed. "But my goal was making partner. I figured the whole 'finding a husband and making babies thing' would fall into place afterward. And now it's possible that neither one is going to happen."

"Well, marriage and babies ain't the happy ever after it's built up to be," Sam said dryly. If Lilly was fresh out of the gate in her career, Sam was the opposite, having opted to stay home and raise her kids. "And I get the whole parents-not-being-supportive thing. Mine are thrilled that I'm here instead of using my poly-sci degree in DC like I wanted."

"You wanted to work on The Hill?" It was an easier question than asking what was going on between her and Brady. They hadn't been friends long enough for Cassie to want to pry.

"I did, but my mom needed surgery so here I am." Sam raised her coffee in a toast. "I wouldn't give up my daughters for the world, but kids change your life. If you want them, nothing's stopping you. Hell, you can make babies and skip the husband."

If only Cassie could be sure that was what she wanted. Her biological clock seemed to be on permanent snooze. When her sister-in-law was pregnant with her niece, she'd waited for it to kick into gear. To see a pair of tiny booties and poof! The got-to-have-a-baby-gene would kick into action.

It hadn't happened. Not then, and not a few years later when her nephew was born.

"I'm a year and change away from forty," Cassie said. "As my mother loves to remind me, I'm running out of time."

"You are not," Lilly insisted. "Forty is the new thirty, right? And you're gorgeous. You'll have no problem finding somebody."

"Sure. Because I'm awesome at dating."

"That's not true. You just went on a date with…"

Cassie waited. "You gonna finish that sentence, counselor?"

Lilly wouldn't be able to because Cassie couldn't remember the last time she'd been on a date either. Her friend wrinkled her nose in frustration.

"Uh-huh." Cassie ripped off half her croissant and stuffed it in her mouth.

It wasn't as if she hadn't been trying, but dating had always been a challenge, and not only because of the hours she put in at work. She was a loudmouthed chick with a take-no-prisoners, badass side, but she *had* to be that way. In a professional landscape where women were often discriminated against, being tough as nails was the only way she could intimidate. Her battle armor was what helped her succeed, from her first mock trial, to her first time in front of a judge to her own firm's conference room. Problem was, that armor didn't work in relationships. Her hard-shell exterior was great in the courtroom, but not so great in the bedroom. Which was why most of the relationships she'd had ended soon after they started.

"Well you've gotta get back out there," Lilly said.

"Men *out there* don't have a tendency to like women like me."

"What the hell does that mean?" Sam asked.

"It means I'm difficult. Abrasive. Too hard to deal with." At least that was what her last few boyfriends had said during their breakup conversations. "Men say they want someone who is hardworking and intelligent, but that's bullshit, because look at me, Ivy League and still single."

Not that she was going to change who she was. If a guy was being a dick, she was going to say so. They couldn't take her heat, then they could get the fuck out of her kitchen.

"Clearly, you've dated some real winners," Sam said.

"They weren't strong enough to take me." Her toughness scared most men off at the first signs of conflict. Cassie shrugged. "Whatever. I don't need a man. I'm perfectly happy on my own."

She glanced at Lilly's collar. At Sam's wedding ring.

If she'd been under oath right now, she'd be perjuring herself.

"It means you haven't found the right guy," Lilly insisted. "You've gotta keep looking. Weren't you the one trying to convince *me* to get out there a few months back?"

"I was," Cassie grumbled.

"And didn't I resist it?"

"Like a stubborn mule."

"And didn't I end up meeting an amazing man and falling hopelessly in love?"

And Cassie had stood by the whole time, terrified her wounded-by-an-ex-boyfriend, vulnerable friend would get her heart broken. "You did. But—"

"But...?" Lilly prodded.

Cassie rubbed the back of her neck. She'd never explained why she'd been so overprotective when Lilly was first dating Jack. It had been a combination of fear and envy, because BDSM was perplexing as fuck. How did it work, when you didn't think you were dominant or submissive, but fell somewhere in between? What did it mean when you liked to fight, but wanted a man who would fight back? Cassie was tough, but what she hungered for was to be taken down—to feel that satisfying push in a way that was both arousing and terrifying.

Just like the grey area of Cassie's genetic makeup, her sexual desires left her feeling like an outsider, uncomfortable and confused.

"But, I'm not sure everyone is that lucky," Cassie finished. "So I think I'll focus on making things happen at work."

Lilly smiled. "Your name's gonna be up on that wall. I know it."

"That's the dream."

They finished their meals, talking about doing more things during the week to get Sam out of the house, and Lilly suggested a shoe-shopping trip that made Sam almost as giddy as it made

Cassie. When they parted ways at the lot where Lilly was parked, Cassie walked home, determined to get her head back in the game. Now wasn't the time for worrying about men or babies. It was time to find the client that would make her a rainmaker, and bring in so much business the firm begged her to become a full equity partner.

And as for her shameful desires? They'd stay buried where they'd been for years. It was easier than hoping she'd find someone who could fulfill them and still respect her—that she could have them fulfilled and still respect herself. She wasn't Cinderella, didn't need any Prince Charming to bring her a shiny slipper. She was going to use her own expensive stilettos and shatter that damn glass ceiling with them all on her own.

And then she'd show Patrick Dunham how satisfying her life could be.

5

"You have someone waiting for you in the conference room, Ms. Allbright."

Cassie stopped in the lobby and stared blankly at Piper, the firm's receptionist.

"I don't have anything on my calendar," she said as she fished her phone from her bag and thumbed over her agenda.

Other than ten memos she needed to hand in, three back-to-back client meetings, finishing document review for an upcoming discovery hearing, and helping Gabe with a motion he needed to get in before midnight.

"He waltzed in as I was unlocking the door and said he'd make himself comfortable until you got here."

"Couldn't you have farmed him out to one of the first-years?"

Piper had worked there as long as Cassie had. She was half admin, half bouncer.

"I tried. He wanted you specifically. Real sleazy-looking kind of guy too."

Fantastic. "All right. Thanks for letting me know." Cassie hurried toward her office. Gabe appeared by her side, coming out of the kitchen with a steaming cup of coffee.

"Buenos dias," he said. "Got a case of the Mondays already?"

"We can't all be chipper like you are." Married to Lilly's brother Nick, Gabe always seemed happy. He was also a partner in the firm, and had been her mentor for years. "I haven't put my stuff down yet, and already there's some dipshit without an appointment making demands on my time."

"I'm sure you'll have him beaten into submission in seconds. Stomp all over him in those fabulous Jimmy Choos."

She stopped to model her favorite glittery pumps. Four-inch heels with a rounded toe and worth every penny. Cassie didn't mind the bit of extra junk in her trunk—real women had curves and all—but if she was able to offset it with some flashy footwear, she was gonna. She didn't spend on much. Her apartment was modest and she budgeted the hell out of her salary to afford her mortgage, putting money aside to save for her capital contribution to the firm. Making partner would mean she'd have to purchase her equity share to the tune of a hundred grand, so she kept her expenditures to a minimum. But when it came to shoes, she was Imelda fucking Marcos.

If Imelda had gotten all her heels from discount racks and outlet shops, of course.

"Good thing I didn't wear my Pradas. I wouldn't want blood on them."

"Don't judge. That could be somebody's kink." Gabe waggled his eyebrows. "And hey, what happened with Schaeffer on Friday? Are we about to celebrate?"

Cassie grimaced. "Nope. No celebrations. Instead our fine Mr. Schaeffer told me I was no longer on partner track."

Gabe's jovial expression vanished. "Do you want me to talk to him?"

His unwavering loyalty made her smile, but Cassie was too proud for that. She was going to fend for herself. "Thanks, but I don't think it'll change anything, and I don't need anyone going to bat for me."

"I know you don't. But the offer still stands." He lifted his mug in a salute. "Give the new dipshit my apologies."

Squaring her shoulders, Cassie dropped off her things, then powered down the hallway to the conference room. A blond guy with a ponytail lounged in one of the chairs.

Cassie strode into the room.

"If you're looking for a place to nap, I hear there's a great hotel up the street."

His grin was all teeth. "Is that an invitation?"

Ew. No wonder Piper had warned her. What was it with these guys? Except unlike Mr. Muscles from yesterday, Ponytail Man was the pompous, moneyed type, a fact that rolled off him from the shine of his shoes to the shape of his smirk.

"It's an invitation to get the hell out of this firm."

"Words spoken like someone who has some clout here. Or did I get that wrong? Aren't you just an associate?"

Just an associate? Oh, she was done here. Crossing her arms, Cassie geared up for the fight.

"Last I heard, being an associate at one of the biggest, most successful firms in Boston wasn't something to sneeze at. Now, if you'll excuse me, I have about two hundred other clients' work to attend to."

She turned on her heel and started out.

"Wait, Ms. Allbright. Please."

Cassie paused and glared over her shoulder. "I don't see why I should."

"I apologize for the way I came off," he said, his grin vaguely less smug. "I needed to make sure you could take a little heat. You're obviously all you're cracked up to be."

That was better. "And what exactly do you know about me, Mister..."

"Grant. Hudson Grant. And I know you graduated summa cum laude from Brown, clerked for the state Supreme Court, and are a qualified and highly recommended lawyer who has played a major role in some of the most complex bankruptcy cases this firm has taken on."

All things he'd obviously found in her bio on the company website, but the words *qualified* and *highly recommended* softened her slightly. It was the ego-stroking she needed after Friday's massacre.

"All true," she replied, turning back around.

"I work with the best, Ms. Allbright. So I'd appreciate it if you'd consider my case."

"And what case is that?"

His hands fell to the armrests, and he gripped them, a little tell of stress. "Bankruptcy, it would seem. Unless you can magically fix my company."

He looked away. Not wanting her to see his weaknesses, Cassie guessed. But if she was going to represent this guy, she'd rather see him lay his cards out on the table.

"I'll need more information, Mr. Grant, if I'm going to perform magic."

He met her eyes and folded his hands, a move more calculating than docile. "I'm Ivy League myself. Princeton. And I'm the President and Editor in Chief of Grant Books. It's a boutique, digital-only publishing house, with elite authors and subject matter. I've put everything I have into it."

"What are the stakes?"

"I have a reputation to uphold, investors to answer to, as well as an ex-wife who'd like nothing better than to see me fail. I need this taken care of quickly, and quietly. Out of the papers, with as little exposure as possible."

She eyed him. Clearly Hudson wanted to keep his catastrophe on the DL, but if he was so high profile, he'd want a well-established attorney attached to his case. Someone who was known. "Why come to me instead of one of the partners?"

"I need someone passionate. Someone ruthless, who believes in what she's doing and is invested in my success."

Passionate. Ruthless. Words she liked when it came to her career. Among other things.

"And what makes you think I'll be invested in you?"

She certainly wasn't *interested*. Not in a guy like him, especially given the way his gaze crept toward her cleavage before snapping back up to her face.

"My company is worth approximately five-point-two million dollars. And you've been an associate for a long time. A win for me could be a win for you too."

Her heart began to pound. She didn't like him, but this could be big. The case she'd been waiting on, the game changer that would finally advance her career. His behavior didn't matter. She was a damn good lawyer, and could advocate for even the slimiest Princeton asshole.

Cassie walked slowly back to the table and settled into a seat, not missing the way Hudson's gaze chased up her legs as she crossed them. Whatever. He could look all he wanted. He wasn't getting any.

"Okay, Mr. Grant. You have my attention. Talk."

* * *

Patrick reared his arm back and hit the ball with a satisfying thwack. It sailed over the net and out of Jack's reach.

"Deuce," Patrick cheered. "Did you know Wednesday is one of my favorite days?"

"Oh?" Jack scooped the ball from the ground with his racquet. "Is that because you leave work early, come to campus and hit on my students?"

Patrick grinned. Their weekly matches at Harvard's indoor tennis court did have their perks.

"I'll always be grateful you became a law professor for the abundance of lovely female scholars surrounding you, but that's not why." Patrick got ready for Jack's next serve, lunging backward as the ball soared to the far left corner. "It's because every Wednesday I get to kick—your—ass!"

Patrick's backhand was his best move. Which was why he was sure he'd been wronged when Jack easily smashed the ball back at him, a slice Patrick couldn't have reached even if he'd been seventeen again and they'd been playing in his backyard court. Jack served again, this time an ace down the middle. The ball bounced against the mesh wall.

"What was that about you kicking my ass?" Jack asked.

"Fuck you."

Jack snorted and walked to the bench to retrieve his water. "You must be tired. All those late nights are getting to be too much for a man your age."

"We're the same age, asshole. And you're the one with the twenty-eight-year-old girlfriend."

Jack took a long sip. "That I am."

His smiles were still something to get used to. Less than a year ago, Jack had been mired in depression, unable to get over the loss of his late wife, Eve. Patrick had spent months trying to get his friend back out there, with no success. The guy had one foot following Eve into the grave, but then he'd met Lilly. Now Jack smiled like he was getting it regularly, from someone he truly loved.

"I always told you sex gives you energy," Patrick said. "Glad you finally followed my example."

"I did. So what's your excuse for being such a pathetic opponent today?"

What *was* his excuse? "Work sucked. For starters."

"You always say that."

"I always mean it. By the way, Brady never called me about that book idea for Samantha."

"Something's going on there, but I haven't asked about it yet. I'm waiting to see if he'll come to me." Jack pointed his water bottle in Patrick's direction. "And we were talking about you and your lack of ass kicking."

Patrick went for his own drink. "What? I'm having an off day."

An off week was more like it. Maybe an off month?

Come to think of it, he'd been off since January, when Cassie Allbright walked into his life and pissed him the fuck off.

"Last night's conquest didn't do it for you?"

"Nah." He was bluffing. There hadn't been a conquest last night to *do* anything for him at all.

They both sat on the bench. Patrick could feel his friend eyeing him.

"You didn't go out last night," Jack said.

Stupid twenty years of friendship. The guy could see right through him. "What makes you say that?"

"Because if you had, you'd be bragging about it."

"I did on Friday."

"For you, going without from Friday to Wednesday is a dry spell."

Patrick shrugged and threw Jack his best I-don't-give-a-shit grin. "I'm being choosy with my options. When you're this good looking, you can afford to be picky."

It wasn't entirely the truth. The truth was he'd been itching to clash with a certain bitchy brunette attorney, to see how much Hudson Grant had gotten on her nerves.

"Don't worry," Patrick added. "I'll be back in fighting form by the weekend. You're going to the pub again, right?"

Their habitual nights at Barrel 'n' Flask had made Friday Patrick's other favorite day.

"Not this weekend. I'm planning something special for Lilly."

Jack's smile widened. Patrick rolled his eyes.

"Be careful she doesn't tire you out too much. I don't want to have to visit you in the hospital. Or see you on an episode of 'BDSM Sent Me to the E.R.'"

"I'll try not to. But, seriously. Don't you ever..."

"Don't I ever what?"

Jack sighed. "Want more than empty, casual hookups?"

"This again?" Patrick lolled his head on the back of the bench. "We've had this discussion before. I'm not like you."

Opening up came easy to Jack. Patrick? Not so much.

"I know you *think* you can't be like me, but—"

"—but it's true."

"But you could be. And this fear that you'll never find someone who'll love you—"

"—isn't something we need to talk about."

Patrick dumped his water bottle in his bag. Fucking hell, he wished he'd never told Jack that. A moment of idiotic honesty a few months back when he'd admitted he envied his friend's capacity to love and be loved in return.

Envy and desire weren't the same things. Love wasn't something Patrick needed. At all.

"Fine," Jack said. "I'll drop it." But this conversation wasn't over. Patrick knew they'd be having it again. "What's going on with work?"

"What's always going on with work? It's my job."

"It's not a job. It's your damn company, for fuck's sake. If you're so miserable, change something."

"You read the paperwork. There's nothing else to be done."

His voice sounded so dead and distant, he wasn't sure it was his own. And there wasn't anything he could do. The proof was right there in the edict that kept Patrick trapped at Dunham and Strauss, his father's stranglehold revenge from beyond the grave.

"The language is vague. We could've contested it. Wills are challenged all the time." When Patrick didn't reply, Jack added, "But it was a shitty thing, what your father did."

"He was a vindictive asshole. You know that."

Jack knew better than anyone what life was like for Patrick growing up in the extravagant and cold Dunham household. "He wasn't the nicest guy. But what he did to you and your mother was harsh."

"Yeah well, she's not such a peach either."

Patrick stood, picked up a ball and started slamming it against the ground. Being the wife of Reid Dunham, CEO and billionaire, was a good gig. One Patrick's mother was so dependent on she ignored the women Reid kept on the side and buried her unhappiness in bottles of wine and vodka. For years they fought one another in silence and ignored Patrick in the process. And for the most part, Patrick had kept that shit to himself. He knew other people had it much worse, and he never wanted anyone calling him a poor little rich boy. But tutors and tennis coaches were no substitute for parents, and by the time Patrick was eighteen, all he'd wanted was to escape.

His acceptance into Princeton was his emancipation, although he'd been expected to follow in his father's footsteps and get a degree in economics. Majoring in English had been Patrick's first rebellion, followed by the double minor of Spanish language and Hispanic studies. The latter choices had been less to bother Reid and more because Patrick had wanted to, which led to his last act of mutiny: instead of coming home after graduation and going to work for his father, he went abroad, wanting to see the sights he'd read about. He spent a year in Spain, falling in love with the language, the music and the food.

He'd fallen for more than that, a fact he'd never shared with anyone.

"It just proves you're capable of love," Jack said.

Patrick tensed, his fist around the ball. "How's that?"

"Taking care of your mother the way you do."

He relaxed a bit, bouncing the ball again as he walked in circles. Movement was necessary when his past started crawling its way out of his skin. He'd never told Jack what had happened in Spain, why his desire to immerse himself in literature, or anything other than sex, had become obliterated after his trip. All

Jack knew was that Patrick had returned home to discover that Reid had died, and he was now at the helm of the family business.

He'd refused the job. He had no clue how to be a CEO, and wasn't so shallow as to take a job he had no experience in because of his last name. And being connected to books in any way had been the last thing he'd wanted.

But Reid had figured on that, and found a way to screw his son even after his own funeral. If Patrick wanted his inheritance, he needed to take a role at Dunham and Strauss. If he didn't, he would lose all his monetary support, and so would his lush of a mother.

So he'd offered the job to Leroy Strauss, Reid's business partner with a lesser share of the company's holdings, and taken on the role of National Sales Director instead. Not that Patrick knew anything about sales either, but it was the lowest position on the totem pole, one the board of directors could easily nurse him through.

He'd watched his mother nurse herself through with alcoholism too. It was a disease; he knew that, one she wasn't in control of. But he wasn't going to be stuck there watching her drink herself to death. So he'd removed all the liquor from her home, and threatened to do whatever it took to cut off the funds he now controlled. She'd finally stopped drinking, but their relationship was strained at best.

"Different kind of love, my friend," Patrick said. "I look after her because I have to."

"I thought you two were getting along better?"

Patrick shrugged. "As well as we ever did. But she's sober, so at least there's that."

He was proud of her for that accomplishment. And he knew he shouldn't resent her. After all, she'd loved a man who cared so little about her, he'd have been content to leave both her and their son homeless.

If only she'd learned early on what Patrick had: that love was an illusion—nothing more than a lie.

His body itched. He needed to move. Patrick grabbed his racquet and twirled it around. "I've had enough of today's therapy session. One more game? Or should I go off to hit on your students?"

"You're such a pain in the ass."

"That's what she said."

Patrick grinned, happy to go back to his routine. Wednesday afternoon tennis. Friday night conquests. They were the only things that stopped him from feeling completely trapped.

Because even though he was now the Executive Vice President of Global Sales at Dunham and Strauss Books, he was doing the same thing he'd begun doing when he got home from Spain. Weekdays with the board hovering over him. Lunches with his emotionally distant mother. Sex on the weekends. And always walking out women's doors first, because he'd be damned if he'd let history repeat itself again.

6

───────

$\mathcal{B}$y Friday afternoon, Cassie had learned everything she could about Grant Books.

Hudson had retained her for an in-depth analysis after their meeting, and Cassie had gone straight to Schaeffer afterward, informing him of her chance to possibly restructure a tanking multimillion-dollar business. He'd said this could be a great opportunity but reminded her to be careful, to vigilantly review everything and double-check her work.

I.e., don't screw up your last chance to make partner.

She wasn't planning on it.

She'd dropped everything, shuffling around other clients and handing off some work she was supposed to help Gabe with to Lilly. And every day this week, she'd been at Grant Books headquarters, a renovated building in Boston's Back Bay area, in an attempt to inventory what the fuck Hudson had done to his company. She'd opened all his books, interviewed his staff and researched his investors. And in between, she'd looked over the earnings of every author he'd published, and examined each piece of art and furniture he owned.

Hudson liked to surround himself with some lavish shit. His

space only housed him, his assistant, his rights coordinator and book formatter, and yet he'd furnished it with high-end brands and suppliers. In Hudson's office alone, there was a writing desk worth fifteen grand. He'd also given himself a hefty bonus every year for no reason whatsoever.

Seeing so much reckless spending made her teeth grind, especially after the way her family had struggled with money. But her personal feelings didn't matter here. She'd analyzed everything and now was back to deliver the news.

"Okay, Mr. Grant. You have two options."

His eyes passed appreciatively over her, but she'd gotten accustomed to that. Hudson liked pretty things, and Cassie used it to her advantage. She'd put on her best power outfit—pencil skirt, a short-sleeved, fitted, black button-down that showed a bit of cleavage, and her favorite pair of Manolo Blahniks—bought heavily discounted of course. She'd even spritzed on her favorite perfume. It did the trick, making her commanding but sexy as hell at the same time.

She needed his attention and respect, but it didn't hurt to keep him a little distracted.

"And what are they?" He settled himself behind his desk and put his feet on it. Like the thing he was resting his shoes on couldn't pay someone's college tuition for a year. Seriously, the *cojones* on this guy.

"Option one, we restructure."

"I like the sound of that. What would a restructuring involve?"

"For starters?" She waved a hand around the office. "This all goes."

Hudson's smile fell. "What all goes?"

"The custom-made luxury table in your conference room. The thirteen-hundred-dollar flower vase in your waiting room. This desk. The entire office space itself. It's all equity, and you need to sell it to put new money back into your business."

He looked horrified, like a kid who'd had a very expensive

lollipop yanked from his mouth. "You want me to sell my building?"

"Yes." *Did I stutter?* "This property is on Boylston Street, one of the eight most expensive places to have office space in North America. Among the seven before it are Royal Palm Way in Palm Beach, the Avenue of the Stars in LA, Pennsylvania Avenue in DC and Fifth Avenue in Manhattan."

It was as if she were naming the most expensive properties in Monopoly. And from Hudson's snide expression, he felt the same way too. "I publish elite authors, Ms. Allbright. An elite building reflects that."

Oh, they'd get to his authors in a minute.

"Having this elite building is in direct relation to your inability to pay your bills. So you either sell and move to an all-online operation, or lease it to a business that will pay you rent."

She took a second to let that sink in. No harm in letting him recover before she went in for the kill.

"I also feel you need to expand the range of people who write for you."

"What makes you an authority on books?" he snapped.

Cassie wasn't intimidated by the sharpness of his words. If anything, she found it amusing.

"I'm not. I'm an expert in bankruptcy law, which is why you hired me. So in addition to going through all your assets, I also met with my firm's financial consultant, and reached out to a few market experts in the field."

She'd done her homework, seeing where Hudson stood in the local and national landscape and only getting slightly sidetracked when coming across the name Dunham and Strauss. Patrick was worth more than Cassie would see in her lifetime, even if she finally made partner and worked until she was dead.

But as far as Hudson was concerned, her experts had all come back with the same feedback: his handling of his money was half the problem. The other half was his business.

"Every one of your authors is a white male. Every book is one of their biographies. Books you assured your investors would be windfalls, but didn't sell as well as you'd hoped. I understand you want your house to be—" Cassie searched for a word that wasn't *snobby* or *borderline racist*, "—unique, but you need to look outside that if you want new contracts. You need cash so you can pay back your creditors, not to mention sending your authors the royalties you owe them."

Hudson's nostrils flared. "What's option two?"

"You claim bankruptcy. Which is an expensive, time-consuming and public thing."

Exactly the opposite of what he'd wanted. Hudson put his feet down and swiveled back and forth in his chair. "How long would the restructuring take?"

"Three, maybe four months."

He stared at her, as if somehow, if he did it long enough, she'd give him a different answer. Cassie shrugged.

"It's your choice, Mr. Grant. Take my suggestions, and we'll consolidate and come up with a repayment plan, so you don't lose your connections or respect in the industry as a whole. Or you can ignore my advice and we'll take our chances in court. You're welcome to see if someone else will give you a different answer, but I wouldn't recommend it, because no one is going to do a better job at this than I will."

And now that she'd said her piece, Cassie gathered her things. She was taking a gamble here, but she'd played hardball with clients before, and had a feeling her hand would play out.

She put her last file into her bag and stood. Hudson looked up at her.

"You're sure that's the only way?" he asked.

"The way I see it, yes."

He rose to his feet and reached a hand out. "Option one it is. Send me whatever paperwork you need to get things started."

Cassie gave him a firm handshake in response. He held on a

bit longer, grinned and reminded her he'd take her up on her offer to hit that hotel up the street any time. She rolled her eyes and pulled her hand away. The guy was a prick, but he seemed to respect her ability to reorganize his company.

She left his office high off her triumph. It was warm and sticky for a mid-September evening, perhaps the last day like that they'd have. Standing outside amongst the brownstones and bustling after-work crowd, she wanted to go somewhere, to meet her friends and celebrate, but Lilly would be at Jack's by now, and Gabe had been nursing a cold all week. So that left having a triumphant drink by herself, or going home.

Screw it. She lifted her chin and went into a bar across the street.

It was a cushy cocktails place, much more her style than the beer-coated floors at Barrel 'n' Flask. She sat down at the bar with a don't-fuck-with-me-because-I'm-awesome confidence and ordered a blood-orange cosmopolitan. It may have been sheer luck that Hudson had chosen her. Maybe he'd liked her face on the company website, who knows. But after years of watching the high-profile cases go to the old boys' club at the firm, and quashing her Cuban side because of it, she was finally on the path to making partner.

You're going to change the world, Cassandra.

The memory came at full impact. If only he was here to see her doing this. He'd never gotten to see her graduate high school or college, wasn't around for most of her adult life, but she'd felt like he was there sometimes. Every time she made an important decision she got a hint of cigar smoke on the air, like he was puffing on it as he watched over her. It happened again when she'd visited Brown. The first time she'd felt those autumn leaves crunch under her feet, burnt somehow and mixed with the scents of apple cider and pine, she'd gotten a whiff of smoke even though the air was clear around her, and known she was making the right choice. She smelled it again when she'd started at Legal

Aid and when she'd gotten her clerkship, but she hadn't again since.

She hated cigarettes, but man, she'd loved the smell of that cigar.

Cassie turned to face the room, people-watching as she sipped her drink. She was enjoying the warm buzz from the combination of vodka and triple sec in her glass when her gaze hit on a familiar face.

A familiar face that was *hitting on* an unfamiliar one.

Patrick fucking Dunham. Did he ever go off the goddamn prowl?

He was hovering over his young blonde prey at a table in the corner, his body language smooth and predatory like a jaguar. In dark-washed jeans, a crisp white shirt, and a sport jacket left carelessly open, he wore a casual uniform of independent wealth. His nose moved past the young woman's ear as he whispered something into it, and Cassie's stomach churned. The man was relentless in his attempts to get in women's pants. He hit on anything that breathed and was a size two or smaller. Why was he like that?

Cassie wasn't a size two. She had curves and thick thighs. And a brain.

She was smart. Smart enough to know Patrick was going to leave this woman in the morning. Earlier than that, if Cassie pegged him right. So why did it bother her so much, watching him seduce this woman? Why did jealousy snake through her gut as the blonde blushed, her shoulders curling inward under the heat of Patrick's undivided focus?

Because she'd been the recipient of that focused attention, once.

As much as she didn't want to think about it, she couldn't help but remember the party he'd thrown at his apartment for Jack's birthday. A swanky, black-tie affair that hadn't stopped Jack and Lilly from getting into their very first public argument. Cassie had been standing off to the side watching the couple face off on the terrace when Patrick moved in beside her.

"I take no responsibility for Jack's behavior," he'd said grimly. "The guy's got his head up his ass."

"I'll kill him if he hurts her," Cassie had growled.

Their eyes met, and her heart had leapt. Not because of his closeness, but at his expression, his eyes so green and intense and...*hungry*.

"What a thing it must be," he'd murmured. "To be under your fierce protection."

"I look after the people I care about."

"I know. It's one of the things I admire most about you."

The memory repulsed and humiliated her. As did the sight of Patrick right now, kissing the blonde's cheek before he stood and walked away. Would he be in that woman's bed later tonight? She was young and perky, but youth didn't hold a candle to experience. It might've been a while, but Cassie had skills that could turn a man into knots. She could do Patrick better than that twenty-something bleach-job could.

She caught herself for the thought. What the serious fuck? She didn't want Patrick. She didn't at all. And there was no reason to be jealous of this stranger. If anything, she should pity her. But Cassie was still looking at Patrick when his gaze landed on her. His brow lifted, his expression morphing into something resembling delight.

Shit. Cassie slid around on her stool and faced the bar.

A glass appeared on the countertop beside her. "See something you like?" Patrick asked.

He couldn't resist, could he? Couldn't help himself from starting up something, his voice warm and amused.

"Nope," she replied. "Other than my drink."

"It's satisfying you, I hope?"

Cassie threw him a glare, but the move backfired. It only got her caught up in his conniving smile and freshly trimmed goatee, his hair that was a little more mussed than usual, curlier and infuriatingly touchable. Why did he have to look so damn good all the time? "Yes, it is."

"Is that a cocktail to pass the time while waiting for someone to join you? Or is something at work stressing you out?"

Since when did he care how her job was? "Neither, actually, I'm celebrating."

"What are we celebrating?"

"Landing a huge client."

His expression shifted, as if he were considering saying something, before it returned to its normal glib state. "Congratulations. I'm celebrating something too."

"What's that?"

He stared at his drink before taking a sip. "Getting through another week."

As if being a high-powered, extremely wealthy executive was so tiring for him. "And that's how you celebrate. By picking up yet another woman."

"Is that envy I hear?"

Anger bubbled up inside her. She wouldn't dignify that comment with a response. "What do you say to these women to get them to fall into your lap, anyway?"

His eyes glittered. "Wouldn't you like to know?"

Cassie turned away and knocked back a sip from her drink, hoping he would move on.

He didn't. "Come on, Cassie. It's obvious you're pissed because I'm doing something you wish you could. That's why you dislike me so much."

No, it wasn't. She was hard up as all fuck, but she had no desire to go home with a stranger every night.

"Unless..." The way he trailed off forced her eyes back to him. "*You* want to be the one falling into my lap."

Oh, how she hated this man. Pure, one hundred percent loathing. But having him this close, she couldn't tamp down the attraction she'd suppressed for months. He wasn't so much tall but thick, his chest and shoulders filling out his jacket. His suit hid it well, but there was a brute strength behind it. She hadn't noticed before, but there were tiny creases by his eyes and the tiniest bit of salt-and-pepper in his goatee. The small signs of his age weren't a turnoff. He was still all man.

Virile, broad-shouldered, sexy-as-hell man.

Cassie found herself wondering what his torso looked like unclothed, how his skin would feel under her fingertips. If he'd be the one to act out the hungers that haunted her fantasies, to hold her down and whisper menacing things to her, to fight her for dominance until he finally, blissfully won.

Disgust rolled over her. Jesus, she shouldn't want these things in the first place, but now she was thinking about them with *Patrick*, for fuck's sake?

She downed another sip of her drink. "You know, you'd be a lot prettier if you didn't talk so much."

Patrick chuckled. The throaty sound sent dual shockwaves of pleasure and annoyance through her. "You think so, huh?"

"Yep. Maybe I should ask Lilly where I could get a ball gag for you."

Patrick nearly spit out his drink. Placing his glass on the bar and wiping his lower lip with the back of his hand, he asked lowly, "Do you know what I know?"

His eyes were bright, scheming, and Cassie considered her answer. Did *he* know what *she* did? Lilly had sworn Cassie to secrecy on the details of her and Jack's relationship, but that had been months ago, right before the night of that fateful party. The two of them weren't secretive anymore, not about being together, but Cassie wasn't sure Patrick knew what they were into.

"I might," she said. "What do you know?"

"I know that necklace Lilly wears isn't *just* a necklace."

"I know she doesn't call him *Sir* just to be polite."

"Then we both know Lilly would know exactly where to get a ball gag, if you were into that kind of thing."

Patrick grinned, a salacious one Cassie couldn't help but mirror. Her heart rate spiked with a rush of adrenaline. It was like a game, trading clandestine information. Their usual verbal warfare was present, but the vibe was different—without the anger, and a hell of a lot more sexually charged.

"Submission is Lilly's thing, not mine. Being on my knees isn't my number-one fantasy."

"What is your number-one fantasy?"

Cassie started to answer, then paused. What was she doing? She'd already confessed more to him than she ever thought she would, but she was buzzing off their banter. And off a little more than that, if she were being honest. Patrick was close enough now for her to catch his scent, all woodsy pine and vanilla and man. For her to look at his lips beyond his bristled goatee, and wonder what it would feel like to kiss him.

And that, ladies and gentlemen of the jury, was her cue to exit. She was too turned on, too captivated with the way he was leaning into her, eager to discover her secrets. The risks of following through on this were far too high. She'd never worried what their friends would think if she and Patrick slept together—everyone knew she detested him, and she had a feeling her post-fuck attitude toward him wouldn't be any different. But she wasn't about to let her guard down. She wasn't going to tell him her deepest desires, or fool herself into thinking he was actually interested.

Like that night months ago, she was nothing more than another chase.

Repeating Patrick's earlier tone, she tipped her head toward his and asked, "Wouldn't you like to know?"

He chuckled again. Cassie reached for her bag, left some cash on the bar and stood. "I think it's time for me to call it a night."

"So soon? I thought things were finally getting interesting."

"I'm always interesting, Patrick. But you wouldn't have any idea about that, would you?"

"I guess not," he replied with a broad grin.

"Oh well." Cassie hooked her bag over her shoulder. "I hope you're able to find someone half as *satisfying* to spend your night with."

She started out, hoping her words landed the punch she'd said them with and knowing full well Patrick's eyes were on her ass. She glanced over her shoulder.

Yup. Still looking.

Power coursed through her as she sashayed to the exit. He was definitely still interested, and leaving him high and dry was the cherry on top of a pretty fuck-awesome day.

Cassie stepped outside and headed toward the T.

"I've always loved your spitfire attitude."

Patrick's voice cut through the night. Cassie stopped and whirled around. He was standing at the doorway to the bar, his arms crossed like a bouncer or a Greek god.

"Have you now?" Cassie cocked her brow and placed a hand on her hip. "Well, you'd love me in bed then. I'm a spitfire there too."

The words popped out before she could stop them, but she didn't regret it. For once, she wanted that bastard to know the chance he'd passed up. Because she might never have been in love and had dated some serious losers, but damn it she knew how to make a man moan.

Patrick dropped his hands to his sides and quickly closed the distance between them.

"Prove it," he said.

"Prove what?"

"That you're a spitfire in bed. Unless all you can do with that mouth of yours is talk."

It took everything in her not to snarl. He was baiting her, seeing how pissed off he could get her, like he always did.

Screw the consequences. She'd had enough of his attitude. This time, she was calling his bluff.

She dumped her bag on the ground and got into his space. "I really don't like you."

"Same here."

Cassie grabbed him by the collar and closed her fist around his shirt.

"Good," she said, and kissed him, hard.

7

*P*atrick had never been thrown by a kiss before. Every time his lips met a woman's, it had been calculated. Planned. He'd never expected Cassie to kiss him. After how angry she'd looked, he'd expected her to spit in his face and tell him how repulsive she found him.

Instead her lips were sliding over his, her mouth open and wet and demanding. Demanding more.

In a move that was half reclaiming his footing, half dying to touch, Patrick found Cassie's hips with his palms. Her soft moan was the cue he needed. He gripped her hard, mapping the curves he'd been aching to feel for far too long before his brain kicked into action.

What the hell? She wanted him?

Forcing himself to break off the kiss, Patrick opened his eyes. Cassie was breathless and glaring at him and hotter than fuck.

"I thought you didn't like me," he said, and damn if he wasn't breathing heavily too.

"I don't. I can't stand the sight of you."

But she was still clutching his collar. And her gaze was darting from his eyes to his mouth and back up again. This was what all their sexual tension had been leading toward. They'd been somewhere in between flirting and taking punches for months now. And if this was how she treated people she didn't like, she could hate the ever-loving fuck out of him.

Wrapping his hands firmly around her waist, Patrick dragged her toward him until her body was flush against his. Her breasts were soft and full, her nipples tight beneath her blouse. He could feel her heat through his jeans.

"Well," he said. "I can't stand *you* either."

Patrick covered her mouth with his and swept his tongue greedily along hers. Cassie's hands went from his collar to the back of his neck, her nails biting into his skin, and he wrapped his arms around her until they were panting on a street corner like two teenagers. They were going to need to move this indoors, fast.

"As long as we're on the same page—" Fuck. He could barely make himself stop kissing her long enough to talk. "—should we go to your place, or mine?"

She pulled back, her brows slanting. A pink flush had stolen over the apples of her cheeks. Her hair fell in dark waves over her face, her lipstick messy now that she'd been kissing him.

It was the hottest thing he'd ever seen. And she wasn't even naked yet.

"My place," she said. "It's closer."

Patrick clasped her hand in one of his and lifted her bag from the ground with the other. Slinging it over his shoulder, he hailed a cab. He could've called for a company car, but he didn't have the patience to wait for it. He wanted her alone and undressed as soon as possible.

She climbed into the taxi's backseat, and Patrick gazed at her perfect ass again. She'd known what she was doing when she walked out of the bar. There was no way in hell he wasn't following her. He'd been compelled to, needing to see more of her, wanting to provoke her as hard as she was goading him.

The glimpse of her cleavage was epic as he sat down next to her.

"Brookline," Cassie said to the cabbie, then gave him a street address.

They started moving, and Patrick kissed her again. He'd never been much of an exhibitionist, but if the driver wanted to watch then so be it. He'd been waiting ages for this and he wasn't stopping now.

Jesus. Cassie. Finally.

The reality of the situation slowed him down. She wasn't someone he was going to be able to dodge after they saw this through. But she clearly wanted this, and he didn't need to explain anything, since she knew his M.O. It was almost unsettling, how into this he was before giving his usual speech; a gentle, *"Just so you know, I can't stay the night"* before things got started. It wasn't the only sign he was way off his game. By the time he'd gotten this far with a woman, he'd clearly stated his intentions, and knew what she wanted once the clothes came off. Patrick didn't have a clue with Cassie.

"Something wrong?" Her tone was low, taunting and tempting as fuck.

"You sure about this?" It was the only question he could manage through his lust-fogged brain. "I don't know if…"

If that drink impaired your judgment. Or if you're sure about fucking someone you hate.

She pulled back and studied him, blue eyes sharp and cautious. If she was doubting this and wanting to put the brakes on, she was smarter than him.

"I'm sure," she said. "Are you?"

"Fuck yes."

"Good." He glanced outside to gauge how much farther they had to go. When was the last time he'd been this worked up on the way back to a woman's home?

He knew when. But he wasn't going there now.

The driver pulled up in front of her building. Patrick fumbled for his wallet, handed over some cash and yanked the door open. Cassie shimmied out and led the way inside. His pulse hammered as he hovered behind her, waiting for her to unlock the door. The second they were inside her front hallway, a narrow space that barely fit the two of them, he slammed the door shut and pressed her up forcefully against it. She dropped her purse and threw her arms around him, and then everything was a blur of hands and mouths. The sensation of her tongue gliding along his raced straight to his cock. Frantic, she went for his jacket, yanking it off him.

"Suspenders?" she asked, palming the elastic bands crossing his chest.

"What? I like the look."

Whether Cassie liked them or not he couldn't tell because she shoved them down and went for his shirt buttons like she couldn't get him undressed fast enough. He wasn't any different, all twisted up with sexual tension. The heat between them was insane. She wasn't the cold woman he'd thought she was, and his mind was reeling instead of calculating his next move. He wanted every inch of her. Like he'd imagined for months. Had she always felt the same?

Shoving her backward, he held her still and growled, "How long?"

"How long what?"

"How long have you wanted me?"

Cassie narrowed her eyes. She opened and closed her mouth, then huffed out a breath. "Since April. Jack's birthday."

Her reply felt like triumph. Patrick grinned. "Me too."

It wasn't the truth. He'd wanted her from the minute they'd met. But she didn't need to know that.

He attacked her again, his mouth on her lips, her jaw, her neck—hard, violent kisses set to bruise. He unzipped her skirt, loving the feeling of her warm skin and bombshell hips as the fabric slid to the floor. She kicked off her shoes, and he stopped kissing her long enough to hastily unbutton her blouse. He wanted to savor the moment of getting a look at her all disheveled in a black lace bra, but he was too worked up.

He needed to pounce. To touch and taste and bite. To get inside this infuriating woman, right the hell now.

Patrick kissed down her throat, sucking and biting as he went. Cassie jolted and arched against him, hand slowing as she tugged at the last of his buttons. He did it again, liking that he'd slowed her down, that he'd found a way to get at her without words. Between panted breaths and frustrated grunts, she finally got his shirt open and wrenched it off. Her hands roamed his chest until she pushed him backward and narrowed her eyes once again.

"Oh, fuck you," she said.

Patrick followed her gaze down his chest. "Is that a compliment?"

Most women fawned over, even purred at the size of his chest, but Cassie seemed angry at what she saw. Her touch canvassed hungrily along pectorals he worked hard to keep in shape with tennis matches, his morning regimen of push-ups and holding himself up in lots of interesting positions.

"Yeah. It is."

He was big in other ways too, something he would be half bragging, half warning her about if he weren't so amused by her irritated distraction. Reaching a hand up, he traced a finger along the cups of her bra. "You're not so bad yourself."

Cassie was worlds better than *not so bad*. She was all curves and steel, sexy as fuck behind her tough-as-nails, fierce exterior. She was goddamn perfect, but he wasn't going to tell her that, either.

His finger grazed her nipple. Cassie hissed and shoved him to the opposite wall. Patrick laughed in surprise, watching as she halted for a moment, as if she were waiting for something, then went for his belt. She unzipped his jeans, dragging them and his boxers down. His cock bobbed low on his abdomen, swollen and hard and wet at the tip.

"Oh, Jesus."

Patrick smirked. "Too much for you?"

She palmed the tip. His breath hitched as she coated her hand in pre-come.

"Not at all," Cassie said, then gave him a catlike smile and dropped to her knees.

"Hey, I thought kneeling wasn't your number one—oh *fuck*."

She took him into her mouth, and Patrick's head knocked against the wall. He'd always had a thing for oral, but because of his size he rarely had it done well. Cassie however, didn't seem to have any problem. She swallowed him easily, then sucked all the way up to his tip. He shuddered, watching as she made another openmouthed plunge. When she hit the underside of his cock with a tiny bit of teeth, Patrick's knees went weak.

"Christ, your goddamn mouth."

She popped her lips off him, and Patrick nearly moaned at the loss until she made a wet circle around his base with her fingers. She moved her hand in unhurried strokes, thumb hitting the sensitive spot that made him jerk involuntarily before she leaned in and lapped once at his tip.

"I said being on my knees wasn't my number-one fantasy. I didn't say I didn't like it."

She repeated the motion, a flick of her tongue before he was once again plunged into perfect suction, soft and wet and hot, and he was powerless to do anything but groan. Fucking hell, she was good at this. Good enough to finish him off embarrassingly soon, if she didn't stop.

Delving his fingers into that silky-smooth hair, he tugged her off him, ignoring the aching protest in his balls.

Her complacent smile was messy, her lips shining. "Told you I could do more with my mouth than talk."

Patrick practically snarled. He needed to get her back, to see her as weak with pleasure as she'd made him. Heaving her up by her shoulders, he got her to her feet. He stepped out of his shoes, kicked his jeans and boxers to the side and hooked his finger between the cups of her bra. Her nipples stood out under the satin, and he rubbed the stiff point of one with his thumb.

"Were you thinking about fucking me every time we argued?" Using the leverage he had, Patrick dragged her closer, enjoying her unsteady movements as she stumbled toward him. "Did you go home from our little spats wet?"

"No."

"No?"

"You heard me."

What a stubborn pain in the ass she was. But shit, he liked it. "I'll bet you're lying."

"You'd be wrong." She lifted her chin, defiant. "I've never gotten wet around men I don't like."

Patrick huffed out a breath in frustration. Clearly she was attracted to him, so was this a deliberate provocation? She took a step back, the move loosening his finger from her bra. When she gazed up at him with a glimmer in her eye and a wicked smile, Patrick realized what she was doing.

She was lying. And she was baiting him. Fucking *baiting* him.

It made him want to bare his teeth—to force the truth out of her until she submitted.

Shaking his head, Patrick went in for a kiss, but stopped when she leaned into him and grabbed her instead, shoving her backward against the wall.

"Why do you have to make everything so damn difficult?" he hissed.

Cassie let out a startled gasp, her shoulders hiking up on a full-body shiver. So this was how she liked to play. To tease and tussle and be shoved a little. He was suddenly overwhelmed by the urge to push this further—to see her helpless. Wrestling her around until her nose was pressed against the wall, Patrick trapped her with one hand on the back of her neck, the other gripping her wrists behind her and pinning her still.

"You don't get wet around men you don't like, huh?" he murmured into her ear.

She arched into him, making it easy for him to slide his cock along the curve of her ass and jamming her more fully against the wall. Her head lolled back, and Patrick released one of her hands and slid his now-free one between her legs. Her panties were sopping wet.

"Dirty, dishonest girl. You're soaked."

"I said I've never *gotten* wet. Past tense." But her voice was strained.

"So it's just because of me then?"

"Fuck y—" A grunt cut off her word as he mapped out her slit and pressed inward. Patrick chuckled again.

"That's what I thought. Now stay put."

He slid his fingers beneath the waistband of her panties and dragged them down her legs. He tapped once at her ankle, and she stepped out of the leg holes, obeying his silent command and bracing her hands against the wall. God, was that a sight to be seen. Reaching a hand up, he drew a line with his middle finger over the small, neat thatch of hair between her thighs, then eased it along her wet flesh. A single stroke over her clit had her going up on her toes and widening her stance.

"More," she whined.

"You want more?" He stood and pressed himself against her. Slipping his hand between her body and the wall, he lightly tickled her clit again. "What if I don't want to give it to you?"

She banged her fists, but she was smiling.

Grinning at her neediness, Patrick unhooked her bra and turned her around to face him. She was lust-drunk, her eyes hazy, face flushed. He took one taut, pink nipple into his mouth, and dipped a hand to her sex again. Lower. Circled her entrance. Pushed inside.

"Pa-*trick*."

Her body bowed off the wall, her hips working in rhythm with the movements of his hand. Patrick tugged her nipple with his teeth, then released it, and gazed up to watch her face. Her mouth was agape, her head tilted back, eyes pinched shut. Seeing the effect he had on her made his dick painfully hard, but he never ceased the thrusts of his finger, searching for her—

"Fuck." Her eyes flew open. "That. Yes."

Patrick relentlessly stroked until Cassie gripped his biceps and cried out. Wetness splashed over his palm.

"Look at you," he said, half in amazement. "You're drenched."

Her cheeks went red as she panted and squirmed. "How are you doing that?"

"Don't tell me no one's done that to you before."

"Not like—" She gasped when Patrick rubbed that rough ridge of flesh a little harder. "God...I need...fuck."

Yeah. So did he. "Where are your condoms, Cassie?"

She threw him a sideways glance. "You don't keep a store of them in your jeans?"

Snarky even when she was being fingered. God, this woman. "I do. I just used them all up this week."

Her pleasured smile vanished. Shit. He wouldn't have wanted to picture her fucking someone else right now either. Patrick slid his finger free.

"I'm sorry. I'm kidding. I actually...haven't."

"Haven't what?"

"Used any condoms. This week."

"Is that a record for you or something?"

"Honestly? Yeah." As a matter of fact, he hadn't even done so much as gotten another woman's phone number. Including the one at the bar tonight.

She examined him, like she wasn't sure she believed him, then pushed off the wall. "Come with me."

She led him through her kitchen and living room to her

bedroom, then flipped on a lamp, illuminating the small room. Her bed took up most of the space, but it felt warm there. Comfortable and lived in. Patrick watched the confident sway of her hips as she walked toward a nightstand.

Goddamn, the curve of her waist. Her thick, solid thighs. He wanted to tell her how fucking beautiful she was, but his capacity for language was shot. He needed to feel. Taste. Smell. Take.

He followed her, sitting on the bed as she bent over to open a drawer. The enormity of the moment hit home as she retrieved a foil packet, ripped it open and glanced at him. He nodded once, keeping his eyes on her face as she rolled it over him. She was silent, focused, and he let her run the show as she climbed onto his lap, his pulse pounding so fast he could hardly breathe. She stayed like that, rocking against him and pausing like she had before.

Since when did Cassie hold back on asking what she wanted?

Unless she wanted him to take control.

Going on instinct, Patrick seized her hips, drew her above him and lined himself up. His cock nudged her entrance, and Cassie's head dropped back on a moan.

"Not so much a spitfire now, are you?" he asked. "All talk."

"Shut up and fuck me."

That was more like it.

Inch by inch, he eased her down, relishing the grip of her hands on his shoulders. His grasp on her hips was equally as strong. God, she was tight. Snug enough that he had a feeling it had been a while for her even if he didn't possess more girth than the average man. And fuck if he didn't like that.

"Okay?" he gritted out when he was fully seated.

Her head jerked in a short little nod. Her belly flexed, hips rolling. "Please."

Oh Christ. The sound of her begging was a tripwire, nearly setting him off before they'd even begun. Summoning his self-control, Patrick found a rhythm, their foreheads pressed together as he thrust up inside her and she pressed down. Within minutes they were both nothing but panted moans and sweaty thighs and arching backs, and he was getting perilously close to the edge. It was too hot, seeing her like this. Unraveled. Unleashed. Her hair damp on her forehead, her neck. Her body surging as she raced him to the finish line.

"I wanna watch you," he said. "Wanna see you fall apart for me."

"Not—yet." Slowing the movement of her hips, she sat up a bit and squeezed her inner muscles around him.

Patrick's body jerked with the immense pleasure. "What the fuck are you doing?"

It was like she was grabbing him, pulling him into her. The sensation was so intense he nearly lost control when she did it again. He growled in his fight to hold on.

"Aww, come on. Don't tell me no one's done that to you before."

He hated her. He truly hated her. Because no one, in fact, had ever done that. Not one woman, in two decades of fucking, had been this good.

He heaved her upward and rolled her onto her back. She fought against him with a smile, her hands pushing at his shoulders. Patrick pinned her wrists to the mattress.

"Thrash all you want, sweetheart. I'm gonna fuck the fight out of you."

Her head fell back on a groan. Bending down to lick the sweat from between her breasts, he started up a pace, deep and frenetic. Her hips met his, thrust for thrust. Cassie whimpered and closed her eyes.

"You gonna come for me?" he asked.

"Close."

Whatever she needed, Patrick was compelled to find it for her. But he had moments left, if that. He took one of her hands and urged it between her thighs.

"Get yourself there, Cassie."

Her fingers brushed against him as they circled her clit, and the idea it afforded was too much. Cassie rubbing herself because he'd told her to, the two of them working together to get her off.

"I'm gonna come," he rasped.

"Me—" Cassie clenched, her orgasm stealing her breath before she could finish the sentence. Burying his face against her breast, Patrick groaned through his release as she shuddered beneath him. Her climax lasted, pulses that drew his out even more, her body tightening around him again until he sagged against her, his brow to her shoulder.

It took longer than usual for him to catch his breath. A lot longer.

When he'd finally recovered, Patrick lifted his head and asked, "Still don't like me?"

Her giggle was a sweet, tinkling sound. He eased out of her and tied off the condom, tossing it into a trash bin beside the bed. She'd stretched out when he turned to look at her. Propping himself up on one arm, he explored things he hadn't gotten to see before. A beauty mark at the base of her neck. The light golden tone of her skin. The soft crease of her navel. God, he could look at her for hours.

"Isn't this usually your cue to make something up?" she asked.

He glanced up. "I'm sorry?"

"When the sex is over. Isn't that when you usually find an excuse to cut out?"

"Usually."

"Well, let me save you the trouble." She sat up, reached over to her nightstand and retrieved an oversized T-shirt. "You don't have to make up an excuse."

"So I don't have to pretend I have a tennis match in the morning, or a work obligation? Sweet."

"Well, I know how you roll. You never sleep with the same woman twice, so what good would it be to hang on you?"

"None at all."

He was mostly joking. He'd thought she was kidding too, but apparently not. She drew the shirt over her head, stood and went to her dresser. "Well it's a good thing I'm not then."

Stepping into a fresh pair of panties, she ran her fingers through her hair.

"Then I'm free to go, I guess," he said, watching her.

"Totally free."

She was giving him an out. Hot sex, with no pesky emotions required in the aftermath, no requests for a repeat performance. It shouldn't have bothered him.

So why did it bother him?

"We're on the same page with this." She turned toward him. "Right?"

A sudden discomfort gripped him. For once, he didn't want to run out the door, but he wasn't about to admit the sudden change in his pattern now. "Totally on the same page."

"And we're not telling anyone about it."

"Not a soul."

"Perfect. Then we can go back to hating each other and no one will be the wiser."

Patrick stood, and Cassie walked him down the hall. His clothes were scattered everywhere, and awkward didn't begin to describe it as she helped him retrieve them.

"Thanks for coming over," she said when he was fully dressed. "I had a nice time."

"That's usually my line."

She stuck her tongue out. "Beat you to it."

He laughed at her playfulness, and told himself to get with the program. He didn't have to worry that he'd taken advantage of her, and Cassie definitely didn't seem like her feelings were hurt.

No, she was making this easy for him.

Patrick checked his pockets for his keys, phone and wallet, and flashed her a laid-back smile. There was no reason for him to feel anything other than relief. Commitment wasn't his thing, and now that he'd had her, he'd be able to move on.

"I had a nice time too."

"I'm glad."

Cassie opened the door. "Good night." She didn't reach in for a hug or a kiss. Which wasn't strange, considering her behavior. What was strange was that he felt the urge to.

Patrick shoved his hands in his pockets. "Night." He went down the stairs and out into the evening, ready to leave this night, and his lust for Cassie Allbright, behind him.

8

———————

*C*assie stared at her phone in disbelief. "I did *not* just get another email from Hudson."

Gabe glanced up from his computer. "You're shouting."

"I'm not."

A drawer in his filing cabinet rolled open. Lilly stuffed a folder inside it.

"Yeah, you kinda are," she said.

"Why are you two ganging up on me?" Cassie's phone buzzed. "And why the hell is he emailing me again?"

"You're still shouting," Gabe sang.

Cassie tossed her phone onto his desk in frustration, then bent over and covered her eyes. "I can't help it. He's a sniveling little crybaby, and I'm already sorry I took him on as a client."

Two days into the week, and he'd emailed her over a dozen times.

"Do I have to sell my desk?"

"How am I supposed to run a publishing house out of my home?"

"Can't you do all this for me?"

Those were the highlights, and they'd been nonstop since Saturday. She'd spent most of the weekend with her phone off drafting a restructuring plan. She'd researched her ass off, ascertaining what made a publishing house fail and succeed, figuring out where his debts were and what his potential future earnings could be. But her computer had dinged once an hour with a barrage of complaints from him.

"You won't regret taking him on when you've made partner," Gabe reminded her.

Cassie kept her hands firmly in place. Maybe she wouldn't regret Hudson. But she did have one regret: sleeping with Patrick.

She totally regretted it. Mostly.

Sort of.

She couldn't believe it had actually happened. Analytical to a fault, Cassie always thought everything through, so the fact that she'd impulsively kissed him wasn't her normal behavior. She'd spent half the weekend wincing at what she'd done, half savoring the way her body felt—her lips tingling from rasping over his mustache and goatee, her body pleasantly tender, stretched and slightly raw. She'd scold herself for the thought, then catch herself staring off into space, recalling the way he'd forced her on her back, demanding she take the pleasure he was going to give her.

And he'd given it. With the right number of inches and damn near perfect girth.

He was a lot bigger than she'd imagined, and she didn't only mean his cock. His perfectly tailored clothes hid the sheer size of his broad chest and muscular arms, but once she'd gotten the jacket off him, those suspenders he'd worn made his chest look even bigger. Like it was behind bars.

It should've been illegal, what they'd done. She half wished it was. Then she wouldn't be wanting it so badly again.

The drawer Lilly was working in squeaked shut as she searched for another file.

"I thought you'd love bossing around a spoiled brat like Hudson Grant."

Cassie's phone buzzed again. She couldn't bear to look at it. "I am, but he's acting like I'm his therapist."

"Didn't you know that's what you went to law school for?" Gabe asked. "It's a juris *doctor* degree."

Cassie uncovered her eyes and sat up. "You know, you two can *besa mi culo.*"

"Oooh," Gabe said. "We know she's mad when she tells us to kiss her ass in Spanish."

Cassie reached for her phone and unlocked the screen. Yes, she was disgusted by Hudson's attachment to money, and she was enjoying telling him what to do, because that's what would save his company, whether he liked it or not. This was part of the fun in being a lawyer. Handling the impossible. Getting. Shit. *Done.* But if he didn't stop whining, she was going to start sending his emails directly to her spam folder.

She scrolled through her notifications and sighed. The last message hadn't been from Hudson. It was a text from her sister.

"I'm gonna head to my office. Elísa wants to FaceTime."

Lilly checked her watch. "At two thirty on a Tuesday? Doesn't she know you're at work?"

"She does. But family is more important, right?"

Lilly made a face. "Hey, you're not off the hook about this weekend yet. We still have to figure out what we're doing for our birthdays. And to celebrate my acceptance into the Massachusetts Bar."

She was beaming on the last part. She'd been promoted from paralegal to associate, and would be sworn in in November.

"It's so cute that you guys have almost the same birthday," Gabe said.

"Yeah," Cassie agreed. "Plus ten years."

Lilly's birthday was on Friday, Cassie's the day after. She'd put off planning anything, because thinking about turning thirty-nine wasn't high on her priority list. Lilly, however, was excited about hitting the last year of her twenties and wanted to do something special.

Her phone buzzed. Hudson. Again. "I'm not sure I'll be able to do anything this weekend. I'll be spending it chained to emails from my favorite client."

Lilly giggled. "I spent most of last weekend chained up, but for different reasons."

Gabe covered his ears. "T.M.I.!"

Cassie would've laughed, but another image of Patrick popped into her mind, this one of his hands on her wrists keeping her immobile. His naked body moving under hers as he thrust up into her. How it had felt when he'd growled and flipped her over, brushing the edges of the fantasy she'd kept under lock and key. She'd been surprised at how strong he was, and it had thrilled her, even frightened her a bit.

The way she'd always wanted it to.

Her cheeks rushed with heat. She needed to stop thinking about him.

"Well," she said, recovering her composure. "I might need to borrow one of your toys to whip this idiot into shape."

Satisfied they hadn't suspected anything, Cassie headed out, texting her sister as she walked. She'd just sat down at her desk and propped her phone up when the FaceTime request came through.

Elísa's smiling face filled the screen. "Hey, sis."

As teens, Cassie and her sister had looked like twins, despite their eight-year age difference. But Elísa had kept her hair long, and her south Florida tan highlighted the azure color of her eyes, so now they barely looked alike at all.

Cassie rubbed the back of her neck. "Please tell me you're not calling about me getting a date for your wedding. Mom hounded me about that last week."

"No, I'm calling to wish you an early happy birthday."

"You, doing something ahead of schedule?" Elísa lived on Latin time and then some. Early wasn't in her vocabulary.

"I know. But Hector and I are going away for a pre-wedding getaway, and I'll be busy. I didn't want to forget."

"Right. Because of all the sex. It does things to your memory," Cassie said. "Mom and Dad are letting you guys do that?"

"They don't have a say in what I do."

"They did when I still lived at home."

Cassie hadn't even been allowed to date until she was eighteen. Her mother had dragged her to church, drilling the concept into her that women shouldn't sleep around and that she should be pure for marriage, while her father sat on the sidelines and nodded along.

It was a complete load of shit too. Elísa had been sleeping with Hector long before they'd gotten engaged, a fact easily forgotten once there was a diamond on her finger. And her brother had never gotten a lecture. Alejándro was *livin' la vida* well into his twenties, bed-hopping until he settled down and was absolved from his sins in the form of two grandchildren. But hey, he was a boy. Boys were allowed to be like that. If Cassie acted the same, she'd be seen as an object, losing all respect.

"Well, you're not at home anymore," Elísa said. "What are you doing for your birthday?"

"Probably nothing. I've got a ton of work to do, and—"

"Nothing?" Elísa's squeak made Cassie flinch. "Come on, Cass. You can't be doing nothing."

"Why? Because the neighbors will gossip when I come home without a man on my arm?"

Cassie could hear the astonished whispers now.

"Can you believe it? Cassandra is here by herself, again!"

"Dios mío, I'll bet all her eggs are dried up!"

"No, dumbass. Because you work like crazy, and you should go out and have some fun."

Elísa's scowl was a mix of earnest concern and exasperation, and Cassie felt bad for going on the defensive. But that was how she dealt with the world, always ready for a fight, which was another difference between them. Elísa was the baby, the most sheltered and free, allowed later curfews, and more at ease with who she was. As the eldest, Cassie had the most expectations thrust upon her. Work hard. Become something important, do something worthwhile, but keep your heritage close.

But now the culmination of all her hard work was finally in sight—the carrot at the end of the stick she'd been following for nearly two decades. Maybe she didn't need to work the *whole* weekend. Hudson's emails could wait a day.

"I guess I could go out. It's my friend Lilly's birthday too. Maybe we'll go dancing or something."

"That's the spirit! Get your salsa on for the big three-nine," Elísa said. "And maybe find a sexy guy to spend the night with after."

Cassie glanced away as Patrick hijacked her thoughts once again. The heat, the passion. His moans of pleasure when she went down on him, the way his hips had kicked toward her mouth. But she couldn't get back into bed with him. She still didn't even *like* him. Not as a person, with his arrogance and player ways. After all, he'd been picking up another woman before he'd seen her on Friday. For all she knew, he could've gone back out on the prowl when he left her apartment.

No. One mistake was bad enough. She didn't want to make it a second time.

But he wasn't the only man out there.

"I think I might." An idea percolated in Cassie's brain. "Have fun with Hector."

They hung up, and Cassie began searching online. After a few minutes, she dialed Lilly's extension.

"I've got a plan for this weekend." She clicked on a link and smiled. "You might need Jack's permission though."

9

*T*hursdays were Patrick's least favorite day.

It wasn't only because they were usually crammed full with meetings. A conference call at eight a.m. with the Rio de Janeiro and Dubai offices. A midmorning video chat with the London and Vancouver branches, then a planning session with his team to review their presentation for Friday's bimonthly Global Sales and Marketing meeting. A board meeting rounded off his day at four. That all sucked, but those weren't the only reasons.

It was because every Thursday at two, he had a late lunch with his mother.

Always at two. Always at the same place, a French restaurant on Boylston, right after her AA meeting. It was a ritual they'd started after he'd marched her into her first meeting and stood guard outside until she was out. Lunch at *La Lutte* was a bribe in exchange for good behavior, to make sure she skipped the wine and went straight for the caviar.

She'd been sober for a decade, but things remained awkward. Not that they ever weren't. For as long as he could remember, his mother was emotionally absent, his father physically so. She, at least, was there most of the time. The only memory he had of Reid at home was the banker's lamp he read by when Patrick was a child, a green glass shade with a touch of old-world elegance. The warm glow stopped coming from his office when he stopped coming home much at all.

It hadn't been hard for Patrick to figure out what was going on. Watching his father traipse into the house late at night with his clothes askew was clue number one. Watching how he interacted with his secretaries and other industry professionals on the occasions Patrick had to follow him around closed the deal. Reid was wealthy and powerful and bored with his wife, and went rampantly through women because he had the means to get away with it. So in theory, Patrick understood why his mother drank. In practice, a visceral, boyish feeling of abandonment remained, even all these years later. He cared what happened to her—only someone totally heartless would let their own mother become destitute. But he'd always felt she'd turned a blind eye to Reid's cheating so she could remain in the lap of luxury, not so she could be there for her son. Whatever her reason, they'd never found a way to talk about it, and he'd come to dread the meals that were nothing more than perfunctory check-ins.

As he left his building, stepping into one of the company's town cars, Patrick wished he and his mother were meeting someplace else for once. Because *La Lutte* was steps away from the bar where he'd kissed Cassie the other night.

Six days since he'd left her apartment, and he'd barely been able to think about anything else.

What happened with her was still a mystery. With other women, he talked to them first. Watched their mannerisms, asked them questions until he figured out what made them tick. He never went in cold with their desires a mystery.

But he'd been so wrapped up in what was happening with Cassie he'd forgotten his usual routine. He'd been spinning off being nasty and flirting, and it had followed straight through into her bed.

It was the only time he'd been "off script" in years, the only time he'd been driven by his own needs and hungers. He wasn't detached, wasn't filling a role so he could escape. He was one hundred percent present, focused and turned-on as fuck. And so was she. No matter how much she barked at him, he knew she liked it—the proof of her pleasure had doused his fingers. And her taunting had both turned him on and made him angry in a way he couldn't explain.

He couldn't explain any of it. He shouldn't have liked the idea that she hadn't been with anyone else lately, shouldn't have felt that possessive urge he never felt for anyone. And he sure as hell shouldn't want to have her again either.

Again was completely out of the question.

One night they could write off, but if they kept sleeping together, someone was going to get hurt. Besides, it didn't matter if he wanted more, because she didn't. She'd shown him the door before he'd even caught his breath.

It wasn't his ego that had been affected. No, she'd pissed him off. Because after all those lectures from her about how he mistreated women, about what a pig he was and how they deserved more than a one-night stand, in the end, that was all Cassie had wanted with him.

She was such a fucking hypocrite.

He arrived at his destination, told the driver he'd call when he was done and went inside. Tightlipped and in her pearls as always, Blair Dunham sat at their usual table, her posture ramrod straight and looking as uncomfortable as Patrick felt.

"Afternoon, Mother."

"Patrick." She leaned over for a mechanical kiss on the cheek. Patrick sat across from her and nodded at the server who handed him a menu he'd practically memorized. "Business is going well?"

It was the only question she ever asked. Not about him or

how he was doing, just inquiries about her louse of a dead husband's empire. The one Patrick had been locked into whether he'd wanted in or not.

He never discussed that with her. She was still drinking when he'd had the choice thrust upon him. And talking about it now was pointless, since there was no way to change it.

"It's going fine," he said, though it wasn't quite the truth.

Things weren't bad, but they weren't great, not the way they were before the golden age of bookstores ended and the dawn of Amazon began. Dunham and Strauss published imaginative literary fiction and nonfiction, coffee-table art books, textbooks, children's books and long-forgotten out-of-print works. They had Pulitzer Prize-winning authors, sold as far as New Zealand and as close as the Harvard Co-Op, but it didn't mean they'd be in good shape forever. That meant constantly figuring out new markets, finding uncharted and lucrative territories. The only tree they'd never tapped was foreign translations, but the way the industry changed, it wasn't a tree to be barking up right now.

The maître d' came by and shared the day's specials. Patrick's mother smiled, no doubt appreciating the distraction as much as he did. When they'd ordered, the silence settled once again, her ease melting away.

"How was your week?" he asked tersely.

"It was lovely. There was a fundraising event at the library—"

"That's not what I meant."

She stiffened and studied her water goblet, her fingers pinching the thin stem. "It's been years since you've had any reason to ask me that."

It was years that he'd watched her finish a three-liter bottle of wine by herself when Reid had spent the night out philandering too. Years when she'd chosen a bottle over being a parent.

But she was right.

"I'm sorry," he said. "I didn't mean to offend."

He could sweet-talk nearly every woman in Massachusetts. Why was it impossible to talk to the woman who bore him?

"You were saying, about the library?"

She began talking again, and he listened, but the story was something to fill the time until they could eat and be on their way.

He was distracted, though, when a few women entered the restaurant chattering in Spanish. Patrick immediately tensed. He hadn't been fluent in years, but he could pick out enough. The conversation was about nothing in particular, but simply hearing the language was enough to trigger him, a tripwire sending him spiraling into the past. Still, as painful as the memories bombarding him were, a few of the nicer ones surfaced. Ones that didn't make him regret the year he'd spent working in Gustavo Perez's bookstore in Asturias, Spain.

A widower with three children, Gustavo was looking for help and for someone to let the vacant room above the shop. Patrick's knowledge of Spanish literature impressed him, and the older man took to Patrick quickly, trusting him in the store and often inviting him to his home for dinners. Patrick in turn had loved how welcoming the Perez family was. One night in their company, and they'd acted as if they'd known him forever. Gustavo's sisters taught him how to dance, his sons taught Patrick *fútbol*. They'd spend hours talking around the dinner table, asking him his opinion on things. They even surprised him on his birthday with a huge fiesta of *tapas* and traditional almond tortes.

All Patrick had gotten from his own family since he was twelve was a card and a check.

No wonder he'd been so desperate for affection. It was probably why he'd been so foolish. So gullible. Why he'd worn his heart on his sleeve from the first moment he met Sofía, then had it stomped on and kicked out the door.

Sofía. Even thinking her name made him wince.

His mother didn't notice. She was going on about the next charity auction, and Patrick hid his frustration with a chug of his water. Twenty years of his life had passed, and not once had she asked why he was forty-six and still single. Never questioned why, during every one of the lunches they'd had, he'd always shown up alone.

Not that Patrick wanted a wife and kids. He had no idea how to be a spouse or a parent, not after the stellar example she and Reid had given him.

The server arrived with their meals. They got through lunch in near silence, parting ways with another mechanical kiss outside her taxi. There was an hour left before his next meeting, so Patrick walked for a few blocks before calling for the car. He needed to clear his head. Get some fresh air.

He needed to connect. With something resembling family.

Palming his phone as he walked, he went for Jack's number, then remembered he'd be in class right now. Thumbing over his contacts, he called another number instead.

"Helios Industries, how can I help you?"

"Brady Archer, please."

"Who should I say is calling?"

"Say it's his other big brother."

After a few seconds on hold, Brady picked up. "Patrick?"

"The one and only," he replied. "Weren't you supposed to call me a week ago? About that book idea for Sam?"

"Crap. I was. Sorry. Things are...tough lately."

To ask or not to ask, that was the question. "Things at work, or things at home?"

A sigh preempted Brady's response. "Home."

Patrick frowned. Jack had been waiting for Brady to come to him, but that wasn't happening. And he wasn't the kid's pseudo other brother for nothing.

"You want to talk about it?"

A beat of silence was his answer. Then, "No. Not right now, anyway."

"Got it. I'm here if you change your mind."

"Thanks." Brady cleared his throat. "You joining in the festivities tomorrow night?"

Patrick reached the intersection of Boylston and Copley Square and looked around. Autumn was still a day away, and already the first breaths of yellow were visible on the tips of the trees. But New Englanders savored what remained of their sunny days, and students were milling around on the green. A young couple was stretched out on a blanket, kissing and laughing.

"What festivities?"

"Cassie and Lilly's birthdays. Jack said we're hitting a dance club Friday night. After the girls are done at Hard Wood."

"The strip club?"

"Cassie's idea. Nick and Gabe are going too. We're meeting up with them after. Unless you feel like joining them for some *Magic Mike* action."

"Not particularly." Part of him wanted to go though, to stand in her face and stop her from ogling other men. To remind her she'd been practically ready to stick a single in his boxers last week before she'd shoved them down. It fueled his renewed resentment of her.

"So, meet at the dance club then? Sam said they should be done by ten."

On the grass, the couple nuzzled one another. "Cassie invited me specifically?"

"Not specifically, but I assumed it was all of us."

Nice. It was Cassie's freaking birthday, and she didn't care if he was there or not.

If she could move on so quickly, then so could he.

"The dance club sounds great. Shoot me the address when you know it. I'll meet you there."

He needed to cleanse his pallet. A new flavor, to get Cassie out of his system. And he was going to find one, right in front of her prissy, fresh-out-of-a-strip-club birthday-girl ass.

* * *

Patrick had only been to Pleasure a handful of times.

It was smack in the Theatre District, an upscale lounge where the über sexy gathered after dark for a mix of hip-hop, old-school rap, Latin and techno. The name matched the vibe, and real-life pleasure was what he planned on seeking when he left. The line to get in was down the street, but Patrick had been on the scene long enough to have connections. He bypassed the waiting people and shook the bouncer's hand before slipping inside.

The crowd was packed with beautiful women. Sleek couches lined the dance floor, the track lights above it switching from blue to purple to orange along with the heavy beat. Patrick had an agenda tonight, one that involved talking to some of those beautiful women, but he needed to make an appearance with his friends first. He'd already arrived an hour later than everyone else.

Weaving through the crowd, he located Jack alone on a sofa, a table full of drinks and coatroom tickets in front of him, his gaze fixed on the writhing bodies in the middle of the room.

"Where's Brady?" Patrick asked.

Jack nodded toward a corner of the room. "Talking to Sam."

Patrick looked off to the side. The couple wasn't talking. They were arguing. "I think you're right about something going on there."

"I agree. I'm bringing it up to him tomorrow."

The words were there, but Jack's eyes were still on the dance floor. Patrick followed the direction of his friend's gaze until he found what Jack was watching: Lilly and Cassie, dancing and laughing and not wearing a whole lot of anything, aside from sashes with the words "birthday girl" printed on them.

Patrick took a step closer without realizing he was doing it. Cassie's tight red dress was low cut. And backless. With tiny straps. And as some guy came up behind her and spun her around, Patrick got a glimpse of her matching red heels, ones with ribbon ties wrapped around her ankles and cinched in a bow.

"Holy shit." Wait, had he said that out loud?

"I know."

Okay, apparently, he had. If Jack thought anything of it, he didn't say. He was too busy watching as the same guy that had twirled Cassie around reached for Lilly. She waved him off, dancing instead with her brother as her gaze met Jack's. They seemed intrinsically aware of one another, an invisible line of heat or ownership or love or all three connecting them. Cassie, however, hadn't so much as glanced Patrick's way. That guy hovered over her again, and it was almost embarrassing to watch. He couldn't dance for shit. Patrick wanted to give him credit for trying, but seeing his hands on Cassie's hips as she moved perfectly to the beat sent an aberrant and fierce wave of jealousy through him.

Jealous. He never got fucking jealous.

Cassie Allbright, finding new ways to piss him off since 2018.

He should go out on the dance floor. Find his own partner to get sweaty with. But Patrick was unable to focus on anyone other than Cassie. If he'd thought she was attractive before, now he couldn't stand to be within ten feet of her without wanting to tear her apart. Not since he'd tasted her kiss, felt her skin, seen the color of her nipples and heard the noises she made when she came.

The song ended, and Jack crooked a finger, motioning Lilly toward him. She bounded across the floor and up the steps to where the couches were. Jack pointed to the empty spot beside him, and Lilly quickly sat, going a bit limp as he kissed her.

It was a kiss of possession, and for the first time, Patrick was envious of what they had.

"All right, little girl," Jack said. "Time to take you home."

Lilly stood, removing her sash. Jack picked a coatroom ticket from the table as she scampered out to say good night to the others.

He glanced up at Patrick. "You found your next conquest?"

Patrick tried not to look at Cassie, but it was too late. She was already headed their way. "Not exactly."

"Well, have fun."

Brady and Sam joined the group as well, saying their goodbyes along with Jack and Lilly. A chorus of happy birthdays were exchanged before they made their way out. Patrick shook hands with Nick and Gabe as Cassie dropped onto the sofa.

"That was fun," she said.

"Sure was," Gabe replied. "But I think the two of us are going to call it a night as well."

"Awww, you guys too? It's not even midnight."

"And Nick and I are turning into pumpkins soon. You'll be okay if we head out?"

Cassie spread her arms along the back of the couch. "Oh, don't you worry. I'm a big girl. I'm sure I'll be able to find *someone* to keep me company."

Someone, huh? She crossed her legs, showing off more skin than Patrick could handle, but she'd yet to acknowledge him. And he was just...standing there.

Gabe kissed her cheek, and Nick followed suit. "Get home safe, honey."

"Thanks for a fun night," Cassie called out as they walked off. She reached for a glass of water and brought it to her lips, still avoiding eye contact. Patrick could've walked away, but if she was acting this rude, he might as well pick a fight with her in return.

"Enjoying your birthday?" His question wasn't really picking a fight, but at least he sounded flippant as all fuck when he asked it.

"It's actually tomorrow, but yes, I've enjoyed the night." She glanced up at him. "The strip club was especially enjoyable."

"I'll bet. Did you get your money's worth?"

"Oh, yeah." She toyed with her straw. Watching her fingers had him recalling her touch with perfect accuracy.

His cock remembered it too. Goddamn it, he was hard just being near her now.

"So." She lifted an eyebrow. "No new concubine thrown over your shoulder? Are you losing your touch?"

She looked both condescending and incredibly hot in the same breath. "I'm not losing anything. My night hasn't even begun."

She swung one foot out, rocking her leg suggestively. "And what makes you sure anyone here is interested?"

She was interested. He could tell from her body language, from the way her eyes were flashing, color rising on her cheeks. Even the way she was showing off those shoes was a sign she wanted him. She might've been combating him with words, but there was a fire behind their banter now, and after all, this was what they did. Their fighting was foreplay.

Patrick got as close as he dared. "I'm sure at least *one* person is interested."

She grinned, full and wide. "Why don't we find out." Cassie uncrossed her legs, sat up and put her drink down. "Go ahead. Try your game on me."

He cocked his head to the side. "You want me to seduce you?"

She shrugged. "If you can."

Patrick's body reacted even more, adrenaline rushing through him. Maybe she was bluffing, but if not, she was throwing the one-time thing out the window. And he'd never wanted a second time with a woman so badly.

He sat beside her and held out a hand.

"Hi, I'm Patrick. Can I buy you a drink?"

10

"**C**an you buy me a drink?" Cassie spat. "*That's* your opening line?"

Patrick smiled mischievously. Cassie couldn't help but give him a smug grin in return.

"You'd be amazed what you can learn about a woman from her choice of drink."

So that was how he got things going. "Okay. Fine."

Reaching out, she shook his hand, enjoying the feeling of his touch more than she should've. She had no intention of going home with him, but what the hell. Let him try.

"I'm Cassie. And sure, buy me a drink."

"What would you like?"

She sat back and crossed her arms. "Surprise me."

As if she was going to make this easy for him. She felt like she was twirling an imaginary evil mustache, and waited for Patrick to holler in defeat. *Curses, foiled again!*

But he simply eyed her pointedly before moving to stand. "A surprise it is."

She watched him walk away, so entertained by what was about to go down she almost wished for some popcorn. Awesome birthday celebration? Check. It had been years since she'd treated herself to a lap dance from some very fine, albeit very gay, strippers, and she hadn't hit a club like this since college.

And she'd liked having Patrick's eyes on her when she was dancing.

A buzz of energy had zipped through her when she'd caught him in the act. It was the only reason she'd let that uncoordinated, yet harmless dumbass touch her. She knew what she was doing out there—her grandfather had taught her to salsa almost as soon as she'd learned how to walk. And knowing Patrick was watching her made her feel powerful. Sexy.

Like the catch he'd never be able to have.

After all, it was only two weeks ago when he'd told her she was jealous because she couldn't do something he did all the time. Why couldn't she do that now? She could give as good as he did, and find someone else to have fun with, thank you very much.

It was why she'd ignored him on purpose when she sat down, not wanting to give him the satisfaction of knowing she was eyeing him too, although he did look incredibly fine tonight: button-down shirt rolled up enough to reveal some very pretty forearm porn. Vest and a pocket square, dark slacks with a faint pinstripe, and why had she never noticed his ass? If she had, she would've spent much more time appreciating it when they were naked.

Which was most certainly not happening again tonight.

Patrick turned from the bar, caught her eye, and grinned. Damn it, she would've kept herself busy by looking at her phone instead of him, but it was locked up in the coatroom along with her purse and her keys. Now he'd caught her watching him again.

Whatever. She could look if she wanted. And she was making a show of looking at everything but him when he returned with a blood-orange cosmo for her and a whiskey sour for himself. Cassie pursed her lips and accepted the glass. He must have called Jack and asked Lilly to tell him what her favorite drink was.

Patrick resumed his seat and motioned at her sash. "I take it you're celebrating something tonight."

Cassie rolled her eyes. "You know that."

He replied with an amused sigh and a shake of his head. He leaned into her, his arm pressing against hers as his mustache and goatee brushed enticingly over her ear.

"Play along, Cassie."

She shivered. The mild order combined with the soft bristles of his facial hair sent a tingle down her spine. Cassie sipped her drink to compose herself, then adjusted her sash.

"Yes. It's my birthday."

"Well, happy birthday. Do you have anything else planned to celebrate it? Party with family?"

"I don't have any family here. They're all in Miami."

"Really?" Patrick looked genuinely surprised. "Is that where you're from?"

"It is, but I moved here for college and never went back."

"Couldn't leave this dirty water, huh?"

She finished the song lyrics, smiling. "Boston, you're my home."

"Why'd you choose the Northeast?"

He was attentive, interested in a way most men weren't. Part of the game, most likely, but he didn't know her background, since they'd never had an actual conversation about themselves.

"Simple. It's where most of the Ivy Leagues are."

He raised an eyebrow. "And which fine institution of higher learning was graced by your presence?"

"Undergrad, or grad school?"

"I want to hear about both, of course."

She nearly rolled her eyes again. Was this how he talked to women? "Brown. I got my JD at Boston University." It wasn't Harvard or Yale, but it had taken a ton of work to get there, and she was damn proud of it. Even if the mountain of debt she'd racked up in the process meant she'd had to kill herself working to pay it off.

"I'm an Ivy Leaguer as well." He lifted his glass for her to clink hers against. "Do you miss home?"

A swift change of subject. She wanted to ask where he'd attended, but it didn't matter. "I do when it's cold. But sometimes I'm glad there's a three-and-a-half-hour flight between me and my family." She paused and leaned in to whisper, "How exactly is this you seducing me?"

He gave another shake of his head along with a playful smile. Putting his drink down, he inched closer.

"Seduction begins with connection," he said, his voice husky and soft. "I'm starting a conversation with you. Looking for something we have in common, so I can get to know you better. Is that a good answer, Ms. Smartypants?"

His eyes twinkled. Fucking hell, whatever he was doing, it was working, and Cassie found herself fighting against his magnetism.

"It is. Thank you for clarifying." Feigning disinterest, she took another sip of her drink and waved a hand at him in a move that said *go on then*. "You may continue."

"Why, thank you. I've never been to Florida. Maybe you could show me around sometime."

Like that was ever going to happen. "Maybe."

She fingered the stem of her glass. Patrick kept looking at her face, his gaze never dropping from hers to the ample cleavage the dress afforded her.

"What about your family?" Cassie asked. "Are they local?"

A shadow crossed Patrick's face, or maybe it was a trick of the eye from the lights shifting colors overhead. "My mother is."

"Just her?"

"Yup. That's all I've got." The darkness in his eyes deepened. "You look absolutely stunning, by the way."

Her stomach pitched from the heat in his eyes, a look so full of lust she could feel the punch of it. But did he mean it, or was it more of the game?

Whatever the answer, Cassie wasn't sure she cared.

"It's the dress. Makes things look better than they—"

"It's *not* the dress." He gave an emphatic shake of his head. "Those shoes, however..."

Cassie swung a leg out. These babies weren't from the sale rack. The red satin Gianvito Rossi pumps had been bought full price during her lunchtime outing with Lilly and Sam to Saks Fifth Avenue.

Hashtag, It's My Birthday Goddamn It.

"...would look better on my bedroom floor?" she finished for him.

Patrick laughed, but his eyes grew hooded as they followed the movement of her leg, sweeping upward and grazing along her collarbone until his gaze met hers in a hungry stare.

"In your bedroom, yes. But not on the floor."

"No?"

"No. I think I'd definitely be making a request for you to leave them on."

Cassie flooded with heat. Her sarcasm was her only defense, an attempt to throw him off, but she was quickly losing ground. The tension between them mounted, the attraction powerful and hypnotizing. She was painfully aware of his size, the broadness of his shoulders and chest beneath his shirt. She wanted to peel it from him, touch him. Taste his mouth. Hear the gritty edge his voice had taken on and feel the rush of being physically controlled again, even if he only did it for a minute.

She hadn't wanted to want this, but now that he'd started, she didn't want him to stop.

"A woman who wears shoes like that knows what she wants." He shifted so his leg pressed against hers. Cassie's body wound as tight as a coiled-up spring when Patrick made a purposeful slide of his knee along her thigh. "What do you want, Cassie?"

What did she want?

She wanted to make partner. To achieve job security and success, and find a way to change the world. To figure out if she was going to have a baby or not. She wanted a man who knew the right way to scare her and please her, who could make her fantasies a reality in a way that wouldn't make her feel ashamed of them.

"It's simple. I want to dance." Cassie put her glass down, pulled her sash off and stood, tucking her coatroom ticket in his shirt pocket. "You coming?"

Her dodge hadn't fazed him, nor had the movement of her fingers. "Oh, I'm coming all right."

Cassie walked out onto the floor. The DJ had started playing a popular song with a Latin beat, one that reminded her of home and nights when everyone would spin around on the lawn until well after the sun went down. But she also needed to get up. To move. Do *something* to get her head on straight. Because after the way Patrick had gotten into her head, she needed to reclaim her footing, literally and figuratively.

They found space on the dance floor, and Cassie was thrown once again when Patrick drew her into a quick merengue. He clasped her hands, lifting their arms and spinning her around.

Goddamn it, he moved like a Cuban.

"When did you learn to dance like this?" she asked.

His expression went flat for a second before he shrugged. "Just something I picked up."

He switched seamlessly to a salsa, and for a second it was as if she'd never known the man in front of her. The feeling that he was a bit of a stranger, one who was surprisingly well-built and commanding, made her tingle with excitement and a touch of fear. Taking her hands and placing them on his shoulders, he effortlessly shifted her weight, encouraging her to move where he wanted her. Was this what submission felt like? She had to wonder, because she'd never felt so alive and yet controlled, so contained and so free at the same time.

She didn't want submission, though. She wanted something much darker. Something anonymous and dangerous and forbidden.

Firmly wrapping one arm around her back, Patrick tipped her backward, then lifted her knee up until her inner thigh grazed his hip. They were nose to nose, their bodies pressed together and surrounded by pounding bass, lights and heat. The look on his face was so intense it took her breath away. It didn't make sense. Patrick didn't do repeat performances, so why was he trying so hard?

"What is it that *you* want, Patrick?"

Another split-second pause before he grinned and twirled her around. "I thought it was obvious. You."

Cassie's heart stopped for a beat or two. "Why?"

"Other than the fact that you're the most beautiful woman here tonight? Or that I've been thinking about you all week?"

Had he? "Yes. Other than that."

"You challenge me, Cassie. You test my mettle. And you piss me off, but I like it. I think you like it too."

"What makes you think that?"

His eyes narrowed, his smirk explicit and mocking as his fingertips splayed out along her back, pulling her snugly against him. She could feel every inch of him.

Every. Single. Inch.

"I can read your little tells of attraction. The way your mouth just opened a little, and how your body is pushing back against mine. I could tell you all the other ways it's obvious you want me, but that would ruin the fun. So tell me—am I right?"

Jesus. What was he doing to her? She swallowed. "Yes."

"I thought so. So, it's simple for me too. I want to crack your code. Figure out your secrets. And be what you want tonight."

The word *tonight* made her stomach plummet, but his thighs, powerful and hard as they slid between hers, provided the distraction she needed. "We agreed it was a one-time thing. And we don't even like each other."

"We don't need to like each other to fuck again."

Her face got hot. It almost felt like sex now, like foreplay with words, are her limbs went suddenly molten, as if liquefied by his heat. The song ended, and he led her to the edge of the dance floor.

"What about your 'never being with the same woman twice' rule?" she asked. Were they really talking about this like it was a business proposal?

"I've been known to make exceptions. It's rare, but it happens."

The reminder of how often he did this had Cassie on the defensive again. "Our one-time thing aside, I'd rather not let a man who's sticking his dick in the rest of Boston 'crack my code.'"

"If it makes any difference, I haven't been."

"Haven't been what?"

"Sticking my dick in the rest of Boston. Not as much as I used to, anyway. It's been a while since I've been like that."

"How long is a while?"

His gaze centered on her. Green. Sharp. Piercing. "January."

Her heart stopped, then went into overdrive. January was when they met. And there it was again, like that night months ago. A moment without his mask on, when he felt open and honest. Real. But she had to be wary. If there was anything she'd learned in her years as an attorney, it was how to know when someone was manipulating you.

"What about last week? Weren't you hitting on someone else less than an hour before you were in my bed?"

"I wasn't interested. Which happens more often than you think." His smile turned sheepish. "Sometimes I've picked up women around you for show."

"Why is that?"

"To get under your skin."

"You got lucky to annoy me? Thank you. I'm flattered." Cassie scowled, which only prompted his amusement. His laugh was loud and wonderful, and it dismantled some of her walls. It was weird and a compliment all at once, knowing he'd been doing that to get a rise out of her.

"You're welcome. But I've been getting tired of luring in new women. It's hard work. I'm probably due a break from it."

"I'd be a vacation from your rigorous schedule of bed-hopping?"

That moment of sincerity was gone, disappearing as quickly as it had arrived. It should've mattered—she should've *made* it matter—but then Patrick moved in close and stroked two fingers along her arm.

"I didn't mean it like that. I meant I'd be happy to focus my talents on you for a while." His eyes met hers. "Very happy."

Up and down his fingers moved, slow and dizzying. "Would you now?"

"Mmhmm. All you have to do is admit your fantasy."

Cassie quirked an eyebrow at him. "Only one of them?"

He chuckled. "All right. Fantasies. Plural."

Fantasies she'd repressed for a lifetime raced through her mind, with Patrick taking the lead role. She pictured him holding her down, providing the illusion of captivity. Shoving her against a wall like he had in her apartment, but harder, with more force. His hand on her throat, restricting her ability to breathe. Teasing her, touching her while he did it, torturing her until she begged for relief. She imagined him forcing his way into her with that gloriously thick cock, making her endure pleasure, bringing her to orgasm whether she wanted to or not.

Cassie's body reacted in that familiar confusing mix—skin rising with gooseflesh with the conflicting sensations of terror and intoxication.

"And what do you get out of it?" she asked.

He zeroed in on the sensitive spot by the inside of her elbow. Tiny, swirling motions that would've felt so much better on another area of her body. "I get to fulfill them."

"That might take more than one night."

"Do you see me complaining?"

Cassie swayed on her feet. His invitation was enticing, but it was a bad idea to agree to something so perilously open-ended.

She could agree to one more night though. After all, this was nothing serious. It was a game. Nothing more than Patrick seeing if he could seduce her again.

"I'll consider your offer. But like any good attorney, I'll need a retainer first. You'll need to prove yourself before I accept anything." And before she made him privy to any of her more taboo fantasies.

"How do I do that?"

She put her hand over his, stopping the movement of his fingers. "I've never been able to come without my clit rubbed before. Think you can make that happen?"

He grinned. And holy fuck, the gleam in his eyes. "I think so."

"All right then," she said. "My place, or yours?"

11

*P*atrick's apartment was as swanky as Cassie remembered. Perched on the top floor of a luxurious door-manned building in East Cambridge, it was all open-concept, with hardwood floors, windows everywhere and one wall entirely made of stacked stone. A double-sided fireplace separated the living area from a kitchen gleaming with stainless steel. The last time she'd been here, she felt vastly inferior—just a mixed-race girl from a working-class family, her six-figure salary a joke in comparison to Patrick's wealth. But she didn't care about that now, not with him moving in behind her.

"I haven't been able to stop thinking about you," he said.

Was this still part of the game? It was hard to keep a healthy sense of mistrust in place with his body so close, his breath heated as he kissed her neck.

"Since last week?" she asked.

"Yes." He kissed her again, grazing the back of her neck before moving to the other side. Cassie shuddered at the feel of his warm skin and beard. "No."

"You want to clarify that?"

"Longer. Since the night we met. You had on a white blouse

with a black jacket and a matching skirt, and I wanted to rip it all off you."

"You remember what I was wearing?"

"Yes."

It shouldn't have made her so happy to hear that, but fuck it. If she were being honest with herself, she'd wanted him that long too.

She reached back to touch him, one hand on his cheek, the other gripping his pants, tugging him closer. "I don't remember what you wore, but I do know you were off in a corner, flirting with some chick I thought was your girlfriend."

"I was being Jack's wingman. Trying to get him out there again."

"You left with her."

"Semantics." He bit down on the tender skin of her neck. Cassie inhaled sharply.

"I didn't like you," she said.

"I know." He went for the back of her dress, leisurely drawing the zipper down. "You were so mad. So obnoxious once you decided what kind of man I was."

Cassie's pulse raced as the dress slipped to the floor. "I think I made some kind of comment about you running out of options at your age."

"You did. See? You piss me off."

"And you enjoyed that?"

"Fuck yeah. It gave me a reason to piss you off right back."

He helped her step out of the dress and urged her forward, fingers wrapped around her waist as he turned her around, then shoved her backward until her hips hit the wall. Cassie's breath caught at the forbidden thrill.

He smiled. "You like that, don't you."

Cassie nodded. She did. More than she knew how to say.

She hoped he'd trap her there, that she'd get to feel that implacable grip even more tightly, but he moved in and kissed her roughly instead. When he bit down on her lower lip and sucked it into his mouth, Cassie hissed and gazed up at him. His eyes were open too, and he was smiling around his bite, mirth in his eyes as he let go and pulled back.

"I think you like *that* too."

"What?"

"Biting."

Roughness. Aggression. That was what she liked. "I might."

"I picked that up last time." There was meanness to his expression, a taunting, sinister flash in his eyes. "I wish you'd told me beforehand, but I guess that's going to be part of the fun with us, isn't it?"

"What is?"

"Finding the right button to push." Shifting to her side, Patrick palmed her belly. His hand dipped down until his fingers teased the edge of her panties. "Then pushing it harder."

Cassie tipped her pelvis toward him, feeling hungry, depraved and empty. She grappled with his arm in an attempt to push his touch toward where she was throbbing, and was rewarded with the feeling of him snatching her by the wrist and pinning her hand behind her.

"You don't call the shots," he whispered, menacing and delicious. The gravelly sound of sex in his voice was mesmerizing.

"No?" she breathed.

"No. Put your other hand behind you."

Willing to play his dangerous game, she did as she was told. Patrick locked one hand around both her wrists, slipping his other one beneath the elastic of her panties to tease his middle finger along the length of her slit.

Cassie's head knocked back against the wall on a curse.

"Now, if I'm understanding you correctly, you don't want to be touched at all here?"

A single, gentle rub had her hips bucking. "Maybe not at *all*."

She didn't want him relying on it, attacking it with the heavy-handedness she'd experienced with other lovers. But that already wasn't the case. He made a slow circle with his finger while grasping her wrists more tightly, and the contrasting sensations had her mouth dropping open.

"No, no." Patrick was practically gleeful. "You wanted to come without your clit rubbed."

He switched to tiny up-and-down motions, then back to circles again. A filthy noise of pleasure escaped her as she arched toward him. Each shift hit her differently—the former she could feel deep inside, the latter bringing the kind of intense pleasure that would speed her toward orgasm. It was difficult to stand like this, especially in three-inch heels, but she spread her legs wider anyway, inviting him in.

He stopped, cruelly and abruptly. Cassie groaned, then panted at the ache that throbbed through her. It felt good in a bad way and bad in a good way, leaving her breathless and confused as she always was over the things she liked and wanted.

"I hate you," she said.

He chuckled, his eyes going dark as he let her waistband snap back against her belly. "You might, by the time I'm finished with you. But that was your condition for accepting my offer, and I intend to comply with it."

God, he looked so good. So sexy when he was taunting her and being just shy of rude.

"Then comply, you pain in the ass."

"Pain in the ass, huh?" he asked. "We can do that too."

Excitement shivered through her. "Good to know."

She'd never experimented with back-door play before, but she didn't want to share her lack of experience now. She'd let him find *that* button and push it harder too.

He released her hands, and Cassie lunged for him, wrenching his vest and shirt off as soon as the buttons had been freed. She spread her hands over the wide expanse of his chest and down to the sinful V of his hip muscles, drinking in the feel of him. He let her play for a minute, then unclasped her bra, tossing it and peeling her panties off next. Undoing his belt and zipper, Cassie dragged his pants down, moving to the floor along with them. Black boxer briefs outlined the shape of his erection, and she leaned in, pressing an open-mouthed kiss to where his tip met the cotton.

Patrick grunted, then twisted his fingers in her hair, tugging her off him. "Oh, no you don't."

"Why not?"

"Because you know damn well how good you are. And that's not how I want to come tonight."

He yanked her to her feet. Cassie gasped in surprise as he hoisted her up like she weighed nothing, strong hands cupping her ass. Now that it was no longer a shock to see how burly he was, she reveled in it, indulging in her fantasy. The power in his arms proved he was physically capable of taking her with force, if he wanted to. She knew she shouldn't want that, but her body rushed with a giddy pleasure anyway, her brain flooding with a high she could hardly process as anticipation twisted through her with a little spark of fear.

He kissed her again, kicking off his pants and shoes, and she wrapped her legs around him. He walked them toward his bedroom, and the world went sideways as Patrick laid her down on his bed. He bracketed her body with his palms and kissed down her neck, her collarbone, between her breasts. His beard scratched over her belly, and once again she was lifting her hips toward him as he kissed her inner thigh, then bit lightly. Cassie jolted off the bed, whining in protest when he avoided her clit and repeated the action on her other leg.

"Poor little princess," he said underneath the heated press of his mouth. "Dishes out an order, then can't live with the consequences."

He moved down to her feet, and everything slowed as he

undid the bow on her left ankle. She watched in awe as he took that shoe off, stroked a finger over her bare heel and then undid the bow on the other. He handled her with such delicate care, she couldn't believe he'd thrown her against a wall moments before. He seemed to be taking her in as he did it too. Studying her.

He made her feel beautiful.

She'd fallen into that trap before—seeing infatuation where there was only lust, dropping her guard for guys who were too weak to handle her and jumped ship at the first sign of her inclement seas. How many other women had felt this way after making it into the elusive Patrick Dunham's bed, only to be shown the door after?

"Is this part of your game?"

Patrick jerked his head up, his brow lined with concern. "What do you mean?"

I mean I don't know how to trust you. Or anyone.

But mostly you.

"Making me feel wanted. Are you still just showing me how you seduce?"

He crawled up her body and hovered over her. His nose to her nose. His forehead touching hers, chest hair scraping lightly over her nipples, arms thick and ropy on either side of her. His body was a prison holding hers captive, but she'd never felt so safe.

"This isn't seduction anymore. This is you and me, two people who've wanted each other for a long time. Let me prove it to you, now."

He claimed her mouth, gentle and soft, his kiss an apology and a promise wrapped up in one. Cassie's palms found a home on his lower back, urging him toward her until his thighs were nestled between hers. He still had his briefs on, and the fabric dragged along her already sensitive clit.

He hummed at her shiver. "I want you."

"So take me."

Rocking against her once more, he pulled back, then hoisted

her up with his hands on her hips, manipulating her onto her hands and knees.

"Doggie style?" she asked. "Classy."

He reached to the side with one arm, and Cassie heard the sound of a drawer opening, then the noise of a foil wrapper. "Someone laid a gauntlet down for me. Fulfilling her request means a deeper angle is required."

"Dangerous, giving away your trade secrets. I might use them against you."

She peeked over her shoulder as the mattress bowed with his movements. He tossed his briefs to the side, then ripped open the condom's packaging and rolled it on.

"I'll take my chances." He knelt behind her, and then Cassie was tipping forward, her hands clenching the pillows as he pumped her slowly with one finger, then two. "You must really dislike me tonight. You're sopping wet."

She would've found something sarcastic to say in response, but then Patrick tipped his fingers upward, thrusting faster. Cassie groaned as her body obeyed the demanding plunges inside her, wetness spilling down her thighs.

"There you go again. Drenching the sheets."

She buried her face in a pillow, trying to stifle her noises. "Fuck...please..."

"I like it when you beg," he said huskily.

He worked her harder, and she whined, shocked at her involuntary response to his touch. Patrick slowed his strokes. "Does it bother you, getting so wet you can't control it?"

She nodded, then shook her head. She didn't know how to explain how it made her feel—her body reacting without her control. Messy and dripping, even when she didn't want to be. She felt like an object. Just a body.

"I love it."

"Fuck." His whispered curse rushed through her, a pulse of heat, his arousal to her response as reflexive as her own. Patrick slipped his fingers free, then eased inside her, and Cassie tensed up and relaxed all at once with the sensation of him filling her.

"You feel amazing," he said, his voice hoarse. "So goddamn good."

Cassie moaned as he withdrew and surged into her again. Each retreat and thrust was slow, controlled, making her feel every thick, hard inch. One of his hands went beneath her to her belly.

"Like this." He lifted her slightly, changing the angle. Cassie whimpered in surprised pleasure as he hit a deeper spot. Her toes curled, her nipples going tight as she rode the new waves of bliss.

Patrick bent over her and kissed her spine. "Feel good?"

She nodded, unable to manage more than that. Holy Christ, he knew what he was doing. He took her hands and placed them one at a time on the headboard.

"How about like this?" he asked, then picked up his pace.

Cassie's arms quivered, her eyes flying open as she gripped the wooden slats. The quick, shallow thrusts hit a new spot that made her gasp. Every time his cock ran over that sensitive area, it triggered a phantom orgasm—an explosive, about-to-come feeling, as if he were stroking her clit from the inside.

"Don't stop," she begged.

"Don't stop what?" He took her hands and helped her back down again, returning to the same position they'd begun in, his thrusts smooth, deep and purposeful. "This?"

"Yes. Fuck."

Once again, his palm found her tummy, lifting her up. "Or this?"

"That. Both. Jesus, I don't know."

She rutted against him, not wanting to think about how he'd gotten this talented in bed. Not wanting to think about anything but what he was doing to her, and how incredible it felt.

Patrick brushed his thumb over her back entrance. "I could do this too."

Cassie pinched her eyes shut, her thighs and shoulders shaking at the new and foreign feeling. She didn't know if she was ready for that yet, but she was enjoying this too much to say no. And wasn't that one of the things she secretly craved? To be brought somewhere she wasn't sure she wanted, then forced to take the pleasure when she got there?

"Don't know. Just—" Her words broke on a moan as he coaxed another shiver from her.

"Gonna come for me?"

She shook her head, but she was closer than she'd ever been without a finger between her legs.

"You sure you don't want that sweet, soft clit of yours rubbed?"

Cassie grunted and trembled. The thought of how good it would feel if she did touch it, if he touched it, how strong those sensations would be, how quickly she would come...

"No, you've gotta—*fuck.*" Her words dropped off when he stopped rubbing her back entrance and lifted her up once again, placing her hands on the headboard. "You've gotta prove you can do it." She was going to hold out if it killed her, despite how badly that swollen spot was begging for attention.

"Is that what you want?" Patrick asked. "Denial?"

He was always asking what she wanted. As if it were easy for her to say. "You might be giving your secrets away. But I...*ohh*... don't have to do the same."

His soft chuckle made the hairs on her neck stand up. "Then I'll—have to—guess."

She loved those little pauses, the breaks in his stride, pleasure clouding his words as he tortured her. Tortured them both. He was so deep inside he was barely moving, fucking her with short, staccato pulses. A dull pain throbbed through her as those not-quite-there strokes once again shocked her from the inside out. Being strung out on the edge like this was torment.

A torment she wanted relief from, and never wanted to have end.

"I don't think you want to come without being touched," Patrick continued. "You want to be brought to the point that you're so close to coming, all it would take is a few quick strokes and you're done for."

Was that what she wanted? Maybe that was part of it, but not all. The thrill was missing. The fight, the sliver of fear. But as he helped her down to her elbows again, fucking her faster, the ability to reach rational thought escaped her.

"Am I right?" he asked through labored breaths. "You want to be so worked up, you barely need to be touched until the last second."

Did he know that second was here? She was teetering so close to the brink that one swift touch would destroy her. "I'm there. Please touch me."

"Does that mean I've proven myself?"

She clutched the sheets, sweating. Desperate. "Yes—ugh, you have. Just, please. Please."

She would've done it herself, but she wanted it from him. For Patrick to be the reason she fell apart.

He slid one hand beneath her. Cassie's breathing turned rapid, heart fluttering in anticipation until his finger finally, *finally* met the tip of her clit. She cried out, her body jerking beyond her control, her whole focus on that one pinpoint of contact as he swirled and pressed. She had seconds to enjoy the fierce crush of pleasure before her orgasm barreled through her.

He never let up as she thrashed, wringing every ounce of her climax from her shaking body. She put a hand over his to stop him, unable to take any more, and then his hands found her hips, fingers digging in as he took her harder, faster, until—

"Cassie, shit...I'm gonna...*fuck.*"

His thrusts slowed, and he shuddered and groaned through his release. When he drew back, Cassie slumped against the mattress and turned on her side. Patrick disposed of the condom and curled around her.

"Incredible," he said, still catching his breath. "Fucking incredible."

He licked up her neck, prompting an aftershock. Spun out, Cassie turned onto her back, her head foggy. She smiled up at him with a syrupy satiation. "For the record, I don't dislike you as much as you think I do."

"Same here."

Her heart skipped a beat. She needed to be careful—she didn't know where this was heading, but it had been so long since she'd been this close to someone. Cassie ran her finger through a line of sweat on his chest, feeling the same dampness on her lower back. She was drenched in the smell of sex, but she could shower later. And she had a feeling Patrick's 1200-thread-count sheets had seen worse.

The thought of other women here bothered her in a way it had no business doing, but then she remembered his offer.

"Did you mean what you said? About focusing your attention on me?"

He was silent for a moment. "I did. Is that you saying yes?"

Was she? Things had certainly changed between them, but she didn't want to rush into this. And she still had so many unanswered questions. Ones she didn't want to ask while they were naked in bed.

"I think I need to sleep on it."

He looked at her intently, then nodded. "Sleep here then."

"Here?"

"Yeah, it's—" Patrick glanced at the clock on his nightstand, "—after two in the morning. And getting chilly out."

"It's not that chilly." Although, compared to Miami this time of year, it was downright frigid.

"Whatever." He snuggled close, tucking her into the crook of his arm. "You'll be more likely to give me the answer I want after a good night's sleep."

"Nice rationalization," Cassie said sarcastically. But deep down, she was touched.

"Is it working?"

She stifled a yawn. The night had sapped her energy. "I *am* tired. And your bed is extremely comfortable. I guess I'll stay."

"Good."

Patrick kicked down the blanket and sheets, getting his feet beneath them and then pulling them up to cover them both. Cassie stretched her arm over his chest and closed her eyes. She wasn't sure how they'd gone so quickly from hating each other to lovers, but she gave in to it, enjoying the feeling of him holding her close.

She breathed in his scent and drifted off to sleep.

12

*P*atrick woke up alone.

He sat with a start, gaze darting around the room. Cassie wasn't there. His breathing went shallow, and his chest locked down until he heard the sound of the shower running. Leaning forward, he put his head in his hands and took a few deep breaths.

Man, Pavlovian reactions were hard to kick.

It wasn't as if he didn't wake up by himself all the time. If a woman was in his bed until after sunrise, it was because the fun had lasted that long. But waking alone unexpectedly was a slingshot into the past, and his accelerated heart rate proved that last night had been the epitome of bad decision-making on his part.

The plan had been to find someone else. To flash some hot, willing, twenty-or-thirty-or-he-couldn't-care-less-year-old in Cassie's face. But somehow, he'd ended up propositioning her instead.

Blinking back the bright sunlight, Patrick yanked off the covers, threw on a pair of boxers and dropped to the floor. He needed to move in order to think. Balancing himself on his hands and toes, he started his morning routine, planning on doing as many reps as possible before his arms gave out or Cassie finished in the shower, whatever happened first.

Maybe it was her smug attitude that had set him off course. She'd thought she was unattainable, beyond his ability to ensnare, and he'd had to prove her wrong. Or perhaps it was another instance of the Dunham-Allbright battle of wits— nothing would piss her off more than getting seduced by him, and he'd been compelled to show her he could both dance, and get her from rude to breathless, without breaking a sweat.

But as he felt the first beads of perspiration on his forehead, Patrick knew all of that was bullshit. He'd gone after her because she blew his goddamn mind. Because her wit and playfulness was as hot as her body. Because one time with her wasn't enough, and he abso-fucking-lutely needed to get at her again.

And that was a problem. Because he never slept with the same woman twice. And now he was offering her a fucking exclusivity contract.

His nose met the floor, arms shaking as he hit his two-hundredth push-up. There was no rationalizing his way out of this one. He'd told her he made exceptions, and that was true—a rare bonus night when he ran across someone he hadn't seen in years and it was clear there was a leftover itch that could use a little scratch. Nothing like chasing someone a week after he'd had her, and nothing like what he'd suggested last night. But it was the look in her eyes, that damn eyebrow when she insinuated one night wasn't going to be enough to satisfy. Most women barely admitted they had one fantasy. Cassie looked like she had so many scenarios cooked up in her head, there weren't enough hours in the night to get through them all.

God, he wanted to get through them all.

No longer able to hold himself up, he flipped over and switched to sit-ups. It was true what he'd told her about picking up women for show—doing it in front of her face, waiting for her to be jealous. Seeing that flash of disgust in her eyes turned him on in ways he couldn't fathom, and he wanted an endless supply of that, wanted her angry and sweaty and gasping his name.

Sex. That was all he was offering. A not-really-friends-with-benefits situation. Yeah, this might've been a change of pace for him, but wanting a sexy woman in his bed on a recurring basis wasn't a crime. And Cassie was totally on board with it.

Not totally. Not at all, actually. She hadn't said yes yet.

Patrick dropped to the floor with a smile. Cassie wasn't an exception to his rule. She was his biggest challenge yet. A whole other ballgame of seduction. He didn't need a reason for wanting to do this, other than one simple thing: most women wanted him. Cassie didn't. And that was enough for him to want to change her mind.

The shower shut off. Patrick jumped up and quickly mopped his brow with a T-shirt before hunting for some clothes for both of them to wear. He wasn't gonna let her walk out that door without giving him an answer, and the second she put that dress and shoes back on, he was either going to need to fuck her again or get her the hell out of his apartment.

Forcing himself to think G-rated thoughts, Patrick got dressed. By the time Cassie had emerged from the bathroom in a towel he'd found something for her to wear too.

"Good morning, birthday girl. I hope you enjoyed your shower."

"I did." She blushed—yeah, *blushed*, looking a tiny bit... uncomfortable? Embarrassed? Cassie nervous was a sight he'd never seen before. And fuck, did it turn him on.

He gestured toward the bed. "I laid some clothes out for you."

"Do you keep extra clothes hanging around for your morning-afters?" she asked, no longer uneasy. No, that snark was back in full force.

"No, smartass. It's just for you. Although I was kinda hoping to put you back in that sash you were wearing last night."

She laughed. "I wish I hadn't left it behind. It got me a bunch of free drinks at Hard Wood."

"And a lot of lap dances, I assume."

"A few. And by the way, you cheated last night. At the bar."

He raised an eyebrow. "I don't know what you're talking about."

"When you surprised me with my drink. Did you find out what I like from Lilly?"

"Nope."

"Then how'd you know?"

"Easy. It's the same drink you always have."

"You've noticed that?"

"We've been going to bars together for months and you always order a blood-orange cosmo. Did you think I wouldn't remember?"

Another part of his propensity to observe and remember everything, as well as a lovely side effect of having an alcoholic mother: he was always aware of what everyone drank, how much and how often. It was why when Jack had lost himself to alcohol after Eve's death, Patrick had locked up his friend's liquor cabinet and stolen the key.

It made him think, though. "Out of curiosity, how much *did* you have to drink last night?"

"If you're asking if I was drunk when I decided to go home with you, the answer is no."

A tight notch in his chest released a little. "Good to know. I'm planning on cooking you breakfast, so you can either put on these clothes, eat naked, or get back in that dress. Which will only end up getting you naked again."

"Cocky, aren't we? Are you so sure I'd want another round?"

Why did he like the way she fought him at every turn?

Patrick took a few steps toward her and ran one finger along where her towel was wrapped securely around her breasts.

"Yes, I am," he said quietly. A noticeable shiver went through her. "Now, what would you like for breakfast?"

"Do you cook for all your conquests?"

No. "I can't consider you a conquest yet. You haven't accepted my offer."

He kissed her then, sweet and easy, his lips lightly brushing along hers. She was holding back, arms still firmly wrapped around her towel, but she moaned and leaned into him. Patrick smiled in triumph.

"So, what would you like to eat?" he asked. "And *don't* say surprise me. I want to know."

She thought for a moment. "Do you have bread?"

"I do. Several kinds."

"Eggs?"

"Yup."

"Cheese? Bacon?"

He did a mental account of his fridge. "I have gruyere and some strips of applewood smoked."

"I'll have all of it. Eggs over easy. Toast crusty. Coffee too. Definitely coffee."

"As the birthday girl commands." Although he would've thought she liked her eggs hard scrambled, not easy. Nothing soft suited her.

How long had he wanted to know what made Cassie Allbright tick? Finding out that one tidbit was a gateway drug, because now he wanted to know everything. Why she'd decided to become a lawyer. The reason she was happy to be away from her family in Florida. How a woman as beautiful and sharp as her hadn't gotten snapped up by some other lucky bastard by now.

He wanted answers to all the complicated questions, and to the simple ones like how old she was.

Nothing wrong with asking that harmless one, right?

"By the way, how many years of Cassie Allbright being on earth are we celebrating?"

She flopped down on the bed and sighed. "Thirty-nine."

Just seven years younger than him? "Not possible. You don't look a day over twenty-five."

She rolled her eyes. "Go cook breakfast."

Patrick laughed and went into the bathroom. Yeah, this was different, and he was enjoying her company, but pushed any concern about it aside. The comfort level was there because they'd known each other for a while, and he had an agenda. He needed to put her at ease in order for her to say yes.

And she was going to say yes.

He did his business, then headed to the kitchen and went to work. He was so focused on the percolating coffee and the pops and crackles on his stovetop he didn't notice Cassie in the room until she'd pulled out a chair at the bar.

She was a sight to be seen in his old white button-down. Her bra was visible beneath it, and when she leaned over the countertop, it gave him an ample glimpse of cleavage.

Nope. No sex. He was making breakfast. *Breakfast.*

"I hope this meets your standards," he said as he checked the sourdough slices in his toaster, making sure they didn't burn.

"It does. Hey, how come you don't have any curtains in your bedroom? It's seriously bright in there."

The light was harsh in his bedroom sometimes, especially when the sun was reflecting off the river. "Aesthetics. I wouldn't want to block out that fuck-awesome view."

But the truth was not having anything between him and the skyline made him feel less alone.

He plated their food, and they both tucked into it. They were silent for a few moments until Cassie looked up at him.

"So." She bit off a mouthful of bacon. "This agreement we're talking about."

He couldn't hold back his grin. "What about it?"

"I need specifics. What would it entail?"

"Still treating this like a lawyer, huh?"

"Damn straight. I need to know the terms of something before I reach a decision on it."

"Fair enough." He put his fork down and crossed his arms. "It entails whatever you want it to." It was too broad an answer, but he wanted to see what she said first.

"At the basics, I'm thinking it involves me making a list of my fantasies, and you carrying them out."

His dick twitched at the thought. "Sounds great to me."

She tapped her fork against her plate. "Have you done something like this before?"

"Nope. You'd be the first."

"Why do you want it with me?"

Because she kept him guessing. Because she made him irritated and horny and happy all at once. Because he couldn't quite peg what it was she craved, and hoped he'd get to find out.

"Is there something wrong with enjoying how I made you scream, and wanting to do it again?"

Her stoic expression didn't change. Patrick offered her an amused sigh.

"It's like I said—I'm getting tired of the hunt. I think I'm due a sabbatical from it. But I'm also incredibly attracted to you. And now that I've proved I can do what you want..." He waited, hoping images of last night would flood her mind. She flushed and smiled. "I'd like to know the rest of your steamy thoughts."

Her smile widened, but she didn't seem convinced yet. She picked up another strip of bacon and munched on it thoughtfully.

"Why don't you do relationships?"

"That's a complicated question."

"Then give me a complicated answer."

He felt stretched too thin, scars from years past protesting at being prodded. "I could ask you the same thing. Why is there no man in your life?"

"You're dodging the question."

"I am."

Cassie threw him that luscious sneer he'd learned to love and hate. "Then I guess I will too."

"Touché. I suppose I have to give if I want to get." He picked up his coffee and swirled the liquid around. "I don't do relationships because it's easier. No hearts involved, no one gets hurt."

He took a sip, hoping she didn't notice his uneasy swallow.

"I guess it's the same for me," Cassie said. "No emotions, no disappointments. I also work like a maniac, so I don't have time to date. Although that could be an excuse." She winced, as if she regretted telling him that, a small show of vulnerability. "I don't have the best track record with dating."

"Why's that?" He felt like a toddler, asking *why, why, why,* but this question had been plaguing him for months.

"'Cause most guys don't like women who are tougher than them."

"You're not that tough."

She bit into her toast with a grin. "You haven't seen me in court."

He hadn't. Suddenly the image of her all powerful, commanding a judge and jury's attention, had him forgetting to eat.

"I'm argumentative," she continued. "But I have to be. Comes with the territory when you're a lawyer, especially a female." She ran a hand over the back of her neck. He'd seen her make that move before. A self-soothing thing, perhaps? "One of my ex-boyfriends called me a battering ram."

Protective instincts he hadn't known he had kicked into gear. "Want me to have him killed for you?"

She laughed and shook her head. "Not necessary. He was one

of many idiots I dated, and most of them said similar stuff. I call the shots when I see them, and don't let up until I get my point across. So while it's true I don't have time to date, when I do meet someone it falls apart pretty soon after it starts."

She focused on her food, and Patrick did the same, stunned by this new side of her. Cassie was tough, but there were chinks in her armor. He'd spent months trying to widen those cracks, poking at them like a schoolboy pulling at pigtails. Now he wanted to solder those openings back together.

"If it's any consolation, I like your battering-ram ways. As long as I get to ram you back."

She chuckled, then placed her fork on her plate. "Can I ask you something?"

"Of course."

"At Jack's party... You said you admired me. Was that true?"

She glanced up with those ice-blue eyes, ones that had so often been filled with hatred when they met his. They were now unguarded and defenseless. It cut into him like a hacksaw, opened his chest up and stole his breath away.

"It was. You're a mouthy pain in the ass, but I respect the hell out of you."

She smiled, one side of her mouth a little higher than the other and fuck if that didn't light him up.

"If you wanted me then, why did you act like you didn't after?"

Patrick started to come up with an excuse, but what the hell. "I thought you weren't interested in me. I wanted to pursue it, but the next time we saw each other you were as..."

"Bitchy as usual?"

He grinned, glad it was her who finished the sentence. "I was going to say standoffish. But yeah. Basically."

"You did the same thing, you know. Acted like your usual dick self."

"I suppose I did."

Their eyes met, then locked. Had they been misunderstanding each other this whole time?

"I wanted more," she admitted. "But I didn't think you did."

Just like that, months of resenting her dissipated like steam. "Does that mean we're doing this?"

Her face changed to something soft. A gentle expression he'd never seen on her before. "Maybe."

Excitement flared, a firecracker in his gut. Patrick reached out again and stroked his pointer finger lightly along her arm. "How do we get that from a maybe to a yes?"

"Persistent, aren't you?"

"Never said otherwise."

Her eyes darted down to his hand. Her breathing shifted. "I'm kind of late to the party on this, but, you've been tested, right?"

"Yes, I have. Recently. All clear, and I always use protection. I can provide you with the results if you want."

"No, I believe you."

He waited before asking, "And you?"

"It's been over a year for me, but I was clean the last time I went. I can get them done again if you want."

A year? Good lord. Were the other men in Boston blind? "That won't be necessary."

She nodded, no longer uneasy. She was back to being confident. All hotshot, businesslike attorney.

If role-play was on her list of fantasies, he was in for it.

"I know I said the opposite before," she continued. "But I think we should tell Jack and Lilly. It'll be easier than hiding. And we'll probably end up telling them on our own, so we should just get it over with."

"Agreed." Hope buoyed in his stomach. This sounded like an accord. "Do you have any other conditions?"

She curved forward, sultry like a cat. "Every agreement should have an escape clause."

He couldn't imagine needing one—not with how they

seemed to be on the same page with everything—but he was fine with meeting her needs. "And what condition frees us from our obligation?"

"We keep our feelings out of it. All sex. No emotions, no disappointments."

Patrick beamed. "No hearts involved, no one gets hurt."

Cassie leaned in and traced a hand along his forearm. "Then it's a deal. I have a short-term claim on you: I come up with the fantasies, and you fulfill them. If someone starts to have feelings, our agreement becomes null and void."

"Sounds perfect." And now the negotiations needed to wrap up, because, yeah, he wanted her again. "Should we put this in writing?"

"Not so long as we both know what we want. I have no desire to fix a bad boy, and I don't believe I'm the one to cure you."

"Good." Patrick moved in to kiss her. "I don't want to be cured."

* * *

At noon on Sunday, Patrick was sitting with Jack at Barrel 'n' Flask, waiting for Brady to arrive. Jack had initiated this lunch the day before, saying he hadn't gotten anywhere talking to Brady on the phone, and hoped having Patrick around would ease the truth out of him.

He'd do what he could. But he had truths of his own to share, and since the younger Archer brother was running late, now was as good a time as any.

Without looking up from his menu, Patrick casually said, "Cassie and I slept together."

Jack didn't look up either. "I was wondering when that was going to happen."

"It did. Three times." The third after they'd finished breakfast, with her bare ass naked on his countertop.

133

"And this is going to continue?"

Hell yeah it was. "For the time being. Cassie has certain needs, and I'm going to meet them."

A quiet *hmm* was Patrick's only response before Jack glanced over his menu. "Just don't fuck it up."

"Meaning, you're afraid I might hurt her?"

"Meaning, I'm afraid Lilly might castrate you if you do."

Patrick coughed out a laugh. "I think Cassie would beat her to it. Don't worry, she and I are on the same page."

Jack nodded, then put his menu down as Brady barreled into the room.

"Sorry I'm late." He dropped into his seat and leaned his head back against it. "Tough morning."

Out of the corner of his eye, Patrick saw Jack's forehead crease in concern.

"What's going on?" Jack asked.

Brady exhaled, scratching his beard before sitting up. "I'm... struggling at work."

"It's Sunday. Were you working this morning?"

"No. Doesn't mean it's not true."

Patrick didn't think work was the reason Brady looked haggard. "Work sucks for all of us, kid. What else is going on?"

Brady stared at the table. "Allegra isn't doing well in school. Behavior problems, refusing to do her homework. It's been a rough transition from summer to getting back into it."

His leg bobbed under the table. Patrick and Jack exchanged glances.

"And?" Patrick prompted.

Brady lowered his chin. "And I think Sam and I might be headed toward divorce."

Shit. He'd been expecting as much, but still. Those two had been together since they were in college.

Jack steepled his fingers together, tapping them once against his mouth. "Do you think there's somebody else?"

"Nah, I don't think it's that. It's—" Brady shrugged his enormous shoulders, still bulky from B.U. football. "She seems annoyed at everything I do. We barely talk, unless it's about the girls. And I can't remember the last time we had sex."

Heavy stuff, but fixable. Patrick tried to lighten the mood. "Maybe you need to shake things up. The two of us can certainly help you with ideas."

"No thanks."

"Why not?"

"'Cause it's weird. And gross."

"It's not gross," Patrick insisted. "Think of it as getting advice from your elders. There's little I haven't done, and if it's getting smacked around that Sam might be into, your brother's the authority on that."

Jack tensed. Brady's head lifted in openmouthed aversion.

"You're the authority on *what*?"

Oh. Crap.

In his attempt at helping, Patrick had forgotten Brady's lack of knowledge on his big brother's proclivity toward dominance. Jack's jaw was stiff as he met Brady's gaze.

"Lilly and I engage in BDSM play. She's my submissive," he said. "So was Eve."

Brady's brow was so furrowed Patrick worried the lines would remain permanently etched. "Hey, buddy. You look far too shocked. Haven't you ever heard of—"

Brady held up a hand.

"The movies. The books. I know. Sam has them." His face contorted as he looked at Jack, like he wasn't sure who his brother was. "You're a Dominant?"

Jack's hands remained steepled. "I am."

Brady rapidly pushed his seat back. "I need some air." He made his way toward the exit. Jack sighed heavily.

"Hey man, I'm sorry," Patrick began, but Jack cut him off.

"Don't be. It was bound to happen. Didn't think he'd react like that though." He shook his head. "You go talk to him. Clearly he doesn't want to speak to me right now."

Yeah, somebody needed to go out after the kid. And Patrick owed it to them to fix this, as best he could anyway.

"All right. Order some nachos or something. Maybe food will help get him back inside."

When Patrick had pushed the pub's door open, he found Brady leaning against the building, facing an empty Fenway stadium. The air was crisp enough to be uncomfortable if the sun weren't so bright. Patrick stepped into the sunshine.

"You want to talk about what happened in there?"

Brady's jaw worked. "I didn't know about Jack. It shouldn't bother me."

"But it does because...?"

"Because I'm not like Jack. I'm...the opposite."

"The opposite?"

Brady's cheeks burned brighter than the Sox flags fluttering in the breeze above them.

Oh. *Oh.* "As in, you'd rather be the one getting smacked around."

He nodded and hung his head. "If being Dominant is what Sam wants from me, if that's the only way I can keep her—" He choked back a sob. The kid's anguish was palpable. "It used to work between us. It used to be good. You don't know what it's like, to be in love with someone, for it to be so damn perfect, and then to feel totally helpless as it crumbles in front of you."

Oh no, Patrick knew what it was like. To wake up one morning and discover that the life you'd planned on living had vanished while you slept. "I'm sure this will come as a surprise, but I do know how you feel."

"You?" Brady asked. "When have you ever been in love?"

Patrick squinted at the sunlight. The gold beams reminded him of the shoulder-baring peasant blouses Sofia used to wear. He recalled every detail about her, from the way she smelled to the deep brown of her eyes. So different from American girls, she had an air of mystery to her, and captured his heart instantly. He'd captured hers, or so he thought, and what they shared together was pure magic.

Then that magic ended, nearly destroying him.

"A long time ago."

"What happened?"

Nope. Not going there. "It didn't work out. But it doesn't mean that's the way it's going to go with you and Sam."

"Maybe," Brady said quietly.

"Have you tried talking to her? Telling her how you feel? Or —" How did he phrase this? "—the things you want in bed?"

Brady responded with a grim shake of his head. "I can't."

Patrick was no king at expressing his emotions either. And he couldn't imagine admitting something like that to your wife. Brady took a deep breath, and Patrick had a feeling the kid was done with their little heart-to-heart.

So was he, to be honest.

"I'm gonna go back in." Brady pushed off the wall. "I need to apologize to Jack."

Patrick retrieved his phone and pretended he'd received an important message. "You go. I've gotta read this. I'll be there in a second."

Once Brady was gone, Patrick pocketed his phone and leaned against the building. Staring at the yellowed leaves on the ground and branches in front of him, he willed away thoughts of the woman who'd broken his heart. He tried to keep them out, because whatever hasty stitches he'd managed to fasten across his heart got ripped open at the memories. Two decades had passed. He should've recovered by now. Should've been able to move on and fall in love again.

He hadn't. In fact, he'd made a point of avoiding connecting with anyone at all.

The fear that he'd started connecting with Cassie crossed his mind, but no. What they were doing was different. Sure he wanted to get to know her, but there was no romance involved. Just an enormous amount of sex, and with a woman who was as adamant about not getting attached as he was. She'd come up with a foolproof stipulation to make sure that didn't happen. If either of them started having feelings, they were out. Game over. Done.

The wind kicked up, swirling leaves in circles around in the street. Patrick pushed off the wall and went inside.

13

"Mr. Grant is waiting for you in the conference room, Ms. Allbright."

"Great. Thanks, Piper." Cassie tapped the speakerphone button and gathered her things. Hudson had pushed this meeting with his investors from Monday to Tuesday, which had been fine by her. It had given her more time to prepare. She'd planned to work on her presentation over the weekend, but that was before she'd ended up spending half of it in Patrick's apartment.

And the other half thinking about what she wanted to do with him.

Sunday morning had begun with another grueling hour on the stair-climber. After a walk home and a shower, she'd set herself up at her desk with her laptop. No matter how hard she'd tried, she couldn't get herself to concentrate. Her mind kept returning to Patrick.

He was offering her a blank slate of possibilities, willing to fulfill every sexual fantasy she had. All she had to do was tell him about them.

Easier said than done.

Some things wouldn't be a problem to bring up. Anal was definitely on her list now, and the idea of being gagged was something she'd thought about since they'd mentioned it that night at the bar. She liked the idea of him tormenting her again—of having her orgasm held off to the point of desperation—and the feeling of being objectified. Body slapping. Name calling, things she'd never allow outside the bedroom. But those were tame cravings. Easier things to say. The rest were a bit harder.

A *lot* harder.

She'd told Patrick the sad truth about her dating history, but she'd only skimmed the surface. Yes, she had a tendency to be argumentative. She got easily frustrated, but whenever a fight popped up, her exes ended things instead of doing what she wanted, which was to fight back. She wanted a man to prove himself—to show that as tough as she was, he could be tougher. Because what turned her on the most was the idea of being physically controlled by someone she couldn't fight off.

Of course she'd never voiced her fantasy to anyone, and she had no idea where this dark, taboo fantasy had come from. But it had always been there, as far back as she could remember. When she was a teenager, she'd lock herself in the bathroom because it was the only place she could get some fucking privacy, and imagine resisting the hold of some faceless, nameless male. Her hand between her legs in the shower, she'd picture powerlessly clawing at him to stop, the pleasure mounting the more she fought back. In her head, he'd whisper threatening things, telling her he was going to fuck her whether she liked it or not.

She'd liked it. So much it frightened and disgusted her.

The throat-grabbing hadn't become a thing for her until college with the boyfriend she'd lost her virginity to. He'd said he wanted to grip her neck while he fucked her, and while he hadn't done more than put his hand there, it had been an *a-ha!* moment for her. One when she realized other people were into some fucked-up shit too.

So she'd done some research, deciding that knowledge was power and if she was going to want to do things, she might as well know what they were called. Breath play was the closest she could come to naming that one. She didn't want to be choked, but there was something about being grabbed that way that she enjoyed. Something that made her feel overpowered and controlled.

Her other fantasy had a name she hadn't expected. It was apparently called consensual non-consent—a mutual agreement to act as if permission had been waived.

It had been a relief to know this was actually a thing, and it didn't mean she wanted to be raped. That, she would never allow. But she'd never understood her desire for a taste of reckless thrills, so she'd shut them down, avoiding them in self-loathing and shame. She was a woman, a lawyer who demanded nothing less than respect. Not to mention she was half Latina. Spaniards conquered indigenous women in the Caribbean and South America. They had sex slaves. And as recently as last year, Cuban women had been lured to Miami on promises of jobs, then were forced into prostitution. How could she want to be treated like an object when her maternal *gente* had been forced into it? When women of all races and backgrounds had?

She shouldn't want it, but at her core, she did. She hungered for things that were risky and dangerous.

Maybe it would be less dangerous with Patrick.

She couldn't imagine trusting anyone with the darkest, most appalling parts of herself, but it seemed more plausible after their conversation on Saturday. His response about relationships was a total non-answer, but she'd let it go, especially after realizing they'd been misinterpreting one another's behavior for months. If only they'd talked to each other before now, she wouldn't have spent so much time resenting and snapping at him.

Then again, they both enjoyed it when she did.

She smiled to herself at the thought. After all, what had their bickering been a precursor for if not some nasty, name-calling, hair-pulling, fist-around-her-throat, raw hate-sex?

Her skin started to prickle, body buzzing with the idea of him wrestling her into surrender. Pinning her down until she struggled under his weight and he took what he wanted, fucking her despite her protests, and letting her give in to the thrill, fear and pleasure of her most depraved needs.

It was the perfect scenario. She was going to explore her fantasies with someone she already knew and she felt safe around, but had zero chance of falling for. Patrick wasn't going to be the guy she lost her heart to. He was worth millions while she'd had to work for everything she had. They couldn't be more wrong for each other, so their escape clause was a moot point. No need for a fail-safe when it was just sex, but she'd put it out there anyway, to make sure she'd covered her ass.

It was the most epic strategy she'd ever devised, like a well-played game of dominoes, or a perfectly laid-out restructuring plan. There was nothing she hadn't thought of. All she had to do was tell him what she wanted.

But she had to get through this meeting first.

Cassie picked up her laptop and Hudson's file. Making her way down the hall, she stopped quickly in the ladies' room and was relieved when she got into the stall. She'd had some breakthrough bleeding this weekend, and the last thing she needed right now was cramps. Her periods had been wonky lately, arriving quicker than before and only lasting a few days, but sex could throw a wrench in a woman's cycle. Thankfully, that time of the month didn't seem to be hitting yet.

She left the stall, checked her reflection in the mirror and got ready to kick some legal ass.

When she reached the conference room, Hudson was pale and sitting in a chair, stupid ponytail and all.

He looked up at her. "I'm a nervous fucking wreck."

"Well, good morning to you too."

She settled her things on the table and tried not to be annoyed. Hudson needed to be babied, and understanding her client's needs was part of her job.

"There's nothing to be a wreck about," she said. "It's going to be fine."

"I'm not sure about that. They're pretty angry."

"Your investors?" She had to clarify, because there were a bunch of people angry at Hudson—his authors, editors and all other employees included. He nodded. "Why is that?"

"Because I haven't been a hundred percent honest with them. Or you."

Cassie stopped moving. "What do you mean?"

She'd spent the last two days listing Grant Books' assets and liabilities, where Hudson's debts were and what his potential future earnings could be. She'd researched his investors, exhausted hours poring over information about the publishing industry and the day-to-day operations of Hudson's business. She'd covered every detail possible to ensure that his and his investors' issues were going to be identified and addressed, creating a plan that fucking *worked*. If Hudson had been keeping things from her, it could turn today's meeting into a toppling house of cards.

"I've avoided telling them how bad it is. They don't know I haven't paid my authors in a few months, and that I haven't signed on anyone new, or done much in the way of marketing. I've been using their money to pay my bills, which I told them about this morning."

He'd been robbing Peter to pay Paul. Cassie knew this, but the fact that his investors hadn't until today didn't bode well for her plans.

"And what haven't you told *me*?"

"Nothing more than that. It's not easy to admit how badly you've run your company to—"

She ground her jaw. "To?"

If he said to a woman, she was dropping his case right the fuck now.

"To the person who's supposed to help you fix it."

Cassie could barely stand the dissatisfied creases at the corners of Hudson's mouth. It pained him to talk about it, when he was the one who'd caused all this to happen. He'd chosen not to pay people what he owed them in order to cover his own lavish expenses. Hadn't anyone taught him how to handle his finances?

But beyond the tight set of Hudson's lips, there was a desperation he'd been hiding. It was why he'd kept his investors in the dark. She shouldn't judge her client. She needed to be on his side, to be sympathetic and patient. And working toward Hudson's best interests worked toward her own. Stability. Job security. Partner.

"I *am* going to help you fix it, but I need you to be completely honest from now on. Understood?"

She half expected him to respond with some kind of obnoxious comment about her helping him fix problems south of his belt as well, but all Hudson did was nod.

"Good. Now, when Bruce and Reynash get here, let me do the talking. Whatever I say is going to happen, don't argue, even if it seems beneath you. If I say we're extending a contract to a homeless street artist in Trinidad because she's become an internet sensation and we can make millions off her story, you agree. The goal is a deal, and you don't put your ego in front of it. Are we clear?"

He bobbed his head again. If felt good, having him subservient. She'd just finished setting things up when his investors walked through the door.

"Mr. Harrison, Mr. Agarwal." She reached a hand out for each man to shake. "Thank you for coming. Please have a seat."

Bruce Harrison and Reynash Agarwal. Two people Hudson couldn't afford to have on his bad side. They were entrepreneurs and venture capitalists with a history of threatening litigation.

Hudson hadn't done his homework when calling on them. He'd found them through Princeton's alumni network, and had used their shared love for their alma mater to hit them up for money. They had a combined wealth fifty times what Hudson had, but these men weren't your run-of-the-mill investors. They were the have-their-own-yacht-and-jet kind of wealthy. The villa-in-France-and-mansion-in-Mumbai type of rich. When they invested in something, they expected to see a high return of profit, and Cassie needed to make sure Hudson's mistakes didn't bite him in the ass.

Once they'd been seated, she stood in front of them, ready for battle.

"As you know, we're here to discuss your current interests in Grant Books."

"*Current* being the key word," Reynash said with a pointed glare at Hudson.

"Of course. We're here to make sure everyone is on board with this restructuring." Cassie started her presentation and pulled up the first slide. "Step one is to show you that the company is doing everything possible to maximize its value."

She took them through her plan, which began with a new clause in their standing agreement with Hudson: clear reporting on what he was doing each month, as opposed to him dodging the phone calls they left with his assistant. Next, she brought up a graph which showed how much they could expect to make from the sale of Hudson's building, explaining which portion would go back into the business, how much would go to paying off his debts, and what amounts Bruce and Reynash could expect to receive from it. The third step was identifying whose goals mattered—and that wasn't only the two men sitting on the other side of the table.

"Authors and readers are our bread and butter," Cassie explained. "They're our biggest constituencies, because without them, a publishing house can't exist. Putting the authors first puts the business first. So we'll be paying them their full royalties, which haven't been sent for three months, then expanding the scope of the business to offer contracts to new and up-and-coming writers. This will require an act of good faith on your part, and the continued funding of Grant Books."

The room was silent for a single, heart-pounding moment.

"Ms. Allbright," Bruce began. "Clearly you've worked hard, but I no longer have the faith in your client that you do. And I'd like to understand why you're trying to convince us to give Mr. Grant more money, rather than explaining why you're not filing for Chapter Eleven."

Movement in the corner of the room caught Cassie's attention. Elliot Schaeffer and Reginald Pierce were standing in the conference room doorway.

Nothing like having two out of three name partners in the room to get your heart rate up, or being surrounded by a group of men who made three times your salary. Bruce and Reynash were itching to bring this to trial, Elliot and Reginald were ready to see her fail, and Hudson was only out for himself. But Cassie never backed down from a challenge.

"I understand your reluctance, Mr. Harrison. But claiming bankruptcy, in this case, does not equal success. Filing for bankruptcy would end a relationship with the people capable of bringing in more income. The plan I've outlined includes an out-of-court restructuring, otherwise known as a soft landing. A hard landing, on the other hand, is one where the process begins with possible hostility between the company and certain parties. I don't think we're there, yet."

She made eye contact with Bruce and Reynash, knowing there was hostility between them and Hudson, but that wasn't the only strained relationship in the room. It also existed between Cassie and the men standing behind Hudson's investors. She might've been protecting her client, but she was also protecting herself.

Everyone in this room had to see her as capable. Everything, *everything* rode on her ability to be a hardass, no-nonsense, straight-shooting attorney.

She moved to stand behind Hudson, literally and figuratively.

"I'm sorry you've lost faith in Mr. Grant. My job isn't to restore that confidence. My job is to see all sides, to create a deal that maximizes the remaining value of a troubled company. A business's most valuable assets are the people who bring it money. In this case, those people are the authors and readers."

The two investors glanced at each other, a silent acknowledgement passing between them, but Cassie hadn't gotten Hudson out of hot water yet.

"As for the two of you, all I can do is assure you that you're not being disadvantaged. Moving forward, no one will be kept in the dark. Everything will be out in the open, to dispel any possible misconceptions."

Reynash swung back and forth in his chair. "And what is our exit strategy, should things not work out this time around?"

An escape clause. Just like she and Patrick had.

"If this happens again, Grant Books calls it quits. The doors close, we liquidate everything, and you get your money back. No negotiations involved."

Cassie hadn't run that by Hudson. He stiffened visibly but remained silent. She felt like patting him on the head. *Good boy.*

"All right, Ms. Allbright," Reynash said as he and Bruce stood. "You have a deal."

Once Cassie had seen out two pleased investors, two even more pleased partners, and one exhausted Hudson Grant, she went back to her office feeling like she could take on the world. She sat down, toed off her classic Chanel pumps and reached for her phone. A text message from Patrick was waiting for her.

"I'm playing hooky from work." It was followed by a picture of him half naked in bed. *"What are you wearing?"*

The cheesy line shouldn't have worked, but Cassie was in too good a mood not to smile.

"I'm wearing what I always wear to the office. A clown suit and thigh-highs."

She giggled as she hit send. Christ, since when did she fucking giggle?

"Kinky," he replied. *"Wanna come over and play?"*

Cassie groaned and flipped back to his picture. Bare-skinned and smiling up at her with one hand behind his head, he looked damn tempting. Going to his place in the middle of the day wasn't what she should be doing, but she'd kicked ass in that meeting. No one would care if she stepped out for a few hours.

"I'm hungry. Will lunch be involved in playing?"

She watched the little dots bounce on the bottom of her screen.

"Tell me what you want and it'll be here waiting for you."

By the time she'd given him her order, she had her things and was heading toward the door. Lilly quickly joined her and hooked an arm around hers.

"I heard your meeting with Mr. Crybaby went well. Are you going out to lunch to celebrate?"

"No... I'm actually going to Patrick's."

Lilly stopped walking, nearly yanking Cassie backward in the process.

"What?" She shook her head and tugged Cassie toward the law library. "No, no, no. You're explaining things. Now."

When they'd reached a quiet section in the corner, Lilly crossed her arms and waited expectantly.

Ugh. Time to fess up.

"Patrick and I slept together two weeks ago. And again last weekend."

"But...you hate him."

"I did. Maybe still do. I don't know. It's complicated."

"That's an understatement. How did this happen?"

"We were arguing and it...somehow turned into sex?"

"Somehow." Lilly put her hand over her heart. "I was yelling at him, Your Honor, and then suddenly his dick was inside me."

"It didn't go exactly like that. But, it happened."

"Twice."

"Three times, if we're being accurate."

"Way to get back out there." Her friend smiled deviously. "So?"

"So, what?"

"So now you're...?"

Hook-up-er and hook-up-ee? They certainly weren't boyfriend and girlfriend. "So now we're nothing. Same as before. We don't like each other. It's just sex. But it's not quite...what do you call it? Vanilla?"

Now Lilly went serious. And quiet. "You're into—wait. What?"

Hello, awkward. "It's not like you and Jack. It's...different. Honestly, I don't know what it is yet. That's kind of what we're doing. Figuring out what I like. I'm not ready to talk about more than that."

"Okay, well. If you change your mind..." Lilly shrugged. "I'm here."

"Thanks." Confiding in her friend had been easier than she'd thought. Maybe she could talk about one thing. "Can I ask you a question?"

"Of course."

Do you sometimes feel mortified about the things you like?

Do you ever ask Jack to force you?

How do you ask someone to scare the crap out of you?

"What do you like about being a submissive?"

"Other than the amazing sex?"

Cassie laughed. "Yes, other than that."

Lilly leaned against the bookcase. "It frees me. Takes me to a place where nothing is holding me back. I do things with Jack I never thought I'd be able to do."

That struck a chord. "How'd you get to that point?"

"It took a while, but I know he won't hurt or frighten me, and we have limits on what we're each willing to do. We always use safewords, in case I get scared. But it comes down to trust, plain and simple."

Cassie tried to hide her confusion. Limits were good, but her limits included allowing Patrick to scare her. And full and complete trust...she hadn't experienced that with anyone. But she did like the idea of a safeword, in case things got out of hand.

"I never thought of myself as submissive," Cassie said. "I thought I was too headstrong. Is there such a thing as a submissive feminist?"

"That's exactly what it is. We make the rules. The Dominants play by them."

That, she liked. A lot. Cassie gave Lilly a hug. "Thank you, again. For understanding."

Lilly squeezed her back. "That's what friends are for, right?"

"It is. Now if you'll excuse me, I have an attractive man waiting to serve me lunch."

"Riiiiight. Lunch."

"We are eating lunch!"

"Sure you are. Enjoy what he puts in your mouth."

Cassie rolled her eyes. The two of them went their separate ways, and when she reached the downstairs lobby, her phone buzzed in her pocket.

"Food's here. Get your sexy ass to my place before I eat it all."

Cassie put her phone away and headed outside.

14

Cassie finished the last bite of her sandwich with a satisfied smile.

"Good?" Patrick asked.

"Very good."

"I'm glad I was able to oblige."

She sat back and gazed around the room. "Full belly and a lovely view. Not a bad way to spend my lunch hour."

"Are you talking about me, or the scenery outside my window?"

"Both."

Now that she'd been here a few times, his place didn't seem as intimidating. Luxurious, yes, and definitely expensive. But there was something about the vast amount of wide-open space that seemed...lonely.

Patrick's leaned across the table, eyes glittering. "My view isn't so bad either."

Cassie's stomach flip-flopped. They held one another's stares for a long moment until Patrick moved to stand. "Give me a second to clean up."

Cassie started to help, but he put a hand out to stop her, gathering the remains of their lunch and bringing it to the sink. His gallantry was surprising—truthfully, she thought a man with his money would have a housekeeper or a team of maids to cater to his every whim. It still felt like he was running his game on her, but whatever, she'd sit and let him do the work.

Wanting a better look at the scenery, Cassie walked over to the windows. The building looked out onto the Charles River Basin. A crew team was hard at work in the water, their paddles slicing through the waves. Beyond that, a sea of autumn colors was splashed along Beacon Hill, so classically Boston and reminding her of what drew her to New England in the first place.

"It's beautiful here."

"Sure is." Patrick moved in behind her and pressed a light kiss to the back of her neck. His goatee and mustache scratched lightly as his nose pushed her hair out of the way. "Here too."

"Such a smooth talker," she said sarcastically. "I bet you say that to all the girls."

"Will you shut up?" he asked, then bit down gently.

Cassie shivered, closing her eyes against the rush. "Never."

"Didn't think so."

He led her to the living room. Cassie ran her fingers across the stones lining the far wall, the jagged surfaces in brown, grey and taupe rough beneath her fingers.

"Have you always lived in Boston?" she asked.

"I have. Are we going to talk about real estate, or about your list of fantasies?"

She wasn't stalling. She wasn't. "I was waiting on you. You're the player. Don't you have some kind of evil master plan?"

"I might. Helps if I know what you want first, though."

"I want a lot of things."

He leaned against the wall and crossed his arms. "Pick one."

God, it would be so much easier if he was fighting with her. If she could avoid speaking the words out loud, and say what she wanted through nasty comments until he shoved her backward, growling and violent in his lust.

Cassie took a breath. She could do this. Like today at the office, this was her show. Her time to get what she wanted. She could remind herself of her own strength, even when what she wanted was for him to take it away.

"I don't know if you noticed, but I like being...manhandled a little."

"I noticed." His voice went deeper. He was barely an inch away, and the air between them cracked like static. "What did you like about it?"

"I like it when you're mean to me. Like when you asked why I made things so difficult in my apartment and shoved me against the wall. I like the feeling of being trapped, and being made to enjoy something."

Good thing she didn't have her hand over a Bible. It wasn't the whole truth, but it was good enough.

"Is that what you want?" he murmured. "For me to trap you? Be mean?"

She swallowed. Her skin was buzzing, heart pounding. She wanted him to move closer. To demand. To take. "Yes. Then make me come whether I want to or not."

Something wild flared in Patrick's eyes. Something fierce and animalistic that made her tremble. "Dangerous fantasy."

"I know, so I think we should have a safeword. Something to say in case—"

"I know what a safeword is, Cassie." His tone was soft and condescending at the same time, and it pushed the feeling of being put in her place. "Do you have one in mind?"

She searched her brain, going with the quickest thing that came to it. "Exit."

He let out a short, amused laugh. "That works."

He uncrossed his arms and finally touched her, his fingertips light on her skin from her hands to her shoulders. Then he gripped them lightly and brought his mouth to hers. This kiss didn't consume—it was yielding. Tender. It was an agreement made with lips and closed eyes and a warm exchange of breath.

He inhaled once, then tightened his grip on her shoulders and shoved her mercilessly against the wall.

Cassie gasped. "What the f—"

"Shut up," he hissed.

Her heart galloped. She could feel it straining in her chest, pounding under Patrick's implacable hold. He held her for a moment, not hurting—just keeping her still, and the corners of his lips turned up in a grin.

Oh, *fuck* yes.

"I will not," she snapped, arching forward and trying to push off the wall.

Patrick held her down easily, fingers spread across her breastbone as he resisted her efforts. He leaned in until his nose met hers.

"Yes, you will."

She struggled against him, scratched at his chest until he wrenched her hands to her sides. Pressing her to the wall with his body, he ground against her, that egotistic, hotshot grin on his face as she started to buck.

"What a little fighter you are. It's cute to watch."

Cassie worked to free her hands, but it was pointless. He was using all his strength now, hard muscle and broad shoulders keeping her pinned in place. He twisted one of her hands up and molded the other over his trouser-clad cock.

"You see what you did? What you always do to me?"

He was like steel, thick and warm. Knowing she'd gotten him this turned on made desire fray every nerve in her body.

"I see." She managed to free a finger, scratching her nail along the length of him. Patrick snatched her hand more tightly. The look on his face was almost violent.

"You like knowing how much I want you?" He released her hand to unzip his pants.

"Uh-huh." Cassie didn't bother to hide the satisfaction in her voice. But when he took that deliciously thick, hard cock from his trousers, she forgot to be sarcastic.

"Well then, you'd better be ready to do something about it."

Patrick grabbed her by the hair and shoved her to the floor. The stones grated against her back through her blouse. It was going to leave marks, maybe even rip her shirt a little.

She'd never been so aroused in her life.

He captured both her hands and held them up against the wall until her arms took the shape of goalposts. "Now stay still while I take that amazing mouth of yours."

Cassie's breathing went shallow, her body flooding with endorphins. She was trapped, jammed against the wall and unable to fight him. This was exactly what she wanted—the push and pull, a constant show of him overtaking her. The satiny head of his cock reached her mouth, already wet with pre-come.

"You gonna behave?" he asked. "Or am I gonna have to make this unpleasant?"

Fuck. Cassie licked her lips to soften the entry as he slid over her tongue.

"That's right. There you go."

She relaxed her jaw to accommodate him, let her cheeks stretch, breathing through her nose and flicking her tongue along the underside of that wide, blunt head. Gliding in and out of her mouth, he groaned with each smooth, slow movement, cursing when she closed her lips and sucked.

Cassie glanced up and smiled around him.

"Proud of yourself, are you?" Patrick withdrew almost

completely, then drove himself past her lips again. "Don't get overconfident. I'm still the one holding your ass to the wall."

Bastard. Prickles of excitement shivered down her body.

She sucked harder with his next plunge forward, letting her teeth graze the underside, and Patrick exhaled a short, sharp sound of pleasure. She tried to take advantage of his fleeting moment of weakness, attempting to shove her way off the wall, but his grip on her wrists was unrelenting.

"I *told* you to stay still."

Something dark and twisted leapt inside her. He thrust deeper, harder, faster, and longing shot through her like lightning. It was so crude, so cruel. So fucking wrong to be used like this, but she liked it.

Goddamn it, she liked it.

Patrick continued thrusting, his expression shifting, mouth dropping open as he looked down at her with an almost pained expression. She could feel him swelling in her mouth, clearly nearing release. But instead of letting go, he slowed himself down, withdrawing until only the tip teased her tongue.

"Too bad you don't like being on your knees. Subservience does you well."

Cassie glared and sucked harder to show him she still had a little fight in her. Patrick's body surged on a combination of a groan, a shudder and a laugh.

"You're such a little bitch."

She exhaled heavily around him. The words hit her just right. Her stomach churned in an angry, white heat as she fought with herself, wanting to claw and fight back, and to have him call her that again. She liked it and didn't. She hated it and loved it. It shouldn't have felt this good to feel so damn bad.

Patrick gazed at her. "What is it? That word?"

She nodded—as best she could with her head and body trapped this way—amazed and relieved that he'd figured it out.

Bracing himself against the wall, he moved in closer, filling her mouth to the point of near gagging. "You goddamn fucking tease. Every time I saw you, every night we argued in that bar, I hated you. Because I wanted you, wanted this. But you got off on fighting me, didn't you? It turned you on, my bitchy little princess."

Cassie moaned her assent, unable to say anything more around his unyielding plunges.

"Well you're not gonna fight me now, are you?" he asked, breathless. "No, you're gonna take my fucking come in your mouth."

His hands clasped her wrists with a merciless force, and he hit the back of her throat. Cassie's eyes watered and she couldn't catch her breath, but she didn't want him to stop, didn't want him to do anything to break this spell. His thighs tensed, his strokes becoming erratic until he gasped and his body caved in.

"Cassie, Jesus—*fuck*."

Swallowing down his release, she glanced up to watch. Mouth open, chin tilted back, his eyes shut and chest heaving, he was beautiful in the throes of orgasm. When the last spurts of his release filled her mouth, Patrick pulled back and let go of her hands.

"Holy shit." He was still out of breath as one sweaty palm found her cheek. "Are you okay?"

"Very okay. That was seriously hot."

Patrick laughed. "It sure as hell was."

He tucked himself back into his pants, helped her to her feet and walked her to the couch. They sat, their heads touching as he drew her legs up and over his. He caressed the back of her neck with his fingers, gentle and soothing. A deep sense of contentment flowed through her.

"Thank you," she said quietly. "For fulfilling that fantasy."

"You're welcome. But I don't believe I've fulfilled anything yet."

Cue another round of shivers. Cassie lifted her head as he made a tentative stroke with his finger over her knee.

"Am I allowed to touch your clit this time?" he asked.

She smiled. "You are."

Patrick slid his hand up her thigh and smiled when his fingertips nudged the top edge of her thigh-highs. "Good. 'Cause I'm gonna make you come now, whether you like it or not."

15

a week later, Patrick couldn't decide which day had been his favorite. Or which night, really. He and Cassie had spent every one together. He was fucking exhausted, but goddamn was it worth it.

He kept waiting to get bored, but his interest only kept growing. Every time she told him something new she wanted to try, he became even more intrigued. Wrestling her until she was flat out beneath him? Sign him up. Making her so wet she cried real tears in embarrassment? He was on board. And he couldn't *wait* to tap that sweet virgin rear of hers, with his fingers or whatever else she wanted to try. He had no reservations with any of her requests, and if literal push came to shove, he had to admit he liked what she wanted.

He'd had rough sex before, but not like this, not in a way that was so aggressive and mean.

He hadn't thought it would come naturally, but as it turned out, he and Cassie were the same in bed as they were out of it. Just as nasty, but...naked. It was fun, and oddly freeing too—not needing to have any filter, taking his pleasure as he liked, objectifying and being cruel to her in ways he'd never imagined.

The look she'd gotten when he'd called her a bitch and fucked her mouth against the wall in his apartment had brought on one of the most intense orgasms of his life.

He had a moment's hesitation wondering why he enjoyed debasing her, but who cared? What he'd wanted was to get inside Cassie's head—to know what lurked behind those bright eyes of hers—and now he was there. He wasn't sure where her desires came from, but it wasn't his job to psychoanalyze. It was to bring her as much pleasure as possible. To satisfy all her depraved little cravings.

And he was doing that. Repeatedly.

God, he loved this arrangement. It was so pristine. So cut and dry. Just sex, smiles, and a *see-you-next-time*. All escape, no hassle. Why hadn't he done this with anyone else?

Because not all women were like Cassie.

She was ballsy and sexy, intelligent and beautiful. And she had no problem having incredible sex and then walking out the door.

Damn it, he was starting to like her. Not in the romantic department—having feelings for Cassie wasn't possible because Patrick didn't have feelings to *feel*. But he enjoyed the fire in her, enjoyed being able to tame that flame and bring it to its knees. They were straying into BDSM play, however. He'd wondered if he should talk to Jack about it, but Patrick could always fake it 'til he made it.

He sure as hell had been doing that with his job for the last twenty years.

With a sigh, he returned his attention to the sales forecast he was working on. The information on the screen in front of him was his biggest responsibility at Dunham and Strauss, right after maintaining the budget and developing new business. The house was doing better this quarter than he'd thought, thanks to a few new partnerships he'd made over the summer. That was what made the Global V.P. of Sales important—their knack for building revenue. Not that he'd ever had any natural skill with that.

He'd been taught by Leroy Strauss and the board. They'd started him off easy, assisting him with developing pricing strategies, sitting in on conference calls while he made deals, and looking over action plans with him afterward to evaluate what market to move into next.

He'd spent so much of his life staring at numbers, he'd gone numb from it.

The spreadsheet he'd been working on was swimming in front of his eyes. That was the way it was in publishing though, something even veteran industry professionals felt—you spend too much time looking at it and it starts to blur. The business was changing at near light speed, and the harder he stared at it, the harder it was to tell what was going on. But this report was due Friday whether he was losing focus or not, and he'd had to cancel his tennis match with Jack today because of it. At least he had a good team to fall back on. Patrick took a hands-off management approach with the people who worked under him. It made them think he trusted them, had faith in them. Which he did, but it also avoided having them see how much he hated this place sometimes.

Feeling that familiar tingling in his limbs, Patrick stood and went to the window. Dunham and Strauss was in the heart of Boston's financial district, a giant of a building with a view of the harbor. A red haze hugged Logan's tarmac in the distance, and beyond the glittering skyline of the ocean, the dark blue of night was setting in.

The view spoke of freedom, beautiful and distracting, and was the only part of his office that dazzled.

His space was a stark contrast to the gilded chambers of the main lobby. Reid had decorated the massive atrium in gold paint, marble floors and decked it out with a large portrait of himself. If his father loved ornate opulence, Patrick had become the opposite in resistance, from the classic cut of his clothes to the decorations in his executive corner office. His father could look up from beyond the grave and sulk all he wanted. Patrick's salary might've been a consolation prize for being so damn miserable, but he wasn't going to spend it here. All he had was a few seats across from his simple, polished wood desk, his father's old nickel banker's lamp sitting atop it.

He hadn't known why he'd kept the thing—there was nothing sentimental about it. Every time he shut it off, it was his way of saying *fuck you, you fucking prick. I'm here, but you mean nothing to me.* Same for the wall of books behind him.

Always behind him, so he didn't have to look at them.

He didn't read anymore. Funny, for someone at the rudder of a publishing dynasty, but he wasn't valued here for his opinion on content. Besides, the last book he'd read had been *El Viejo y el Mar.* The Spanish edition of Hemingway's *The Old Man and the Sea* had been on Gustavo's desk, and he'd loaned it to Patrick, telling him there was a lot he could learn from it.

He'd been almost finished when he'd met Sofia.

He hadn't read a single work of fiction since.

His cell phone rang, the name *Brady Archer* reading out on the screen. Patrick accepted the call, relieved for the distraction.

"Hey, kid. How's things?"

"Dude. I'm almost forty. When are you going to stop calling me kid?"

"Never."

Brady snorted, and Patrick laughed at the sound. It was a nice change from the last time he'd seen him this past Friday night. Samantha had joined Brady at the pub, present even though things between them were noticeably strained.

Patrick's focus, however, had been on Cassie.

She'd been playing pool with Lilly, sauntering around the table and throwing out wiseass comments between shots, and he'd sat there with a mildly amused grin, enthralled with the way she moved. With her ass as she bent over the table. With the sly grin she'd thrown his way when no one was looking.

He'd enjoyed watching her. Bantering with her. Enjoyed knowing he was going home with her.

He'd been so entranced, he hadn't noticed Red Sox Girl until she was standing next to him. She'd placed a hand seductively on his shoulder, and Patrick had immediately glanced at Cassie. The lighthearted, easy smile she'd had disappeared, her features drawn tight as if a portcullis had rolled shut over it.

He had two options: entertain his former conquest and make a promise to call her that he'd never follow through on, or do something to ensure Cassie's trust.

He'd disentangled Red Sox Girl with a gentle but firm, "Not tonight. Sorry."

When she'd left with a shrug, Patrick had managed to catch Cassie's eye. A bit of her smile had returned, and the look on her face was one of almost non-belief.

Her doubt wasn't necessary. Patrick was many things, but a liar he wasn't. Brady, however, felt the need to point out the obvious.

"Did you turn away fresh blood?" he'd asked, incredulous and uncomfortably loud.

Patrick shrugged. "She wasn't fresh blood. She's old news. And you know my rule about dating the same woman twice."

That same look had momentarily darkened Cassie's face, but she didn't say anything. Not then, not on the cab ride to her apartment, and not when he'd spread her across her bed and buried his head between her thighs in a silent apology.

She tasted like candy. If getting drunk was an option for him, he'd have done it on Cassie. He'd gorge himself on her until he'd had his fill and relished in the hangover.

"So," Brady said, snapping Patrick back into the here and now. "About that festival this weekend."

"Right. You guys want to go?"

Bringing up the Lit Crawl had been his diversionary tactic after Brady's comment. The yearly event was a full weekend of readings, performances and literary games. Dunham and Strauss was a sponsor, which meant Patrick had free passes to spare.

"Definitely. Sam seems super into it, and I think Allegra and Hope would love it too."

Samantha hadn't seemed *that* into it, but maybe her point of view had changed, especially if her daughters were involved. Either way, Patrick could hear the desperation in Brady's voice.

Thank God it would never get that way with him and Cassie. When it was time for things to end, they'd be adults about it, stopping in as businesslike a matter as they'd started.

"Then it looks like I'll be seeing you all on Saturday morning."

When they hung up, Patrick kept his phone out. He hadn't asked Cassie specifically if she wanted to go as well, and wanted to remedy that now.

He pulled up his last text to her and sent her a new one.

"You interested in going to that Lit Crawl on Saturday?"

He should've put his phone down, but found himself waiting, staring at the screen until those little dots bounced at the bottom of it. *"It's like a pub crawl, right?"*

"Yup. Except with books instead of booze."

"Hmmm..." More waiting. More watching little bouncing dots. *"What's in it for me?"*

A wink emoticon followed her question. Patrick typed back quickly.

"My dazzling company, of course."

There was a pause before her next reply came through. *"Just you?"*

His stomach sank. It shouldn't have, because time alone together outside the bedroom wasn't part of their agreement.

"No—I think it's gonna be me and the whole Scooby gang."

"LOL. Okay, so Lit crawl during the day...and maybe crawling of another type back at your place after it's over?"

Now Patrick's stomach tightened with excitement. As did his pants.

"That's definitely a possibility. See you Saturday at ten."

The promise of another intense night with her both revved him up and settled his nerves. Patrick sat at his desk, and returned to the sales forecast with a smile.

* * *

Saturday morning arrived with the kind of brilliant freshness you could only find during the peak of foliage season in New England. Columbus Day weekend brought what F. Scott Fitzgerald would've called football weather—crisp air, clouds dappling the sky, the ground littered with leaves the color of fire. And at ten a.m., Copley Square was bustling with people.

Patrick stood by the fountain and waited for the remainder of the group to arrive. Brady and family had already collected their tickets. He'd looked tired as he mumbled a thank-you, his eyes on Sam like she was going to disappear as Allegra and Hope dragged them toward the children's pavilion.

Lilly and Jack turned up with Nick and Gabe next. They collected their tickets and programs, then walked off in different directions as Patrick continued to hang around. After fifteen minutes, however, he began checking his phone and gazing through the crowd.

Where was she?

A hollow feeling sat in his belly. Maybe Cassie wasn't coming, which was fine. Things came up. Work. Life. It was an inconvenience, that was all. But she could've at least told him.

"Waiting for someone?"

Patrick turned around and was nearly knocked over by the

sight of her standing behind him in jeans, a black sweater, scarf and sneakers.

How the hell did she look so sexy in *sneakers*?

"I am, for someone who was supposed to be here twenty minutes ago, as a matter of fact."

She snapped her ticket from his hand. "The T was running behind, dumbass."

Patrick laughed. It wasn't quite relief filling the well in his stomach. Just reassurance that the day was going to go as planned. He gestured toward her shoes. "I thought everything you owned came with a three-inch spike."

"Almost everything," she said with a wink. "I knew I'd be walking around all day, so I went with these instead."

As much as he loved what a pair of heels did for her figure, the faded blue Chucks were completely adorable. Patrick waved a hand toward the green. "Shall we?"

They moved out, looking at the vendors' tables as they walked. A band was sound-checking on the center stage, and carts of books stretched from one corner of the lawn to the other.

"Does your company sponsor all this?" Cassie asked.

"Not everything. The musicians and the food trucks pay to be here, and a lot of the poets and playwrights contribute. We put a chunk in every year as part of our angel patronage."

"How philanthropic of you."

He shrugged. "Nothing benevolent in supporting the arts. If people aren't reading, we go out of business."

"Good point."

He followed Cassie toward a reading in a tent. They stood in the back, and she listened attentively, her lips slightly pursed, her tiny upturned nose dusted with sunlight.

Yeah, he was kidding himself over pretending he wasn't relieved she was here. She was fucking beautiful, and he wanted to find a quiet corner to drag her into.

She glanced up and caught him staring. Patrick grinned. Guilty as charged.

He made sure none of their crew was around before he moved in close and whispered, "You're killing me today, by the way."

"Oh? Why is that?"

Cute sneakers aside, and the jeans that did amazing things for her already amazing ass, she was standing differently—one hand casually tucked into a pocket, her movements unhurried, her breathing even and calm.

"You seem relaxed. It's nice."

"I am. It's nice to be away from the office for a half a second."

He tried not to be pleased that she'd taken that break to be with him. "I read somewhere that the more successful you are, the more your life is hell."

"Then I'm heading straight there. My newest client might be my big break, but he's driving me bat-shit crazy."

She had to be talking about Hudson. "Why could he be your big break?"

"Because if I successfully restructure his company, I'll finally make partner at my firm."

Whoa. That was a bigger deal than he'd thought, and not at all what he'd imagined when he'd sent Hudson her way. He considered telling her he'd been their matchmaker, but it didn't seem like the time. The reading ended, and they applauded with the rest of the crowd before stepping back into the square.

"How'd you get into law, anyway?" he asked.

"Simple. It's a job where I get to argue."

"You? Argue?" he replied dryly.

"Shut up."

He raised an eyebrow. "That's my line."

Cassie grunted, her cheeks heating with an obvious rush of desire. Yeah, it got him there too. He kept talking to distract himself. "Aside from the arguing, what do you like about it? Would you say it's your passion?"

It was the kind of question he'd ask when seducing a woman, pretending he cared about her answer. Except this time, he did.

"I suppose. I like the 'saving the day' aspect of it. You feel like a superhero when you can fix something that's gone completely wrong. But I got into it because my grandfather told me when I was a kid that I was going to change the world. That he was counting on me to do it. He meant a lot to me, and I knew pursuing law would make him proud."

She got a faraway look in her eyes, and she looked up at the sky. For a moment she seemed...softer. Younger.

"Is he still around?"

"No, he passed when I was sixteen."

Patrick didn't know what to say. He'd never known his own grandparents, and had little experience with grief. Reid had put a nice roof over Patrick's head, and Patrick wouldn't be alive if it weren't for him, but other than acknowledging that he certainly hadn't mourned his father.

So all he said was, "I'm sorry."

"Thanks." She took a breath. "What about you? How'd you get into the sales end of publishing?"

Patrick covered his grimace with a cough as another sponsor walked by. He couldn't let everyone here see the disdain he had for the job he'd been strong-armed into. "I just...fell into it."

"You don't *fall* into being an Executive Vice President."

He should've known she wouldn't stop there. "You're correct, counselor. But it's a long story."

Cassie stopped at a vendor's booth. Books were spread across his table, foreign ones with their native language texts on one side of the page, the English translation on the opposite. It was done by a small local press, and was the kind of thing he'd like to acquire, but the board would never sign on. It simply wouldn't be considered lucrative enough.

"A long story," Cassie repeated, touching the delicate texts. "Did your parents read to you when you were a kid? Did you have some kind of huge old-school letterpress where you wrote your papers?"

His parents reading to him? That was a joke. "No giant typewriters in my house, no."

"Did you get into it for a love of reading?"

"Is this a cross-examination?" Clearly she wasn't backing down, so he went with a shortened version of the truth. "I got into it because it was the job I needed to take. I actually don't read much."

She threw him one of her looks of sarcastic disdain. "You run a publishing house, but you don't read?"

"It's not my job to read. It's my job to make money."

"Is that what matters to you? Money?"

"It's what matters when you're in charge of sales at a huge corporation which bears your name."

"You don't enjoy being The Great and Powerful Oz of Dunham and Strauss?"

Of course he didn't. And he wasn't great and powerful at all. But it made sense that she'd see him that way. His whole life was smoke and mirrors—everything an act, a show. Even his apartment was one more trick in his magician's hat, keeping him hidden instead of showing what was behind his curtains.

"Objection, your honor," he said with a grin. "Leading."

Cassie rolled her eyes. "What's *your* passion, then?"

"Sex."

That allotted him another eye roll. "What? It's true." In a life where his whole function was to chase the almighty dollar, sex was the only enjoyment he had. "Speaking of that, what were we saying about you crawling?"

"Cassie!" Sam's voice rang out in the crowd. They both turned to see her waving from one of the food trucks.

Cassie waved back and then flashed Patrick a grin. "Guess you'll have to wait and find out."

He did wait—all day while they sampled food and listened to snippets from memoirs, through roundtable discussions on art history and literary criticism, and a read-aloud from a picture book Allegra and Hope loved. He waited until they'd parted ways with their friends and were on their way back to his apartment. By the time they got inside, a vicious hunger had coiled itself inside him, needing to be turned loose.

He led her to his bedroom and tackled her against the wall. Her grunt was a filthy, satisfying sound.

"Tell me what you want, Cassie," he growled against her ear. "Tell me now."

She tried to wrench herself away from him, and grinned when she couldn't. "I don't actually want to crawl. But there's something else I want."

"What's that?"

Her breath rushed out on a shuddery exhale. "I want you to slap me."

He held himself still, even as his heart began to pound. "Slap you?"

She nodded, her arousal clear in the way her body undulated slightly toward his. Patrick felt the ground shift. They were heading into new territory now, moving from rough play to acts of violence. He'd never hit anyone before, nothing more than a playful swat.

"Where?" he asked, because fuck, there were things he didn't know. Did she bruise easily? Had she had surgery anywhere he could possibly do damage? How hard did she want to be hit?

"Breasts, thighs, if you need some suggestions. And don't be gentle, either."

"You want me to do that while I'm touching you, or...?"

He trailed off, desperately needing her to finish his sentence.

Slapping alone wasn't enough to go on, and he was too turned on to think straight.

She huffed out an irritated sigh, like she'd been watching a movie and someone's cell phone had rung. "Yes, while you're touching me."

"You're sure?"

Something like defiance burned in her eyes. "What, the famous player can't figure out how to make it hurt so good?" Her eyes sparkled, her chin lifted in a dare. "Come on, Patrick. Don't tell me you can't slap me and make me come at the same time."

There she went, goading him again, and his palm itched to smack. Lord, this was messed up. Seriously erotic and twisted. But he couldn't deny the twinge of excitement rippling through him, and there was no way he was shutting down Cassie's unique form of kinky deviance. He was pretty familiar with her body by now, and this was consensual, after all. If she wanted to push both their boundaries like this, then fuck yeah, he'd do it.

And somehow try to be incredibly careful in the process.

Patrick pushed her against the wall, hips grinding against hers. "You know damn well how hard I can make you come. I've seen it. Several times. But I'm happy to give you a reminder."

Cassie shuddered, a sharp *fuck* dropping from her lips. Patrick grabbed the bottom of her sweater and dragged it forcefully over her head. He went for her bra next, yanking it down. The sight of her exposed breasts spilling out the top of it sent his pulse hammering. He unzipped her jeans and shoved them down to her ankles, then jammed his hand inside her panties. Parting slick folds, he drove in deep.

"Sopping wet already." He caught her nipple with his other hand and pinched until she squirmed, then released it and slapped her breast. It was experimental, not terribly hard, but enough to make her skin go pink. Cassie hissed, her teeth clenching as her pussy tightened around his finger.

Narrowing her eyes, she glared at him. "More."

"More? The little bitch wants more?"

The question tumbled out of him, but it felt right, and Cassie moaned loudly in response. The name-calling was a flare going off, a burning blaze that hiked her shoulders up and directed him where to go. Patrick wasn't sure if it was the words, the smack, or his finger inside her that made her do it. Regardless, it was a hell of a sight, one he needed to see again. He repeated the motion, a stinging slap to the same spot. He leaned down to suck and bite her nipple, tugging sharply with his teeth and making her skin angrier. Cassie tilted her head back and groaned.

He struck her other breast, giving that nipple the same cruel treatment. "You're enjoying this, aren't you?"

He was half provoking her and half checking in. Not that he couldn't tell. Her grinding hips was all the proof he needed, but he had to be sure.

She bared her teeth at him like an animal. "No."

"No?" Was she playing? She hadn't used her safeword, and her skin was still flushed.

Going on instinct, he curled his fingers upward in faster strokes that once again had her spilling over his palm. She whined and pinched her eyes shut.

"Do you hear yourself? Hear how wet I've made you?" Patrick reveled in her wince. "You can lie all you want. Your body is telling me how much you like it."

"Fuck—" He added another finger. She panted. "—you."

Patrick worked her harder, just to prove what he could do. She was so wet her panties were drenched. God, he'd never been this hard.

Cassie tried to wriggle away from him. "No," she moaned. "I can't."

"You can't what? Can't take any more?"

He smacked her thigh with his other hand. Cassie cried out, her eyes closing as her body started to shake. She was close now, and Patrick wanted inside her so badly he couldn't stand it.

"Yeah, you can take it. And I don't like it when you tell me no. So I don't think I'm going to listen."

This was dangerous ground, words that strayed against consent, but it got her even wetter. And him even harder. Jesus Christ, was he a closeted masochist? The urge had to have been buried inside him, because here he was, fingering her roughly while slapping her until he saw his handprint on her flesh, saying shit he'd never imagined he'd say.

Mean. He was being mean. And he really. Fucking. Liked it.

She snarled. "You'll fucking listen to what I—"

He slapped her face. "I will not."

It had been a smack like all the others, but this one hard against her cheek. Cassie went rigid. Suddenly tipping her hips away, she frowned, blinked and stared at the floor. Patrick froze.

Shit.

"Are you okay?"

She swallowed. Blinked again. "Exit."

Without thinking, Patrick pulled his hand from her panties and gathered her in his arms, one hand cradling the base of her neck as the other wrapped solidly around her. They'd never hugged before, not like this, and he doubted the move until Cassie burrowed into him. She held on tightly, chin digging into his shoulder.

"The face slap?" he asked. "Was that what did it?"

She nodded and clung to him. "I didn't like that."

Her voice was barely a whisper. He rocked her gently. "Okay. I'm sorry. I didn't know."

"Neither did I."

Patrick kissed her cheek. The spot he'd struck was warm. For all that he enjoyed taunting her, that was only with the knowledge that she liked it too. He hated knowing he'd actually hurt her.

"Do you want to stop? Go home?"

Please don't say yes.

"No. But could I have a glass of water?"

He nodded quickly and helped her with her clothes, then walked her to the living room couch. He'd have put her in the bed, but he didn't want her out of his sight. After wrapping her in a throw blanket, he hurried to the kitchen, keeping an eye on her as he filled a glass. He'd been dying to fuck her less than a minute ago, but now sex was the furthest thing from his mind. He wanted to do whatever it took to make her laugh. To order her favorite delivery food and turn on a TV show she liked. To not let her leave so he could make sure she was all right, and hold her until the sun rose.

Those weren't feelings he was supposed to have.

Those weren't feelings he *ever* had.

And Patrick didn't know what to do with those feelings at all.

16

$\mathcal{C}$assie glanced at the time. A quarter to five, and nearly time for her annual review. At least the partners had the decency to hold it on a Friday, so she could have the weekend to collect herself if it didn't go well.

It would go well. It had to go well.

Her phone buzzed with a text. A ridiculously stupid smile spread across her face when she saw it was from Patrick.

"Good luck," it read. *"Not that you need it. You're going to do great."*

Sitting back in her chair, she reread his words several times. It was amazing, how different things were between them now, even more so since last week.

Everything seemed to be split to a time that existed before The Hug and after it.

She'd loved play-fighting with him. The arguing revved her up, made her belly tighten and her skin tingle like she was getting ready for a smack-down in court. But she felt a little bad for how things had gone afterward. She hadn't known what to expect from the slapping, and had started to lose herself to the sensation. The pain made the pleasure sharper somehow. Each stinging blow to her breasts left a ripple behind, hijacking her attention before it returned to the plunges of his fingers. He was getting her to a point she'd craved—bringing the wall down between her body and her mind, releasing her from the life sentence of guilt her fantasies had imprisoned her in.

And then he'd struck her cheek, and everything had screeched to a halt.

It hadn't hurt—not exactly, not physically anyway—but it took her by surprise and she'd had to blink back tears. She'd never stipulated he should avoid her face, because she hadn't known she'd react that way, but it made something sick roil in her stomach, made her feel foolish and ashamed.

And Patrick had understood.

There was no criticism, no irritation. He'd simply stopped what he was doing and held her, even seemed remorseful that she'd gotten upset. And he'd found other ways to chase her pleasure when she'd recovered.

Cassie typed back a thank you and a smiley emoticon, then put down her phone.

She still had yet to understand her own desires. Out of the bedroom, she demanded respect, fought hard for it, and refused to be seen as anything less than fierce. In the bedroom, she was the opposite. In her professional life she liked to fight and win, but sexually, she liked to lose.

Her head felt like a courtroom, with the warring parts of her psyche arguing their cases before her own judge. She could see the caption on the court docket now:

State of Massachusetts Supreme Court, County of Boston, the Honorable Cassie Allbright presiding. Cassie Allbright, a.k.a. lawyer-with-her-head-on-straight, Plaintiff, against Cassie Allbright, a.k.a. woman-who-likes-to-be-forced, Defendant.

It didn't make sense. But she supposed that was part of what she and Patrick were doing—trying things out, seeing what she liked and didn't, discovering where her limits were.

What she needed in order to feel safe, to trust the person she was with.

Did she trust Patrick?

She wasn't sure, but she *had* started to like him, which was weird. She hadn't seen him since the weekend—a side effect of her period coming on Monday. But she'd enjoyed spending time with him at the book festival, even if she'd found his attitude toward his career irritating. He headed a publishing house, but didn't read. He was a businessman who saw dollar signs, whose only passion was sex.

Not that she was complaining. She was benefitting from that passion at the moment.

But being in his arms, having him hold her and rock her...that was different, as was how she'd been feeling since. His embrace was a place she wanted to be now, and she had to wonder if that meant she needed to hit the eject button.

Not now. They weren't in a danger zone yet. After all, who didn't like getting hugged when they were upset? And she had more important things to worry about.

Attempting to distract herself and make the time go faster, she checked her voicemails: one was a reminder about an upcoming event with the Bar Association, another was a request from a former coworker at Legal Aid asking her to take on a rash of pro-bono cases. The third was Hudson's real estate agent requesting copies of the final paperwork from the sale of his building.

Jotting down call back numbers for the last two messages, Cassie got a bit queasy. The former provided assistance to low-income families who had nowhere else to turn. The latter was proof that she was helping a wealthy man stay in business, which she was doing in order to get ahead in her career.

Sure she was helping his authors, but only inadvertently. It was Hudson the partners wanted her to help, to keep the cash flow coming in.

How was that changing the world?

It wasn't. But she couldn't do that until she changed her own, i.e., made partner.

Fighting back the feeling that she was selling her soul, she ignored the message from Legal Aid and called back Hudson's agent. Assisting Boston's impoverished could happen down the line. She had to secure a future for herself first.

By the time she'd finished the call, it was five o'clock.

Cassie gathered her things, ready to prove how awesome she was. When she reached the corner of the building where William Forrester, Elliot Schaeffer and Reginald Pierce's three big offices were, she was greeted by Pierce's assistant, Hannaleen.

"You're gonna kill it, girl," Hannaleen said. "I've been listening to them talk in there a tick. I'd be gobsmacked if they're not about to offer you partner, and a massive bonus."

Cassie smiled, marveling at the other woman's way of carrying herself. Half European, half South African, Hannaleen had grown up in London and still spoke in British slang. Her Afrikaans accent was thick too—her a's sounded like flat e's, and she hit her consonants like a machine gun. With her toffee skin highlighted by gold eye makeup and her hair wild and curly, Hannaleen was unapologetically herself.

Unlike Cassie, who kept her mixed-culture background under wraps.

Hannaleen herself hadn't believed Cassie was biracial at first. But once Cassie had launched into flawless Spanish in the privacy of the executive kitchen, the other woman was convinced. They were among the few minority employees at the firm, even though Hannaleen wore her heritage more openly than Cassie did.

Cassie wanted to be like that, sometimes. To not always keep such a tight lid on the brown side of her background. But as much as the firm touted the importance of multiculturalism, Cassie couldn't forget that every partner was a white male. Her chances of competing were better when she was simply Cassie Allbright, and not *Cassandra Flóres* Allbright.

Hannaleen's phone rang. She picked it up, then nodded. "They're ready for you."

Cassie stepped into the lion's den.

A half hour later, when she and the partners had discussed her evaluations from coworkers, her billable hours, strengths and weaknesses and her current progress with Grant Books, Reginald Pierce brought up the topic she'd been waiting for.

"And now comes the part where we discuss your future in the firm."

Cassie's skin prickled. The shortest of the three name partners, Pierce was also the most intimidating, often hiding what he meant behind a not-so-benevolent grin.

"You've learned a complicated industry," he continued. "You're reliable, and you have a can-do attitude your clients respect. You're hardworking, and know without having to be told when to adjust your plans to work. As a matter of fact, you remind me of me when I first began."

"That's certainly quite the compliment," she said.

Partner. Say the word partner.

"You're doing well," Schaeffer added. "That's a feat in itself. It's hard to excel here, because everyone who makes it onto our roster is extraordinary. But we're not an 'up or out' firm. We're not going to show you the door if you don't make partner."

Cassie sat up in her seat. She was here to prove her worth, and she wasn't going down without a fight.

"I understand, but it's what I want. You told me I hadn't brought in a huge client, so I went out and got one." Although the reason Hudson had chosen her out of all the bankruptcy attorneys in Boston was still a mystery. "I *am* invaluable to this firm. My successful turnaround of Grant Books will prove that."

They went quiet for a moment and looked at one another.

"Do you have the funds you'll need to purchase your equity stake?" Forrester asked.

"I've been saving for it for years."

Pierce chuckled again and shuffled his papers into a neat pile. "See? Exactly like me."

Cassie's skin tingled. "I hope so. I'm determined to have my name on the firm's wall someday."

"Forrester, Schaeffer, Pierce and Allbright?"

"Works for me." She was going to make this firm her bitch.

When the meeting had adjourned, Cassie headed to her office flush with energy, like a boxer at the end of a match, her gloves held high in the ring. And there was only one person she wanted to celebrate with.

She packed her things and stepped outside. The sun had set, the mid-October chill making the air sharp and dry. Inhaling, she waited for it—that mossy sweet scene of cigar smoke, the apparition that told her she was headed in the right direction—but no dice. Oh well. She fished her phone from her purse and called Patrick.

He picked up on the first ring. "How'd it go?"

His voice was husky and smooth, warming her from the inside out.

"It went great. What are you up to?"

"Waiting for your call and wondering when you were getting your fine ass out of work so I could see you."

"My fine ass, huh?" Cassie glanced into a shop window and stopped in her tracks. Her pulse quickened. "What if I said I was ready for you to do some things to my fine ass tonight?"

A hard exhale was her answer. "I would say, time and place."

"My place around eight?"

"I'll be there. Anything I should bring?"

Feeling incredibly fiendish, Cassie stepped inside a store she'd never set foot in before. "You bring yourself. I'll bring the toys."

17

*C*assie put the finishing touches on her makeup and sat on her couch, waiting for Patrick's arrival. She'd put on her favorite little black dress and those new red shoes she'd gotten for her birthday, giving her the extra boost of confidence she needed. A bottle of wine was chilling in an ice bucket on her coffee table, two glasses beside it, and her recent purchases were on her nightstand.

A quick knock sent her pulse hammering. She checked her reflection in the foyer mirror before putting one hand on her hip and opening the door.

Standing in her hallway with his coat folded over one arm, he was sexy as always: navy slacks, that massive chest framed beautifully by a white button-down, heather-grey vest and pocket square. But his clothes were nothing compared to his grin—sultry like a fox, sly and ready for the hunt.

"Hey sexy." Patrick pulled her to him, kissed her like he was a betting man and she was his lucky pair of dice. He didn't just kiss with his mouth either. He devoured her with his entire body, hands in her hair, hips grinding against hers.

"Miss me?" she breathed against his lips.

"Incredibly."

"It's only been a few days."

"A few days too long."

She closed the door behind them. She took his coat and folded it over a chair, then led him toward the couch. Her place was small enough that it wasn't a far walk, but he tangled their fingers together anyway, as if he didn't want to stop touching her for a second. Sparks chased down her spine. She motioned to the chilled bottle.

"Would you like some wine?"

"I think I can allow myself a glass."

"Only one?" She'd need more than eight ounces of liquid courage if she was going to bring up what she wanted him to do to her tonight.

"I always only have one drink. It's my rule."

Really? "I've never noticed."

He shrugged, the move casual and distant, his face twitching into that mask of indifference for a brief second before he worked it back into a smile. "Let's hear about this meeting."

When they'd settled on the couch and she'd poured them each a glass, she said, "Things are finally turning around. The partners are happier with me, thanks to this huge case I brought in."

"The bankruptcy case you mentioned, I assume?"

"Yeah. Totally fucked company, but if I can fix it, I'll finally make partner."

"I'll keep my fingers crossed." That mask seemed to slip back on, but then he put down his drink, brought her hand to his mouth and kissed her fingertips. "Now about those toys you mentioned."

"Getting straight down to business, aren't we?"

"Mmm-hmm." He ran the pad of her middle finger over his bottom lip and licked. Pleasure jolted through her. "I want to see them."

"Now?"

"Yes. Now."

Cassie didn't need to have been a submissive to obey that command. Eager and full of nerves, she stood, knowing he was watching her hips sway as she went into her bedroom. She returned with four objects and sat back down beside him. Patrick plucked them one by one from her hands.

"A ball gag, a bullet vibe, an anal plug and a bottle of lube." He examined the gag, rolling the ball around. "My, my. Someone was busy this afternoon."

"I was. Are you pleased with my purchases?"

"Depends on who the gag is for. You did say I'd be prettier if I didn't talk so much."

She laughed, momentarily regretting having said that.

"It's for you to use on me. They all are, if you're up for it."

"I'm very up for it. That being said..." He turned the plug over and pressed his fingers around the widest part. "This was a bit ambitious. You're not ready for something this big."

Cassie frowned. "How do you know?"

He reached around behind her with his free hand until his palm found the bottom of her dress. Lifting it up, he grazed over her rear.

"You're pretty tight, my dear. A plug this big needs working up to."

Frustrated and disappointed, Cassie lowered her gaze. It was embarrassing how inexperienced she was compared to him. If she'd known she needed working up, she wouldn't have bought it.

Patrick put the toys on the coffee table and cupped her face, drawing her eyes back up to meet his. "Hey, no pouting. This is uncharted territory for you, and your eyes are bigger than your... back door."

A small giggle bubbled up from her chest. And having his

large, warm palms on her cheeks was comforting. It settled her, like The Hug had. "I suppose you're right."

"I know I am." He dropped one hand down to where it had been, a teasing squeeze to her other cheek. "Don't worry. We can still play that way."

Cassie felt her smile return. "Oh yeah?"

"Definitely. There's plenty I can do with my fingers."

His middle finger found the space in question, pressed down and slid back and forth. The sensation was a shock—violating but strangely pleasurable. Her eyes fluttered shut, her mouth dropping open around a silent *oh*.

"I think you like that," he said quietly.

She nodded and held on to him while he played, pressing, rubbing, circling. A little more pressure, and she gasped and fisted his shirt. Patrick chuckled, then stopped his ministrations to reach out and retrieve the gag.

"And this I think we're both going to like."

She shivered as he dangled it from his fingers. He was already driving her to the point of utter powerlessness. What else could make her feel as helpless as having her ability to protest muffled?

"Tell me what you fantasized about doing tonight, Cassie."

"I want..."

I want you to take me. Force me. Show me your strength and I'll surrender to you.

She struggled with the words, because for all they'd done together, for all the badassery she knew she had, she still didn't know how to ask to be violated.

He leaned in to kiss her neck. Cassie jolted at the bristles of his facial hair, the wet sensation of his tongue on her skin.

"If you don't tell me your fantasies, Cassie, I can't live them out."

God, she wanted to live this out. She was safe with him, but she wanted the illusion of not being so. And he would make that happen, if she asked him to.

"I want you to be mean like you have been, but more. I want it to be hard. I don't want to be able to say no."

"Jesus." His head lolled back against the couch, and he reached down to adjust himself.

"Is that a bad thing?"

"Not at all. It's sexy as hell. The shit you like, it makes me crazy. But I need you to be more specific."

"So I don't end up getting upset again."

"No, silly. So *I* don't do anything that *gets* you upset again."

"Oh." The fact that he was taking responsibility floored her. Patrick twirled the gag around his finger, waiting.

Specifics. Okay. She could do this.

"I want you to use the gag on me, and play with my ass, and maybe even scare me a little. Make me want it, even when it seems like I don't. Make it so good I can't help but come."

"Tall order."

"You asked for specifics."

"I did. And you gave me exactly what I wanted—a very detailed fantasy." There was a heated glint in his eyes. "But you need to be able to show me if you're not okay. Hard to say a safeword with a piece of rubber shoved in your mouth."

She looked around. On her desk was a stress ball she'd had since law school. She pointed to it. "I could hold that. Throw it if I get scared."

He glanced over, then gave her a quick nod. "Get it. Then lie on your bed. Face up."

She scrambled to her feet, clumsy in her excitement. Patrick went into her bedroom, unbuttoning his shirtsleeves as she retrieved the ball. He put it with the rest of the toys at the foot of the bed, then pulled his vest and shirt off, revealing that broad, powerful torso. Just watching him, she could already feel the bulge of his shoulder muscles under her hands, the sheer size of him as he pressed her to the bed, chest hair scraping over her nipples. She liked that there was nothing manicured about him under his clothes. That for all his grooming and wealth, beneath it all he was simply a man.

"Towel?" he asked.

Cassie nodded toward the bathroom. He returned with dark blue terrycloth, dropping it on the bed as he loomed over her and crashed his mouth against hers. Hot and fast, tongue darting into her mouth in short, teasing moves, he kissed her like she was fresh fruit off a vine. Her head was spinning when he stopped to take off her dress. He didn't rip, but was rough as he yanked it down her arms, her bra and panties next. Nuzzling her exposed breast, he bit until she hissed, then licked over the pain he'd caused. Cassie dug her heels into the blanket.

"My shoes..." she said when he'd gotten her naked.

"Leave them on."

"God." Cassie arched her hips toward him. "Please."

He ducked back and knelt on the floor instead. She scowled at him, and his grin was infuriating. "What? Did you think you were going to get what you wanted so easily?"

He gripped her thighs and spread them open. She struggled, trying to break away and drag him back up but his thumbs dug painfully into her.

"Don't make this more difficult than it needs to be, Cassie."

There it was—the power and danger she needed, the hint of a fight in his voice.

"And what happens if I do?"

"The more you protest, the more I'm gonna take what I want instead," he said. "And what I want is that." He fit his mouth against her sex, sucking lightly on her clit.

Sensation shocked through her, and Cassie gave up the fight. Two of those big, warm fingers slid easily inside her and curled upward as he flicked his tongue over her tight mass of nerves, and Cassie bowed off the bed, defenseless to the crush of pleasure. This was perfect. *He* was perfect. How had they avoided this for so long?

One of his hands came down hard and flat on her side. She squeaked in surprise at the sudden smack. "What are you doing?"

"Whatever I want."

"I thought these were my fantasies we were acting—oh *shit*." He did that thing that made her crazy again, rubbing so fast and hitting so deep and making her so wet she wanted to hide her face in embarrassment.

"Little whore doesn't know what she wants, does she?" He slapped her again. Sucked harder. Fingered faster. She couldn't take it. She was almost there. "Asks for one thing, then complains when she gets it."

He slid his fingers free, and Cassie groaned at the agony of being that close to release, then left hanging at the edge. He discarded the rest of his clothes, and she took in the perfect planes of his chest, his thick legs dusted with hair and long, hard cock. He smiled at her as he stroked himself. Longing stirred, hot in her belly, as he fanned his hand open, his palm running along the underside of his dick.

"You like watching me?"

"Mmm-hmm," she said, entranced.

"Something we have in common. Because I'm about to enjoy watching you too." Patrick stopped stroking. He reached for the gag. "Open."

A heady thrill shivered through her. She sneered up at him. "You're gonna have to make me."

He paused, something like hesitation passing over his face. Cassie pinched her brows together and gave a tight shake of her head.

Don't break the spell.

Make it feel real.

He blinked in understanding, then his posture transformed. Shoulders back, arms taut, he bent down and glared at her. His angry look made something sharp leap in her stomach. "Then I guess I will."

In swift moves that didn't give her time to think, he dropped the gag, then gripped her hands and shoved her on her back. She thrashed but he held her down.

"Don't fight me," he said. "Or there will be consequences."

Fight me, is what she heard. *Then enjoy the result.*

Cassie tried to wrestle him off, but he was stronger, and oh, that feeling of him grappling her still. With his legs jamming her against the bed and one thick arm like a steel beam across her chest, he smiled.

"What a pathetic little fighter you turned out to be. All bark and no bite."

She snapped her jaw at him—the only recourse she had. Patrick's brow lifted, a teacher scolding his pupil. "You gonna bite me like the little bitch you are?"

Heat flashed through her. Keeping her immobile with one arm, Patrick reached down with the other and played with her clit. Cassie wilted beneath him, conceding the fight because it felt too good not to. The pads of his fingers swirled and stroked, up and down, around and around. It was unfair how quickly he'd found all her buttons, how easily he could crack her open and make her beg for more.

His hand slipped lower and plunged inside. Cassie's head fell back on a groan.

"You're a mess," Patrick said with a laugh. "A beautiful, drenched, horny mess."

She arched toward him involuntarily, needing more, but she wouldn't let him win completely. "Is this what you call consequences?" she asked through clenched teeth.

He chuckled, then withdrew his fingers and slapped her clit. "No, this is."

The smack ricocheted through her in a bullwhip effect, pain that reverberated from that tiny point into a warm, heavy pleasure. But she didn't have time to absorb the sensation.

Seizing her by the crown of her head, Patrick gripped her hair, brutal as he jerked her upward.

"Be good now," he warned, letting her go to retrieve the gag. Cassie shivered as he thumbed along the side of her jaw, coaxing it into her mouth. It felt bigger than it looked, and fear pulsed through her until he whispered, "Breathe."

She did—one inhale, one exhale, adjusting to the invasive feeling. The ball was punched open with holes she could take in air through, and once he'd fastened the strap, he sat back on his knees to look at her.

"You have no idea how sexy you look, all helpless like that."

Her heartbeat kicked up a notch. She could feel wetness everywhere. Between her thighs. On her chin from her own sloppy breathing.

"So pretty with something shoved between her lips." Patrick tweaked each of her nipples, rolling them between his fingers and thumb. "Unable to be her rude, bitchy little self."

Her groan came out muffled around the gag. Patrick slapped her breast, then picked up the stress ball.

"Exit," he reminded her, and pressed it into her palm.

Cassie nodded, and they stared at one another for a moment. Something passed between them, although she wasn't sure what. Affection? Respect? She wanted to try to say it, to spit out the words wreaking havoc in her head, but she couldn't, rendered silent by a toy he'd put there.

With a lethal calm to his voice, Patrick leaned in and hissed, "Now, up on your hands and knees before I force you there."

The threat in his words had her shaking harder. Cassie turned over and held herself up on all fours.

"Trembling like a little flower," he said through harsh breaths. "Trust me, my dear. You haven't begun to shake yet."

When he knelt behind her, she heard a cap pop open, and then cool, thick liquid drizzled over her backside.

"I'm gonna have a little fun now, and if you don't struggle, you might enjoy it too."

Anxiety and excitement mounting, Cassie clutched the ball and pushed back against him. He spread his fingers across the middle of her back and pushed her downward until she was stretched out on the bed.

"Legs open," he instructed, and she widened them as far as they could go, her head to the side on the pillow. Cassie closed her eyes as Patrick stroked between her thighs and back into where she was aching.

Heaven. Agony. So much and not enough. She moaned into the gag, feeling herself get even sloppier.

"Your pussy is so greedy," he said, thrusting in and out. "So sloppy."

She trembled, surrendering to it all. Her jaw hurt but the rest felt so good—the pressure of his elbow on the small of her back, his incessant plunges inside her. She spread her legs wider and rocked against the comforter, needing friction at her clit.

"So desperate to come you're fucking the bed."

She exhaled hard. Patrick's free hand crept downward until one finger—his pinky?—made a lazy path through the lube on her cheeks, searching, seeking. He slipped it along her back opening.

"Now, you're gonna take this," he murmured. "And I'm going to stroke that tight little ass of yours until you're coming all over my fingers."

Cassie held tightly on to the stress ball. Her breathing sped up, and she tried not to clench as his finger slipped past the first tight ring of muscle. It burned, but along with it came a deep plunge into her pussy from his other hand. He slid a little deeper into her backside, and she let out a long, muffled groan.

"That's it." He sounded almost amazed. "There you go. I knew you'd like it."

She did. It felt strange and violating and wrong, but

incredible at the same time, and her discomfort dissipated as he found a rhythm. One finger, then the other. In and out, working in opposition. His forearm pressed into her lower back, forcing her to take, to feel.

"Now, what was that you said before, about not being able to help but come?"

He stopped fucking her with his fingers and twisted his body around. Cassie heard a buzzing sound. The bullet vibe switching on.

Easing his hand beneath her, he fitted the vibrator against her clit. The quick, steady pulses rocketed through her, but Cassie's gasp was silenced by the gag. She was sweating now, her hips bucking. Patrick's pinky rode even deeper into that unfamiliar back passage as he penetrated her with his fingers once again. Cassie whined loudly. He was kidnapping her body, her mind lost to the way he was working her. Her face was a mess—she could feel drool everywhere—but she couldn't care, not when it felt like this.

She was seconds away from coming when Patrick bent lower and whispered, "Take it, whore, and come. I don't care if you want to or not. We both know you're going to."

Cassie broke apart, the climax so intense she screamed around the gag. Patrick pushed her down as she writhed, forcing her to take more. She clutched the pillows and arched away in an instinctive reflex, trying to escape from the vibrations, but he made her endure it until another orgasm seized, hot on the tails of the first. When he finally, mercifully, slid his fingers free and removed the vibe, Cassie sagged against the bed.

"That looked like you enjoyed it immensely," he mused as he toweled off his hands.

Her throat was too raw for her to reply. It was the closest to her fantasy she'd ever experienced, but it was missing something. Missing the fear, missing the sense she couldn't escape, that she was being taken against her will.

What the hell was wrong with her?

Suddenly she couldn't catch her breath. The shame at wishing he'd been even harsher made tears spark in her eyes. She tried to stop them, but the dam was broken, and she couldn't hold them back.

She shoved the stress ball in his direction and pinched her eyes shut.

"Okay, shhhh. Hold on, I'm taking the gag off."

He unlatched the strap, and Cassie yanked the gag out of her mouth, curled into herself and started to sob. The only respite was the warmth of his body as he wrapped the towel around her and tucked her head beneath his chin.

"I'm here," he said. "I don't know what I did wrong, but I'm here."

"You didn't do anything wrong," she babbled, her voice scratchy. "That was great. Incredible, actually."

"Then why are you crying?"

"Because of the things I want. They're fucked up."

"What—orgasms?"

Cassie snorted despite her tears. "No, it's..."

She teetered on the edge, the words waiting to come out the way you'd wait to careen off a cliff. Sharing this awful truth with anyone, let alone Patrick, had always felt impossible. But this was all just sex, wasn't it? And there was something about being with him that felt anonymous. A step outside reality where she could whisper her sins to the darkness, and he'd absolve her of them, taking her secrets with him when their time together was done.

"...My fantasies disgust me."

Cassie knew he'd heard it—the meekness in her voice, the sound of her armor peeled away. But he held her more tightly. "Why?"

"Because I want to be treated as an object. You don't think that's fucked up?"

"Should I?" He rubbed soothing circles over the towel. "We

like what we like. It doesn't mean there's something wrong with us."

Us. That helped a bit. Calmed her at the same time as it bolstered her nerve.

"I've always been ashamed of the things that turn me on."

"I don't see what there is to be ashamed of."

She wiped her face and looked up at him. Hiding had always been easier than trying to trust someone, or even understanding her desires herself. But here, in his arms, she felt safe enough to try.

"Because I want to be taken against my will. That's the messed-up part. I'm a woman. I'm a lawyer. I'm half Cuban, for fuck's sake. Everything I've ever known tells me I shouldn't want what I do."

Patrick went strangely still. "You're half what?"

"Cuban," she repeated.

He leaned away from her. His expression wasn't what she expected—blinking and stunned, and not in a good way.

"But your last name. Allbright, it's American."

"German, technically. My dad's a native Floridian. My mother is Cuban." She was annoyed, but his disbelief wasn't a surprise, so she did what she always did to prove it. "*¿Te he sorprendido? Pobrecito bebé, deja que mamá lo bese.*"

Did I surprise you? Poor little baby, let mommy kiss it.

As quickly as if she'd stung him, he pulled away and swung his legs over the bed.

Cassie's skin prickled as she stared at his bare back. "What just happened?"

"I need a minute."

"For what?"

"Hearing you speak Spanish—it...took me by surprise, okay?"

Wait, seriously? Everything she'd said and he was freaking out because she was biracial?

Cassie's armor began clipping back into place. She sat up and wrenched off her shoes, not wanting to be anything resembling sexy anymore, at least not for him. "Was discovering I'm technically a minority such a blow to your rich-white-man frame of mind? You can't believe you've been fucking a half brown-skinned girl this whole time?"

"Jesus. No, that's not it at all."

"What is it then?"

"I'm—I just...fuck!" He jumped to his feet. Cassie thought he was going to leave when he tugged on his boxers, but then he began to pace, marching back and forth in silence. She threw her shoes to the floor and hauled the blanket up to cover herself, kicking the toys off until they hit the ground with a thump.

She crossed her arms. "You have two options, Patrick. Explain yourself, or get the hell out of my apartment."

"All right!" Patrick stopped pacing. "All right," he said more softly. "I'll tell you everything."

18

*S*taring at Cassie on the bed, Patrick felt genuinely sick.

She was holding the blanket like a taut shield over her body and her eyes were hot enough to make him think she could set him on fire and dance on the ashes. But that wasn't the thing making him panic. He could take her up on her offer to leave—he'd walked out women's doors for far less—but he wasn't going, not now. This thing between them wasn't ending like this. And not letting that happen meant telling her the story he'd never spoken aloud to anyone.

He made a slow path back and forth in front of her bed. Where else to start but the beginning?

"My mother was an alcoholic," he said. "She's been sober for years, but she was drunk for most of my teens, and my twenties. Not that I could blame her—" even though he did, "—if I were married to a philandering jackass, I'd drink myself into oblivion too."

Cassie was quiet for a moment. "Your father cheated?"

Her question came out a bit detached, as if she were examining a witness on the stand. He didn't mind. If anything, it made talking easier. "Repeatedly."

"And your mother knew?"

"She did, but she numbed herself to it by drinking. They had a shitty relationship."

"Did they fight a lot?"

"No. They barely spoke to each other, even less to me, and when they did, it was cold. Empty. I spent most of my childhood desperate to get out of there."

He'd hid it well, though, behind the smiles he'd learned to paste on. They covered his feelings of shame, the emptiness he faced at home. He never invited anyone over, save for Jack, too embarrassed for anyone to see what life was like behind the wrought-iron gates.

"That sucks," Cassie said, still distant. "But what does this have to do with—"

"You?" Patrick stopped pacing and caught her tight nod. God he did *not* want to talk about this. But she'd laid out the options— tell her the truth, or walk out the door. "I'm getting there."

She eyed him carefully, mistrustful. Patrick leaned back against her bedroom wall.

"I went to Princeton—Dad's alma mater—with the explicit instruction I follow in his footsteps and get a degree in Economics. So I took literature classes instead, just to piss him off."

"He ran a publishing house. How would that be an issue for him?"

"Because he wanted me to be like him, a perfect little copy."

She looked at him, her arms tight across her chest, her body language closed off. "I know what you're thinking," he continued. "Rich-kid problems, right? I had money so I shouldn't have complained. But I didn't want to be like him. I wanted to be something more."

Cassie held still over another beat of silence, then asked, "What did you want to be?"

"Last week, you asked me what my passion was. If you'd

asked me that question twenty-five years ago, my answer would've been different."

"It wasn't sex? You didn't fuck your way through college?"

"I was a virgin in college."

"Seriously?" Patrick flicked a glance at her, but she just shrugged. "Sorry, I find the idea of you being a late bloomer hard to believe."

"Surprise," he said. "I didn't understand how a normal relationship worked, not after watching my parents. And I wanted my first time to be with someone I cared about. I wanted it to mean something."

He didn't look at her on the last bit. Admitting his naïve dream of finding love before he had sex was embarrassing enough without having to see Cassie's expression of incredulity about it.

"So, you spent college a monk," she said.

Patrick's short huff of a laugh was hollow, without mirth. "Not completely. I fooled around, but nothing serious. My real love affair was with words."

"I thought you don't read much."

"Not now. But back then, I spent more of my time reading than not."

He recalled the quiet of it, the peace. The smell of old books in the library. He'd be immersed for hours, lost in a collection of sentences. The prose he'd read, the way the authors painted pictures with words, made him feel alive for the first time in his life. It was a world he'd wanted to bury himself in—to read and never stop.

"Your passion was with literature?"

"Spanish literature," he corrected her. Now he made eye contact. Purposely—to make sure she was listening. "One course and I was hooked. After that I took every class I could—soaked it up, packed on the credits, even went from beginner's to advanced Spanish in a semester. By my senior year, I was fluent."

One plus of having a great memory. Languages were super easy to learn.

Cassie raised an eyebrow. "Fluent?"

He raised one right back. "Don't believe me?" She didn't seem to, so he narrowed his eyes and leaned over the bed. *"Pobre pequeña princesa, deja que papá la bese."*

Poor little princess. Let Daddy kiss it.

It was a purposeful turnaround of her snarky comeback before, and oh, did it do the trick. She shifted under the blanket, a pinched V between her brows. She was angry at being bested, and if he wasn't mistaken, she'd gotten a bit turned on. But now wasn't the time for that.

"My father was pissed but told me at my graduation I could 'still be an asset to the company anyway.'" Patrick remembered the anxiety, the frantic need to do anything but lead by that bastard's side. "I was supposed to come home, shadow him and move into a management position. I skipped town instead."

"A multimillion-dollar business was your birthright, and you ran away from it?"

"Like I said, I didn't want to be like him."

And yet, he'd become that way anyway. Wealthy. Angry. Sleeping around.

God, he was disgusted with himself.

"I came home for Jack and Eve's wedding, left a note for my parents, emptied the one bank account I had access to and was on the next flight to Spain."

He could see the rugged coast of it now—the mountains and medieval architecture. He could smell the food, hear the music. The rushing current of the waterfall outside the bedroom he'd spent far too many nights in.

"What did you do there?" she asked, anchoring him in the present.

"I backpacked around, taking on odd jobs and staying in hostels until I landed in Asturias."

"Spain was where you learned to dance, wasn't it?"

His glance back at her was sharp. "Spain was where I learned a lot of things."

She shifted again, this time uncomfortable. Cassie was nothing if not good at understanding the subtext: Spain was where he'd gotten so good in bed.

"So what happened? Did you gamble away your inheritance at a casino in Madrid or something?"

"Not quite. I got a job in a bookstore and stayed with the man who owned it. He took me in, and treated me like family." Patrick's jaw tightened, his eyes meeting the floor. "And then I met Sofia."

One, two, three beats of quiet. "Who was she?"

There was a flat note of jealousy in her voice, peeking through despite her attempt at being casual. If he hadn't felt so damn nauseous he would've enjoyed it.

"She was a cashier at a high-end clothing shop in town." With wild, thick hair, and a body he'd dreamed about for weeks. "It was love at first sight for me. But I didn't have the guts to talk to her."

"You? Shy?"

"I told you I was a late bloomer. I was terrified to approach her. She didn't speak much English, and wasn't in town on the weekends—at the time I didn't know why—so I wrote her a letter. A long, lovesick schoolboy's poem."

His face burned at the memory of the words he'd written in Spanish, asking for her name, her time, her heart. How trusting, how foolish he'd been, pouring his soul out on paper like that.

"No one's written me a love note before," Cassie said.

"Well that's insane. Somebody should've."

"I would've had to have been in love for that to happen."

Patrick's gaze snapped toward hers. "Never?"

Cassie shook her head. He didn't know how that was possible, but after what she'd shared about her past relationships, it wasn't such a surprise. He wanted to go to her, to touch her, but she hadn't moved her arms from her middle, and he wasn't ready to sit yet either.

"Well, love isn't the fairy tale people say it is."

Patrick could hear the bookshop's bell tinkling happily, the elated leaping of his heart when Sofia finally walked through the door, yellow peasant blouse and beaming smile and his note in her hand. The past rattled in his skin, too many emotions to fit inside. He started to pace again.

"Our first in-person conversation lasted for hours. We went to a café, and talked until they closed and she asked me to go home with her. I was so excited, I could hardly breathe."

"Was she your first?"

Patrick nodded. "And having sex made me fall even harder."

He couldn't go there, couldn't play back those feelings. He moved instead, cut a narrow path between the foot of her bed and the TV across from it. Ten steps from the windows on one side to the door on the other, glass frames on one wall, exposed brick above her headboard. It was cozy. Comfortable.

Another reason he hadn't wanted to leave.

"How long were you with her?"

"Six months." The second half of the happiest year he'd ever known. He had a job he liked, a family to spend time with, albeit borrowed. And love, or so he'd thought. "It wasn't all sex, although that was a big part of it. We spent countless nights together, talked about everything—books, politics, art. She opened up a world of intimacy to me, and I loved her with every stupid, hopeful bone in my body. But none of it was real."

"What do you mean?"

His pulse pounded. "I wanted to stay in Spain, to spend all my time reading and discussing books, work in the shop and marry her. It was my childish version of a happily ever after, and I spent every cent I had on a ring." Patrick could feel his heartbeat in his throat. "Turned out, she already had one."

"What?"

He turned around to catch Cassie's startled expression. "Yeah, turned out she was engaged, and had been the entire time to a businessman her father had set her up with. That's why she was never around on the weekends. She went back to the countryside to be with him."

"She told you when you proposed?"

That would've at least been decent. "No, she waited until after we'd made love, and I'd fallen asleep beside the woman I thought was going to be my wife. I woke up the next morning alone, the ring on top of a note explaining that she wasn't in love with her fiancé, and had wanted one last fling before she tied the knot. She never expected to care for me, but she wasn't going to run off with me, either."

He could recall every detail of that morning. The quiet of her being gone. The anguish. How devastated he'd been to read her words, the future he'd imagined with her evaporating like warm breath on a cold day.

"She ended the note with the words *'Lo siento, y adios para siempre, amante mío.'*"

"I'm sorry, and—"

"—goodbye forever, lover of mine."

The shame was thick on Patrick's tongue at the translation.

"A Spanish woman was your first love and your first heartbreak," Cassie said. "No wonder you freaked out on me."

Patrick winced. Hearing her speak Spanish had sent him catapulting into the past. "I'm sorry about that. It was a knee-jerk reaction. Emphasis on the jerk."

"It's okay, I guess." She shrugged. "At least I understand now."

Okay I guess didn't mean she was okay. She still had her back up, and that guard didn't come down easily. Which was why he was surprised as all hell when she pushed back the covers, inviting him back beside her.

A small gesture, but one he hadn't known he'd been waiting

for. Gingerly, he sat on the bed and stretched his legs out. She curled up beside him.

"What happened then?"

He'd stopped being the boy he was. Started being the man he became, whoever that was. "I packed my things the next day. I couldn't be there anymore. Everything about Spain, about books, reminded me of her. Of how foolish I was."

It still did.

"You weren't foolish. You were in love."

"And foolish. I was so focused on this life I thought I had that I couldn't see how badly I was being played."

Cassie held him more tightly, and her arms felt like a brace, holding down that need to move. Gustavo had been sad to see him go, but had given him that tattered old copy of *El Viejo y el Mar* as a goodbye gift, saying one day he'd find more meaning in it.

It had been untouched on his bookshelf ever since.

"So I sold the ring, bought a plane ticket and went home, only to find out my father had died, and the CEO position at Dunham and Strauss was waiting for me. And he'd put a stipulation in his will saying if I didn't work for the business, he'd deny me my inheritance and cut my mother off from her monetary support as well."

"Nice guy."

"Yeah, he was a real winner." Her humor lifted his mood, as did her cheek, warm against his shoulder. "I didn't care about the money. I would've walked away from it all. But my mother would've ended up on the street. I wasn't going to abandon her."

Even if she'd never offered him the same courtesy.

"You couldn't challenge the will?"

"Trust me, I tried. There was a no-contest clause."

"So if you fought it and lost in court, your inheritance would've been forfeited."

"Bingo. Not a risk I was going to take. Jack pored over the will until he found the loophole—I only had to be in a position of authority to satisfy the conditions, not run the ship. So Director of Sales, I became."

And resigned himself to being trapped in his life, his fancy home and his steady cash flow.

"You never wanted to be in charge?" Cassie asked.

"I'm not in charge now. I just have a larger share of the stock. And the joy of doing something I hate."

"I didn't know you hated it."

"It's not what I imagined doing with my life. That's for sure."

"You wanted to continue your love affair with literature," she said. "Sex isn't your only passion."

But it was his escape. "Maybe, but since Sofia, I don't get involved. No emotions, no one gets hurt."

Especially not him. Because not a day had passed when he hadn't thought about her, and he'd spent his life since avoiding connections, leaving women first because he couldn't stand the idea of waking up alone like he had that morning long ago, and making damn sure he knew how to protect himself from something like that ever happening again.

"What's your fantasy?" she asked quietly.

Patrick searched his mind and drew a blank. "I don't know that I have one."

"None?"

"I prefer fulfilling other people's fantasies. It...gets me out of my head. Anyway, it's too late for me to pursue my passions. I've sold my soul to Dunham and Strauss. I wouldn't know how to start over now."

He wouldn't know how to change either, how to break from the life he'd started living, spending money because he figured he was stuck in this situation, so he might as well get what he could out of it. Expensive clothes. Lavish apartment. His home was as closed off as he was, luxurious and lonely.

Except when Cassie was there.

He hadn't realized it until now, but that was another reason he hadn't wanted to walk out her door. He didn't overthink when he was with her, didn't worry about the future or fixate on the past. He didn't need to become someone else either. He was just... himself.

Cassie touched him, slim fingers against his chest. "Why didn't you tell me any of this?"

"I've never told anyone about Sofia."

"Not even Jack?"

"Nope."

"Why tell me, and not your best friend?"

"I didn't want to talk about it." He rubbed her knuckle like it was a worry stone, then turned her hand over and ran his thumb along her palm. "I told you because you needed to know my reaction tonight wasn't about you. And because I trust you, which is weird as all hell, since I've spent the better part of this year seeing how angry I could get you."

She smiled and melted into him. Patrick liked it, knowing he'd made her feel better. And telling her everything had made *him* feel better. He hadn't realized how much that story had been eating at him until he'd finally told someone.

Not someone. Her.

It was like exposing a wound that refused to heal, somehow helped by contact with the air. The anger had festered in the darkness, growing more bitter as it flowed through his veins. He'd been so ashamed, unwilling to explain to anyone how badly he'd been duped, why his future was meaningless and his past was a mess. But it had felt right to tell Cassie. The sense of calm now that he'd done so was palpable.

He nodded in the direction of her living room. "My mother is also the reason I don't drink much. Hence the one glass of wine."

"That makes sense." She nuzzled his chest, a tiny, sweet motion. "Thank you for telling me all that."

"You're welcome."

She got up on her knees, the sheet giving way to curves and soft skin as she kissed him. She took control, tongue sweeping into his mouth, and as she got more demanding, suddenly it all made sense—her feisty temperament and zero tolerance for bullshit. How she radiated femininity and sex appeal, even when she was being impossible. Her ability to chew someone up and spit them out while still being seductive, provocative and fiercely loyal to her friends.

Cassie was Latina. Maybe only half, but still.

He didn't understand why she kept it under wraps. He was caught between wanting to get her talking, and to find the best ways of shutting her up.

He'd seen her with her clothes off, but Patrick had a feeling he hadn't truly seen her naked. Now he was getting to see the real her—the woman behind the defense she so often kept in place. A whole new Cassie was in front of him, and he wanted to know everything about her.

He eased off the kiss and tapped her bottom lip.

"And now that I've told you all my secrets, it's time you did the same."

19

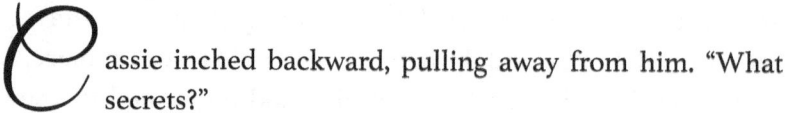

assie inched backward, pulling away from him. "What secrets?"

She'd thought the last hour of talking had been about him. And absorbing all that new information had been more than she'd expected—hearing about his family, his time in Spain and Sofía. She'd always assumed Patrick was too callous to have given his heart away, and never having been in love meant Cassie didn't know what it felt like to have your heart broken. But his story proved that not only was he not the man-whore she'd thought he was, but he'd had a relationship the depths of which she'd never known.

"Why do you hide your Cuban side?"

Cassie hooked a hand over the back of her neck. "I don't know that I hide it. I just don't flaunt it."

But she didn't exactly embrace it either.

"Why not?"

"Because."

Her hackles were rising, and she kneaded harder at her neck. It was impossible to explain this—the stress of growing up with two identities, the murky area of who she was.

Patrick reached up and covered her hand with his.

"I won't judge you, Cassie. I hope that much is obvious by now. And I told you my story, so I'd love it if you'd share yours."

She looked at him, at the sudden sincerity in his eyes. That mask of his was gone, and he *had* just bared his soul.

Why did she always see a problem where there wasn't one? She lowered her hand, the heavy weight of her guard dropping.

"It's...personal. It's hard for me to put into words."

"I understand."

Instead of her rigid massage, Patrick's fingers smoothed over the tendons in her neck, slow and calming. "How'd you know this would calm me down?"

"Easy. You always rub the back of your neck when you're nervous."

Of course he'd noticed that. It was her stress response—what she did when she wanted to fight but knew she couldn't.

"I don't know where to start," she said. "They call being Cuban-American 'life on the hyphen' because you're not one or the other. I'm not Cuban or Anglo. I'm a hybrid—a *Cubanglo*. I have two cultures, but I don't belong wholly to either one."

He waited, continuing to coax the tension from her neck. Cassie snuggled a little closer. "Growing up, we only spoke Spanish at home—well, Spanglish, really. A mix of Spanish and English. But I'm fluent in both, and it was hard to know which language to speak, which Cassie to be."

And no one who saw her outside the house knew which Cassie she was either.

"Hey mami, you white or Latina? With that skin and those hips, I can't tell."

"My Dad speaks Spanish too, albeit a bit softer than my mom. He was always this quiet, logical voice of reason in a very loud house."

"Loud?"

"Cubans have two decibels: loud and louder."

Most of the time, she loved the quiet, the peace and privacy she had in Boston. The only way any of her family got up in her business was by text or phone. But now, talking about it, she missed them. Missed the ease of talking to her father, who rarely was the one who called. Missed her brother, so busy with his own family they only connected every once in a while. Missed Elísa and her mother yapping at each other, the bustle of home, the noise.

She missed the part of her she'd left there, but it didn't fit anywhere else.

"Finances were tight," she continued. "Dad worked a lot while Mom stayed home. He tried to retain our Cuban culture, but snuck me and my siblings out for fast food whenever we needed a break from rice and beans."

Patrick chuckled. "That was a staple growing up?"

"You couldn't tell?" Cassie asked dryly. "This thick Latina body came from years of fatty and high-sodium food." How anyone was expected to stay trim and fit on a Cuban diet was beyond her.

Patrick slid a hand beneath the blanket to graze her thigh. "I like your thick Latina body."

She grinned and shivered. Good to know.

"Did you ever go to Cuba?" he asked.

"Nah." She'd skipped out on the trip her family had taken together after Castro died, saying she was too busy.

Maybe that had been her excuse.

Maybe it was always her excuse.

"My whole life, Cuba was this paradise, this homeland my grandfather had been exiled from, but meant nothing to me other than the stories he told."

"He left when Castro came to power?"

Cassie nodded. "He ran a casino in Havana but had to leave when the government was overthrown and the gambling establishments were seized. He talked a lot about the fall of Batista, how dangerous it was for him and my grandmother crossing the Florida Straits in a flimsy watercraft."

"They abandoned everything?"

"Everything. They arrived in Miami with nothing but their clothes. But my grandfather found a way to work the system. The nightlife was booming there, so he took out a loan and opened a bar."

And despite all his success, he seemed to live with his bags packed, yearning to return to *La Cuba de ayer*, the Cuba of yesterday.

Patrick turned on his side so they were face-to-face on the bed. A smattering of his chest hair was visible above the sheet, and Cassie longed to rest her face against it, to feel the coarse hairs and his warmth on her skin.

So she did.

Her tension deflated on an exhale as his arms came around her.

"Sounds like a pretty cool guy," he said.

"The coolest. He was a proud man—he didn't like taking charity—and had to enlist in the Cuban Refugee Program to get the loan. But he made sure to pay back every dollar with interest. He's the one who drilled that 'stand on your own two feet' mantra into me. And taught me how to dance too."

Patrick's chest rose and fell, a quiet pause she couldn't read, but she let herself fall into the pattern of his breathing until he asked, "Is your grandmother still alive?"

"No, she passed away before I was born. It's part of what made my grandfather retire."

"Is the bar still there?"

"Yeah, our extended family runs it. I think he was happier actually, not being in charge. He spent most of his time being 'Señior Casimíro,' a Miami legend, content to do nothing but play dominoes and smoke cigars. Which weren't even Cuban. They were Dominican."

She tried to recall the scent, the heady mix of tobacco and leather and smoke. The smell reminded her of him, of innocence, of a time before grades and boys. Before she realized there was such a thing as being biracial and having to figure out how to blend all the parts that made her up. Before she had to learn how to decide which side of her ethnic background she viewed things from.

"Sometimes, when no one is smoking nearby, I swear I smell his cigars and I know he's there, watching over me."

"That's a nice thought to have," he said. "Tell me more about him."

Cassie sifted through memories, picking happy ones instead of the ones that brought the wistful pinch of tears. "I made him teach me how to play dominoes when I was seven. I insisted not teaching me was communism, even though I had no idea what that meant."

"Sounds like something you would do."

She grinned. "He gave in, and every day after school he'd wrap the ring from his cigar around my finger and teach me how to match the tiles, to strategize and guess my opponent's moves. It was kind of my early introduction to the legal battlefield."

"Is that when he told you that you were going to change the world?"

She blinked a few times, astonished that he remembered. She shouldn't have been. Elephant memory and all. "It was. It became the driving force in my life, propelling me toward my goal of becoming a lawyer."

She valued the struggle her grandfather went through. It was why she was trying so hard. To show she was thankful for his sacrifice.

If she didn't do that, she'd have failed him.

"So why law?"

"Laws change the world," she said simply. "I wanted to become one of those badass women who blazed trails and influenced history forever. Like that statue on Wall Street of the fearless girl and the charging bull, braving the discrimination and gender gap."

"I wanted to run with the bulls."

"In Pamplona?" She lifted her head in disbelief. "You're crazy."

"I always regretted not doing it." He put his fingers up in horns. "Toro, toro!"

She laughed, appreciating the break in the heavy even as she batted his fingers down.

"You were saying?" he asked.

"I didn't want to be a famous Cuban-American actor or a musician. I looked up to ambassadors, cabinet members, congresspeople, and journalists. Gilda Oliveros, the first Cuban-born woman mayor. Raoul G. Cantero III, the first Hispanic Justice on the Florida Supreme Court. Jim Acosta, Soledad O'Brien. Ted Cruz, Marco Rubio. All Latinos."

His eyes searched hers. "If you're proud of things they've done, why hide the Cuban in yourself?"

"You mean you haven't figured it out despite my convoluted attempts at talking around it? Come on, Patrick. Read my mind!"

She was stalling, but hey, wasn't paying attention his specialty?

"If I had to guess, I'd say your heritage means a lot to you, and you're proud of it, but you don't quite know how to...*be* it."

Damn. He did pay attention.

"You got most of it right." Cassie rolled over onto her back. It was easier to admit this when he wasn't looking at her so intently. "I've always struggled to figure out who I am, from work to relationships to filling out forms. Which little box do I check?

Latina or Caucasian? There was no multicultural option back then, I could only choose one. So I chose to be white."

"Did something happen to make you choose that?"

She slanted a pointed look at him. "People treat me differently when they find out."

"I'm sorry, I—"

"No, don't. It's not just you. It's been my whole life. When I'm Anglo, I'm respected. When I'm brown, I'm ignored. I love a lot about my heritage, but no matter how far we've come in America there's still an undercurrent of racism, and as much as I hate to admit it, my eye and skin color have given me opportunities others don't have, especially at work. I don't look Cuban, and that's made life..." she shrugged, "...easier."

Easier to be one than stuck in the middle. Easier to keep silent and hide under a cloak of Caucasian features. It was a horrible thing to say. A horrible thing to feel. A horrible way to honor her grandfather's sacrifice. How could she long for her heritage and reject it at the same time?

"You've clearly worked hard to get where you are though," he said softly. "I'm sure your grandfather would be proud."

"I feel like he might, sometimes. I have his drive, his desire to avoid charity. Not having a loan over my head is important to me. I want to make my own way. I don't want anything handed to me."

Patrick went quiet for a moment.

"What?" she asked.

He shook his head. "Nothing. I just had no idea you'd struggled that much."

She was still struggling. "I've gotta work crazy hours and put everything into proving I can do a man's job—a white man's job. A lot of my female coworkers cut their hours to raise their children, or left the practice completely. I can't do that, not if I want to make partner."

"You want kids?"

The was a question she didn't know how to answer. So she went with honesty instead.

"I know I'm *supposed* to want kids, but I've never had that ovary-exploding, biological urge, so I put it on the back burner. It's certainly what my mom wants from me though. She's constantly on me about when I'm going to get married."

"Is she now?"

Cassie rolled her eyes and turned back on her side. "All the time. I mean, she's proud of me, at least I think she is, but it's like —" she smacked her hands together several times in succession, "—where's the husband and babies, Cassandra? Tick-tock!"

He laughed. "Well I don't have that problem. I don't think my mom cares much about what I do. And kids are..."

She looked up at him, at the sudden darkening in his expression, his gaze far away.

"...I don't think they're for me," he finished.

"I get it. I'm too old at this point to change my routine and my budget—my savings is for my investment in the firm. And like I said, I've lost my patience with dating. I hate all those games you have to play. Be independent, but never let a man think you don't need him. Demand respect, but act demure. Act sexy, but don't let them treat you like an object."

Patrick grinned and brushed his nose against hers. "But you like being treated like an object."

Cassie's pulse spiked uncomfortably. "That's a problem too."

"Your fantasies?" The huskiness in his voice made her tingle. "Objectification, name calling, slapping—those are hot. Not problems. Not something to be disgusted with."

So he remembered what she'd said. Felt like a year, not an hour ago. "But it goes deeper."

"I know. You like it when your body isn't in your control. Like when I get you crazy wet. It makes you mad and it turns you on. And that makes you madder. Which turns you on more."

"True, but I haven't told you the fantasies I'm really ashamed of."

Her body went tense, and her breathing sped up. She felt naked despite the blanket, raw and vulnerable without the armor she'd gotten so comfortable hiding behind.

Patrick brushed his knuckles over her cheek, caressed her softly a few times before slipping his hand around to the back of her neck and anchoring it there. "The idea that you have even dirtier fantasies makes me want you even more."

His smile was genuine, his eyes shining.

She inhaled slowly.

Jumped off the cliff.

"Breath play is one."

He gripped her neck a little harder. Whether it was in excitement or discomfort or an attempt to keep her steady, she didn't know. "Okay. What does that involve?"

Cassie's breathing shifted—still fast, but it wasn't tinged with fear. She didn't feel that usual sense of revulsion she always harbored about her perverse hunger to be forced and taken and claimed.

"I don't want to be choked. I just want the threat of it, the feeling of a hand around my throat."

He looked at her neck, brought his hand around to the front and experimentally tightened his fingers. Cassie inhaled, surprised by the pleasure that coiled through her at the restriction, at how nervous and safe she felt at the same time. The sensation was dizzying.

"Have you ever done that?" he asked quietly, hooded eyes focused on her throat.

"Once. A long time ago." But she wanted more than that fumbling grip from a boy who posed no real threat. She wanted Patrick to do more than tease her.

She wanted it to feel real.

"Have you?" she asked.

He released her throat, pressed his palm to her sternum, his breath hot on her face. "No. Does that bother you?"

"No."

"Good. Tell me about the other fantasy."

Cassie's nipples puckered up. She was lightheaded, her blood rushing. "Consensual non-consent."

He stilled, his eyes blazing. "Rape play."

The words thudded as loudly as her heartbeat. Cassie nodded.

"Have you always wanted that?"

"Yes. I've tried to push it back, but it's always been there."

"Did anybody ever..."

"Rape me for real? No. Which makes me feel crazy guilty because of what actual rape survivors have been through. But I do...want it."

"And that's something you want to do with me?"

His throat bobbed on a swallow. He was turned on, as aroused as she was, her fantasies the sparks that always set them both on fire. "Not right now, but, yes."

"Specifics," he gritted out. "Please."

It was easy, now, to tell him. Now that he knew everything. "I want the rush, the fear and excitement of trying to fend off someone stronger than me. I want to be taken when I don't expect it, to feel like it's anonymous and believe it's real. To be scared and fight until I have no choice and my body gives in."

He nodded, like he was taking it in, filing it away. "And if we do that, what do you need? After, I mean."

After he'd pretended to assault her? "I need to feel safe, I guess. Tethered. Grounded." She reached up, traced her fingers along the back of his hand, secured over her heart. "What do you need?"

His jaw worked, and he pulled her close, arms tight around her, his lips at the crown of her head. "Don't leave," he said. "No matter what happens, don't leave."

Something sharp flashed in her throat, something jagged and raw. "Okay."

She wasn't sure how they'd gotten here, but somehow Patrick had become the person who gave her the most comfort, the person she was willing to share her deepest secrets with. And she guessed the same was true for her to him. It was still just sex, she knew that, but it was okay.

Everything felt okay, as long as his arms were around her.

They stayed like that, breathing quietly together until Cassie fell asleep.

* * *

Patrick awoke a few hours later. It was the middle of the night, and Cassie was still there, warm and pliable and soft in his arms. He'd been in and out of sleep since she drifted off. His mind was reeling with all she'd shared with him, her history, the things she craved.

It had felt like a privilege, to learn so much about her. But worries niggled at the back of his mind. Like her grandfather, she wanted to make her own way in the world. How would she feel if she found out he'd sent Hudson to her? Would she see it as a handout?

He'd have to keep that one to himself. And make sure Hudson didn't tell her either.

She shifted in her sleep, bare legs rubbing against his, skin soft and silky smooth. He wanted to let her sleep, and tried to steel himself against his burgeoning erection, but his mind went into overdrive, awash with the things she wanted him to do to her. How rough she wanted him to be.

Not rough. Cruel. Brutal.

Jesus, this woman. Passionate and spirited, wild and difficult to break. But she wanted to be broken. Wanted *him* to break her.

He was so fucking gone for her.

She opened her eyes, heavily lidded and drowsy. "Hey. Sorry I passed out like that."

"'S'okay." He ran his hand down her back, up her side, needing her close, needing more. Instead of hungering for escape he wanted to be present. To be totally enveloped in her.

She touched his face. "You all right?"

A prickly tightness started up in his chest. "Cassie, are we..."

Coming too close to having feelings? Should we shut this thing down?

"Are we what?" she prompted.

"Are we okay? We sort of had a fight tonight, I guess."

Leaning in, she kissed him. Light. Gentle. Her tongue a wet swipe in his mouth.

"We're okay," she said against his lips. "Besides, we're used to fighting."

Desire spooled low in his belly, anticipation flooding through him in a rush. This. This was a language they spoke well. Whatever they couldn't say with their mouths, they could say with their bodies, and suddenly Patrick was done with the talking.

He kissed her, and turned her onto her back with a growl. She'd released something in him. Something unfamiliar and desperate he couldn't control.

He reached over to her nightstand, fumbling with the drawer until he found a condom and shoved his boxers down. She held on tight when he pressed inside her. She wasn't as wet as usual, sleepy as she still was and their regular foreplay absent, so the entry offered him more friction. A confusing shameful lust drove him wild as he thought about what she wanted, about forcing his way into her. It doubled the intensity, sheared the edge off his restraint, but he made himself slow down, teasing her with shallow pumps until the slickness of her pussy eased him deeper inside.

"Not like this," she whispered. "Give it to me hard."

God, yes.

He seated himself in one smooth stroke, then reared back and started a frantic pace. Cassie's eyes closed as she absorbed his pounding, and Patrick did the same. He didn't want to think about how messy this was getting, or focus on the past anymore. He wanted to be with her, in her, to fill the gaping hole inside him with this gorgeous, complicated woman, and take, take, take until everything they'd left behind them were distant memories again.

20

*P*atrick reared his arm back and readied his serve.

"Love-thirty," he said, then tossed the ball into the air. It landed smack in the middle of the net. He pulled a second ball from his pocket, then missed again.

Across the court, Jack cracked a grin. "You suck today."

"Fuck you."

He *was* sucking. Majorly. Again. But he had an excuse—he was distracted, and had been for five whole days.

His next shot made it over the net. Patrick ran to meet Jack's return, but his brain wasn't there. It was on Cassie. Thoughts of her had him struggling to concentrate, here and everywhere else.

Her request last Friday had woken up something primal in him. But it worried him too.

She wanted to be taken savagely. Without her consent.

He wasn't sure he could go through with it. Where was the line between fulfilling a fantasy and committing a crime? How could he avoid crossing it while still making it good for her?

He was determined not to fuck it up. Being asked to do this, to be trusted *that much*, took what they were doing to a new level. They were definitely in BDSM territory, and as much as he'd played at things over the years, he was completely out of his element.

Jack scored, winning the match. He threw Patrick a shit-eating grin. "You need a rest, old man?"

"You're an asshole."

But a rest would be good. It would give him a chance to ask his friend some questions. Patrick gathered up a few wayward tennis balls and made his way to the net.

"Looking to get your ass kicked a third time?" Jack asked.

"Actually, I'm all played out. Do you think we could head over to your office for a bit?"

Jack raised an eyebrow. "I thought you weren't going to be hitting on my students for a while."

"I'm not. But I need some—" He paused. He'd never done this before. "—*lifestyle* advice."

Jack's face went serious. His jaw ticked in understanding. "Let's go."

Jack had always been extremely confidential about his sexual proclivities, living the BDSM lifestyle in private. He was a professor at Harvard Law. If people found out he got his rocks off spanking and flogging and tying women up, he feared it might affect his career. So he was all about discussing things in secure places.

By the time they got to Jack's office, Patrick couldn't feel his fingers. It wasn't that chilly—it was certainly going to get worse— but it was cold enough.

Fuck. He needed a vacation.

Jack closed his door behind them. "What do you need?"

Patrick leaned against a chair. "Things with Cassie have progressed, and I'm wondering what you can tell me about breath play and consensual non-consent."

Jack's eyebrows shot up. "Try not to kill her, to start."

"Don't be a dick. I'm serious."

"So am I." Jack sat at his desk. "I thought you two were just fucking. Have you gone beyond that point?"

He didn't know. "Things got kind of...intense last weekend."

"Intense how?"

Taking her in every orifice, intense.

Gagging her and making her come so hard she cried, intense.

Telling her things I've never told anyone, not even you, intense.

"It's complicated."

"That's a fucking understatement." Jack frowned and steepled his fingers together. "This is dangerous stuff, Patrick. They call it edge play for a reason. It requires a shit-ton of trust, and being able to read one another. Are you sure she wants this? Are you sure you do?"

Patrick pushed off the chair and paced around the room. Cassie wanted this. He knew that. They'd talked more about it over the phone since last weekend, and she'd said she liked the idea of being tied up as part of the fantasy. To have her mouth covered when she started to scream. Patrick should've been disgusted. Appalled. Anxious as all shit over the idea of her wanting him to be so vicious.

But, fuck. It turned him on.

"What does it say about me if I do?"

Jack was silent for a beat too long. "I guess the question is, why do you want it?"

"Because she asked me to."

"So these are Cassie's fantasies," Jack confirmed.

"I thought they were—hers I mean—but I want them too."

"And that bothers you?"

"I don't know that it *bothers* me..."

He hadn't been bothered by anything they'd done together, from telling her to shut up to gagging her. He'd thoroughly enjoyed watching her struggle to speak, rendered helplessly silent. He'd loved her body's reaction when he'd had his fingers inside her pussy and her ass too, his elbow shoved against her spine, making her like things she'd never tried before, feeling her give in. And, God, hearing the strain in her voice when she finally broke under the force of all that pleasure...it was the hottest, most powerful thing he'd ever experienced.

He wanted it too. To take her by surprise. To feel her thrash and hear her protest and knowing he could have her anyway.

"I think it bothers me that it *doesn't* bother me."

"And why is that?"

Patrick continued to pace. Stupid law professors and their stupid Socratic methods. This was why he'd never needed a therapist. He had Jack asking him questions until he ran out of air. "You know I'm kind of an asshole, right?"

"Your words, not mine."

"Well, with her, I can be that—not the nicest. I can let this heartless beast out, this part of me that's angry at everything, the part I try to shut down and sublimate through empty sex with strangers because I can't do a fucking thing to change it. She likes it pretty goddamn rough, and I can...give in to that. But I'm not gonna actually hurt her. What she's asked me to do, it's this deep-seated fantasy she doesn't even get, and it woke up stuff in me too. And we're not just fucking. We talk. Sleep together. Make breakfast in the morning. Shit I never do, with anyone."

Patrick stopped talking, stopped pacing too. He turned to face his friend.

"So, Cassie is different," Jack said.

"Yeah. She is."

Relief came like a linebacker, suddenly knocking the wind out of him. Everything with Cassie had been a break from the ordinary, and maybe that's why this was coming to the surface. Maybe wanting this was something he'd buried, because when would he have figured out that he liked this on a one-night stand? No woman would meet a guy in a bar and say the things Cassie did. But perhaps this was what had always crackled between them—a dark, intense attraction that had driven all their verbal clashing. A secretive thing they both shared that he'd never known he wanted before.

It was why he couldn't stop himself. Why be broke his own rules to be with her, again and again and again. The desire had always been there. Cassie just lit a fuse in him. She was the burning match, but he was the kindling, and he wanted to chase that fire until they both exploded.

"Then I don't think wanting that says anything about you," Jack said. "Except that you've found someone who trusts you with the most secret parts of her being."

He put his glasses on, turned to his computer and started typing. Patrick settled into a chair.

"There's no safe way to do breath play," his friend began. "But if you're going through with it, you have to know what you're doing. Never apply serious pressure to the front of her throat. Listen to make sure her breathing doesn't get too shallow. Don't wait for her eyes to lose focus, or for her to struggle, for you to stop. And always, *always* make sure you can feel her pulse."

"Got it."

"Have you taken a CPR course?"

Patrick nodded grimly. "We have one at work every few years."

"Good. I'm assuming you're smart enough to have established a safeword?"

"Of course," Patrick scoffed. "I do actually know a thing or two about this."

"You came to me for advice. Now shut up and take it."

"That's usually my line."

Jack rolled his eyes, typed a few more things and clicked on his mouse. "I'm sending you some articles. Read them thoroughly. If you have any questions, let me know."

"And take two aspirin and call you in the morning."

Jack did not seem to appreciate the lighthearted commentary. His lips were tight in a way Patrick had never seen before.

"I'm warning you, Patrick—do not hurt her. Or you won't only have Lilly banging down your door. You'll be answering to me as well."

He'd never seen his friend's Dominant side, and he had to admit, it schooled him.

"Understood."

They grabbed a bite to eat after that, changing the subject to the situation with Brady and Sam over a pint and sweet potato fries. They were talking about Jack and Lilly's plans to give the troubled couple some space by babysitting Allegra and Hope for a weekend when Patrick's phone buzzed with a text.

Cassie's name read out on the screen. His stomach pitched with happiness.

"This day can suck a big bag of dicks," her text read.

Patrick couldn't hide his smile. *"Is that an invitation?"*

"Unfortunately, not tonight. I have more work to do, and I'm exhausted."

"Pobre cosita."

The teasing Spanish words for *poor thing* came to him quickly. Amazing, the pieces of language that had stuck in his memory after all these years.

"Don't you dare get me horny. I have to stay focused."

He replied with a frowning emoticon. He was disappointed that he wouldn't be seeing her—five days already felt like an eternity—but it was all right. Given the several articles Jack had sent him, he had plenty to keep him busy.

Her next message came in quickly.

"I'm taking a personal day tomorrow to get some stuff done. Call you when I'm finished?"

Yeah, he was way too happy to read that text.

"Sure. I take a long lunch on Thursdays. Maybe I won't go back to work afterward."

"Tough life."

He sent her an emoticon with its tongue stuck out. *"Don't work too hard."*

He pocketed his phone and looked up to find Jack staring at him expectantly.

"What?" Patrick asked.

"You haven't heard a thing I've said, have you?"

Patrick mirrored Jack's shit-eating grin from before. "Nope." He was pretty sure that was the way his face always got now, whenever he was talking to Cassie.

Jack chuckled and knocked back a sip. "It's okay to let yourself be happy, you know."

Patrick didn't know how to respond to that. The truth was, Cassie made him happier than he'd been in...ever? But telling Jack that would mean explaining the rule the two of them had made up when they started this thing. The escape clause he should've invoked when he and Cassie were in bed the other night.

Mentioning it then, or now, was like pointing to the eight-hundred-pound gorilla in the room. And Patrick wanted to put that shit off as long as possible.

He smiled and reached for his beer instead.

* * *

Once Patrick was home, he sat down at his computer and opened Jack's email. There were dozens of other ones he should've given his attention to—ones from Strauss, his team, and he needed to get in touch with Hudson as soon as possible, but right now he had other things on his mind.

He clicked open the links and read through the posts on breath play first. Jack's warning that there was no safe way to do this was no joke. Depriving her brain of oxygen would put her in hypoxia, which would enhance her orgasm, but he was literally going to have her life in his hands. He'd do anything to fulfill

Cassie's fantasies, but he wasn't confident he could pull off this one without leaving a corpse behind.

He needed to dial things back. She didn't want to have her breathing cut off—just to feel the possibility of it, so that was as far as they were going to go.

The pieces on consensual non-consent drew his attention in a different way. It calmed him in a way he never expected, reading through women's accounts of what they liked about it, even defending it. And the more he read, the more he understood there was nothing wrong with either of them wanting this. They were simply two consenting adults engaging in role play. Doing this was totally fine, if you were with the right person.

Patrick wanted to be the right person for Cassie.

He hated that she'd been so ashamed. And he suddenly felt fiercely protective of her, wanting to shield her from the frustrations of her life, how she struggled with being biracial and the strain she felt from her job and family.

Her mother was pressuring her to have a baby. The image bothered him, because Cassie being pregnant meant he'd no longer be in the picture. Sure he might've wanted kids, in some alternate universe where he had a clue on how to be a parent. And what shit could he pass on to them? Addiction? She didn't seem to want kids, though. At least, not right now. And he certainly shared her feelings of ambivalence on the subject.

He pulled out his phone and read over their texts, smiling at her quippy little lines. There was a lot on her shoulders, but it was more than that. Cassie didn't give herself permission to be who she was. She was hard-hitting, but also surprisingly vulnerable. And he wanted to give her what she needed. To ruin her for every other man by acting out her last two fantasies and making them incredible.

Wait, were they the last?

Patrick searched his memory. She'd only said they were the

two fantasies she was the most ashamed of, but they did have an air of finality to them.

He didn't want this to be over. The very thought of it nearly had him bolting out of his chair, his legs itching with the need to move. But the desires gnawing at him were hypocritical at best. This claim she had on him was short term—that was always the deal, and he'd been all for it. He never wanted commitment, just a break from luring new women into his bed.

The thing was, he didn't want a new woman.

He wanted Cassie.

Somehow, he'd gone beyond liking her. He liked the certainty of knowing he was going to see her, craved the intimacy they shared. It wasn't only her pleasure he longed for, but her laughter, her fearless attitude, her flirty text messages and the familiarity of her body next to his.

And that was a bad sign.

It was time to put some distance between them. Maybe it was a good thing that these two fantasies might be her last, because that gave him a reason to cash in his chips.

He could do that, right? Say things were getting too deep and walk away unscarred?

Goddamn it, he didn't think he could. Not without feeling a very palpable loss.

He'd been determined to never fall in love again, because Sofía had broken his heart into so many pieces it never managed to work right afterward. But the ache in his chest right now made him aware that his heart was working again, and it didn't want to let Cassie go.

21

*C*assie paged through magazines, trying to stay busy. There wasn't a lot she could do while sitting on a table in a paper gown, but if she wasn't distracted, her thoughts flipped back to Patrick.

It was still dizzying to realize he wasn't the man she'd thought he was. She'd only seen his wealth and cavalier behavior, but there was so much more to him, so much he hid behind his mask. And after last weekend she couldn't help feeling like the stakes had changed. It was still just sex, but they'd become more to one another. Deeper friends, maybe? Perhaps when their arrangement came to an end, there'd be a newfound understanding between them.

She frowned at the magazine. She didn't like the thought of this ending. They hadn't put a date on it, so she guessed it was her call when it did. He'd promised to see out all her fantasies, and she still had plenty left to play with.

The door to the little room she was in opened. "So, Cassie, how are you feeling?"

Cassie smiled at her ob-gyn. Talking about her menstrual cycle wasn't what she wanted to be doing, but at least the appointment would be over quick. She'd ordered her plane tickets to Florida this morning, so once this was over, she'd be home in time to FaceTime with Elísa during her final dress fitting, then head to Patrick's for some late afternoon fun.

Fun that maybe wouldn't involve condoms after another month.

"Mostly fine. Although my periods have been a little wonky."

"Describe wonky."

"They've been coming every three weeks and lasting around four days. It's one of the reasons why I wanted to go on the pill. I'm hoping it will make me more regular."

Her doctor opened her file. "How long has this been going on?"

Cassie shrugged. "Six to eight months."

Luckily her period hadn't gotten too much in the way of their sexy times, but she'd been counting her cycle to schedule their time together around it, and to be sure she wasn't late.

Another reason for wanting the birth control. What a cluster fuck that would be.

"Any irritability?" her doctor asked. "Moodiness?"

Two words that described Cassie well. "Yeah, but that's nothing new."

"What about a reduced sex drive, or vaginal dryness?"

Hah. Not so much a problem lately. "No, none of that."

"No hot flashes or sweating?" Cassie shook her head. "Okay, just the irregular periods. You've recently turned thirty-nine, correct?"

"Correct." Thanks for the reminder.

Her doctor closed the file, then made a face. Cassie did not like that look at all.

"It's possible that you're in the first stages of perimenopause."

Cassie liked the sound of that even less. "What's that?"

"It's a completely normal stage that comes before menopause. Most women don't know it exists because it happens while you're still menstruating. The actual change could be several years off. Typically it starts in the mid-forties, but for some women it can start in the late thirties."

"And *it* means what?"

"Your estrogen and progesterone levels may be in the beginnings of their decline. Your fertility will be decreasing, but pregnancy could still be possible, if you want it to."

Oh. So, basically, it was her body's way of saying, *Hey, we're closing up shop soon! Are you suuuuuure you don't want a baby?*

"We could do some blood work to be completely certain, but it's nothing to be worried about. Think of it as an opportunity to take stock of your life—a time to consider what changes you'd like to make, if any."

"Meaning, the clock is ticking." She could hear her mother's voice in her ear.

"If having children is something you want, then yes."

Well, fuck. She'd come here hoping to go on birth control, not to find out it was time to make a decision about growing a tiny human. She could only imagine what Patrick's response would be to this.

Not that he was the one she was going to have babies with. He'd said it himself—kids weren't for him. She wasn't sure they were for her either, but she thought she'd have more time to figure it out. Now her body was making the choice for her.

Her doctor stood. "Let's get the exam going, okay? And I'll write you up that script. Then you can let me know if you have any more questions."

By the time she'd picked up the prescription for birth control and gotten home, a chilly rainstorm had started. She'd just gotten her coat off when her phone started vibrating.

"I'm coming, I'm coming," she yelled at the incoming FaceTime request. She found her phone in her bag, plopped down on the couch and accepted the call.

Elísa's face filled the screen, a myriad of voices behind her.

"Cassie, look." Her sister held the phone out so Cassie could see her in the mirror looking radiant in a veil and a sparkling white gown. "*¿Qué piensas?*"

What did she think? She blinked back tears. "I think you look amazing, honey."

"Thank you! I wish you were here."

For the first time in ages, Cassie wished she was there too. She wanted the bright southern Florida sun and gentle sway of palm trees and the exuberant feeling of her little sister's tight hugs. She wanted life to slow the hell down for a minute, so she could figure out what she wanted.

Elísa turned the phone around. Her face immediately fell. "What's wrong?"

Shit. What had her sister seen in her expression? "Nothing. It's nothing."

"Cassandra," Elísa warned. "*Dí me.*"

Tell her? Tell her what? That she'd found out that her eggs were slowly dying inside her, and the guy she was seeing for some casual sex wasn't at all husband material?

Before Cassie could answer, her mother stole the phone.

"*Hola, mi vida.*" She walked to a line of couches. Squished onto them were Cassie's sister-in-law and niece, along with several Flóres-Allbright aunts and cousins, and Elísa's future mother-in-law. "Everybody say hello to Cassie."

A chorus of voices greeted her. Annalisa climbed into Cassie's mother's lap.

"*Tía* Cassie, when are you gonna get married?"

Cassie couldn't hide her grimace. On the screen, her mother kissed her niece's cheek. "Good question, *niña*. I've been asking her that for ages."

Cassie ground her teeth as the Spanish chatter in the background turned on her.

"*Trabajas demasiado, Cassandra. ¡Necesitas encontrar un marido!*"

"*¿No quieres tener un bebé?*"

Yes, she worked too much. No, she didn't need to find a husband.

No, she didn't know if she wanted to have a baby.

And this wasn't what she wanted to deal with right now.

"Okay, everyone. It's not my day, it's Elísa's. *¡Entonces porque no me dejan sola, carajo!*"

She didn't often curse in front of her niece. Or tell her family to leave her the fuck alone.

Elísa snatched her phone back. "Okay, everyone lay off Cassie. And you—" her sister stared into the screen, "—call me later and tell me what's going on."

Cassie nodded. "Sure."

She wasn't going to. Not about this, not when her sister had so much to celebrate.

Elísa ended the call, and Cassie stared at her phone. Her first thought was to call Lilly. But the person she wanted to talk to was someone who knew her deepest desires and all her nervous habits, and could soothe her in a way no one else had before.

She dialed.

"Hi," she huffed after Patrick picked up. "I need to come over, now."

* * *

Patrick watched the darkened sky as he waited for Cassie's arrival.

He'd been more than happy to cut his lunch with his mother short when she called, especially since they'd been sitting there saying nothing to one another. Plus it was pouring out—the kind of ugly, cold rainstorm that sucked the warmth straight from your bones.

He didn't know what was on her mind. Maybe she'd found out about him sending Hudson her way. Maybe she'd decided they'd gone too far last weekend and she didn't want to do this anymore. Perhaps she'd come to terms he couldn't, and knew it was time to put that escape clause into action.

The elevator dinged. Patrick waited as the door rolled open.

"Hey," he said.

She stepped inside and ripped off her coat. "Hey."

He took her coat, shook off the raindrops that had beaded up on it and folded it neatly over one of his barstools. Cassie stormed past him into the living room. She was her own violent, windy squall, full of power and fury. But for once he didn't want that ferocity unleashed on him.

She collapsed on the couch and he sat down beside her.

"Tell me what happened."

His voice sounded stern, but he was experimenting with his tone. He'd seen her struggle to get words out before. She'd probably stew forever in her head if he let her. Even if this was about them, he wasn't asking her to talk to him right now. He was telling.

"It's my fucking goddamn family."

His anxiety dissipated. She wasn't mad at him. This he could work with. "And what did your fucking goddamn family do?"

Humor. Element number two in battling Cassie's anger. She glanced at him, and her scowl morphed when she caught his smile. He opened his arms and she crawled into them.

"Today was my sister's final dress fitting for her wedding, and when I FaceTimed to watch, my mother started harassing me again about being single."

Jesus. What was the big deal? He reached up and ran his fingers over the back of her neck.

"Your sister is getting married?"

"Yup. You'd think that would be enough, since my little brother is married with two kids, but no." She shook her head and exhaled heavily. "It's gonna be worse when I go down for the wedding. All my mother is gonna talk about is why her eldest daughter is still shamefully unhitched."

Patrick stroked gently up and down until her eyes closed. Yeah, he enjoyed soothing her as much as he liked tormenting her. And right now, he wanted to calm her. To take care of her, and make her problems go away.

"When is the wedding?" he asked.

"Thanksgiving."

"Is that the only thing bothering you?"

Cassie stiffened, then relaxed into him. "It is right now."

Okay, that was enough. He wanted to make sure there was nothing else upsetting her before he suggested a solution.

"I could go with you to Florida. Be your human shield, so to speak."

She looked up at him. "You'd do that?"

"Take a trip to a warm climate in the middle of this disgusting weather? Get to see a gorgeous woman in a beautiful dress, and maybe a bikini too?" He grinned at her. "Why wouldn't I want to do that?"

It was the perfect plan: protect her from her family's questions, and go someplace luxurious and tropical where they could act out her fantasies.

But Cassie didn't smile. She looked...flustered.

"Because you'd be pretending to be my boyfriend."

And that wasn't what he was. The reminder was a punch to his rib cage. His unease over that sent off all kinds of alarm bells in his head, but he ignored them. Making Cassie happy was all that mattered.

"I don't usually have something to look forward to this time of year," he said. "Spending Thanksgiving with your mother who you barely speak to isn't as much fun as it sounds. And I was thinking I needed a vacation. So we'd be doing each other a favor."

Her eyes went from hard to glittering. Maybe a little scheming too. "You'd be a great defense. My mom would eat you up."

"Then count me in. On two conditions."

She raised an eyebrow. "And they are?"

"We go on that tour of Miami you promised me, and you let me take care of the hotel."

"Couldn't we split it?"

"No." He wanted to know the space. To plan it out. To be completely in charge of it. "I know that's a boyfriend thing too, but *technically* we'll be dating while we're there." He leaned in and grazed his nose along hers. "Which means I can spoil you a little."

Pink stole across her cheeks, and fuck, there it was, that smile he'd come to adore. No longer angry, her eyes were bright— sparkling, real and authentically Cassie.

"Good argument, counselor," she said. "I believe you've won your case."

22

"Hey, Dad." Cassie bowed her head against a blast of wind. "You busy?"

"Not for you. What's up?"

She started to answer, then blinked against another gust. A week before Thanksgiving and already it felt like the dead of winter. Her office building's doorway was shielded from the blustery chill, but once she'd made her way down Congress Street and onto the busy intersection with Exchange, she needed to hold on to her non-proverbial hat. At least this weather gave her an excuse to wear her favorite Alexander McQueen boots.

Not that she needed one.

"Okay, great. I needed to ask you something. Well, tell you something, really."

"Hit me."

"I'm bringing someone home next week. For Elísa's wedding."

"And you're telling me this because..."

"Because I know it's last minute and I wanted to make sure I could bring a guest."

Cassie turned a corner, hoping he would buy the lie. She knew better than anyone that Flóres family members were known to show up at events with one, two, or even five extra guests. She'd had cousins from out of town sitting on one another's laps at her own *quinceañera*. But she was dodging her mother, hoping to avoid the Cuban Inquisition and have her father relay the news.

"It's fine," he said. "I'll let your mother know. I'm sure she'll be thrilled."

"Thanks, Dad. I appreciate it. I would've called earlier about it but things have been crazy at work."

"Crazy in a good way? We're getting closer to the partner offer, right?"

Another exhalation. Her father never dismissed her goals and aspirations the way her mother did. Or at least, he never held up marriage and children and asked her why she was the only one of his children on Latin Time as far as that was concerned.

"If I can close this one matter I'm working on, I should make it before the year ends."

And that was easier said than done. Despite the sale of Hudson's building and a slew of new authors signing on, it hadn't been enough to get him out of debt. Bruce and Reynash had agreed to allow him to pay what remained of his debts to them over future profits, as long as he was able to find another investor to bring him into the black. She'd been so busy balancing his neediness among her other clients, she'd barely seen Patrick, let alone gone to the gym or left the office at all over the last several weeks. She'd also had a follow-up call from her friend at Legal Aid, which had sucked. She hated turning the cases down, but she simply didn't have the time.

Helping Boston's impoverished wasn't possible at the moment. She was too busy helping a filthy rich person who'd overspent his money make more of it, so her rich bosses could get richer.

It made her sick, but this was how it was in corporate law.

Soon she'd be finished with this case, and would be able to call herself partner. Then she could do things differently.

"That's great, Pumpkin. I'm super proud of you."

She smiled at her father's pet name for her, and his adverb of choice. His expression of affection might've been different from her mother's Spanish ones, but "super" was Miami regional slang, similar to Boston's "wicked." It made her miss him, miss home in that familiar, complex way that left her longing and confused.

"Thanks, Dad."

"So, this guy. Is it serious?"

Cassie's neck tensed at the question. "No. I mean. I like him, but it's not serious."

It was the best she could do. After all, there was no way she was telling her father they had an arrangement involving lots of kinky sex, and that she was bringing him home to shield her from her mom.

"Well I'm looking forward to meeting him either way," her father said. *"Te amo."*

Why was everything always easier talking to him? "Love you too. See you next week."

She reached Faneuil Hall Marketplace and ducked inside. The indoor shopping area was both a respite from the cold, and home to the bakery she'd been headed toward. She wanted something delicious to sweeten both the good and bad news she had to deliver to Patrick.

She was about to get in line when a high-pitched shriek came from a table behind her. Startled, she turned around and caught a flash of red hair. It was Samantha, yanking a lock of her younger daughter's hair out of the fist of her elder daughter's.

"Allegra, stop it." Sam's words came out around clenched teeth, her usual calm demeanor swapped for wild eyes and what looked like an about-to-snap patience.

Cassie stepped over to them. "Hey there."

Sam glanced quickly over her shoulder. "Oh, hi Cassie." She picked up her purse and fished out a few dollar bills. "Here. Both of you go and pick out something to bring home for Daddy."

Her daughters pushed out their chairs and sprinted toward the bakery line.

"And stay where I can see you," Sam called after them, then slumped into a chair.

Cassie took one of the girls' abandoned seats. "Tired?"

"You have no idea. I need these two off school for two days next week like I need a hole in the—" Her expression morphed into anger. She shot up in her seat. "Allegra Mackenzie Archer!"

Cassie had no idea what was happening behind her, but she had a feeling it was best not to look. Geez, there was no better birth control than watching your friend's kids misbehave.

Samantha resumed her slouch. "How are you?"

"I'm okay. I'm sorry you're stressed."

"Part of the package when you're a stay-at-home mom and one of your kids is adjusting to her new ADHD meds." She reached for her coffee and took a sip. "So when are you gonna fess up about you and Patrick?"

Cassie froze. "You knew?"

"I figured it out at the Lit Crawl. You two couldn't have looked more smitten." Sam smiled behind her cup. "I figured it out about Jack and Lilly too, ages before they told us."

"How did you know?"

"Because I'm me," she said simply. "I'm a very good observer, but it wasn't hard to pick up. It was written all over her face. And her collar."

Cassie stared at her friend, stunned. "You knew...*that*?"

"I know what BDSM is. I'm a mom, not a nun. Although with how little Brady and I have been having sex, I might as well be."

Cassie made a face, not knowing what to say. She hadn't gotten far enough into a relationship to see the sex dwindle, but she could imagine if she and Patrick got that way, it would be the end of them.

"You still haven't confirmed," Sam teased.

"That Patrick and I are a thing?"

"Yes."

It was probably too late to deny it. "Yeah. We're a thing. But it's no big deal. It's just—" her neck tensed again, "—sex."

Why was she having so much trouble saying that?

"Whatever. I'm not judging." There was a glimmer in Sam's eye. "Glad he's not still being a dick."

"Well, he still is sometimes, but I like it."

Sam's grin grew wider. "Ohh, that's the way you two roll. Interesting."

Her daughters returned with a box. Allegra placed it on the table. "We got Daddy a donut," she said, then turned to Cassie. "You work with Aunt Lilly."

They called Lilly their aunt now? "Yes I—"

"Hey! I wanted that."

Cassie sat back, trying to stay out of the way as Hope picked up the donut box and Allegra tried to yank it from her sister's hand. Sam stood to intervene, but then Hope held out the box in her tiny hand.

"I was holding it for you," she said to her sister. "I want you to give it to Daddy."

Something painful shoved at Cassie's heart.

"That was nice of you, Hope," Sam said. "I think it's time to go home."

She reached for the girls' coats, getting them situated as she turned back to Cassie. "How's work going, by the way?"

"Okay." She watched Allegra help Hope with her gloves. "Sometimes I don't feel like I'm doing anything worthwhile."

"You mean case-wise?"

Sure. That was what she meant.

She'd avoided thinking about her current childbearing

situation, too busy with work to think about it much. And when she did, she still didn't feel it was the right choice for her. But now, watching Sam's daughters sweetly hold hands while they waited for their mother to be ready...

God, ambivalence was a bitch.

"Yeah, work isn't rewarding at the moment."

"When was the last time it was?"

Legal Aid had been a mix, satisfying because of the civil cases she worked for low-income families, but grueling because of the pay. She couldn't remember a time when working for the firm had been rewarding in any way that wasn't paying off her loans, or getting her closer to her goal.

"Working for the justice, maybe? It was exciting, but I was a clerk. I didn't have any real clout."

"Ever think of going back there?"

"And give up everything I've spent the last decade working toward?" Cassie shook her head.

Sam put on her coat and shrugged. "If that's what you want. But if you want to change the world, you've gotta be on the ground level. Laws change the world. Not lawyers." She gave Cassie a hug. "Something to think about."

As if she didn't have enough on her plate. "Thanks. I've gotta run too."

Once she'd picked up what she came for, Cassie took a taxi to Patrick's office. He had a work event that night but wasn't leaving yet, and she'd wanted to surprise him.

The car pulled up in front of a towering building near the water. The postmodern high-rise was a mix of granite, gold and glass, reaching far into the sky. Inside the gleaming rotating doors was a long, ornate atrium. The lobby's gleaming marble floors were framed by bushes and plants. A fountain was at the base of the far wall, a piece of artwork the size of a billboard above it.

And she'd thought the outside was swanky.

The reception desk was manned by several people, and above

them sat a large gilded painting of two men. One she didn't recognize, but he had to be Strauss because the other was an older, more hardened version of Patrick. Same dark hair, same sharp green eyes, caught perfectly by the artist's rendition, except now she knew his history and could see the meanness in his expression.

A likeness of Patrick should've been somewhere too, but it was strangely absent.

She could see him turning down an offer of a portrait, though. He never wanted to work here. He would've given it all up to stay in Spain for love. Would've walked away from his family's empire entirely, if it weren't for his duty to his mother. She'd thought he was like Hudson—arrogant, wealthy, no shame when it came to his treatment of women. But the two of them were nothing alike, nothing at all. Aside from them both being Princeton men—a weird connection she hadn't made until now —they were entirely different. She couldn't even imagine Patrick being friends with someone like Hudson.

What a different man he'd turned out to be.

She walked up to one of the receptionists. "Hi, I'm here to see Patrick Dunham."

The young man looked up at her. "Do you have an appointment?"

"No." Hadn't thought about that part.

"Do you...know Mr. Dunham?"

Biblically. "I do. My name is Cassie Allbright. Could you let him know I'm here?"

He did, talking quietly into his headset. His brows lifted as he looked up at her. "You can head on up. Thirtieth floor."

Her heart pounded strangely as she rode the elevator. When she reached the executive level, a smiling young woman led her down a long hallway to Patrick's office. It was a large space, but furnished simply other than the massive wall of books behind him. He was on the phone, looking unbelievably dapper in a crisp black suit. Cinched at the waist, the cut only accentuated the broadness of his shoulders and the power in his arms. She'd bet it was imported Italian wool and expensive as shit, but she wouldn't have minded wrestling it off him if she wasn't in the state she was in.

He hung up the phone and walked toward her, closing the door behind them. "Hey. This is a surprise."

"I know. Hope that's okay. I had something I wanted to tell you, and—" she held the box up, "—I brought treats."

"You're the only treat I'm interested in." He nudged her coat open, thumbs brushing over her hips. One kiss to her neck had her shivering. Stupid, stupid cycle. "But whatever it is, it smells amazing."

They sat down together, and she untied the string securing the box. "It's a preview of the sugar and carb-fest we'll be having in Miami next week: fried dough nuggets and cinnamon churros."

He took a bite and closed his eyes. "Goddamn. That tastes almost as sweet as you do." His gaze swept over her again as his grin grew fiendish. "I wonder what it would be like to combine the two."

"Wish I could."

"Some reason you can't? That door locks."

Time to share Exhibit A. "I have my period, which is good and bad news. Bad because I'm physically out of commission for the next week."

"Bummer. I'd looked forward to eating you out on my desk."

He lapped at the powdered sugar his last bite had left behind on his upper lip. Cassie groaned at the sight of his tongue.

"What's the good news?" he asked.

"The good news is, when it's over, we won't need condoms anymore."

"We won't?"

"Nope. I started the pill a month ago. Been through a full cycle on it."

"Why didn't you tell me you were doing this?"

"Surprise," she said. "I wanted to wait until I'd gone through a whole pack and saw the placebo pills worked. They do, so I think we're good to go."

"I guess I won't need the mega box of Trojans I bought for the trip."

She giggled. "No. But we probably shouldn't hang out this weekend. I'm gonna be cranky as hell, and not the best company. It's best to leave me to my heat pack and container of gelato."

"Uh-huh. And what flavor will I be bringing over later?"

She couldn't stop her wide smile. "Caramel."

"Done." His phone buzzed with an alarm. "Crap. I've gotta get going."

"That's okay. I need to get home. I have to start working on my maid-of-honor speech."

"Nothing like waiting till the last minute, huh?"

"Hey, my sister's worse than I am. She only picked out bridesmaid dresses a few weeks ago. I finally had it fitted this week."

They finished the last bites of their snack, stood and gathered their things. Patrick buttoned his suit jacket closed. "What's this dress going to look like?"

"Black lace. Floor length and sleeveless."

"Nice. You bought shoes for it yet?"

She laughed. "I assume that means you've noticed my shoe obsession."

"I have." His eyes sparkled in the last remainders of daylight streaming in through his windows. "What's the deal with that?"

"My shoe fetish?"

He grunted. "Don't say fetish."

Cassie slipped her fingers beneath his lapels. God, she'd miss this flirting when their understanding came to an end—the brief, passing company of this delicious and powerful man.

"I'll never be a size two, but shoes I will always fit into. And they make me feel sexy and confident."

"You're confident and sexy regardless of what's on your feet." He skimmed his nose along her neck. "What's your shoe size?"

"Why are you asking?"

"Why do you think?"

She slipped backward. She should've said no—she wasn't comfortable with him buying her anything more than the hotel room she'd agreed to—but she couldn't stop herself. "I hope you're not planning on buying me glass slippers, my friend. I'm no Cinderella."

"And I'm no Prince Charming. But I like fucking you in fancy shoes."

"That's a deal I can't pass up." Cassie kissed him. "Size seven. See you later tonight."

23

*T*he day before Thanksgiving, Cassie was on a late-night flight to Miami with Patrick.

It had been a stressful couple of days at work, but it looked like Grant Books was going to come out on top. A new investor had finally come on—a CEO of a private equity fund with a share in a new e-book publishing software platform, one Hudson would use as part of the deal. The investor was also interested in finding new representation, and had his eye on Forrester, Schaeffer and Pierce.

It was the trifecta of deals, an exchange of handshakes that would make everyone happy. She had a meeting bright and early Monday morning putting everything into motion, but for now she could leave it all behind her.

She glanced out the window as they hit cruising altitude and the glittering New England coast faded away in the darkness. "I'm amazed you were able to get a seat on this flight."

"And that I was able to bump us to first class?"

"That too."

She'd never flown first class before. She would've felt bad

about it, but fuck it. She had a blanket on her lap, and legroom for miles, and she was going to enjoy it.

"Coming down was easy," he said. "Coming back I can't do, since someone wouldn't change her return flight and everything else was booked."

"I told you, I can't take a redeye. I need to be rested for that meeting."

"And that's why I'll need to take a later flight home, you silly pain in the ass." He grinned and went back to the newspaper he'd been reading. "It's fine. It's not like I won't be seeing you when we get back anyway."

That was far more comforting than it should've been. "What did you tell your mother?"

"About Thanksgiving?"

Cassie nodded. She'd found it strange that he wasn't expected to spend the holiday with her, regardless of the state of their relationship.

"I said I wanted some warm weather, and that I was going out of town with a woman."

Her heart seized. "How'd she react to that?"

"With mild interest. I've never done that before."

"Never?" He shook his head. Cue more seizing. "Well, *I've* never taken anyone home with me, so be prepared. I'm sure everyone is eager to crawl up your butt with questions."

He leaned in, eyes sparkling. "There's only one butt I'm interested in."

A rush went through her, excitement and relaxation combined. It was as if he had magical powers, because she always felt better when he was around. He made everything seem lighter and easier to manage. She'd thought about sharing her ob-gyn's diagnosis, thinking he could probably help her work out her feelings on it, but it wasn't something she felt like talking about now. For the moment, she didn't want to overthink or plan. No strategizing and measuring. She wanted to enjoy his company, and the four days of eighty-degree weather.

By the time they touched down, it was close to midnight. A buzzed kind of exhaustion and airport coffee kept her awake as Patrick secured their rental car. Stepping outside for a moment, Cassie stood with her suitcases and closed her eyes, basking in the warm, breezy weather of southern Florida in the fall.

She'd missed it here.

She dozed on the drive—he'd rented something sleek and expensive that suited Miami perfectly—and when Patrick nudged her awake, they were turning off the palm tree-lined streets of South Beach, passing cool white buildings lit with colorful lights and into the roundabout entrance of the Ritz Carlton Bal Harbour.

"You did not," she muttered.

"Surprise." He shrugged with that irresistible boyish charm Cassie had first hated, then adored. "Told you I was going to spoil you."

She was too tired to argue. And part of her wanted to be spoiled by him. They parked, and a glittering fountain two stories high and a team of valets greeted them. The hotel lobby was as lush and extravagant as the outside promised, as was the suite he'd booked.

"This is almost like being in your apartment," she said. "Aside from the curtains."

With huge windows adorned with sweeping white drapes, its own private balcony overlooking the ocean, and a bathroom the size of her living room, this was luxury at its finest. Patrick came up behind her, his thick arms surrounding her, facial hair offering a bristly tickle to the back of her neck.

"Curtains can be opened, but I might keep them shut. Make sure no one but me sees all the ways I'm going to defile you in here."

Pinpricks sparked along her skin. Cassie shuddered despite

her fatigue. When his hands found her hips, she turned around in his arms.

"No condoms, right?" His voice was gravelly with the question.

"Right." She reached up and threaded her fingers into his hair. "When's the last time you did it without?"

"Never."

"Never?"

"Not once." The flush of excitement was clear on his cheeks. "You?"

"Same." None of her relationships had lasted long enough to warrant it.

"Well then. We're both virgins tonight." He walked her to the bed, yanking clothes off them as they went. "I'm warning you, I may not last long."

Neither of them did. The feeling of contact, of bare, hot skin against skin was so intense Cassie didn't need the fantasy of danger or a fight. The sex was quick and dirty, and Patrick's groans and hard thrusts jerked the climax straight from her.

She dropped off to sleep in the king-sized bed with a smile.

* * *

The next morning, they ordered room service, which Cassie waited for while lounging in the bed and watching Patrick's morning push-up routine. After eating a delicious breakfast, they ventured into the sunlight. As they waited for the valet to bring the car, Cassie stretched her arms out, smiling at the sky. They didn't need to be at her parents' house until later, and she was grateful for the alone time together.

"Are we starting my official Miami tour?" he asked.

"Yes, and we need to find you something to wear for the rehearsal dinner before the stores close."

"I still don't understand why you vetoed my suit."

She flipped open the sunroof and grinned. "Your tux is fine for the wedding, but you're going to want something more casual for tomorrow. Besides, you'll need to match me in my *guayabera* dress."

"Remind me what that is again?"

"It's traditional Cuban formal wear—short, and kind of see-through."

"I like it already."

As they drove down Collins Avenue, Cassie was able to get a passing glimpse of the ocean: brilliant, turquoise and tropical. One peek at the sandy shore and she could feel the coarse grains between her toes.

"I want to check out that shore-side patio restaurant," she said.

"We're having brunch there tomorrow. It was supposed to be a surprise." A devilish smile turned up the corners of his lips. "I also have a few other surprises for you."

"The shoes?"

"Maybe."

"But that's not a surprise."

"Who said that was my only one?" He popped on a pair of shades. "And my surprises aren't all PG-13."

Cassie winged her legs open, craving contact. She'd worn a short, flouncy sundress, and Patrick's hand found a home above her knee. Once they'd made their way over the Causeway and through the brightly painted walls of Wynwood, she directed him down a side street and to a parking lot.

"Welcome to *Calle Ocho*, the main drag of Little Havana."

Dade County, Florida was the exile capital, a glittering refugee camp with over a sixty percent Cuban population, and this spot was the center of all of it. It was a place where Cubans and other Latinos attempted to recreate a world that no longer existed but came alive for a small strip of shops, art galleries and restaurants.

Patrick took her hand and curled his fingers around it as they meandered down the street. Hispanic culture permeated everything, from the colorful murals to the pulsating beats of traditional music to the rich aroma of Cuban coffee. When they came upon one of the many life-sized painted rooster statues dotting the avenue, Patrick stopped walking and looked at it with curiosity.

"Okay, explain the roosters to me."

Cassie had to drag her eyes away from the cut of his forearms. He'd worn a dark, short-sleeved polo, and his well-hewn muscles stood out in stark contrast against it, as much a work of art as the sculpture before them.

Why had she agreed to give him this tour? They could've stayed in bed.

"Roosters are an important symbol in Cuban culture. They represent strength. Local artists were commissioned to paint them. They're all over the city."

Pulling her close, he murmured, "Now I get why you like it here—all the cock."

She laughed, then led him into a touristy shop on the corner. He reached for a T-shirt and read what was on it. *"How To Keep Your Cubanita Wife Happy: Tell Her She Is Always Right."*

"It's the truth." Cassie grinned and reached for another one. *"'Made in America with Cuban Parts.'* Oh, look. It's me."

"No." He held up one with a drawing of a woman bent over in fishnets and heels. "This one is."

Cassie dissolved into giggles. She couldn't remember the last time she'd had this much fun over something so silly. She handed him a magnet that read, *"Keep Calm and Don't Piss Off a Cuban Girl."*

"I think you need that," she said.

He shook his head and put it down. "I already know it."

They went through an art gallery, stopped at one of the street-side windows for tiny shots of strong espresso before going into a shop filled with linen tops and short-brimmed panama hats. Cassie picked out a classic look for him—a black, short-sleeved, pleated shirt and matching, pinch front hat with a white sash. Then they were back on the street and at the entrance to Maximo Gomez Park.

"This is where the locals gather to play dominoes," she explained as they stopped to watch. The tables were full of senior citizens hunched over their games, the movements of their dominoes as fast as their Spanish. "It's become a bit of a tradition. These people are serious business about their games. There's rules and everything."

"Did your grandfather teach you here?"

"No, we did that at home." But the click-clack noises and the conversations about politics reminded her of him. As did the smoky-sweet scent of cigars, puffed on by men and women alike. "But the smell makes me feel like he's here, now."

Cassie let the aroma wash over her, grief mixing with comfort.

Patrick kissed her cheek. "Thank you for sharing this with me."

They returned to the hotel, and when they arrived at their room, he handed her an envelope. "Surprise number one. You're getting a massage at the hotel spa."

She started to protest, but accepted it at the hint of warning in his eyes.

"Good. Now, on to surprise number two."

He went to his suitcase and retrieved a shoebox. It had a name on it that despite Cassie's love for heels, she'd never been able to purchase. Her hands trembling, she flipped open the top. Her breath caught at the black patent-leather heels and signature red soles.

"I can't accept these."

"Why not?"

"Because." Because they had to have cost half her mortgage payment. It was too extravagant.

"Because you think it's some kind of charity?" He chuckled and shook his head. "It's a gift, Cassie. And an entirely selfish one, because I can't wait to see them on you. And do other things with them on you."

She flushed, then ran a finger over the elegant craftsmanship. The peep-toe, five-inch sandals were embellished with black bows and were made of a sheer mesh that created the illusion of lace. "I've never worn Christian Louboutins before."

"Well now you will." His voice was quiet. Soft. Not at all how he sounded when he was demanding and rough in bed. "Do you like them?"

"I love them."

"And will they match your dress?"

"Perfectly."

"Good. Then they're yours. Now get your butt down to that spa."

Once she'd stretched out on a heated massage bed, Cassie wondered if this was how it would be all the time, if she were with him for real. Pinching her eyes shut, she pushed the thought from her mind. This was never going to be real. It was sex, nothing more. She'd never wanted to be Cinderella, and he wasn't her real-life prince. He was her momentary man. Her make-believe boyfriend. So this line of thinking needed to stop right the hell now.

By the time they got to her parents' house, she'd almost gotten her head on straight.

"I hope you're ready for this." Halfway down the walkway, and Cassie could already hear her family's raucous voices coming from inside.

His brows lifted in amusement. "Now I get why you always sound angry."

She shrugged. "We're not yelling. We're Cuban."

The second they entered, a shouted chorus of greetings in both Spanish and English started. Elísa practically tackled her, then kissed Patrick's cheek and led them both into the kitchen. Cassie was swept into her mother's boisterous hug, followed by her father's gentler embrace, then ones from her niece, nephew, brother and future brother-in-law. As Patrick received the same welcome, Cassie took a minute to stand back and take it all in.

The decor hadn't changed a bit over the years. Warm orange walls were decorated with plates and artwork, upside-down wine bottles were broken open and used as hanging lights. The stereo in the background was booming with the heavy tinges of salsa, and on the stove, spicy and savory foods simmered in a myriad of pots and pans. But her father's Miami Dolphins memorabilia was present too—a framed, signed jersey that he always said was the first thing he'd grab if the house was on fire, and the giant jar of peanuts he loved to snack on while watching games was stashed in its usual spot on top of the fridge. It was everything her apartment in Boston wasn't—wild, colorful. Cuban and American.

Home.

"So, Patrick," her mother said. "We haven't heard how you and Cassandra met."

Cassie cringed. Let the inquisition begin.

"Through mutual friends, actually," he replied.

"When did you meet?"

"The beginning of the year. January."

"January! Why are we meeting you now?"

"Because I couldn't stand him at first," Cassie said.

Elísa laughed. "That should've been a sign for you, Patrick. Cassie never does anything easily."

"I've picked up on that."

Cassie made a face of exasperation at him. "You couldn't stand me either."

Her mother gave him a playful, accusing look. "Is that true, Patrick?"

Patrick's gaze met Cassie's. "A little. We butted heads a bit at the start—"

"More than a bit," she interrupted.

"—but then one night, everything changed. And I realized what an amazing woman was behind that spitfire attitude."

A floating sensation flooded Cassie's chest, a bubble of hope that she hid behind a smile.

Mr. Allbright pointed to his wife. "She gets the spitfire attitude from her mother."

They all went into the dining room, each carrying a plate of food.

"Welcome to a Cuban *Sanksgiving*," Cassie told Patrick. "Dinner will be *masas de puerco, ropa vieja,* and *arroz con frijoles*."

He worked through the translation. "Fried pork chunks, shredded beef, and rice and beans."

"Well done. And *flan* for dessert." She stared at the plates and sighed. "I'm gonna gain ten pounds on this trip."

Patrick nudged her shoulder and winked. "I'll work it all off you."

Cassie tried to hide her shudder. They sat down to eat, and she watched in amazement as he fit in beautifully, easily switching from English to Spanish. Her brother winked at her from across the table, and it came up like a wave that knocked her down—how much she'd missed all this. When it was time for dessert, she and her sister cleared the table while Patrick was dragged into the living room by the kids to play a game of dominoes.

"He's perfect," Elísa said. "Anglo like Dad, but completely fluent. You've gotta keep this guy."

"I don't think that's gonna happen."

She couldn't keep him—that wasn't the deal. She'd known all along this was going to end. That she was going to have to watch him return to his normal behavior, luring other women into the bed she'd spent so many nights in.

The idea made her sick.

Her sister leaned in by her as Cassie stared across the kitchen to the couches where Patrick sat, laughing with Annalisa and Antonio. "No way, Cass. You're gonna marry that guy. I know it."

As if an invisible line connected them, Patrick looked up. And as soon as Cassie got caught in that sharp green gaze and boyish, carefree smile, she felt it happen. She'd broken the rule, passed over the barrier she'd made up for them, her condition for ending this thing they had.

She'd thought this through. Analyzed the situation and made a plan. She thought she'd know when her strategy wasn't working, and when it was time to jump ship. But she hadn't banked on this one uncontrollable default:

She was in love with him.

And that was going to destroy everything.

24

*T*he following morning, Patrick let Cassie sleep in. They'd fallen into bed the night before without getting intimate—a first for them, but they hadn't gotten back from her family's place until well after midnight. He'd hadn't minded, having enjoyed the food and her family's company a lot more than he thought he would. Even though her home reminded him a bit of Gustavo's—with the combination of stucco and butter cream yellow tiles and wrought-iron terraces—he wasn't bothered by the connection at all.

He'd loved watching Cassie slip into a different version of herself too. She went back and forth between Spanish and English, and the melodic sound of hearing her speak had him captivated. They didn't have to be at the rehearsal until three today, which gave them plenty of time for brunch, and for the other thing he'd planned.

Once they'd enjoyed a delicious meal at the outdoor restaurant, surrounded by soft breezes and a fantastic view of the ocean, Patrick led her back to the room. She was wearing some kind of short, billowy thing and another set of her fabulous heels, and from the moment she'd put them on, he'd been dying to get it all off her.

He walked her backward to the bed, prowling over her like a panther and tugging at the bottom of her dress. "I like this a lot. But it needs to come off. Now."

She glanced at the clock. "Do we have time?"

"Plenty."

And whether they did or not, he wasn't stopping now.

Their clothes shed, he laid her down on the bed and kissed her, deep and sensual explorations of her mouth that had her arching off the bed. Taking his time, he moved down her body, suckled each nipple, brushed his goatee over her navel. His hands on her hips, he nuzzled the hollow above her pelvis, then along the trimmed thatch of curls below it. Her hands delved into his hair as he licked a path along her slit and slid a finger inside.

She was searing hot, and so damn wet. It took all his self-control to make himself wait. One time without a condom wasn't enough to slake his thirst for her.

He was beginning to think nothing was.

One, two, three pumps and he easily found the spot that made her body jolt. He flicked her clit and rubbed that rough little ridge, savoring her like she was a decadent dessert or a precious jewel, something he both craved and protected. When he'd teased her long enough, he made his way back up and fed her a taste of herself with one slide of his tongue along hers.

"Please," she whimpered. "Take me."

"Shhh." He wound one hand through her hair, holding her by the back of her head. "I had more surprises for you, remember?"

She nodded. "And not all of them were going to be PG-13."

"Uh-huh." He had a whole section of his suitcase devoted to his plans, with everything he'd thought he'd need down to a first-aid kit.

He wasn't sure he was going to be able to do everything she wanted, but he was sure as hell going to try. Patrick stroked the back of her neck a few times before moving his hand and wrapping it firmly around her throat. Cassie's eyes grew intense —alert, observant and filled with lust.

Yes, princess. We're doing this now.

When she didn't push away, he tightened his grip. "Safeword?"

"Exit," she breathed.

Good. She could still talk. For a minute, he just held her, experimenting with the sound of her inhalations, his pointer finger and thumb beneath her jaw. Finding his balance, he wedged himself between her open thighs and put his weight on his knees, careful not to add any pressure to her throat as he lowered his other hand to work her clit.

Her gasp was thinner, more strained, her neck flexing under his hand, but there was no doubt in his mind that she was enjoying this. Her sweet, thick hips arched with every slow swirl of his fingertips, and her nipples had constricted to taut points. He bent down to take one in his mouth, biting hard in lieu of a slap. She jerked and squirmed, trying to get away before he circled faster over that knot of nerves and she gave in under him.

God. *God*, there was nothing like this. Nothing like the feeling of this strong woman pliant beneath him.

Adding a little more pressure to her throat, he watched her face. Her eyes were closed, her mouth open, and fuck, it was like a light bulb had been turned on, a switch thrown. He'd never seen himself as a Dominant, and maybe he still wasn't. But there was something hot as all fuck about controlling her this way and how her throat felt in his hand. The look on her face, seeing how turned on she was—the power play was such a rush. None of his experiences held a candle to what he did with Cassie.

It was hotter. Dirtier. So wrong. And so fucking right.

"Look at me," he murmured.

He demanded it half to see her dazed expression, and half to see if her pupils had dilated too much. They hadn't, and Patrick's heart raced with her raw expression of hunger.

"You like this?" he asked.

She answered by reaching up and pressing on his elbow.

More, the move said.

He cut off a little more of her air, and she drew in a reedy breath. It didn't seem like play, nor did it seem dangerous, even though he knew it was both. What it seemed like was the closest he'd been to another person.

Under his restricting grip, he felt her pulse pound as her breathing grew shallow. Her eyes widened as she tried to inhale, and Patrick loosened his fingers without her saying a word. They didn't need a word. He knew where too much was when they got there, knew her signals, knew her.

And he wasn't done with her yet.

Patrick quickened his strokes between her thighs, rubbing until her eyes slammed shut and her head crashed back against the pillow. She came with a shout, and Patrick didn't give her any time to compose herself before he pressed his lips to her cheek.

"I'm gonna fuck you now, Cassie."

She made a thirsty sound, deep in the back of her throat. Patrick positioned himself and sank inside her wet, tight heat.

"Squeeze me," he ground out. "Like you did that first night."

She tightened around him, and Patrick's shoulders hiked up on a curse. It was so much more intense when he could feel every slick inch of her. Cassie did it again, then shuddered and started to writhe.

"Is the little whore gonna come again?"

She nodded, strung out on the edge of another release. Patrick fucked her harder.

"Greedy bitch. You'd better get there fast, because I'm not gonna wait. I'm just gonna pound that wet cunt until I come."

Crude words, but it got her there, got them both there. He collapsed into her, still breathing hard. What they'd done seemed to chisel away at the wall he'd kept around himself. He'd never seen sex as a way to connect to someone, but now he understood it was nothing less than that. Every game, every toy, every act—they flayed away the mask he'd worn, opening him up to her with nothing less than unabashed honesty.

He also knew he cared for her far too much for the rules she'd made.

No emotions. It was what she wanted, so this was going to have to end.

But they were here for two more days. And for now, he'd be what she needed. He'd play any damn role she wanted, if it meant he got to be with her a little longer.

When they'd trekked out to the rehearsal site, the wedding party was waiting. Cousins, aunts, uncles, friends, they kissed him on each cheek, acting as if he were already a member of the Flóres-Allbright clan.

As Cassie and her family ran through the service in the chapel, Patrick roamed around. The ceremony was happening at a monastery on Miami Beach, and he strolled through the open-air hallways, stopping to read about the building's history. It had been built in Seville in 1133 AD and purchased in the 1920s by William Randolph Hearst. The structure had been disassembled brick by brick and shipped to the United States, but remained in storage due to Hearst's financial struggles until it was purchased by a philanthropist and presented to the Bishop of Florida.

Feeling like his younger self traveling through the Spanish countryside, Patrick touched the stone structure, marveled at the columns and lanterns, the archways and medieval architecture, and finally, as he returned to the chapel and leaned against the farthest pew, at Cassie.

Her outfit was a shoulder-baring white dress with pockets and a little bow in the front, and she looked fucking incredible. Sure it was a bit see-through, but it covered enough to leave him picturing every dip and swell beneath it. And it accentuated the parts of her he'd come to love. The curve of her back. The perfect handful of her rear. The tender spot on her neck.

But it wasn't just her body he saw. He saw her—beautiful, lush and sweet, despite the barbs she often wore.

When the priest said, "man and wife," her family broke from the rehearsal like a rugby team from a scrum, and Patrick got swept up in it, ready for the carnival-like atmosphere he was sure was ahead of him at her grandfather's bar.

When they arrived at the lounge, Patrick had to smile. Its open-air entryway with neon sign, large green-and-white awning and classic art deco decor looked straight out of 1940s Havana. But it was the name that got him grinning.

"His bar is called *La Lucha*?"

"It is. It means—"

"The struggle." It was the Spanish version of *La Lutte*, the name of the French restaurant where he and his mother ate lunch every week. How fitting that they both translated to the same English words.

The name, however, didn't match the atmosphere. Cassie led him past the colorful and lively bar, down a hallway covered with a collection of artwork, framed newspaper clippings and advertisements. The courtyard behind the lounge was reserved for the wedding party—an outdoor area with globe lights strung from a canopy of banyan trees. Cushioned benches framed either side of a long table. A bongo drum and guitar player jammed in one corner, and in the other cigars were being rolled by hand. A counter to their right was filled with photographs and candles, and he caught sight of one of an older man with a young Cassie.

He pointed to the frame. "Is that you and your grandfather?"

"Yes. That's all pictures of family members who aren't with us anymore."

She grew misty eyed. Not wanting her to get caught up in grief, he asked, "And what's that dress you're wearing?" It had the flag of Cuba emblazoned on it, with ruffles at the sleeves and bottom.

"It's a *Bata Cubana*, a traditional Cuban Rumba dress."

"Do they come in adult sizes?" Patrick kissed her cheek, let his lips graze over her ear. "So we can dance and then I can rip it off you?"

Blushing, she hid her face in his neck. "Not now."

Yes, now. Always now, with you.

"Cassandra," her mother yelled, then fired off some sentences in Spanish. Patrick attempted a quick translation.

"Stop standing around and come help before she..."

"Throws her flip-flops at me," Cassie finished for him. "It's a Cuban thing." She shook her head and sighed. "One day with my family, and already I'm exhausted."

"They don't seem that bad."

They'd certainly wanted her attention, something he imagined she saw as pressure, but without a large and warm family of his own, Patrick could see their intentions for what they were—wanting Cassie to be happy.

"They're on better behavior with you here."

He tipped his hat at her. "I'm happy to be of service then. And you were right. These clothes are much more appropriate." And classic. He felt in his element, like he fit right in.

They joined the party, which was filled with lively conversations in Spanish and the best *empanadas* he'd ever tasted. After the meal, the speeches started, and Patrick excused himself to use the restroom, getting lost in a bookcase he discovered on the way back. It was full of the pieces written by the authors he'd come to love both at Princeton and abroad. Cervantes. Fuentes. Cortazar. Guillén. He passed his hand over the weathered spines, looking at each one carefully until he came to one that stopped his heart.

"My grandfather loved Hemingway."

Patrick glanced up as Cassie moved in beside him. "Oh yeah?"

"Rumor has it he came to my grandfather's casino. He was kind of a legend in Cuba. His favorite drink was the *mojito*, which is the drink of the house here."

His hand was still on the book. "*The Old Man and the Sea* was my favorite."

She touched his hand, one finger tracing over his and the faded and slightly worn cover beneath it. "What did you like about it?"

"There was something about the story—Santiago fighting against defeat, struggling even though it's clear the battle is hopeless." At one point he'd seen himself as the old man, dedicated to his craft no matter how impossible. Later, he'd seen that futile battle as the story of his life. But he'd never finished it, so he didn't know how it ended.

"Why don't you read anymore?"

He stared at the book. "Hurts too much."

It was all he wanted to say. He'd successfully escaped the past since they'd gotten here, had been able to avoid overthinking, hadn't even paced at all, and he wanted to keep it that way.

Cassie bumped his side. "If you could've done anything, what would it be? If your life had been different."

"Honestly, I would've wanted to go into publishing, but not sales. I would've been involved in the actual books. Ideally the foreign ones. It's not something I allow myself to think about often." He breathed in deep, turned to face her and took both her hands in his. "And you, my dear, have a party to get back to."

She smiled, her cheeks rosy. "Maybe someday we'll travel. Go to Cuba. Or Spain. And you can finally run with the bulls. After all, I've shown you Miami, so now you owe me."

Something flared in his chest. A sense of belonging. Of rightness. "You'd want that?"

She was about to answer when Annalisa ran over to them. "*Tía* Cassie, come dance with me!"

Cassie complied, and as her niece tugged her toward the

musicians, Patrick imagined a different picture than the one he saw before him. He saw Cassie, with a baby.

His baby.

The thought shocked him. He'd never pictured that, not even with Sofía, and certainly not in the time since. It was a ground-shaking change, to go from no commitments to thinking about raising a child, but something about it seemed to fit. Something about all of this fit. The culture, the music, the food. This family, energetic and loving. This gorgeous woman, who'd awoken him to sexual desires that had been lying dormant. Could she have stirred the same feelings toward fatherhood?

Could she want that with him too?

She thought she'd figure out having a family after she made partner. That was in her sights now, so did that mean maybe she did want a baby? And she wanted one with him?

She was talking about the future, so there had to be a chance she didn't want this to end. That she wanted more from him than their short-term deal but didn't know how to ask. She'd told him her deepest secrets, showed him the most vulnerable side of herself, and for all those things, he'd had to nudge her along, even shove her along at times, bring her in the direction she wanted to go.

Maybe he needed to do the same with this.

He wandered over to the cigar table where Mr. Allbright, Cassie's brother, Alejándro, her future brother-in-law, Hector, and several other family members were smoking and watching the festivities. Cassie's mother was there as well, and she and her husband exchanged pointed looks before she went back to the crowd.

Mr. Allbright handed Patrick a cigar. "This is the part where I'm supposed to ask you what your intentions are for my eldest daughter."

Patrick hid his nerves behind the light Alejándro gave him. After a deep puff, he glanced at Cassie. The other children at the party had gathered around her like she was a princess or the pied piper. Watching her smile and twirl, it was hard to imagine he'd ever seen her as cold and unfeeling. She was a hardass for sure, intelligent and driven, but she was also incredibly playful, as well as caring and trustworthy. Somewhere amongst the crazy hot sex, he'd found everything he could ever want in a woman in her.

She tossed her head back and laughed, and when their eyes met, his heart fucking lit up. He was in love with her. Ridiculously, embarrassingly, do-anything-to-see-her-smile in love with her.

Sex aside, Patrick realized it wasn't true what he'd told her that night in her apartment about not having a fantasy of his own. *Cassie* was his fantasy, and maybe he could do the whole commitment and marriage and kids thing, if he did it with her.

"My intentions are to make her happy. For as long as she'll let me."

And that needed to be longer than the next few days.

Her father nodded, and Patrick mimicked the move, nodding more to himself than anyone else. He'd devised a plan for while they were here: to give Cassie a safe space to give in to her cravings, to feel powerless even though she was anything but. He still had a few more surprises left, and was going to make sure they were good for her. More than good. Amazing.

But after that, he had a new plan. One much more permanent. Having emotions meant the two of them were out, but maybe they needed to be out of this situation, and in a new one. Then they could start over again, and make it different.

Make it real.

25

*E*arly Saturday morning, Cassie was picked up by a limo and brought to her parents' house to help Elísa get ready for her big day. Patrick would be arriving at the ceremony later, but waking up next to him in cool, white sheets with the ocean lapping silently outside their windows had made her not want to get out of bed. She'd cuddled close to him, tracing the lines on his face until he'd squinted one eye open.

"Creeper," he'd mumbled over a kiss. Groaning, she'd heaved herself out of bed and into the shower, where'd she'd tried to wade through her thoughts.

Asking him yesterday about traveling to Cuba and Spain had been a test. A careful analysis to see his reaction. He hadn't shot it down, but he hadn't enthusiastically replied either. She didn't know what to think, unsure what she wanted, or what the future held. It was odd to notice though that she hadn't been fighting with herself since she'd been back here, hadn't been struggling with which Cassie to be. Instead she was simply herself: lawyer, sister, daughter...girlfriend. No one had asked her any questions, the pressure she was usually under lessened with Patrick by her side.

It was only a show, but was it? Patrick had always been good at playing games, from his seduction of her through pretending to be her boyfriend. But it all felt too real to be fake, from the way he'd looked at her at her parents' house to the way he'd surprised her yesterday morning.

When she'd stepped into those beautiful new shoes, her heart pounded at the feel of them sliding on. The bottoms were a bit slippery—she was going to hate scuffing up that red on the concrete, but it was the only way to break in a new pair. Thank God she had solid calf muscles because these babies were seriously high. Walking in them, she felt like a tightrope walker and a princess at the same time.

The same way she'd felt yesterday morning in bed.

The memory of his hand around her throat had sent shivers pinwheeling down her spine. He'd been completely in control, and she'd felt even more bound to him than if he were inside her.

She craved the feeling now, of being bonded like that. But thinking about a future with him was fruitless. After all, she was supposed to be taking stock. Figuring out what she wanted. If she wanted kids, or if she was going to marry her career. Patrick didn't want children, but if she somehow decided she did, where did that leave her on the odd chance that he wanted to pursue more than this short-term thing?

It left her needing to figure out what the hell she wanted. And to get her ass downstairs.

Her morning was full of maid-of-honor duties—getting her sister ready, consoling her tearful mother, making sure all the bridesmaids were set. Dressed in variations of black lace and carrying bouquets of vibrant red roses, they went one by one down the aisle. Cassie found Patrick immediately in the back row, looking like royalty in a sharp black tux and red pocket square.

The ceremony went off without a hitch, and Cassie got tearful over the *I do's*. She remained her sister's shadow afterward, tucking up her bustle and organizing the receiving line. Once

Elísa and Hector were off to take pictures and the guests were traveling to the reception site, she and Patrick finally had a few moments alone together. He kissed up her neck as soon as they were in the rental car.

"You look incredible," he breathed.

Cassie closed her eyes as his hand strayed across the gearshift to where the lace of her dress played against her cleavage. "Gonna get me all messed up," she protested, but it was a weak objection. She wanted him to mess her up, and get her wild and unkempt the way he always did.

"Later," he said, then broke off and stared at her with a deep, steadying breath. "Later."

The reception was at a club in Coral Gables with a Spanish tile roof and candelabras everywhere. A band played before a shining dance floor, the exposed beams were draped with brilliant red fabric, and black lace runners lined all the tables. Patrick stayed close by Cassie's side, smiling and clapping when the newlyweds were introduced.

"They look happy," Patrick said.

"They are," she replied, watching her sister on the dance floor.

"And you? Are you happy?"

She looked at him, got caught up in those eyes that glittered with sinful mischief and felt like a safe haven all at once. "I am. Right now."

With you.

The first dance ended, and the band invited everyone onto the dance floor. Annalisa ran up to Patrick and asked him to dance. Cassie told them to go on, and Patrick accepted the invitation, looking carefree and relaxed as he twirled her niece around. Cassie waited for that moment, for her biological clock to finally kick into action as she watched the man she...yes, she had to admit it now—loved—dance with a child.

It didn't.

The band started up a quick reggaeton dance—the rhythm a mix of Jamaican reggae, merengue, salsa and house beats. Annalisa ran back to her parents, and Patrick strolled over to Cassie and held out a hand.

"Shall we?"

A mess of emotions ran through her, but she wanted to feel this with him, one more time. He led her to the floor, and they easily found the beat, picking up a quick salsa. With one hand tight on her hip, his eyes stayed on her the way they always did—careful, hungry and paying attention.

"I'd say we're stealing your sister's thunder, if you hadn't been stealing it already," he said.

"How am I doing that?"

Patrick slid his hand down her leg, pulling her against him. "Don't you know? You're the most beautiful woman here."

Melting was the only way to describe what he was doing to her, and yet he was setting her on fire at the same time.

"And I was lying when I said I'd wanted you since we met," he said.

Cassie tensed, ready for him to say this had been a ruse and to blow it all apart, but he shook his head.

"It was more than just wanting you. You tested my mettle. Challenged me in a way no woman ever had. We've both got walls up, but you knocked mine down. You made me remember what it was like to care again. And everything I've learned about you since then has only made me care about you more."

Her breath got stuck in her throat, along with her heart. "I was wrong when I said I didn't like you," she said. "You're kind of perfect for me."

He smiled that dazzling smile before pushing her back out and spinning her around, and the truth of what she'd said hit home. Patrick wasn't the masked playboy she'd imagined. She knew the man behind that wealthy exterior now, knew what troubled him and what made his eyes blaze with hunger. He was passionate and intelligent. Commanding and sexual, he was strong enough to fight her and comfort her, to defile her without losing respect. And he'd made her comfortable with her desires, erasing the guilt and shame she'd felt about them.

Suddenly, she wanted to make time stop, or undo that rule she'd made. To go tell herself not to make that awful devil's bargain, because she'd been wrong, so wrong about everything, and she didn't want admitting emotions to be her way out. She wanted it to be their beginning.

The song came to an end, and he rubbed his nose along hers —a soft, sweet move.

"You're kind of perfect for me too," he said.

And in that moment, everything became clear.

She didn't want kids, and that was okay. She was all right with who she was—a powerhouse attorney. A biracial woman who was a lady in *la calle* and a freak in *la cama*. And she wanted to be that person with him. He didn't want kids either, and she knew he didn't get involved, but they were already involved, weren't they? He cared about her, and that was most definitely an emotion. Maybe he was feeling the same things she was.

Maybe this didn't have to end.

Her mother called out for her. Cassie glanced over her shoulder, then back at Patrick. "Can we talk more later?"

"Of course."

The party went late into the evening, and Cassie allowed herself to celebrate, skipping a cocktail but indulging in the *medianoche* sandwiches and several of those guava and cream cheese *pastelitos* she'd been craving. Bring on the calories—she'd dance until her feet throbbed to compensate. Elísa had skipped out on the customary Money Dance, because no way was she letting anything get pinned to her gown, but had kept the traditional Cuban wedding cake—a coconut *tres leches* flavor filled with ribbons on the bottom layer, one of which was attached to a ring. It was the equivalent of the bouquet toss, and

Cassie conveniently busied herself with seeing out a few older family members when all the single ladies were called the dance floor.

She didn't want to risk not being the one to find the ribbon with the ring, because for the first time, she wanted it to be her.

When the last guests had finally left and the bride and groom were on their way, Patrick ushered Cassie into the car. She dozed on the drive back to South Beach and was out of it as they made their way through the lobby. She slapped her cheeks to wake herself up in the elevator, wanting to be alert enough to talk to him about the future. Thinking some ice water would help, she grabbed the bucket, insisting she was fine to go fill it when Patrick protested. She needed a minute alone to compile her thoughts.

The full bucket in one hand, Cassie used her key card to buzz the door back open with the other, but everything was dark when she stepped inside.

"Patrick?"

No answer. Was she in the wrong room? No, the key card wouldn't have let her in. She took a step farther in inside. "Patrick? Are you here?"

All of the sudden, Cassie was violently slammed against the wall.

The bucket clattered to the floor. Fear shot through her. Her heartbeat went on overdrive as an arm locked across her back, forcing her still as she tried to breathe. She started to yell, but a hand clamped over her mouth.

"Oh, you're a tough little bitch aren't you." A deadly calm chuckle sounded in her ear. "Go ahead. Try to fight me off. But you're not gonna win."

26

P atrick.

Cassie's senses were off—she was still woozy from the drive and the dark made it difficult to find her bearings. She knew it was him, knew what he was doing, but this felt incredibly real too, and any comfort she felt in his presence was coupled with the razor's edge of fear.

Cassie fought back, but Patrick's grip tightened.

"Keep trying. Watching you struggle just turns me on more." Even his voice was different. Sharp. Gritty. "It's up to you, princess. This can go easy for you, or it can go a lot harder."

Excitement and rage shivered through her. Cassie made herself go limp.

"Good decision." Patrick let go of her mouth and wrestled her arms behind her back. "I wanted to be nice, but you've been teasing me all night in that dress and those shoes. And now I'm going to get you back for it."

She tried to shove her way free, but Patrick's hold on her was vicious as he easily pinned her body between his and the wall. Seizing her by the hair, he wrenched her head back so she was looking up at him, then wrapped his other hand around her throat. The threat of pressure and his thumb on her jaw had Cassie's heart pounding. He'd never been this rough with her.

"I guess you're not as smart as you look." His cutting remark was as cruel as his expression. "Looks like we're gonna do this the hard way."

He kissed her then—mean, sharp kisses that scraped and bit and hurt. Desire tinged with adrenaline, the pleasure of his hot, wet mouth meshing with his relentless and cruel hold. Fire lit through every limb, burning her with the need to run and the need to stay exactly where she was.

She bit at his lower lip until he broke off the kiss. "Fuck you."

Patrick grinned. What little light there was caught the mean streak in his eyes. "Oh, you're gonna."

He yanked her backward, dragging her into the bathroom. When he threw the light on, she got a glimpse of him in the mirror. He was still in his crisp white shirt and tuxedo pants, and his erection pushed at the fabric. Cassie tried to fend him off, but it was useless. She couldn't get her balance back, not in these heels. With a strength she hadn't known he possessed, Patrick knocked her to her knees and then forced her down until her torso made contact with the floor. His weight came down on her, his body caging hers. Cassie heard the sound of fabric rustling— his tie coming loose?

"Get *off* me!" she shouted.

He leaned in by her ear and hissed, "No."

He held her down and unzipped her dress, cruelly yanking it down. Her nipples betrayed her, growing hard as they raked across the cold tiles. He heaved her sideways and managed to get the whole thing off her, kicking it to the side. Cassie tried to use the moment to work her way out of his grasp, but he pressed her down with a Herculean might and began binding her upper arms with his tie.

"I could've gagged you with this." His breathing was labored with the effort of what he was doing, hogtying her until she was immobile and helpless. "But I have other plans for your mouth."

"What makes you think I'm gonna do anything for you?"

One hand formed a fist in her hair and wrenched her head backward. "You don't know when to shut the fuck up, do you?"

Her breathing quickened with that delicious edge of fear and arousal, and her neck burned when he let her go. Something sharp bit into Cassie's wrists, and then he grabbed her by the hair again, dragging her up until she was kneeling. Her spike heels dug into her thighs, and the pain of his grip at her scalp made her eyes water until he let go and came to stand in front of her.

"Look at you, all tied up. You're like my own little present."

He bent down, hands braced on his thighs. She didn't know what was biting into her wrists, and for the first time this felt real enough for her to truly be scared.

"What are you going to do to me?"

Smiling his jackal smile, Patrick stood and unbuttoned his pants. "Whatever I want."

Panic spiked. He was himself and not. Ruthless, heartless in the moment, but still her Patrick.

Her Patrick.

His pants hit the floor, forming a puddle around his shoes. He tugged his boxer briefs down and palmed himself, his cock thick and red and wet at the tip. Cassie's tongue came out to moisten her lip involuntarily, her eyes trained on his hand as he stroked.

"You're gonna make me feel good, aren't you?" Moving toward her, he grabbed a fistful of her hair. "Yes, you are. You're gonna behave and put that mouth of yours to good use."

He guided himself toward her lips, and Cassie glared up at him as she tried to hold her head back, but she couldn't escape. When his swollen tip glided over her tongue, she tried another tactic. Knowing it would knock him off balance, she drew him in deep, exhaling around that intrusion until her nose brushed the coarse hair at his base.

"Fuck."

There it was—that sound of surprised pleasure, and Cassie knew she'd gotten to him. The momentary crack in his façade made her smile around him.

"Smug all of the sudden?" Patrick's hands came up on either side of her head. "Let's fix that."

Shoving himself deep, he fucked her mouth, moving her head with his hands. Cassie struggled to breathe, and tension swirled in her stomach even as her pussy ached. Slick and hot, she could feel how wet she was.

Wet, kneeling on a bathroom floor in nothing but her panties and heels with her arms bound behind her. Only he could get her like this, turned on and frightened and not sure what was going to happen next. The knowledge was powerful enough to make her eyes sting with tears. A few let loose and slipped down her cheek.

Patrick looked down at her, then pulled back. He hooked his thumb into her mouth, pulling at her cheek.

"There's no *exit* to this. I hope you know that."

His eyes blazed, green and sharp and hot. He was reminding her of her safeword, of her way out. This was her game, her show, her decision to end it all...if she wanted to.

She sucked on his thumb, then grazed it with her teeth until he slid it free. "We'll see about that."

I'm fine. Keep going. Don't stop now.

He slapped her breast. "Talking back, are we?"

"You're an asshole." Her skin stung, the pain echoing in the wet throb between her thighs. "What's around my wrists?"

"A zip tie."

When the hell had he bought those?

"I have another one I can use for your ankles if you don't do what I say." Patrick bent down, put one hand around her inner thigh and yanked until he'd forced her legs open. "Now, let's make sure you're ready for me."

He shoved her panties down around her hips, glancing over her clit while the other hand rolled and pinched her nipple. Cassie tried to arch her body away—she didn't want it to feel good, but he was thrumming his fingers just right. Finding the buttons he knew would make her moan.

"Look at you," he said. "Trying to pretend you don't want it."

She would've protested, but then he stopped stroking. The loss made her cry out until he started again. Then stopped. Started. Off. On. Stroke. Pause. The second the pain of missing his touch hit her, it folded back into pleasure. A low sound of need escaped her.

"Little whore doesn't know what she wants, does she?" He switched to the other breast, fondling, then pinching so hard she yelped. "Oh, yeah. You're gonna come whether you want to or not."

He was right. A shuddery orgasm was bearing down on her. Cassie's hips rocked with his fingers, a release she didn't want and couldn't live without seconds away, until he stopped once again, landing a hard slap on her clit. Cassie's teeth clenched and she hunched forward, trying to catch her breath.

He used the hand he'd been touching her with to grab her chin, smearing her wetness over her face.

"I'd do it, you know. I'd make you come. I'd force you to endure it the way you made me endure looking at you tonight. The whole night, I wanted to find some room to drag you off into and fuck you until you screamed."

Was that why he'd been looking at her that way? "I guess that's too bad for you."

Patrick released her face and slapped one of her breasts. "Did you know how badly I wanted you?"

"No." She hadn't, and the knowledge made her heart pound in a completely different way.

"No?"

He hooked his hands beneath her underarms and heaved her

to her feet. She was unbalanced, her panties still around her legs, her nipples and pussy tender and her knees stiff. He smiled as he stripped the rest of his clothes off.

"Well you're gonna pay for it anyway."

He picked her up and threw her over his shoulder. When they reached the bed, he threw her facedown onto it. There was a pair of scissors on the blanket, but before she could shimmy away, he covered her body with his, smothering her with his weight. With one hand on her hip, he yanked her panties off and drove a finger deep inside her.

"Do you even know how wet you are?"

He drove it in and out, soothing that hungry ache and making it worse at the same time.

"Stop," she moaned, but she didn't mean it.

"Stop?" He added a finger and hit that spot that got her humiliatingly soaked. "You don't really want me to stop, but it's cute how you think you have a choice."

Three fingers now, and his thumb brushed over her rear.

"No." She tried to push up, and was rewarded with the intoxicating feeling of him shoving her back down.

"You can say no all you want. You can even think this spot between your legs belongs to you. But it's not. It's mine."

It was. All of her was. And as he fucked her with his fingers, thumb putting more pressure against her ass, Cassie's head started to spin. He was getting her to that point she'd been desperate for, the point when fear and pleasure mixed together, when she couldn't refuse, couldn't do anything but be pushed over the edge and feel.

"And I...intend..." The tie came loose. Something cold and hard pressed against her arms. The scissors. "To take...what's... mine."

A snap and the zip ties popped off. He flipped her over, one big hand on her middle, squeezing her breast, the other on one of her ankles, forcing her open. Forcing her to do nothing but lie there and take it.

His cock slid past her pussy lips, and there was nothing gentle about the way he rammed himself home. Cassie cried out, her hips lifting even as she tried to push him off, but he held her down and started to thrust. He was beautiful and fierce, muscles leaping as he reared back and drove forward. Their eyes met, and even through the farce, through this new mask, the one he'd put on for her, she saw him. Her Patrick, giving her what she needed.

"Something you want to say?" he asked through panted breaths.

I love you.

"I hate you," she gritted out.

He grinned. "I hate you more."

If he meant the same thing she did, Cassie didn't know. But he picked up his pace, using his torso to wedge her legs wider apart. She tried to fight, but she didn't want to anymore. Every deep, hard thrust was driving her closer to release. Closer to him. Patrick let go of her breast and brought a hand to where they were joined.

"*Eres mío*, Cassandra," he whispered menacingly. "*No importa lo duro que luchar, siempre va a ser cierto.*"

You're mine, Cassandra. No matter how hard you fight it, it's always going to be true.

His thumb found her clit, and then yes, it didn't matter how hard she fought. Her body belonged to him as much as her heart did, and she gave in, surrendering to an orgasm that took her breath away. He kept at it as she thrashed, didn't stop even when she started shaking her head, unable to take any more. His thumb still thrumming, he brought his other hand to her throat and squeezed until her oxygen was restricted. Gasping, Cassie stared into his eyes, watching the meanness in his expression fall away and her Patrick returning as another sharp release took hold.

He let go of her throat and pulled back, leaving a slick, raw emptiness between her legs. She tucked her knees up at the loss and covered her face with her hands, her whole body shaking, although she wasn't crying. It was simply the only thing she could do after the most terrifying, most sexually satisfying event of her life.

And Patrick had given that to her.

"Are you okay?" he asked. When she didn't reply, she felt his hands at her face, gently urging hers away. "Did I push it too far? God, I'm sorry, Cassie. Please tell me you're okay."

He kissed her cheeks, her shoulders—worried kisses peppered everywhere from her face to her wrists. Everywhere he might have injured her. She tried to find her voice, stuck in a woozy space she didn't quite understand. It was hard to come back to herself, but Patrick was getting frantic.

"Cassie, talk to me. Did I hurt you? Did I fuck this all up?"

"I'm okay," she mumbled. "I promise."

His body stilled, and he lingered at her belly. His voice was small and quiet when he asked, "You don't hate me, right?"

The words were a gut punch to her heart. How could he even think that?

She reached out for him. "C'mere."

A soft exhale was her reply. Patrick crawled up her body, wrapped his arms around her as he buried his face against her neck. "You enjoyed that?"

"I did."

His breathing was still fast and he was shaking. When she could finally think again, she touched his back, running soothing strokes with her fingertips until he calmed. His softening erection pressed against her thigh.

"You never came," she murmured.

"I was too focused on you. Making sure you weren't scared."

"I was, but in a good way."

He picked his head up. The look in Patrick's eyes as they searched hers reached a point deep inside her.

"I don't ever want to hurt you," he said. "It terrified me that I might have."

"You didn't." She stroked his cheek. "Kiss me, Patrick."

His lips caressed hers, gently at first, then with more passion. Cassie shivered when their tongues touched. Shifting beneath him, she reached down and stroked his flesh until he was hard again. Patrick groaned and pressed his forehead to hers.

"You sure you're ready?" he asked through grated breaths. "You haven't exactly recovered."

"I don't need to recover," she said, and guided him inside.

He inhaled sharply and his hips shot forward. "Christ, Cassie, yes."

Patrick gripped her shoulders—not with the same brute force as before, but as if he were holding on to her now. Like she was his raft in a sea he didn't know how to cross. She drew him in deeper with her legs around his, her heels he'd wanted to fuck her in dragging over his calves. He kept his eyes on hers until pleasure forced them shut, and she kissed him, drinking his groans like so much champagne, tasting the sound of his pleasure.

He rolled off her, and she quickly sat up to undo her heels, setting them gently on the floor as she lay back down. They huddled together in the dark. Cassie couldn't believe how relaxed she felt after something so violent and passionate. She'd spent so long stifling what she wanted, but he'd given her a safe place to indulge in her most base, sinister longings.

Somehow, while making her completely powerless, he'd set her free.

She wanted to say all that and more—she knew they still needed to talk, but her eyelids had grown heavy, the day hitting her and sapping her ability for cognitive thought.

So for now all she could say was, "Thank you. Not just for this. For everything."

There was a pause before his reply came. "Thank you for trusting me. Not just with this. With everything."

Cassie turned on her side and tugged on his arm until it was snuggled protectively around her. Their breathing was syncing, and she was so tired she wasn't even sure what she was saying, but as she turned back to kiss him good night, the words tumbled out of her.

"Eres mía también, ¿sabes?"

You're mine too, you know that?

He kissed her cheek. *"Sí, mi amor. Sí."*

---

27

*P*atrick put their suitcases in the trunk, tipped the valet and climbed into the car. Cassie was stretched out in the passenger seat, relaxed in a pair of sunglasses, a tank top and shorts. She was all long legs, bare skin and smiles, and he was going to be sad to lose this version of her when they got back.

But maybe he wouldn't have to lose *her*.

Anxiety formed a knot in his stomach as they drove back to her parents' house. He had so much he wanted to say to her—to ask about the future. To make sure last night was everything she'd hoped it would be. He'd wanted to talk when they woke up, but they'd slept in until right before checkout, and he didn't want to discuss their future while cleaning up broken zip ties and checking over her bruises.

She wasn't too worse for the wear. She'd said her scalp was tender, and her wrists and knees were a little sore, but that was all. She'd kissed him in the quick shower they'd shared before they left, and it had made any lingering worries disappear. Because there had been worries. From the moment they got back from the wedding until he'd woken up beside her this morning.

He'd had to psych himself up for it, before she returned from getting the ice. But once she walked in the door, he'd been swept up in the scene, acting as awful as he could. No filter. Just punishing words and angry, mean sex. He had no idea he could be that horrible and enjoy it, so lost in what he was doing he wasn't sure where the act ended and the two of them began again.

When it was over and she'd covered her face and curled up in a ball, he'd yanked himself out of the role, sure he'd screwed it all up. Certain she regretted it. Convinced he'd wake up in the morning and find her gone.

None of that had happened. Instead she'd burrowed into his arms and told him she was his.

Now he needed to solidify that.

The bride and groom's family were all together for a brunch at Cassie's parents' house. Paper plates were balanced precariously on every flat surface. Patrick had a feeling this was how it usually was there, with family on top of family, always something going on and the house full up with people and life. He envied the closeness, the love that was evident there, even in their teasing and yapping, but if all went as planned, he'd still be a part of it, even after they returned to New England.

When they sat down to eat, Cassie's father asked her for an update on things at work.

"I have a big meeting tomorrow," she said. "If everything works out, you'll be looking at Forrester, Schaeffer and Pierce's next partner."

"That's great. I'm proud of you, Pumpkin."

Patrick smiled through his bite of food. It seemed he wasn't the only one who had nicknames for her. He leaned in to Cassie and whispered, "Pumpkin, huh? I'm glad he doesn't call you princess."

She elbowed him in the ribs.

"Patrick," Cassie's mother said from across the table. "What do you think of that?"

"Of Cassie making partner?"

"*Sí.*"

He tried to read the subtext. Was she asking if he was proud of her too? Or if he was okay with her having a position of authority? "I think Cassie's drive and determination is the sexiest thing about her."

It was true, and a chorus of *awwws* were the background to their short, sweet kiss.

Later that afternoon, after they'd said their goodbyes and headed to the airport, Patrick's heart pounded in his chest. She'd been busy with her niece and nephew when he'd spoken to her father, and now there was a sense of urgency. He couldn't let this weekend go, couldn't allow her to get on a plane without him without making this happen.

Their flights were a few hours apart, but when they got through security, hers had already been announced. They ducked into restrooms to change into the heavier clothes they'd stashed in their carry-ons. When they reached her gate, Patrick put their bags down and pulled her against a column.

He took a breath. "I know we said we said this was going to be short-term, that it was only about sex and living out your fantasies, but..."

She looked up at him, her smile open and willing. "But?"

That face. Those eyes. Only she could make him this tongue-tied. "But I don't want this to end."

She exhaled heavily. "Neither do I."

"You don't?" His heartbeat was choking him.

"No. Not at all. I—"

Too elated for words, he kissed her. Everyone in the terminal had to be watching, but Patrick didn't care. Let them look. She was his. Cassie slid her fingers into his hair, laughing through their kiss. He smiled and pressed his forehead to hers.

"I know we weren't supposed to have feelings. I know that was the rule but—"

"Rules are overrated."

"Fuck the rules. I don't want any more rules. I just want to be with you."

"Me too."

"Good. 'Cause we're gonna do this." Patrick wasn't sure he'd ever felt joy like this. "I didn't want to feel this way again about anyone, but you've changed me, and I can't hold it back anymore."

"You fell for me against your will?" she asked with a touch of sarcasm. "How romantic."

"It's true. You won me over. You're the most intelligent, beautiful, pain-in-the-ass woman I've ever met, and—" She smiled wide, blue eyes shining as bright as the ocean. He was going to say it. Right here in the airport. "I want to marry you, Cassie. I want all that crazy stuff I never thought I'd want. The house and white picket fence and dog and kids. I've already talked to your father, and he gave his blessing. I love you and I want it all, if you'll have me."

Her face changed. Her smile dropped off, and a little V formed between her brows. "You...what?"

"I asked your father for your hand in marriage." He was proud of it too. Figured if he was going to do this, he should do it the right way.

"I heard that part," Cassie said. "It's the kids part I'm not sure about."

Patrick laughed. Yeah this had to be disorienting as fuck for her. "I know you said you were putting kids on the back burner—"

"And *you* said, 'kids aren't for me.' Those were your words."

Always fighting him. Oh, Cassie. "I know what my words were."

"So, what? You...changed your mind?"

Why was she fixating on that? Did she not hear him say he loved her? "I did. After this weekend being with your family, seeing you with them, it changed everything for me."

Cassie's expression shifted. Her mouth pressed into a thin line and her eyes went icy cold.

"I said I wanted this to continue, and see about having a relationship. Not that I wanted to be the mother to your children. But I don't even think this is about me. I think you spent a weekend with 'Latina Cassie,' and it reminded you of Sofía. And now you're projecting a fantasy on me that has nothing to do with me at all."

He stood stock-still, his face burning as if she'd slapped him. The most humiliating thing to ever happen to him, the thing he'd trusted her and no one else with, and she'd thrown it in his face.

"Is *that* what you think? That I'm reliving the past?"

Cassie shrugged and crossed her arms. "Am I wrong?"

He thought so, but who cared? She'd cut him too deep for him to fight her anymore. "I think you've made your own decision, so it doesn't matter what I say."

Her flight was called over the loudspeaker. Cassie picked up her bag and retrieved her boarding pass. "Look, we had our thing, and it was great. But if children are what you want, you should feel free to pursue that with someone else. You've fulfilled my fantasies, and now my claim on you has ended."

"Thank you for clarifying that." He picked up his own bag. "I hope you have a safe trip home."

"You too."

Patrick walked away without another word. He'd done it again. Handed his heart to a woman and she'd thrown it back in his face. There was no point in telling her having children wasn't what mattered. That wasn't what had changed.

Having her claim him for good was what he'd really wanted.

28

*C*assie typed up what was going to be her last official email to Hudson and hit send. Staring at her screen, she sat back and breathed a sigh of relief. Grant Books was finally solvent. A slew of new authors had sold their books to him. All the house's titles had been re-released using the new e-book software he'd appropriated, and his investors were satisfied. To put an extra cherry on top of her cake of legal badassery, Bruce and Reynash had also signed on with the firm, adding to Reginald Pierce's roster of incredibly wealthy clients.

She'd done her job. Done it well. No matter how crazy Hudson had made her, she kept his company together. She'd retained its value, with her client's best interests in mind.

If only she'd been smart enough to do the same with herself.

A week and half had passed with no contact from Patrick. In the time since, she'd tried to look at things as a bankruptcy lawyer would—one who'd failed at her job. Cassie knew from her years of experience that you never fucked with the deal. You get in, solve the problem, and get out. She and Patrick had entered into negotiations in an attempt to navigate the labyrinth of her desires, and once that was done, they were supposed to wrap things up and move on. She hadn't, ignoring all the warning signs that hollered she was on a sinking ship.

That ship had become the Titanic in Miami International Airport.

She slowly swung her chair around until she faced the window. The entire situation still aggravated her. They were supposed to have been on the same page. They *had been* on the same page before he went and dropped that bomb on her.

He wanted children? What the serious fuck?

She shouldn't have gotten so angry, but her fight reflex had come charging in. Maybe she'd gone too far saying what she did about Sofía, but it made no sense that he suddenly wanted babies with her. The idea that he wanted to marry her in itself was insane. They'd barely known each other a year. Had hated one another for months. The only rational explanation was that he'd seen the family he'd wanted to be a part of in Spain in her family. Saw the woman he'd proposed to in her. That made a shit-ton more sense than him suddenly wanting things he'd railed against for half his life.

Whether it was true or not, she'd never know. She'd thought about contacting him to apologize, or to at least explain why she'd flown off the handle, but she didn't have the courage to say the truth: that she'd finally come to terms with the idea of not becoming a parent. That she'd figured out what she wanted, which, as it turned out, was him.

Why did she have to fall for a playboy, only to have him become a family man?

She needed to put him out of her mind. She'd made the right decision. They had conflicting interests, which meant she had no choice but to invoke that escape clause. She had to preserve the business, which in this case was herself.

A light knock at her door got her attention. Cassie gave her chair a determined shove and faced her desk. "Come in."

Elliott Schaeffer stepped into her office. "Is this a bad time?"

"Of course not, Elliott. What can I do for you?"

"You've done quite a lot lately, it would seem."

If he meant Grant Books, fuck yeah she had. "Just doing my job for the firm."

"Well, the firm would like to show you its appreciation."

He handed her an envelope. Cassie's pulse thumped as she took it from his outstretched hand.

"The letter is a formality. We'll discuss the capital contribution and changes in your benefits package once you've officially accepted."

She opened the envelope and read the letter addressed to Cassandra Allbright, Partner, Bankruptcy. The crisp linen paper on company letterhead was what she'd been waiting for—two decades of hard work paid off, the future she'd been working toward finally within her grasp.

So why did it feel so hollow?

"Thank you, Elliott." Her voice sounded stiff and mechanical. "I'm honored."

"You've proved yourself invaluable to the firm, Cassie. I'm sorry I told you otherwise, but it looks like that was the firecracker you needed to bring in an incredible amount of business." He went back to the door and smiled again. "Congratulations."

He walked out, leaving her in silence. They'd lit a fire under her ass, and she'd performed, making her rich bosses even richer for a chance at a slice of their pie. She didn't feel like a charging bull. Didn't feel like she'd broken through any glass ceiling. Instead, she felt trapped under it.

Was this what her grandfather had meant when he told her she'd change the world?

There was another knock at her now-open door. Cassie looked up to find Lilly and Sam standing there with eager grins.

"Is that what I think it is?" Lilly asked, pointing to the letter.

"Yup."

She rushed into the room with a squeal and plucked it from Cassie's hands. Sam retrieved Cassie's coat from the hook on the back of her door.

"We're celebrating," she said in her usual no-nonsense attitude. "Don't argue. We already have reservations."

It took until they were seated and had ordered a bottle of wine for Cassie to snap into focus.

"Why did you have reservations? You didn't know Elliott was going to talk to me today."

Lilly didn't say anything at first. She tugged on her braid and looked over at Sam. After a few moments of silence, Cassie couldn't take it anymore.

"Spit it out, ladies."

Sam tapped her fingers on her menu. "We've actually been planning an intervention."

"An intervention?" Cassie's gaze darted between the two of them. "For what?"

Lilly scrunched up her nose. "We haven't wanted to bother you because you've had a lot of work to do..."

"...but?"

Sam dropped her menu and crossed her arms on the table. "What happened with Patrick in Florida, Cassie?"

It wasn't a question. It was a strange sort of demand—calm and yet unyielding, the way Patrick was when he got her to talk. Cassie heaved a heavy sigh.

"He asked me to marry him."

Lilly's mouth dropped open. "Are you serious?"

"Completely."

"And you said..."

"No, obviously."

Sam nodded slowly. "Catch us up on the 'obviously' part?"

"Because he wanted kids."

That stopped them. Lilly's eyes went wide. "Wow. I never saw Patrick as the fathering type."

"Neither did I."

"And you've decided kids aren't what you want," Lilly verified.

"As it turns out, I found out last month that I'm in the early stages of menopause, so..." Cassie lifted her glass in a toast. "Decision made."

Lilly frowned. "You didn't tell me that."

"It wasn't something I was ready to talk about."

Sam leaned in closer. "Early stages doesn't mean you can't, right? It means that—"

"—the decision's gotta be made now," Cassie finished for her. "I thought about it. I watched him with my niece and asked myself if that's what I wanted, and I don't. I'm okay with not having kids. I'd literally *just* figured it out, and then he decides he wants to have a family with me."

"Well, at least you figured it out," Sam said. "You could've ended up with two kids who fight all the time and a husband who can't remember to watch his language around them, let alone attempt to seduce you, and tries to make up for your lack of a career by getting you to publish your Instagram posts."

She knocked back a hearty sip of wine. Cassie exchanged glances with Lilly. "You gonna need an intervention next?"

She waved them off, the tension in her expression disappearing into a smile. "Brady has good intentions. He just doesn't know how to make me happy. But I've got my dirty books to keep me busy. No intervention needed." Sam sat back in her seat. "I don't know that Patrick is the right person for you anyway. The sex might've been great, but he's still a bit of ass, no? Your classic wealthy alpha-hole?"

It was how Cassie would've described him before. Then she'd seen the real him.

"He comes off like that, but it's a mask. There's much more to him to that." She reached up and rubbed the back of her neck.

It had felt better when Patrick did it.

"How is he?" She hated having to ask, but they were her only connection to him now.

Sam shrugged. "Brady hasn't said anything."

Lilly twisted her braid around her fingers. "He's been blowing Jack off. Avoiding having to answer any questions about you, I guess."

A part of her was happy to hear that, but knowing he was struggling too made things harder. If he'd gone back to his regularly scheduled programming, it would've made it easier for her to stay mad, and eventually forget about him.

"Is it the baby thing that was the problem?" Lilly asked. "Or did you not..."

"Love him?" At Lilly's nod, Cassie replied, "I did. Still do, I guess."

"Does he know that?"

She thought back to his face at the airport. How fucking wrecked he looked.

He'd told her he loved her.

She hadn't said it back. She'd watched him walk away instead.

She would've said yes, would've thrown her arms around him, moved into his beautiful apartment and enjoyed everything that came with being Mrs. Patrick Dunham, if he hadn't drawn that line in the sand.

He'd turned the corner, and she'd heard his plea from that night when they'd told each other everything—that no matter what happened, he didn't want her to leave. But in the end, he was the one leaving. After all, it was what he was good at.

"I don't know, but it doesn't matter." She raised her glass in a toast. "Today is a day to celebrate. I'm finally on the road to changing the world."

"To changing the world," Sam said, clinking her glass. "What's your first order of business?"

Cassie put her glass down. Her mind was startlingly empty.

"You know, I had this weird feeling when Schaeffer gave me the envelope. Like it was..."

Lilly waited. "Was what?"

Like it was the wrong thing to do. "An empty victory."

"It's like I said before," Sam said. "Laws change the world, not lawyers." Lilly eyed her, but she ignored it. "You've done all this soul-searching on having kids. Are you sure partner is what you want too?"

"Of course I am."

She was, right?

They enjoyed their meal, polishing off a second bottle of wine. After thanking her friends for caring so much about her that they'd gotten her tipsy, Cassie went for a solo walk through Boston Commons, hoping the December chill would clear her head.

As she walked along the Freedom Trail, fresh white snow crunched under her boots. The air was clean and cold, icy enough to make her eyes water when the wind hit. She breathed in deep, smelling the different scents—grilled food from restaurants bordering the park, balsam fir, the murky smell of the river and a hint of weed.

It wasn't the bouquet she'd been hoping for.

Fishing her phone from her purse, she called her mother.

"*Hola, mi vida.* We haven't heard from you in a while."

"I've been busy with work."

"And with Patrick?"

Shit. She hadn't told her. "Oh. No. That's...over."

"Oh." The reply was followed by silence.

Cassie frowned. Why was she was calling. For approval? For a connection to her grandfather she no longer had? "I got my partner offer letter."

"Wonderful, *pero, ¿que pasó con* Patrick?"

What happened with Patrick? Was that all anyone could ask her?

"I reached a major milestone in my career today," she snapped. "Could you ask me about that before harassing me about being single again?"

"*No es* harassing." Her mother sighed. "Ay, Cassie. Why is everything so difficult with you?"

She'd heard that before too.

"I'm not trying to be difficult. I just want to know why you don't want me to succeed."

"I do. But I want to know you're taken care of too."

Cassie stopped walking. "Taken care of?"

"Yes. With a nice man. And children to look after you when I'm gone."

Oh, God. "Is that why you push it? Because you're worried about me?"

"Of course it is."

Tears pinched Cassie's eyes, stinging against the frigid air. She walked up Beacon and down a side street to get out of the wind. "I don't need a husband and kids to be taken care of, Mom. You know that, right? I can take care of myself."

"I know. But I don't like the idea of you all alone up there."

"I'm not alone. I have my friends. I have—" She didn't have Patrick. But she'd finally been in love, and was cool with who she was and what she liked, and she had him to thank for that. "—a lot of people I care about."

"Is that enough?"

"You mean, not having children?"

"*Sí.*"

"I don't need children to feel complete. If I'd wanted them, I would've found a way to do it by now. It's not the right choice for me."

"And a husband?"

"I'm still working on that part." She held her breath, waiting for judgment. For disappointment. Sadness.

"Okay. I respect your decision. And I am proud of you."

295

Cassie's lungs released in a rush. "You are?"

"Of course. It's a big thing, being made a partner. And I'm happy with it if you are." She paused, so Cassie stopped moving too. "Are you happy?"

Patrick had asked her the same question at the wedding. There, she'd been sure of the answer. She was happy with him. She didn't have him, but was she happy with her life without him?

Once upon a time, she'd felt good about her choices, felt like she was accomplishing things. At Legal Aid, when she was helping people. When she'd clerked for the justice and was a part of the lawmaking process. Then she'd been hired at the firm and started chasing numbers, waiting for the rich client who would prove her worthy to three rich men.

"Cassandra?" her mother prompted.

Cassie looked up at her surroundings. She'd stopped in front of the Massachusetts State House—the legislature building where she'd clerked.

Laws change the world, not lawyers.

"No," Cassie said, a bit dazed. "I'm not."

She'd gone off-track somehow, but not in the way her bosses or her mother or even she had thought. She'd put herself on this path, thinking partner was the single measure of success. She'd cut off pieces of herself in pursuit of that goal, from her hair to her Cuban side to her own desires, thinking it was the only way she could change the world.

It wasn't.

"I'm not happy. But I know a way I can be."

Cassie smiled, feeling...something. A calmness, an inner peace she'd been missing.

The wind shifted, and she jerked to attention. She looked around to make sure the smell wasn't coming from anyone nearby. It wasn't, and disappeared as quickly as it had arrived— the scent of her grandfather's cigar.

---

29

*A*nother Wednesday skipping tennis. Another Friday not chasing tail.

Patrick had dodged Jack for a second week in a row yesterday because he didn't want to risk a discussion about Cassie. Even hearing from Hudson that she'd wrapped up his case was too much. When he'd called to gloat, Patrick was going to ask him not to mention the connection between them, but decided not to bother. There wasn't much point now anyway.

There hadn't been much point in hitting the bar circuit last weekend either, so he'd stayed home. Going on the prowl had always afforded him the release he'd craved, but it was nothing like being with Cassie.

And nothing was hurt as much as the feeling of her being gone. Not even when he'd lost Sofía. The comparison made him cringe.

Maybe Cassie was right—maybe what he'd wanted had nothing to do with her. Maybe the whole kids thing had been a desire to be a better parent than his own had been. Maybe it was him thinking he'd found something he'd lost in Cassie, projecting everything he'd felt years ago in Spain onto her. The big Latin family, the fast-and-furious affair...fuck, he'd done everything short of dumping his bank account and buying her a ring. He couldn't deny the obvious parallels, but he couldn't deny how he'd felt about Cassie either. He loved her, no matter how similar the rest of it was.

Countless women. An infinite number of sexual encounters. And there was nothing more he wanted than to wake up with her by his side. *This* was why he'd sworn never to fall in love again. Because waking up alone and wondering if he'd be like this for the rest of his life was no walk in the park. But this? This fucking sucked.

The early December chill ripped through him as he stepped out of the company car and into *La Lutte* for his Thursday lunch with his mother.

The same table. The same empty conversation. The same endless cycle of the same shit. He felt like a snake itching to shed its skin. He didn't want to be here. Didn't want this life.

They ordered, and she started talking about another charity event, another way she spent the never-ending supply of money she received as a result of his sacrifice.

He couldn't listen to another word of it.

"I'm fine, by the way," he said. "Thanks for asking."

Her startled expression at his interruption irritated him even more.

"Actually no. I'm not fine," he corrected, because why the hell not? "I'm fucking miserable. But please, go on talking about yourself."

Her mouth opened and closed, like he'd punched her in the face with reality. "I didn't know you were miserable."

"Of course you wouldn't. You never ask."

"I don't know *how* to ask." She sounded as cagey as he did. "I don't understand you, how you are. You act this way and I don't know why."

"You don't know why." He shook his head on a sigh. "Of course you don't."

He sounded unnecessarily sharp, and regret churned with frustration. This was how he always felt around her—a mix of hostility and guilt at trying to take care of a person who'd stopped trying to take care of him. A *"you chose booze over me!"* feeling his logical mind had fought against for years.

Fuck logic. Fuck sitting across this table and pretending he didn't still resent her. Fuck pretending to be happy when the only person he'd given a damn about in decades had just walked out of his life.

"I'm unhappy because I'm stuck in a job I hate. Which Dad forced me into, because of you."

She flinched. Clearly he'd cut deep, but he couldn't stop himself. This storm had been brewing for too long—decades of anger in hibernation—and he didn't feel like shielding her from it anymore.

His mother raised her chin. "I know."

"What do you mean, you know?"

"I know about the will."

Patrick froze. "You know about the will." Repeating her words was all he could manage through the horror locking down his chest.

"I do." She took a breath. "But there are reasons for it. Things you don't know. Things about your father and I that happened when you were abroad."

Two topics he could barely stomach. "I'd rather not—"

"*No.*" She'd never sounded so forceful. She glanced around the restaurant, threw a smile toward the maître d'. Her tone tempered, she said, "No, you need to hear this."

"All right." Even though he wanted to bolt out of his chair, he folded his hands and forced himself to listen.

"Your father and I married because it was advantageous. I had the connections, he had the money. I thought things between us would change eventually, but they didn't. Not when he was always—" She pinched her lips. Swallowed. "Busy elsewhere."

"Busy," he repeated. "What an interesting way to put it."

"I knew what he was doing, and I hated it, but I was... comfortable. In our house, in our life. I didn't think I could survive on my own. So the only thing I could do was escape."

Compassion for her warred with bitterness. He knew what it was like to get locked into an existence you hated. The difference was he'd diverted himself with sex instead of booze. And that he'd never had children.

"You could've left him instead of drinking. You could've left and taken me with you."

"I thought it would be better for you, if you at least had the structure of a family. And your father's money to take care of you."

"I would've preferred to have had parents." He sounded childish, but he felt childish. Cassie may have left him, and so had Sofía, but his mother did it first.

His abandonment issues all stemmed from Mommy. Freud would've had a field day with him.

"I understand why you're angry at me," she said.

"Do you?"

His voice was cold. The ice they were skating over was too thin, the abyss beneath it too deep.

"Yes. And I'm not going to make up excuses. I..." Her hands shook. She clasped them together. "I couldn't see a lot of things when you were growing up. And a lot since you've become a man. You have been quite cold, but I was wrapped up in my own problems. My own grief."

"Your *grief*?" he spat, ignoring her comment about his behavior. He'd learned to be cold by watching her. "You mourned that fucker?"

Tears shone in her eyes. "When you were away, your father and I reunited. He came home one night after he found out he was sick and apologized for everything. He said I was the best thing that ever happened to him and he loved me. We spent the last year he was alive happy, but when he died, I started drinking again. He worried that might happen, and that perhaps you wouldn't be willing to help, so he put that clause in the will. To keep us together."

He stared at her. Just fucking stared. "What?"

"I know it sounds awful, but he did it out of love. He linked your position to my dividends, binding us together through the publishing house. So it would stay in the family and I'd be taken care of."

Patrick had no idea how to absorb this information. He'd thought Reid had done it because he hated him, because he wanted to exact revenge on Patrick for defying him. The idea that he'd done it out of any kind of benevolence toward his wife made Patrick's brain hurt.

But it had still forced Patrick into a life he hadn't chosen for himself.

"Why haven't you told me this?"

"I was supposed to—your father asked me to—but I couldn't find a way because our relationship has been so strained." She swallowed and looked at the table, opened her hands and flattened them against it. "And because I'm selfish."

"Selfish." At least she was the one to have said it. But he didn't know exactly what she meant.

"Yes, because...there's a way for you to get out."

Patrick didn't understand. What *out* could there possibly be? "The will can't be contested. The clause is clear. Jack found the only loophole. It can't be changed."

"No. But you can walk away."

"And then you lose all monetary support."

"No, I won't." Another uneasy beat of silence passed between them, but this one was unlike all the others. It was loaded. A gun cocked and ready to be fired. "There's a trust set up to take care of me, if you did leave your position, or the company. It's not the same as what I've been getting, but it'll be enough to get by."

"Are you kidding me?" he barked. "So I could've clicked my heels together years ago and been done with a job I hate, and it wouldn't have affected you at all?" It was more than that. He'd never needed to be in it to begin with. "How the hell could you keep this from me?"

"Because I was terrified of losing you!"

That shut him up. He gaped at her.

"We have nothing," she said. "Nothing but these weekly lunches which we barely talk through, and the business. For a while I pretended this was the only way. When I was drinking, I rationalized my way through it. If you weren't forced to stay here, then you'd be gone from my life and I'd never see you again. But I had no idea how much you resented your life. No matter how things are between us, you're my only son. You're all I have left in the world, and I won't keep you here if you're miserable."

Patrick's legs twitched with the need to move and felt like lead at the same time. He understood her fear of loss, because fuck if that wasn't his biggest fear too, but he was still furious.

"You should've told me," he said.

"I know. I should've done a lot of things differently." There was a carefulness to her expression he didn't recognize. Something hesitant he vaguely labeled as concern. "Would you be less miserable if you left? Maybe go somewhere with the woman you're dating?"

That pinched at him in a whole other way. "That's over," he said, irritated at her sudden interest in something so personal, even though he'd been waiting years for her to do that.

"I see."

Patrick pushed his chair back. She was reaching out, but he wasn't ready for that. Not ready at all.

"I'm sorry. I need to go."

His could barely think straight the whole ride back to his

building. He walked through the rotating glass doors and into the golden atrium, replying with muted nods to the calls of, "Afternoon, Mr. Dunham," that came from the staff. He stared at the portrait of his father as he waited for the elevator. It was as if his entire world had flipped upside down.

Slamming his office door shut, he didn't know what to do with himself, other than pace and be angry at the world. Looking for a distraction, he walked toward the window. The trees along the waterfront were bare, the harbor half frozen and capped with ice. Years of staring at this same landscape flashed before him, the seasons flipping by like pages on a calendar. How long had he gazed at this view, wishing for freedom, not knowing he could've had it all along?

He had the option now of being released from this prison, if he wanted to. For the first time in over two decades, he had the free will to do what he wanted.

What was he going to do with it?

Needing something to grasp on to, Patrick turned and faced the wall of books behind his desk. Slowly, he approached the shelves, reaching up until his fingers ran over the spine of the one he was looking for. Pulling down *El Viejo y el Mar*, he opened it and paged through to the point he'd stopped reading. Engaging himself in the melodic language, he sat and read, waiting to find the meaning Gustavo had told him one day he'd find.

He hadn't found it yet an hour later when there was a knock at his door.

"This had better be important," he bit off, because he didn't want to deal with work now.

The door opened and Patrick regretted his tone. There were only a few people allowed past the lobby and his staff without asking first.

Brady was one of them.

"Now's not a good time, kid."

Brady hovered in the doorway, hulking shoulders filling the

whole space. "Sorry. I needed to get away from the office and ended up here. I'll go."

His eyes were bloodshot, his hair rumpled like he'd been making fists in it. Fuck. Patrick couldn't send him away now. "Forget it. I'll make time." Patrick waved him in. "Close the door."

Brady shuffled in and thumped down in a chair. Patrick didn't need to ask what was going on to know.

"Things still bad with Sam?"

"Yeah. That book idea I suggested for her was a total flop."

Patrick could've predicted that one. "You guys fighting?"

"We're not fighting, but we're not...anything, anymore."

Patrick stared at the ceiling. The feeling was familiar. "Wish I had some advice to offer you, but I'm fresh out of words of wisdom today."

Out of the corner of his eye, Patrick saw Brady eyeing him. "You look like shit," the kid said.

"I feel like shit."

"What's up?"

"I thought you came here to talk about you."

"I did, but it looks like we need to switch sides." Brady crossed his colossal arms, looking surprisingly intimidating. "You gonna talk, or am I gonna have to call Jack and have him whip it out of you?"

Patrick snorted. "Dickhead. Don't put that image in my head. I won't sleep for days."

What could he say? Tell Brady how pissed he was about things that had happened half a lifetime ago? That he'd been in purgatory for years while the person who could've let him out of it sat by and watched?

"It's too much to get into. Let's leave it at I found out someone's kept something from me, and I'm pissed about it."

"Someone I know?"

"No." Brady's interactions with his mother had been few and far between.

"Does this someone know you're pissed?"

"She knows."

"She?"

Patrick shook his head. "It's not what you think."

He didn't want to talk about Cassie. She wasn't the one Patrick was pissed at.

"What is it then?" Brady asked.

"It's—"

He was mad. Really fucking mad at his mother. And he was still mad at Sofia. But up until now, he'd used them as the reason he'd been stuck in his life. He lived in the now, but he couldn't forget what had happened. Always looking backward, his brain and capacity to remember things locking on to the past and keeping him there.

It was his blessing and his curse. Because while his observation skills were a handy thing in seduction, they also acted as a kind of hyper-vigilance—keeping his former hurts in his current frame of view to avoid getting hurt again. And he did it constantly. Using sex as an escape. Using his mother and his job and his heartbreak as his rationale for why he could never move forward. As a reason to stay disconnected and never get involved with anyone. To love anyone. To trust them.

"It's me," he finally said.

He'd been in a prison of his own making. Sure, the events of his life had put him there, but he'd decided to disconnect as a result, to separate himself from everything and everyone. And like his mother, he'd gotten comfortable. Complacent with his money, and a job he hated but didn't have to try at.

He didn't have to do that anymore. He could do anything he wanted.

"If you could do anything, what would it be?"

"I'd would've wanted to go into publishing, but not sales. I would've been involved in the actual books. Ideally the foreign ones."

"Dude. What's 'you'? You're not making sense."

"Sorry, I'm thinking about something Cassie told me."

He'd admitted his lost passion to her, back when it seemed unattainable, had trusted her with the desires he'd buried. And hadn't trust been the real high when they were together? It hadn't come from the outlet for the aggression that she'd given him, or the kinky acts themselves. It was her showing him who she was. Him doing the same to her.

"Cassie?" Brady asked. "Are you two a thing?"

Might as well come out with it. After all, he was going to see her again eventually. And better to let Brady know than have him point out the obvious tension between them later. "We were a thing. We're not anymore."

"Do *not* tell me you fucked her and left."

"No, I asked her to marry me."

Brady blinked. "Seriously?"

That was a little more than Patrick had planned on saying, but oh well. "Yeah. She said no."

"Whoa." Brady looked like a cartoon character who'd been hit on the head with an anvil. "That sucks, man. But marriage is no walk in the park. You had it right, the way you've been doing it— just sex, not getting involved. It'll be easier to go back to that, right?"

No. It wouldn't.

Brady's cell phone rang. He looked at it and grimaced. "Sorry, it's work. I've gotta take this."

He walked to the rear of the office, head bowed as he rattled off things about servers and code. And in that moment of semi privacy, Patrick returned to the last few pages of his book. When he'd finished it, he sat back with a smile. He'd thought it was about a struggle. A battle between an unlucky man and the thing that was fighting him.

That wasn't what it was about.

The true lesson was how a man could be destroyed but not

defeated. That heartbreak was inevitable, but it wasn't what defined him.

Patrick had been avoiding heartbreak, terrified of being abandoned by people he loved. He'd been acting the way he had to shield himself from rejection, but it happened again anyway with Cassie and he'd survived. He needed to accept the shit that had happened in his life, to stop being stuck in a pattern of escape and avoidance. And as he put the book back in its revered spot, he remembered what it was like to be fully immersed in something he loved. To be lost in the beautiful power of words strung together, in the meaning and magic that came from it.

Only one other thing in his life had made him feel so grounded, so *connected*, and that was when he was with Cassie. He wanted to find that feeling again, and chase it in whatever way possible. Not just in sex, but in life. And now that he was free from his obligation to his mother, he could.

He wasn't going to keep looking for escape. He might've hated the role he'd had at Dunham and Strauss, but he'd learned a lot doing it. Learned what sold and what didn't. And he could use that for the future.

He needed to stop looking backward, let go of the past and look forward for once.

Feeling almost giddy, he reached for his phone. Because, yeah, he'd figured out some shit about his life, and the first person he wanted to tell was Cassie. But calling her now would be a mistake. He'd like to tell her about it eventually, but she might not care either way, and he needed to fix things for himself first. To become a version of himself he liked, regardless of whether he got to be with her.

As Brady ended his call, Patrick cued up a different number, put the phone on speaker and set it down. "Sit tight, kid. Looks like I'm gonna need your brother over here after all."

"Why's that?"

"It's time for me to revisit some paperwork."

30

 $\mathcal{C}$ assie heaved another bunch of files from her cabinet and dumped them into the open banker's box on her desk. Lilly sat in a chair and pouted.

"I can't believe you're leaving," she said.

"I'm leaving the firm, not the city. It's not as if we're not gonna see each other."

"I know, but it won't be the same."

Cassie glanced up at Lilly and laughed. Her friend was still wearing a reindeer-eared headband left over from the firm's holiday luncheon earlier that day, and it bounced at Lilly's sigh.

Lilly crossed her arms, looking like a super fierce Rudolph. "You can't laugh at me when you're abandoning me!"

"I'm not laughing at *you*," Cassie insisted. "I'm laughing at the headband."

"Wearing this was the only way I could get through your last party here."

"I thought my Cuban Rum Cake got you through it."

She'd asked her mother for the recipe, and had gone to three different shops looking for the right banana liqueur. It had been a pain in the ass but worth it in the end, not only because it was delicious, but because it felt good to finally let her Cuban side shine. She'd let her hair grow out a bit as well, and she liked the comforting feeling of it brushing past her shoulders.

"That helped too." Lilly rubbed her belly and groaned. "I feel like I gained ten pounds today. Please tell me we'll still be going to the gym together."

"Of course."

Her phone buzzed with a call from reception. Cassie hit the speakerphone button.

"What's up, Piper?"

"Mr. Grant is here for you."

Without an appointment, of course. Why would she have expected otherwise? "Tell him I'm on a call. Make him wait ten minutes, then send him in."

"I will." Piper lowered her voice. "Glad it's the last time I'll be saying that, for me and for you."

"Your new firm is lucky to have you."

Lilly bent over and covered her face with her hands. "Why is everyone leaving me?"

The reindeer-ears bobbed, and Cassie stifled a laugh. "Maybe you could recruit Sam for Piper's job. It's part time. Might work for her."

Lilly popped her head up. "You're brilliant."

"I know." Cassie hauled more files to her desk. Some were staying at the firm and some she was taking across town, but the rest were going into storage. Her new office was significantly smaller than her current one. She looked around the space and breathed through the mix of sadness and excitement. Her name wasn't going up on the wall here. But if she was lucky, it would be printed in other, far more worthy places.

Gabe popped his head into her office. "I caught the mailroom guy on his way down the hall. Grabbed yours as well as mine."

He handed Cassie her pile, then pulled her in for a hug.

"I can't believe you're leaving us," he cried dramatically. "Whose fabulous shoe collection will I live vicariously through?"

She kicked up one of the black, knee-high, fuck-you-world boots she'd put on that morning. "We'll have to hit the gay bar scene more often. Get you and Nick dressed up in drag."

Lilly bounced in her seat and clapped. "This needs to happen. As soon as possible."

Gabe grinned and parked himself on the chair next to Lilly's. Cassie flipped through her mail, tossing most of it until she came upon a small white envelope sealed with a red waxed stamp. Her breath caught when she turned it over and saw who it was from.

"Patrick."

She had trouble getting her lungs to restart as she peeled the envelope open. Inside it was a sheet of parchment paper, covered in Patrick's tight, angular handwriting. And all the words were written in Spanish.

"*Querida Cassandra,*" it began, and Cassie's brain got itself tangled over her heart, one organ beating too fast for the other to translate effectively. She took a breath, and started again.

Please don't be angry that I've sent you this. I'm not going to repeat any of the questions I asked you in the airport. I know how much they upset you. And I wouldn't have written at all, except for the fact that I had to, and every woman should get a love letter at some point in her life, especially when she's celebrating a change in vocation.

She looked at Lilly. "How did he know?"

"About you leaving the firm? Jack told him."

Cassie glanced at Gabe, who was smiling too widely to be surprised. "Who else knows about him and me?"

"We all do."

"Nick and Brady, too?"

"Yup."

"Carajo." She leaned against her desk for support and kept reading.

I also needed to tell you that you were right, at least partially anyway. You were a fantasy—the ultimate escape—but you were wrong about the why. Escaping into some alternate reality wasn't what my fantasy was. It was never about marriage and children, or being with a Latina woman, never about the amazing sex. You were my fantasy, Cassie. And I've never felt more connected and present than when I was with you.

I know I wasn't supposed to fall in love with you, but I did. And I never cared if we had ten babies or it was the two of us until we were old and arguing in matching rocking chairs. I wanted you, because you changed me—changed everything about me. Your fire and passion for life made me want more out of mine. And I can never thank you enough.

I'm sorry I won't be with you while you change the world, but I couldn't be happier for you, and I'm so proud of what you've accomplished. I wish you the best of luck in your career, and everything else.

Yours,

Patrick

She put the letter down, stunned. He never cared about having babies. She was his fantasy. But he didn't want to get back together either, and this letter had dredged up too many different emotions for Cassie to process them all. She was annoyed with him for not having been clearer. Upset at herself for misunderstanding him. Touched that he'd cared enough to wish her well in her new job. Confused over the need to run to him and throw herself in his arms. Angry at the whole fucking mess.

What a goddamn pain in the ass he was, telling her this now.

The spasm of heartache gripping Cassie's chest was

interrupted by Hudson knocking at her door. She quickly tossed the letter onto her desk.

"Am I interrupting?" he asked, one haughty eyebrow raised. "Reception sent me here."

Lilly gave Cassie a hard look, her eyes wide with the sentiment—*are you okay?*

Cassie nodded. If there was nothing else she'd learned in fifteen years as an attorney, it was how to bounce back when she was rattled. "You're never interrupting, Hudson. I'm always happy when you drop by."

The sarcasm dripping from her voice had Lilly snorting. She and Gabe walked out, and Hudson gave Lilly a once-over before grinning at Cassie.

"Festive," he said, but he wasn't looking at Lilly's headband. His gaze instead was making a path down Cassie's red sweater dress.

So predictable.

"'Tis the season," she replied. "You look relaxed."

No more scowl or curled shoulders on him. He perched himself on a chair and crossed one ankle over the opposite knee —the casual posture of someone who didn't have a care in the world.

"Why shouldn't I be? I'm not in debt anymore, and my operation is running so smoothly I might even take a vacation."

Cassie barely resisted rolling her eyes. "Looks like you got everything you wanted."

"And it looks like you didn't." He jutted his chin in the direction of her box. "Why are you packing? Did your bosses not offer you partner after all the business you brought in?"

"They did. I turned them down."

"Another firm offered you more money, huh?"

"Nope. I'm moving into government. Well, moving *back* into government, actually."

The justice she'd clerked for had pulled a few strings, put in a few good words, all the while insisting Cassie's resume and experience spoke for itself. And now she'd been offered a chance to serve as Deputy Legal Counsel to the Governor. Instead of bringing in money-making clients, she'd be in charge of advising on legislation and implementing regulations, as well as collaborating with the Attorney General's Office on litigation. The change meant a hefty pay cut, but at least she'd be able to live with herself.

And get to work on changing the world.

"Wow." Hudson crossed his arms. "I guess congratulations are in order."

She gave him the first genuine smile she'd ever had in his presence. "Thank you. Same to you."

"So if I'm no longer your client, and you no longer work for a firm that represents my investors, does that mean we can go back to discussing that hotel up the street?"

"I haven't turned you down enough that you've lost interest?"

"Hope springs eternal."

Cassie bit off a laugh, then gave Hudson a once-over of her own. If it weren't for the ponytail, he wasn't a bad-looking guy—he had nice eyes, and given his attitude, he'd probably be more than willing to give her what she wanted in bed.

But he wasn't Patrick. And even if the two of them weren't getting back together, she wasn't ready to move on yet.

"Actually, there's somebody else," she told him. "But thank you for offering."

"If that ever changes, keep me in mind."

He stood and started toward the door. Cassie returned to the task of sorting her files.

"You know," he said. "When my buddy gave me your name, I had no idea what I was in for."

She'd stopped wondering a while back how he'd had gotten

her name, but finally finding out would be interesting. "What buddy is that?" she asked absentmindedly.

"Patrick Dunham."

Cassie dropped the file she was holding. "I'm sorry—who did you say?"

"Patrick Dunham. An old friend from Princeton. He's in publishing too."

"Yeah, I know the name." Her body went cold. "*He* sent you to me?"

"Yup. Told me to do whatever you said. He sure as hell was right."

Cassie's pulse raced, her fingers tingling. Patrick. Fucking Patrick had sent Hudson to her. A good old boys network had been the reason she'd been offered partner, with Hudson gift-wrapped and sent over to her as what—charity?

How could he have done that to her, especially once she'd told him how she felt about earning her own way? She'd talked to him about this case too, what the stakes were. It made her fume, knowing he'd kept this from her all this time.

Fuck his letter. She was going to give Patrick Dunham a piece of her mind.

"Hudson, I need to step out," she said. "Good luck with everything."

She grabbed her coat and brushed past him, throwing it on as she stormed down the hall. A simple phone call wasn't going to suffice. She needed to look Patrick in the eye and ask him why he'd lied.

By the time the taxi got to his building, Cassie was barely able to contain her fury. Racing past the Santa ringing a bell on the street corner, she pushed through the large rotating doors and into the lobby of Dunham and Strauss Books.

"I'm here to see the VP of sales," she said to the receptionist. "Patrick Dunham. And no I don't have an appointment."

The young man behind the desk looked at her strangely. "Mr. Dunham is no longer a VP, ma'am."

"No longer a—what?"

"Mr. Dunham is in a different department now."

She shook her head. This was one too many surprises for one day. "Fine. Whatever. Just tell him Cassie Allbright is here and she needs to see him. Now."

He dialed and spoke quietly, then hung up and nodded. "You can head up. Seventh floor—"

She'd already turned on her heel when he was telling her the department. Adrenaline screamed through her on the elevator ride. She was revved up, ready for a fight.

The door rolled open, and she stepped out into a hall with elevator banks. Beyond that, the floor was an open space that looked raw and unused—just some sparsely decorated cubicles and a lobby with a few chairs, as if it were an area for storage that had just been cleared out and made over. Before she could process any of that though, Patrick was walking toward her.

"I assume you got my letter?"

God, she'd forgotten how attractive he was. Hair sex-mussed, goatee trimmed, his sturdy body barely hidden beneath the confines of a sweater and dark black jeans. But what Cassie was fixated on was his arrogant smile, and the twinkle in those infuriatingly gorgeous green eyes.

"Why did you send Hudson Grant to me?" she snapped.

His mouth dropped open. He shook his head. "Seriously? After everything I wrote, that's why you're here?"

"I'm here because I want to know why you lied."

"I didn't lie." Something cautious tightened his features, a pitch and flare of aggression and heat in his eyes. "Jesus. Did my letter mean anything to you?"

"Answer me, Patrick!"

"I sent him because I knew you'd teach him a lesson," he yelled back.

"Oh, is that why you sent him? Because I'm such a bitch? Or was it because you didn't think I'd be able to get a client like that on my own."

Patrick let out a growl. "Fucking listen to me, goddamn it." He took several steps toward her, large shoulders invading her space. "Hudson Grant is a chauvinistic pig, and I knew you'd chew him up and spit him out, in that way you're so good at doing. I sent him to you because you're a pain in the ass and argue better than anyone I know, and I knew you'd be the best person to whip that jackass's company into shape."

She wasn't sure if she wanted to smack him or fuck him. Cassie narrowed her eyes, her breath sharp with adrenaline and lust. As much as she was ashamed to admit it, she'd missed this— the fights, the banter, the energy that charged like a live wire between them, gasoline waiting for a spark.

"Why didn't you tell me?"

He sighed and pinched his eyes shut. When he opened them, they were soft, like they had been that night in Miami, checking her for injuries, full of regret.

"Because I wanted you to be proud of what you were doing. I didn't want anything to get in the way of you making your goal. I figured hearing that Hudson had gotten your name from me would get inside your head until you believed it was some kind of welfare, instead of knowing you were right for the job."

Oh, God. Patrick's words were getting past the steel fortress she still kept around herself, her iron starting to crack. Her guard was up, but he knew how to take it down.

"You didn't do it out of charity?"

"No." He smiled a little. "Although I was looking forward to hearing how much he pissed you off."

Cassie laughed, the anger seeping out of her, the tension broken. She glanced down at the space between them. He'd walked her backward against a wall, and she shivered with the knowledge of how easily he could overpower her, how it felt for him to take her with wild abandon.

She wanted him to do it again. Not here, but again. Soon. And if she wanted that, she owed him a few admissions of her own.

She needed to be the one to fix this now, in the hopes that they still had a shot.

"I'm sorry about what I said at the airport."

He exhaled, his shoulders caving in slightly. "You don't have to—"

"Yes. I do. I jumped to conclusions. I do that a lot. I always fight, it's my instinct. You touched a nerve so I fought back when I shouldn't have. I do that, I push people away, but I shouldn't have pushed you."

Hesitant, he touched his fingertips to hers. "What nerve did I hit?"

She took a breath, finding the strength to tell him the truth. "Before Florida, I found out that having kids is something I'm running out of time to do, unless I do it right now, and when we were down there together, I realized I don't want to right now, or ever. I don't need children to be complete."

"What do you need?"

You.

Instead of saying it, she did what she did that first night long ago. She took him by his shirt, leaned in and kissed him. Patrick inhaled sharply before his hands claimed her hips. He drew the kiss out, slow passes of his lips over hers, nudging her into corner before he offered her a light slip of tongue.

She had to stop to catch her breath, wrapped her arms around him and held on tight. The room was spinning. Christ. No other man had made her dizzy with a kiss. Which meant it was time for another admission.

"I love you," she said.

Patrick's short exhalation rushed out—soft heat over her cheek.

"You do?"

"I realized it in Miami but I think I've known it for longer than that. I've known it since I met you, but I was too stubborn to say so." Cassie tightened her grasp around him. "I love you, and I hope I'm not too much of a pain in the ass for you to still love me."

Patrick chuckled. "You're the perfect amount of pain in the ass, Cassie. And no, it's not too late."

It was like winning the lottery, or waking up on Christmas Day—the idea that she could have both a career that was satisfying, and this amazing man for her own. A man who'd changed the course of his life too, it seemed.

She glanced at the sign over his shoulder. "Foreign acquisitions? You work here now?"

"I do." He beamed. "Seems that it's not bad to have the last name Dunham after all. I told the board I was leaving, they asked what they could do to keep me, and here you see it. Brand new department. Just put a new team together and moved in here a few days ago."

So she'd been right about the space. "But that means you broke the conditions of your father's will."

"I did."

"But your mom—"

Patrick put a finger over her mouth, a gentle silencing. "It's a long story, but everything with my mother is okay...ish. Or at least it's going to be."

He lowered his finger, grazing her chin with his thumb before taking her hand. Cassie gazed at him. He looked different—calmer, more comfortable with himself. "What made you decide to do it?"

"Someone I know reminded me what my passions were. She's the most passionate woman I know, and she's gonna change the world one day, so I thought it was time I tried to do the same."

Cassie's heart leapt into her throat. She burrowed herself

against his shoulder as he nuzzled her cheek. Good lord, was it even healthy to be in love? How did people survive feeling like this?

"It's gonna be a challenge for us to make those trips to Spain and Cuba," she said. "Since we've both taken some pretty serious pay cuts." Although she could use what she'd saved for her capital contribution on that.

Or she could buy a hundred new pairs of shoes…

"We'll find a way." Patrick reached one big hand around to stroke the back of her neck. "My strong spitfire of a woman. By me, you were suitably conquered."

"Conquered?"

"Yeah. You're the fearless girl and I'm the charging bull."

"Is that so?"

He skimmed his nose over hers. "Toro, toro."

She laughed. "Well you'd better stand your ground, my *conquistador*. Because this fearless girl is about to knock you down."

A low growl purred out of him. Grasping her hand, he led her down a hall to an office half the size of the one he'd had before and closed the door. Backing her against it, his hands mapped her waist, forehead pressed to hers.

"Tell me what you want, Cassie," he said, his breath rough and his voice shaky.

His words got stuck in her chest. In her body. Something flared, heat blooming between her thighs. "Other than for you to spread me across your desk?"

He swallowed and nodded. "Other than that."

What did she want? It took a second to find the right words. "I want you to claim me as yours, every night and every morning, and never walk out my door again."

"I wouldn't mind fulfilling that fantasy."

"Then do it, you pain in the ass."

"Oh, I'm the pain in the ass now, am I?" Patrick grinned and palmed her bottom. "We still haven't done *that*, you know."

Cassie's grin grew wide as he slid one finger tantalizingly over that forbidden back entrance. Oh, the things this man was going to do to her. Assuming she let him.

She twisted her fingers in his hair and skated her teeth over his neck to his ear.

"Consider that the first thing on our new fantasy list."

he room was mostly dark when Patrick blinked his eyes open. Groggy, he reached around for the warm body beside him, fingertips crossing a naked stretch of skin with practiced ease. He'd stopped checking for her weeks ago, no longer needing to reassure himself she was there.

He knew she wasn't going anywhere.

Cassie was still asleep, her gentle breaths even on the pillow next to his. He turned on his side and curled up behind her. Spooning had become his favorite way to wake up in the past month, one hand on the soft curve of Cassie's hip, his cock growing stiffer as it pressed against her bottom in her bed.

Correction. *Their* bed.

Patrick's move from his apartment to Cassie's was one they'd both agreed upon, although the idea had been hers. They needed to consolidate, she'd said. Combine their resources. She'd acted like it was simply a sound business decision, not that she simply wanted to move in together, and he'd agreed. He liked her part of town, liked the classic Boston feel of it. And in her home, he felt his issues slipping away. He felt calmer, had stopped overthinking as much and started reading more, at home and at the office, where that banker's lamp no longer sat. As part of his attempts to let the past go, he'd given it away. He'd even looked up Gustavo on Facebook. Sadly the old, wise gentleman had passed, but Patrick had reconnected with his children, and that was something at least.

He knew he still had problems, but something about Cassie's love, and waking up in her bedroom, was transforming him. The morning sun crept up quietly through the trees, slanting in through the curtained windows in the muted, white-gold tones of winter. It was a softer way to wake up. Gentler, like his hand on her skin.

But Patrick wouldn't stay gentle for long.

"Wake up, princess." Nosing under her hair, he ran his chin over the sensitive spot on the back of her neck he'd gotten to know so well, grinning when she shifted and pressed back against him. "Good morning. Happy Friday."

"Too early," she mumbled. "Don't want to get out of bed yet."

"Who said anything about getting out of bed?"

Her little groan stiffened him even more, as did the way she teasingly pulled away. "We don't have time. You'll make us late for work."

Patrick slid a hand around to her belly. Cassie's words didn't match the reflexive pitch of her hips when he lightly pressed down. She wasn't really protesting. It was part of the game they both loved to play, the one where she fought and he fought back, although she'd realized lately the anonymous way he'd attacked her in the hotel wasn't for her. She didn't want it to feel like she was with some angry stranger. She didn't want it faceless. She wanted to know it was him. A man she trusted.

A man she loved.

"Well you'd better not make it too hard for me then." His words were half playful, and half a threat.

The fact that she loved him still sent him reeling, as did the low, hungry noise that came out of her. It was a green light, a gun fired at the start of a race. Patrick pressed down lightly on her belly, possessive and demanding. Her hips rocked in time with his hand, her breath quickening.

"Now, show me you can play nice, and this will be enjoyable for both of us."

He reached between their heated bodies and rode one finger lightly down her panties, tapping at the crack of her ass until her breath caught. Her right hand reached up, seeking purchase on the pillow, and he grabbed it with his other one, holding her down as he drew a circle around her back entrance.

"You gonna show me how much you like this?" he asked. "Gonna show me how wet you get?"

"No," she groaned, another feeble objection.

"No?" He urged her onto her stomach. "You saying no to me?"

A grunt was his answer as he released her hand. He dipped the other one lower, between her thighs to the soaked patch on the cotton.

"Dirty little liar. You're saying no to tease me."

He yanked her panties down, then shoved her harder against the bed, fingers spanning between her shoulder blades, careful and brutal. There was a fine line between scaring her and pleasing her, between tormenting her and pleasing himself, and every time they got down and dirty together, he edged it further, found a new boundary to push. Being with Cassie was like being with a different woman every night, but it was always the same. Always her. And he never wanted anyone else.

"Fuck you," she whispered, and the words went straight to his dick.

"Oh, gonna be a bitch now, are we?" He wedged his thighs between hers and pried them open. "Gonna make me be mean?"

"You think I'm gonna—ohhhh, *God.*"

What was that?" He drove his fingers inside her, unapologetically rough, seeking out that little ridge that made her soak the sheets.

"Shit. Don't. Please."

Harsh breath skittered over Cassie's words. There was a part of her that didn't want this, and a part that did. It embarrassed and shocked her, how he got her body to react, but it was a button he loved to push, one he was going to push right now.

"Don't what? This?" He did it again. Again. Faster. Harder. She tried to buck him off her, even as her pussy drenched his fingers. The dichotomy of her struggling and giving in was fucking glorious.

"Please," she said, but her tone was different now. Not a complaint, a request—a hungry, desperate one.

"Please what?"

"Please." She panted. "Do it. Get it. Make me like it."

He knew what she was saying. They'd played at her back entrance on and off for weeks, getting her ready, preparing her. "Is that what you want?"

She nodded. He slid his fingers free and pushed himself up to kneeling. "Stay put."

He was out of breath when he angled himself toward the nightstand, his cock straining at the confines of his briefs. What she did to him was insane.

"Make you like it," he murmured, preparing the toy. "You've liked the feeling of my pinky back there, haven't you?"

She nodded again. Her nightshirt had ridden up her back, and he gazed over the sinful bend of her spine, the dimples above that luscious, round bottom. He might have to ask her how she felt about spanking because seriously, goddamn. Positioning himself behind her, her drizzled lube on that puckered, tight hole, then eased the plug into it.

"Breathe," he said, then pressed down. Slowly. So slowly. He paused when she hissed and he felt resistance, helping her along by sliding a finger from his other hand inside her. "Take it for me, princess. Take it and I'll make it so good for you."

Gentle in-and-out pumps stopped her from bearing down. Cassie whined and turned her face into the pillow.

"That's it," he said. "There you go."

Patrick watched in amazement as her body surrendered to him. When the toy was fully seated, he sat back and stared. Facedown. Honey-thick thighs open. Glittering jewel in her ass, her pussy pink and open for him.

She was open. That was the true elixir—Cassie with her armor shed, trusting him completely.

"You have no idea how sexy you look."

She responded with a tight shake of her shoulders. He tapped once at the plug's base, and her shoulders hiked up on a gasp.

"Good?" he asked, even though he knew the answer.

"Yes." Her voice broke on the word. "I want—"

An experimental squeeze to her butt cheeks, thumbs easing them away, then back together, drew a delicious and heady noise from her. Patrick kicked his legs behind him to yank off his briefs. Hands on her hips, he maneuvered her onto her back, listening to the hitches in her breathing as the toy hit her in different places. Gripping her wrists lightly, her pinned her down, affording them both the feeling of capture.

"What do you want, Cassie?"

They were words he always asked, simply because he wanted to hear her answer.

She looked up at him, and her eyes were glazed over, clouded with pleasure. "You."

"Me too." Patrick proved that to her with a slow, tender kiss.

They were still kissing when he lined himself up and sank inside. She was scorching, snug and sloppy wet. Knowing he'd gotten her so completely aroused, and that there was a toy up her ass he'd put there nearly triggered an immediate orgasm. He could feel it inside her too, pressing at both of them through the lining of her body. Cassie rocked against him, breaking away from the kiss in first a cry, then a frantic, wild sound she'd never made before. There was a shocked look in her eyes.

"Touch my clit," she begged. "Fuck, can't believe...gonna come."

Oh, Jesus. "Me too."

She was dragging him over the edge with her, involuntary spasms of her body jerking him toward his own release. Letting her wrists go, he held himself up with one hand against the bed, and slid the other between them. Three quick swipes over that tight, slick knot and she crashed into it, bucking and thrashing beneath his pistoning hips. He held out until he felt her clench a second time, and then the pleasure ripped him inside out. He emptied himself into her, her name almost a sob when the last tremor hit.

Spent, Patrick dropped his head to her shoulder. "Still don't like me?"

"I hate you."

He kissed the sweaty column of her throat. "I love you too."

Cassie winced as he pulled out and slid the toy free, but her discomfort was short lived. A lazy, relaxed grin spread across her face.

"You make it way too hard for me to want to get to work on time."

"You can't be late. Greatness awaits you at the legislature." Patrick nuzzled her forehead. "Come on, let's get cleaned up."

* * *

By the end of the workday, Cassie was still smiling. A good chunk of it was another awesome day at the office. The rest was Patrick.

She exited the T, amazed at how much had changed. One

month ago, she and Patrick had reconciled. One year ago tonight, they'd met. And a handful of hours from now, they'd be celebrating both anniversaries in their own special brand of twisted and kinky. But first, they'd be spending a night with their friends.

She pushed through the heavy doors at Barrel 'n' Flask. The blast of heat she felt inside helped her fingers to thaw as she shed her coat and found her gang at a table in the back.

"Sorry I'm late," she said, taking a seat on Patrick's lap instead of the empty one beside him.

"We didn't miss you much," Gabe teased, then nodded toward the bar. "Nick's getting drinks. Patrick already made sure he ordered you a blood-orange cosmo."

Patrick kissed her shoulder. She could feel his smile behind it. Cassie angled her chin toward him.

"Thank you," she said to him. "Did you have a good day?"

"I did."

Another kiss to her shoulder punctuated his words. He was so much happier now, so relaxed. She wasn't sure if it was them, the new job or the fact that he and his mother had reconciled. Cassie had met her at an intimate Christmas dinner, followed by a raucous New Year's Eve-slash-moving-out party at Patrick's apartment that Cassie's family had flown up for. He also read frequently now, often making their breakfast with a book in his hands, doing the same in bed on the rare nights they didn't reach for each other before sleep.

A snort dragged Cassie's attention back to the table. Brady was rolling his eyes.

"You guys were more fun when you argued."

"Oh, we still argue," she insisted. "Just not in public."

Patrick grunted quietly and surreptitiously adjusted himself when no one was looking. Sam arrived a few moments later, followed by Nick and a carefully handled bunch of drinks. They'd ordered some food by the time Jack and Lilly arrived, both of their faces flushed. Cassie would've thought it was from the cold, except for the way Lilly's blush lingered and the way she was clinging to Jack's side.

"What's the deal, you two?" Cassie asked, biting off the end of a French fry. Fuck it. She'd work it off in the gym tomorrow. Or have Patrick work it off her.

Jack put an arm around Lilly. "What are you all doing four weeks from tonight?"

Cell phones were picked up, calendars checked. When it looked as if no one had plans, Lilly took off her gloves and revealed a sparkling diamond ring. Cassie jumped up to congratulate them, unable to stop smiling amidst Lilly's infectiously happy glow. As everyone else swarmed the couple, Cassie settled back down sideways in Patrick's lap, a buzzing sensation in her belly. They hadn't discussed his proposal since that night in the airport, and she'd been looking for a time to bring it up again.

Seemed like as good a time as any.

"You think that could be us one day?" she asked as she picked at his sweater, totally cool and casual.

Not.

"Are you reconsidering my offer?" She nodded, and Patrick made a show of smirking at her. "You sure you want that?"

"I am. I think marrying you would be very..." She searched for a word. "Satisfying."

He snorted. "If your version of satisfying is being legally bound to arguing with you for the rest of my life."

Cassie smacked his shoulder. "Shut up."

"Shut up?" Green eyes blazed. She could sense the switch flipped in him, that mean streak going. He squeezed her tightly, almost forcing the breath out of her. "You're gonna be sorry you said that when I get you home."

She smiled at him, at this man she once thought she hated, a man who controlled her because she let him with that perfect blend of rough and romantic. She might've been too tough to be Cinderella, but she was happy being his princess, and she had the shoes to prove it.

She leaned in close and let him see the playfulness in her own eyes.

"Yes, I will. I'm counting on it."

THANK YOU!

I hope you enjoyed *Her Claim*. Cassie and Patrick first showed up as background banter in *His Contract*, then quickly proved they had plenty to say for themselves. Their story wasn't always easy to write, but I hope I did them justice.

If you loved their chemistry, laughed at their sparring, or wanted to throttle them at least once before they figured things out, I'd love to hear what you thought. Reader reviews help books like this reach new readers who enjoy sharp banter, strong personalities, and a love story that doesn't take the easy road.

If you feel like sharing, you can leave a review wherever you purchased the book, or on Goodreads. Even a few words make a real difference.

 Rebecca Grace Allen

ALSO BY REBECCA GRACE ALLEN

Legally Bound:

His Contract

Their Discovery

Portland Rebels:

The Duality Principle

The Hierarchy of Needs

The Theory of Deviance

Shakespeare in the City:

Taming Sugar

Hunter Pains

Decades Duet:

Find the Cost of Freedom

Smells Like Teen Spirit

EXCERPT FROM
THEIR DISCOVERY

"O kay." He went around her to the breakfast table and pulled out a chair. "Please sit?"

Sam paused. Was this another joke? It didn't seem to be as he stood there, expectant and waiting. He wasn't being sarcastic. His request had been soft and low, and his face was calm, his eyes filled with a deference she didn't understand. One that made her feel elevated and catered to.

It was unnerving.

"All right."

She immediately felt better—she wasn't used to that many hours in heels—and her breath caught when she felt his hands at the bottom of her hair.

"May I?" he asked.

She was caught off guard. He was just brushing the ends, but each soft tug stimulated all the nerve endings on her head. "Okay."

He continued combing the last inch of the locks, rubbing them between his fingers. She'd assumed he'd forgotten how much she enjoyed this, but then he ran his fingers through her hair, lifting it from her face and gently easing out any tangles.

It was the most intimate they'd been in years.

He did it again, deliberate and slow. Brady had large hands, and she missed what he could do with them. He was even better with his mouth. It had taken time and direction, but once he'd figured out her spots, his tongue had been fucking magical.

He moved in closer, starting at her temples and combing at the roots before running his fingertips down the strands. The sensation was hypnotic. Jesus, if he'd done this instead of joking, the fight never would've started. With him standing so close, Sam got a hit of his scent. It was the same heady combination he'd always had—wood spice deodorant and peppermint soap mixed with an earthy bit of sweat.

Years ago, she'd worn that smell on her like perfume.

He gathered her hair and put it over one shoulder. "Better?" he asked.

She paused, unsure about the dynamic between them. The fight seemed to have dissipated, but there was a strange vibration now—a different kind of energy. Like the charge in the air before a snowfall.

"Yes, better." But she hadn't asked him to stop. She didn't like that he had.

He went back to the counter. Sam watched as Brady put away the rest of the dishes, then stepped toward the sink and turned on the water.

"Thank you," she said. "For helping."

"It's not that I don't want to," he replied softly. "I'm just not sure how to do it right. Like your system for putting things into the dishwasher."

She did have a system. A way to stack everything for maximum efficiency. She didn't know he'd noticed.

"And I don't know how you know where everything goes in the cabinets without looking. It's hard for me to keep track."

Sam frowned, guilt stabbing. He'd always had issues recalling things. It was why they'd met in the first place. Why was she never patient with it? Staring at his profile, she threw out some sarcasm to lighten the mood.

"Well, silly. If you can't figure out where things go, I'll fucking tell you."

She wasn't sure if he'd missed the lightness in her tone, or if he'd caught it and was embarrassed regardless, but from this angle, she could see his chin lower slightly as a swallow constricted his throat. It was a small tell, something he used to do when she was tutoring him, ashamed because he'd gotten an answer wrong. Back then she'd soothe him, put a hand on one of his giant arms and tell him it was her job to help him get things right. He'd blush and smile up at her, eyes sparkling and hopeful.

He wasn't smiling now. But a strange part of her...liked his discomfort.

"I don't mind telling you what to do, you know," she added. "Being your wife is like training an excitable puppy."

Brady went rigid, his muscles tensing beneath his T-shirt as color rose on his cheeks. It had been a long time since she'd seen him react like that, even longer since she'd seen his brow wrinkle and his head sink down more, a surefire sign that he was turned on. It was what he'd do back in the day, when she'd taunt him for wanting her so badly. What he'd done every time she'd ordered him to her dorm room and teased that he must've sprinted across campus to have gotten to her so fast.

When she'd *ordered* him over.

Was that it?

She stared at him. He was waiting, barely moving.

"Maybe that's all you need," she said. "To be given a little—" she paused, testing out the effect of her words, "—discipline."

A noticeable shudder went through him.

Holy shit. She'd read moments like this in her books. Scenes when the Dominant would give his submissive a command, and everything would change. Was that happening now?

She wanted to push Brady harder. To see if she was right.

Sam stood and padded slowly over to him, but he remained frozen, as if he were a helpless animal and she was a lioness stalking her prey.

"You want to see me happy?" she asked, and even she was surprised at how soft and seductive her voice sounded.

Brady didn't look up from the sink. "You know I do."

Moving in behind him, she put her hands on him. His T-shirt was soft beneath her palms. His breathing went shallow as she caressed all those bunched muscles in his lower back. God, he still was a specimen, his torso thick, a dip at the base of his spine leading to the ass she'd once loved to grab and squeeze.

She pressed herself against him. Her chin barely cleared his shoulder blades, but she rubbed her upper body back and forth, testing to see if he could feel her tightened nipples through her tank top and robe. There was the slightest buck of his hips.

Humming softly in approval, Sam went up on her toes, got her lips as close to his ear as she could and whispered, "Then you go back to washing while I have a little fun."

Rebecca lives in southern Florida with three cats who firmly believe they are the main characters. When she's not immersed in fictional love stories, she can usually be found chasing strong coffee, good workouts, and the kind of books that balance heart, heat, and humor. She writes romance for readers who like their happily ever afters earned, their characters flawed, and their love stories a little messy in the best possible way.

www.ingramcontent.com/pod-product-compliance
Lightning Source LLC
Chambersburg PA
CBHW031148120726
47905CB00006B/1864